A TREE ACCURST

Right down through the woods yonder, if you could

see it through the trees and brush, is where the cabin

stood that Frankie and Charles Silver lived in. And long

after they were dead and gone the house fell in, and later

another home was built over the foundations. . . . But

there was a tree that grew near where the old house was.

They claimed that if you got up in it, that you couldn't

get out. And my mother said that she thought that when

I was just a child and we went up there that I got up in

the tree and they liked to have never got me out. I don't

know if that was because of the curse or because I didn't

want to be got out. —Bobby McMillon

A TREE ACCURST

BOBBY McMILLON AND STORIES OF FRANKIE SILVER

DANIEL W. PATTERSON

The University of North Carolina Press *Chapel Hill & London*

© 2000

The University of North Carolina Press

All rights reserved

Designed by Richard Hendel

Set in Adobe Caslon & Smokler types

by Tseng Information Systems, Inc.

Manufactured in the United States of America

The paper in this book meets the guidelines for
permanence and durability of the Committee on
Production Guidelines for Book Longevity of the
Council on Library Resources.

Library of Congress Cataloging-in-Publication Data

Patterson, Daniel W. (Daniel Watkins)

A tree accurst: Bobby McMillon and stories of
Frankie Silver / Daniel W. Patterson.

p. cm.

Includes bibliographical references and index.

ISBN 0-8078-2564-6 (cloth: alk. paper)—
ISBN 0-8078-4873-5 (pbk.: alk. paper)

1. Tales—North Carolina—Mitchell County—
History. 2. Murder—North Carolina—Mitchell
County—Folklore. 3. Oral tradition—North
Carolina—Mitchell County—History. 4. Silver,
Frankie—Legends. 5. Mitchell County (N.C.)—
Folklore. 6. McMillon, Bobby—Contributions in
folklore. 7. Silver, Frankie. I. Title.

GR110.N8 P37 2000

398.23'2756865—dc21 00-036385

04 03 02 01 00 5 4 3 2 1

For

Bobby McMillon

in respect, appreciation,

and friendship

CONTENTS

Acknowledgments *xi*

Introduction *1*

1 Bobby McMillon and Oral Tradition *8*

2 Frankie Silver Lore as Performed by Bobby McMillon *30*

3 The State versus Frances Silver *43*

4 A Story That Happened: The Legend of Frankie Silver *65*

5 The Ballad "Frankie Silver" *99*

6 A Tale of a Governor *121*

Conclusion *149*

Appendix A.
  Variants of the Frankie Silver Legend Cycle *165*

Appendix B.
  Variants of the Ballad "Frankie Silver" (Laws E 13) *178*

Appendix C.
  Artistic Treatments of the Frankie Silver Story *181*

Notes *183*

Works Cited *203*

Index *219*

ILLUSTRATIONS

Bobby McMillon in 1998 *9*

Bobby McMillon in San Diego *12*

Bobby McMillon with his grandparents and cousin *13*

Bobby McMillon at age nine *16*

Mae ("Maw Maw") Shultz Phillips *21*

A sign in the churchyard at Kona *27*

A display in the Silver family museum *28*

John Robert Donnell *45*

William Julius Alexander *46*

Henry Spainhour *49*

Nicholas W. Woodfin *55*

Burgess S. Gaither *56*

Col. John Carson *62*

H. E. C. ("Red Buck") Bryant *68*

Muriel Earley Sheppard *69*

Lattimore ("Uncle Latt") Hughes *70*

A map of the Toe River country *74*

The log house of Jacob Silver *76*

Catherine and Greenberry Woody *77*

A "criminal's farewell" broadside *116*

Bobby McMillon and Marina Trivette *119*

David Lowry Swain *122*

Matilda Sharpe Erwin *126*

Eliza Grace McDowell Woodfin *127*

Quaker Meadows *139*

ACKNOWLEDGMENTS

This book is dedicated to Bobby McMillon, and appropriately so, for he was not only its subject but also my chief collaborator. He gave unstintingly of his knowledge, judgment, time, and friendship. I hope the book in some measure repays him. Tom Davenport, my colleague in many an endeavor over the years, was equally generous, and without his nudging, I would never have taken up this labor. He made available all the material he had recorded with Bobby. My wife, Beverly Patterson, and her colleague Wayne Martin had interviewed Bobby extensively, too, and gave me use of their recordings and of Beverly's transcriptions of them. Beverly did a great deal of additional spade work on the Silver case, pondered the material with me, read the manuscript with a helpful eye, and was ever "ready with wise counsel."

But I am indebted to many others, too—a host of earlier researchers who found, transcribed, published, and wrote about documents concerning the Frankie Silver case, the oral legend, the historical and legal narrative, the history of British and American law, the history of the confessional literature of crime, North Carolina social history, and many another topic. Footnotes will acknowledge my indebtedness to them, but I need to thank by name those who gave me direct assistance during the research. It would take a second book to describe all their kindnesses. I hope they will all accept my sincere gratitude, even though I simply post their names in an alphabetical list: Lloyd Bailey, Bruce Baker, Patricia C. Ballard, Patricia Bryan, Anne A. Connelly, Richard Eller, Helen B. Erwin, Fran Farlow, Randy Folger, Linda Garibaldi, B. J. Gooch, Jeffrey T. Gray, Steve Green, Nina Greenlee, John Harrod, Ann Parks Hawthorne, Loyal Jones, Matthew Jones, Barbara Laughon, Erika Lindemann, Claire McCann, Sharyn McCrumb, Jim McGee, William C. McKnight, James C. McNutt, Frances Manderson, Wayne Martin, Lynwood Montell, Ron Nalley, Gladys Nave, Jocelyn Neill, Jon Nichols, Dan W. Olds, Cheryl Oxford, Panaiotis, Charles Perdue, Clara Lee Riddle, Gerald Roberts, Charlotte Ross, Michael Ross, Robert R. Shields, James D. "John" Silver, Wayne Silver, Michael Taft, Richard

Taylor, Marina Trivette, Michael Trotti, Paul Wells, David E. Whisnant, Howard Williams, the late Lawrence E. Wood, Perry D. Young, Charles G. "Terry" Zug III, the American Antiquarian Society, Berea College Library, the Historical Society of Pennsylvania, the Library of Congress, the Morganton-Burke County Public Library, the Texas State Library, the Transylvania College Library, the Library of the University of Texas at Austin, and especially the dedicated staffs of the North Carolina Collection, the Southern Folklife Collection, and the Southern Historical Collection in the Library of the University of North Carolina at Chapel Hill and of the North Carolina State Archives in Raleigh. The staff of the University of North Carolina Press—in particular Elaine Maisner and Pam Upton—deserve my thanks for all their help and patience.

In closing, I want to acknowledge my indebtedness also to the Kenan Research Fund at the University of North Carolina, which provided funds to offset some of my research costs, and to the National Humanities Center, where I was coddled by the staff and helped by many colleagues, in particular Mary B. Campbell, Barbara Hanawalt, John N. King, Kent Mullikin, and Jay M. Smith, all of whom gave me very fruitful suggestions. Six of the book's chapters were written in the stimulating setting of the Center.

A TREE ACCURST

INTRODUCTION

Bobby McMillon came home from work one afternoon in 1992 and found he had a telephone call from Tom Davenport. Tom, an independent filmmaker from Virginia, was stopping overnight near Bobby's home town of Lenoir, North Carolina, on his way back from videotaping Gary Carden, a storyteller in a community to the west. Tom had just recently begun filming on videotape and editing footage with a computer, and he was exhilarated by the ease and economy of this method. Would Bobby like to drop by the motel, he wanted to know, so they could try taping some of his stories, too? Bobby hurried over. Between them they settled on a ballad and related legend cycle about Frankie Silver. The subject—a North Carolina murder commemorated in a ballad and local legends—is important to Bobby, and he had earlier sent Tom a story he had written about it under the title "A Fly in Amber." Bobby simply sat, sang the song, and then for thirty-one minutes offered his account to the camera in a single, uninterrupted take. From that seed, this book grew.[1]

Tom sent me a videocassette of his unedited footage to use in my folksong class at the University of North Carolina at Chapel Hill. I had introduced him to Bobby many years earlier, after I had myself gotten to know Bobby in 1974 through Cody Lowe, a student in the class. "My high school buddy," Cody told me, "sings all these old songs." Soon he brought along his buddy to the class, and that meeting developed into a long friendship. Bobby, only twenty-three years old then, was already working full time in a furniture factory. As soon as he started singing and talking about ballads, it was obvious to me that he was one of the most important Appalachian tradition bearers of his generation in North Carolina. This means that, as a singer and storyteller, he was very different from the performers so popular then in the "folk scene": slick college boys like the Kingston Trio or political activists like Joan Baez who took up the guitar, went on the concert stage, and sang a repertory of songs learned from books and recordings, dressing them up in harmonies and vocal stylings calculated to win a middle-class audience. Bobby was more akin to Almeda Riddle, Roscoe Holcomb, Mance Lipscomb, Dewey Balfa, Doc Watson, and other traditional artists brought to public attention in those years through the efforts of people like Alan Lomax, Ralph Rinzler, and Mike Seeger. These musicians performed the music of their own families, regions, occupations, and religious denominations.

Since the 1970s, Bobby McMillon has become widely known across North Carolina and has performed outside the state at such events as the Smithsonian Festival of American Folklife in Washington and the World's Fair in Knoxville. He has been the subject of a number of articles and a master's thesis, and his performances have been included in two recordings.[2] In 1995 the North Carolina Folklore Society saluted his extraordinary service to Appalachian traditional culture with its Brown-Hudson Folklore Award, and in 2000 the North Carolina Arts Council honored him with its Folk Heritage Award.

Only a small part of Bobby McMillon's knowledge and artistry is documented and explored in the Tom Davenport videotape *The Ballad of Frankie Silver* and in this book. Bobby performs many kinds of Appalachian songs and tales. He has filled notebooks with the words to nearly four hundred songs he has collected and sings, and he knows more stories than songs.[3] But Tom Davenport and I chose to focus on one song and its related stories that are of particular importance to Bobby McMillon. The materials tell of Frankie Silver, a young woman in the Toe River country of western North Carolina, who was tried and convicted in 1832 of using an ax to murder her husband Charlie, a murder made more horrific by the subsequent dismemberment and burning of his body. Among other striking episodes in the tale are Frankie's escape from jail, her recapture, and her hanging.

The North Carolina Arts Council awarded Tom a tiny grant for making his documentary film with Bobby. My wife, Beverly Patterson, and I served as consultants while Tom and his gifted assistant, Matthew Jones, worked with the footage. Their edited video showed performances of the song by Bobby McMillon and Marina Trivette, his sister-in-law and singing partner, and Bobby's telling of much of the legend cycle. Some of the footage comes from that first rendition in Tom's motel room. But Tom and Bobby, with the help of folklore student Jon Nichols, subsequently filmed portions of the story again on location in and around Morganton, where Frankie Silver was executed in 1833, and in the Kona community in Mitchell County, where the murder took place and where Bobby learned the stories about it in his childhood. Tom and Matthew also included interviews with Wayne Silver, Assistant Attorney General Jeffrey Gray, and others, and at the close of the film added an epilogue, "The Making of a Ballad Singer," in which Bobby and Marina talk about why the old songs are important to them.

When the first edit of the video had been completed, Tom circulated copies and suggested I draft a background booklet for teachers who wanted to use the video in their courses. We had prepared similar study materials for some of our earlier film collaborations — *Born for Hard Luck, Being a Joines,* and *A Singing Stream.*[4] As source material, I had hours of transcribed interviews Tom had recorded with Bobby, two other interview sessions recorded for the North Carolina Arts Council by Beverly Patterson and Wayne Martin, and a two-day interview that Bobby recorded with me. I also went seriously to work exploring both the early documents and the recent writings about Frankie Silver. The film, it soon became clear, contained several factual errors. Tom made a second edit of the video to remove these, to add some important material from the raw footage, and to strengthen the structure. He finished this edit early in 1999 and released the film for the second time. By then the booklet had grown into this seven-chapter book. Its core, Chapter 2, is a transcription of the ballad and the stories as performed by Bobby McMillon in the session Tom Davenport filmed in 1992. The rest of the book explores the background, nature, and implications of this material.

A hundred and sixty-eight years after Frankie Silver's death, her case still has a powerful hold on many people in North Carolina. Her story has been told and retold since 1903 in newspapers, magazines, memoirs, local histories, and folklore collections. Senator Sam G. Ervin Jr. more than once published his assessment of the case.[5] In 1935 Muriel Earley Sheppard gave the tale currency outside the state by including it in her book *Cabins in the Laurel* as both an account in prose and a poem of her own composition.[6]

In an article for the *Journal of American Folklore*, reprinted in a special Frankie Silver issue of the *North Carolina Folklore Journal*, Beverly Patterson describes a flood of recent treatments of the Frankie Silver case.[7] In addition to Tom Davenport's film, videos produced by David S. Mull and Richard Eller also tell the story. Since the early 1970s, there have been stagings of three unpublished plays about Frankie—one by Susan Graham Erwin, a sister-in-law of Senator Ervin, and the other two by Howard Williams and Maxine McCall. The composer Panaiotis has taken the murder as the inspiration for a ballet entitled *The Ballad of Frankie Silver*. The Tanz Ensemble Cathy Sharp premiered this work in 1992 in Basel, Switzerland, brought it to the 1996 summer Olympics in Atlanta, and had plans to return with it on an American tour in 1999; the group's performance has been filmed. Appalachian author Sharyn McCrumb, a descendant of one of Frankie's brothers, uses the same title for her well-received "ballad novel" published by Dutton in 1998, and Fran Farlow, a writer in Gastonia, has completed another novel, still unpublished, about the murder. In 1998 Perry Deane Young, a journalist, authored *The Untold Story of Frankie Silver*, in which he debunks errors in earlier treatments of the case. For the past six years, Jo Ball and other eighth-grade teachers at the Heritage Middle School in Valdese have used Frankie Silver as the focus of a five- to six-weeks' study unit drawing together virtually everything in their curriculum, from social studies to North Carolina history, math, science, English, creative writing, art, and music. The project climaxes in an improvised dramatic production, the students' re-creation of the trial of Frankie Silver. As recently as 1994, Ball's students petitioned Governor James B. Hunt on behalf of Frankie Silver for a posthumous "pardon of forgiveness." In Kona, where the murder took place, Wayne Silver has given Frankie Silver exhibits a prominent place in a Silver family museum housed in the former Kona Baptist Church, near which Charles Silver lies buried. Patricia J. Dowd, a local artist, made a color print entitled *Frankie and Charlie Silver Cabin* and released it in 1998 in a print run of five hundred copies. Jim Harbin, another member of the Silver family, has privately issued a booklet entitled *Nancy's Story: To Right the Legend of Frankie Silver,* which brings together information and photographs about generations of Frankie's descendants.

With the exception of the composer and choreographer, all those described have roots in the region where the murder took place. Bobby McMillon himself spent time as a child in the community where Frankie lived; he is descended from an uncle of her husband, Charlie, and is also related by marriage to the daughter of Charlie and Frankie Silver. For Bobby, this is not only regional but family history. It is even personal history. Hearing the tales of Frankie Silver remains one of his most vivid childhood memories.

The folklore—the ballad and the stories—kept the memory of Frankie Silver alive across the generations and gave rise to all these current activities, but that fact has failed to gain universal approval for the oral traditions. Objections to the story come from several sides. Although interest in the Frankie Silver case has remained strong in western North Carolina and the broader Appalachian region, some outsiders find it distasteful. When Tom Davenport submitted his video to the North Carolina Center for Public Television, for example, its director—who is not a native of the state—rejected the film as too violent and as neither enriching nor educational. In light of the Center's other programming, his stated objections were puzzling. Two of its long-running prime-time features are *The Lawrence Welk Show,* for which few would claim any enriching educational content, and the British series *Mystery,* which is based on a formula that requires weekly homicides. At the time when the Davenport film was rejected because of its "violence," the Center was broadcasting a serial dramatization of Minette Walters's novel *The Sculptress,* which opened with quick but bloody shots of a double decapitation. Since Davenport's video presented no visual images of violence, the Center's reaction to it was perhaps a tribute to Bobby McMillon's power as a storyteller. But it was equally likely to reflect a dislike of any expression of Appalachian vernacular culture not softened by a romantic haze.

A similar embarrassment was confessed recently by one programmer for the local affiliate of National Public Radio. In an interview, she reported feeling an obligation to prepare and broadcast a short memorial tribute when Bill Monroe died. But she had great difficulty finding any recording by him in which he did not sing. Her sophisticated Research Triangle audience, she was sure, would be offended by his "high lonesome" vocal style.[8] Of course, people sympathetic to bluegrass would recognize this quality as the very soul of Monroe's music and wonder at the programmer's fastidiousness. Apparently, some people in the region are dedicated to presenting only a "progressive" image of the South. They seem particularly uncomfortable with the culture of blue-collar Appalachia.

Those who take an intelligent interest in regional material like the Frankie Silver case may have other objections to the traditional accounts. Even in Frankie's own day, many people began to believe, after their initial horrified reaction, that she had been wronged both by her husband and by the law. The number of people taking this position has grown, especially in the last twenty years. Feminists, in particular, find the legend cycle reflective of male bias. Other people, vigilant guardians of factual truth, disdain the ballad and the legends as demonstrably inaccurate — as "only folklore." All these objections are understandable, but I hope this book will provide answers to them, showing why we need to take the oral traditions seriously and what kinds of truths we can find in them.

To do this requires laying out the historical background of the case, which I do in Chapter 3. Others have covered this ground before me, and I am deeply indebted to their discoveries. Like virtually everyone who has worked seriously on the case, I have also made discoveries of my own among the old documents — some in manuscripts directly bearing on this case and others in writings that offer perspective on it. I have also pushed the interpretation of these materials in fresh directions, particularly in assessing the professional conduct of Frankie Silver's attorney. Chapter 6 explores another historical dimension of the case: why two governors of the state failed to act favorably on petitions sent them in Frankie's behalf. This topic had been little explored, and it discloses a second tragic story, that of the Swain family, which forms a curious counterpoint to the story of Frankie and her own family. The stories show, I believe, that Frankie's fate was determined not only by her actions but also by those of her family, by the legal system then in place, by the personal limitations of her attorney, by Governor Swain's private family dilemmas, and by two contrasting social codes of the era.

Some may think the value of these chapters is that they set straight some of the errors in the Frankie Silver ballad and legends. I disagree. Much in the case remains — and always will remain — a mystery, but the ways in which the local lore diverges from known historical fact highlights what the traditional community saw as significant in the distressing events. Comparing oral tradition with the historical record helps us to recognize the peculiar character of the ballad and the legends. These two forms of folklore, however, present differing views of Frankie, and I explore them separately. Chapter 5 argues that the Frankie Silver ballad is best understood as a survival of a very old feature of the ritual of public execution. The singers' perception of the ballad, however, calls into question a fashionable political interpretation some recent scholars have made of this tradition. Chapter 4 interprets the legend cycle, using the historical facts, various theories of narrative, the peculiar structure of this cycle of historical legends, and Bobby McMillon's explanatory comments. I get my personal say too, of course, but I have tried to indicate where Bobby and I may hold differing opinions. Bobby also read the manuscript and discussed it with me in a second lengthy interview that I recorded and from which I quote, and he annotated and commented on passages in a later draft of the manuscript. I have incorporated all his insights.

Bobby's is ultimately the informing perspective in the book, so I have framed the core of my narrative with chapters about him. Chapter 1 describes the lifelong passion that turned Bobby from a delighted participant in the oral traditions of his family and neighbors into a self-conscious collector, student, performer, and interpreter of old songs and stories. The Conclusion brings his understanding and my own to bear on the case of Frankie Silver.

Frankie's disquieting crime has provoked many people to attempt narrative reconstructions of her life—the lawyers at her trial, the gentlewomen who petitioned for her pardon, generations of journalists and local historians, and now teachers, a choreographer, playwrights, videographers, and novelists. Their accounts no more capture the historical Frankie Silver than does this book or the traditional ballad or the legend cycle. That is not really the point of telling the story. Bobby McMillon says that "anything so tragic as that story" would naturally leave behind some residue, "a 'haint,' a ghost."[9] With "a bloody ax in her hand and flaming eyes a-shining," to use his phrase, that ghost stalks our consciousness as it does Bobby's. Crafting these fictions, even arguing about them, helps us all to lay Frankie's spirit, making it, we hope, less perturbed—and less perturbing.

I've been fortunate that I was born
just in the nick of time, you might say,
to learn a lot of these tales and stories
that I never would've gotten if I'd been
born any later.

— Bobby McMillon

BOBBY McMILLON AND ORAL TRADITION

Between the ages of twelve and sixteen, Bobby McMillon came to realize, he says, "where the meaning of my life was at": a passion for oral traditions. It grew from "not just the songs, or how old they were, or where they had come from (which was fascinating to me too)," but from the realization "that these living, breathing people that I lived with, sang them" and had learned them from mothers, grandmothers, and other people close to them. It impressed him that they found deep meaning in the songs.

Bobby especially felt a spiritual kinship between himself and Maw Maw Phillips, an elderly member of his father's family who loved to sing and to share songs with him. Hers had been a difficult life. Bobby says she was what people called "a base-born child," or illegitimate. In her teens, Phillips went to work as a hired girl, and later she endured a difficult marriage. Because of "the hard times that she experienced and the different people that she met," Bobby says, she was a person with the gift to "wonder at the world." She had "learned through that" about life, "and through songs that they would sing."[1] Bobby describes himself in

Bobby McMillon, storyteller and ballad singer, in 1998.
(Photograph copyright © Tom Rankin)

similar words. As a child, he thought of the old traditions as "just being something wonderfully entertaining, something that I wanted to hear more of."[2] But eventually, he says, all of these things came to have "some kind of meaning in my mind that I could ponder on."[3]

It was unusual for a youngster in Bobby McMillon's time and place to have this depth of feeling for the old traditions. The Appalachia into which Bobby was born in 1951 was far different from popular stereotypes of it as a world of isolated coves in which an illiterate population lived in log houses. Long before Bobby's childhood years, industry had entered even the small mountain community of Kona in Mitchell County, where Bobby spent time as a child with his grandparents Rosa and Dewey Woody. After working first as a carpenter for mines in Matewan, West Virginia, and then on the railroads, Dewey Woody spent twenty years at Harris Clay Company in Kona, eventually becoming head mechanic and "trouble shooter," ready day or night—whenever the whistle blew—to go and repair a faulty machine in the mines. Bobby's grandmother Rosa managed a general store across the road from the old Kona Baptist Church. In later years they ran a store in Caldwell County, at the foot of the eastern slope of the Blue Ridge.

A house fire had driven Bobby's other grandfather, Henry Clay Mc-Millon, off his farm near Cosby, Tennessee. He got a small farm near Lenoir, North Carolina, but like many other rural southerners in the first half of this century, Henry McMillon and his sons then entered "public work." If they had lived in Kentucky, they might have gone into the coal mines or moved out of state to find work in the automobile plants in Michigan. If they had been in the Piedmont region of North or South Carolina, they might have taken jobs in a textile mill. As it was, they picked from options available in their part of the South. The oldest son, Goldman, became a truck driver. Amos became an electrician and moved to San Diego. Ken, after he grew up, served in the Navy and then settled in San Diego, too, also working as an electrician. Gordon, Bobby's father, worked mostly as a carpenter but also put in time in a furniture factory in the early 1950s. In the 1970s, Bobby started working in the furniture assembly lines, and except for a few years when he got appointments to perform traditional arts in the schools, the factory is where Bobby made his living.

Their work experiences had an impact on the political views some family members held. Although Bobby's Woody relatives in western North Carolina had always been Democrats, in east Tennessee his father's family had been strict Republicans and thought "a man ought to be happy with an honest day's dollar." It seemed to Bobby that "the strongest Republicans was always the ones that had the least, in Appalachia. And it was like they adamantly defended their right to feel that you *shouldn't* have anything." Bobby himself originally registered as a Republican out of loyalty to his father, but he worried for a week and then went back to the courthouse to change his voter registration. Bobby's father also had begun to shift his political allegiances. In California, he had been tempted to join a labor union but held back because he knew his own father would be against it. (Joining a union was never an option in the factories where Bobby himself worked—the few efforts at unionizing them failed.) Eventually Bobby's father amazed him by turning Democratic, in his views if not his official registration. "He really was an unbiased man," Bobby says, and he "knew where the money was coming from, and seemed like when we were under a Democratic administration that jobs got a little better and more money came out and people could live a little bit easier."[4]

Many younger members of Bobby's immediate family were also able to get schooling that had not been available to earlier generations in the mountains. His mother, his cousins, and Bobby himself were all high school graduates. Bobby loves to read. As a youngster, he devoured stories by Edgar Rice Burroughs, H. Ryder Haggard, and Sir Arthur Conan Doyle. His reading later turned toward folklore collections and books on Appalachian history like Altina Waller's *Feud: Hatfields, Mc-Coys, and Social Change in Appalachia, 1860–1900*, which he respects as a work that matches his own sense of the kinds of personalities and economic realities that have marked mountain life and history.

Members of Bobby's family also showed a growing interest in American popular culture. His grandfather Woody owned a phonograph and recordings. His grandfather McMillon's musical preferences included swing. When Bobby's father was growing up, he went every Saturday to a theater to watch cowboy films. The family was quick to buy a television set when these became available in the 1950s. Comparing their families, both Bobby McMillon and Sheila Kay Adams, another brilliant Appalachian ballad singer and storyteller, agreed that "the people that grew up in our parents' day were looking at all the new stuff and looking ahead." They "wanted to drop everything . . . that they had grown up with, 'cause they had grown up in real bad conditions, and it changed and got better."[5] Bobby recalls that one of his uncles in California seemed ashamed for people know that "when he grew up they had to go out to a little house behind the big house to use the bathroom. . . . A lot of people of my mother and father's generation got to be ashamed of it after World War II, when everything opened up and they begin a different kind of life away from the farm."[6] Attachment to the oral traditions also "skipped a generation."[7] Bobby considers himself "fortunate that I was born just in the nick of time, you might say, to learn a lot of these tales and stories that I never would've gotten if I'd been born any later."[8]

Bobby suggests a number of reasons why he himself came to center his life on learning traditional stories and songs. A theme running through them is his awareness of contrasting ways of life. Both his father's and his mother's families had moved into Caldwell County from homes

Bobby McMillon, aged seven years, in San Diego. (Courtesy of Bobby McMillon)

farther back in the mountains, and thus they were, to a degree, outsiders. Bobby's sense of otherness was compounded by another move his family made:

> When I was six years old, my father, who had two brothers living in California with their families, decided to move out there and take a strike at making a living in the West. And so on my sixth birthday, in 1957, we went west to east San Diego. And I didn't like it at all. We stayed there through '58 and '59. And I came home — we left San Diego on the second day of February 1960 and that was on a Monday. And we got home about 1:30 on Thursday afternoon. I was that anxious to get home. I kept track of all of it, and it's never left me.[9]

His parents took him to California a second time in 1960, but when they came home on a visit later that year, Bobby would not go back with them.

Bobby McMillon at the age of three, with his grandparents Dewey and Rosa Woody and his cousin Pat Burgin. (Courtesy of Bobby McMillon)

He thinks his refusal was in part due to an aversion to the landscape, "the absence of wood and water." [10] But it was also because he felt very close to his Woody grandparents, who had taken care of him as a baby when his mother became ill. They kept him again when his parents returned to California. "After that move to California," Bobby says, "I always just felt a little out of place everywhere I was at."

Since Bobby's grandparents were "the stable element" in his life, he feels that he may have needed to identify with their world, because doing so "made me not be as afraid of ever being uprooted again." But there were positive sides to Bobby's growing awareness of the differences in the ways people lived. Being so much with his grandparents, he "got curious about their life" and about the lives of the people around them. The general store drew a variety of customers, and Bobby was fascinated with "all these funny characters . . . that would seem to pop out of the woodwork."[11]

Equally stimulating to him was a trip he took deeper into the mountains. Bobby's father had left Tennessee for North Carolina in 1946 at the age of fourteen; in 1955 he decided it was time to go back "to have a little reunion with everybody." He drove there in "an old '39 Ford, a white one," and took his wife and Bobby along. Although Bobby was only three or four years old, he vividly remembers the trip and the ways of living and the strong characters he met in Tennessee. "Daddy took us all back in that country where he was raised, and back then, even in the '50s, it was just dirt roads." It was a region in which Bobby could see "the older type of mountain living . . . still going on." The women were still "going to the creek and washing." Maw Maw Phillips, whom he met for the first time on this trip, "wore them old-timey long dresses, not wide dresses, but like granny women would wear, and an apron over the dress." Her young boys were "out a-running with the dogs." His aunt Ethel Whitlock was "cooking salads—you could smell that stuff everywhere." She had married "old man Gibb Whitlock, and he was a bear hunter. And he'd been dispossessed when the Park bought out the land, and he fought a war with the Park for the . . . rest of his life, fifty years, I guess. He would hunt bears in the Park every chance he got. He made liquor, and even got mad at them one time and set the Park on fire, tried to burn it down. He didn't have no conception of how big the Great Smoky Mountain Park was." Bobby calls that tour in the mountains around Cosby, Tennessee, one of the "brighter spots of my childhood." It brought to life for him all the stories his father's people told about moonshine stills and bears.

The storytelling was especially fascinating to him and he says that on later trips there he took a strong interest in it. Maw Maw Phillips, his grandmother McMillon, and others, when they told about things that had happened, took you "back into another world," a world his grandmother called "the wagon days" before 1915. His father's people would say, " 'This old man rid across the hill on a horse, and he come to tell Maw that he knowed who it was that robbed her and Grandpap, and he didn't want to die before—.' I mean I was just spellbound, my tongue hanging out, when I'd hear this. . . . To me to hear these tales was . . . something far better than I could ever see on TV."[12]

In the community where Bobby's Woody grandparents lived, tale telling was also part of the fabric of everyday life. Bobby says:

People always were telling stories. I mean when you set down at the table, some of the older folks they would go to relating what had happened that day. You'd have to sit there and listen to them. I mean it was some kind of narrative *all* the time, whether it was fabulous or whether it had really occurred. Sometimes, if they wanted you to get out of their hair, they'd tell you some tale or something to get you quiet, and sometimes you'd be out in the field a-planting, a-working, and occasionally somebody would tell something.[13]

Bobby was ten or twelve when he first began to seek out stories "beyond what I knew just at home." He recalls learning stories from his first cousins on his mother's side and going with them to hear tales from their grandparents Lounette and Isaac Hopson, who lived at Green Mountain, about six miles down the Toe River from Kona. Paw Hopson

had a lot of tales from the late eighteen hundreds that happened to him. He'd been bushwhacked twice. I think he had a bullet in his shoulder that a bushwhacker had put in him one time. And he could just tell hours and hours of stories of what happened to him. He was the one, I guess, that first started telling me a lot of booger tales and witch tales. And me and my cousins would just sit and listen to him. And his wife, she was Granny Hopson, and she would tell stories about her family.[14]

His cousins' father, Charles Hopson, told them tall tales about hunting "as if *he* was a-hunting, and he seen these wild cats that fit all the way to the top of the tree and the last time he seen them the fur was still flying. I reckon they fit till there wasn't nothing but fur. And then the snake that bit its tail and swallowed itself up."[15]

Bobby's deep interest in folksongs was partly sparked by his discovery of narrative songs. "The first time I ever heard my third cousin William Nathan Gortny sing 'Lord Thomas and Fair Ellender,'" he says, "I liked to fell off my chair." Bobby was not struck just by the contrast between the "old man in overalls" and his song "about lords and ladies and milk-white steeds." What most affected him was that the ballad's story of love

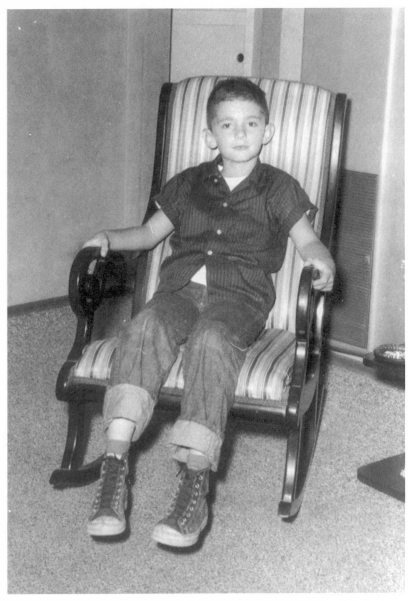

Bobby McMillon at age nine, when he was growing interested in songs and tales.
(Courtesy of Bobby McMillon)

and betrayal and jealousy "sounded like something that had really happened."[16] Bobby says, too, that by the time he was twelve he realized that many of the newer songs he was hearing "had stories" and that the stories "I had heard as a child came back and seemed to go with them, and I realized that the stories and the songs were all sort of together."[17]

By this time Bobby already had a familiarity with folk and other vernacular music stretching back into his earliest childhood. Since before he can remember, his family had taken him along to services at Hollow Springs Primitive Baptist Church, where his grandfather McMillon served as the elder. This denomination has a strong tradition of unaccompanied singing of traditional melodies, and the Hollow Springs congregation included members like Gene Watson, a cousin of Doc Watson and himself a gifted vocalist, who was later the elder there.[18] In Bobby's childhood, this church used at least one hymnbook that contained words only, requiring that the tunes be sung from memory, and another with tunes printed in shaped notes. Hollow Springs also held an annual shape-note singing using another book, Elder C. H. Cayce's *The Good Old Songs*. One church member, Carl McGee, took Bobby to annual Christian Harmony singings at Etowah, southwest of Asheville. It was at the 1969 singings at Etowah and Hollow Springs that Bobby and I, we both believe, actually first met.

Bobby also grew up hearing gospel music in the Missionary Baptist church his Woody grandparents attended and listening to recordings that his grandfather Woody owned — songs, for example, by Smith's Sacred Singers. "I *loved* to hear them sing!" he says, especially his favorite piece, "He Will Set Your Fields on Fire." He remembers his grandmother McMillon's recordings of the Chuck Wagon Gang. Bobby also enjoyed the gospel singing of the Crossroads Quartet on Arthur Smith's television shows, broadcast from Charlotte. By late childhood he had already developed a more than casual interest: "I would make lists of songs that I knew the titles of or little bits and pieces of. I probably knew three hundred gospel songs, before I even begin to pay attention to the older music, just simply from churches."[19]

The awakening of a serious interest in secular songs came through listening to recordings on his grandfather Woody's wind-up phonograph. Bobby recalls songs by Ernest Stoneman and Uncle Dave Macon and, especially, the Carter Family. "I realized fairly quick," he says, "that they were singing some songs that people out in the community knew, that weren't always to be found in song books. And so I began to learn just a little bit about the different versions of things, and that really whetted my appetite. . . . And then I began to get my family members to sing the songs that they had heard in the days . . . even prior to the time that they had phonographs and talking machines."[20]

By the time Bobby was a sophomore in high school, his interest in the old music was becoming a passion. It led Bobby to discover such compendiums as *The Frank C. Brown Collection of North Carolina Folklore* in the public library. His English teacher, Louise Walker Adderholt, encouraged his enthusiasm. She knew Bobby's family well. Her father was a deacon of the Primitive Baptist church where Bobby's grandfather preached, and her own mother, Bobby says, "was and still is just a wonderful shape-note singer." Adderholt was the faculty sponsor of a folklore club Bobby organized a year later. In 1969 she took him to a meeting of the North Carolina Folklore Society, where she introduced him to professors Arthur Palmer Hudson and Amos Abrams. She had taken a course in folklore taught by Dean Cratis Williams at Appalachian State University, and she took Bobby up to meet Williams, too. Bobby says Williams "talked to me a lot about how to document what I was learning and what I had learned."[21] And Williams added words that at the time "just baffled" Bobby, but later came to seem deeply prophetic: he said that one day these songs would come to "hold more for me in life than what I imagined right then."[22]

Perhaps Louise Adderholt influenced Bobby most significantly by inspiring him to want a tape recorder like hers. When he was sixteen or seventeen, he persuaded his father to buy him one. They got it on an installment plan, and Bobby mowed lawns to help pay for the machine. He said to himself, "Now, if I can get any of my folks to sing, I'm going to do it."[23]

Bobby found he had a good deal to learn about collecting songs. "It's been my experience," he says, that if you ask mountain people for something,

> You should never do it directly. They have an aversion to direct requests. It's not that they mind doing anything . . . but they sort of like you to beg a little bit. And so they'll say, "Well, last three or four years my voice has went downhill so bad, I just don't know whether I can sing or not. Lord, I had bronchitis the other week, and it's just about got me on the go-down. I don't know if I'd be able to sing a tune or not. I couldn't carry a tune in a bucket no way, never could. I might,

you know, could start off with a little *some*thing, you know." And then if you kept on, "Oh, I'd really love to hear it. Wasn't there something in there about something a-happening?—I heard so-and-so say that in that old love song that somebody killed so—." "No, that ain't the way it was! They never could get that'n right. I might could go over a little bit for you." And so they go into a verse or so, then sort of stop, and if it looked like you was real interested and just dying for more, then they'd get wound up and after a while they'd just go right on and on. What they really want, they really want to know that that's truly what you want. They wouldn't want to embarrass themselves by coming out singing and maybe making a mischord or something like that.[24]

Bobby met with some disappointments in learning to use the tape recorder. On one occasion, he and his cousins had walked up to the house of a brother of one of his great-uncles:

He was a real queer man, but he was one of these colorful old mountain characters that talked with a voice that people outside the mountains would have real trouble to understand—but he knew all these wonderful stories about growing up and being serenaded and finding dead people in the river. He had went with his brother to Tennessee to kidnap his fiancée and bring her back, and her mother and her brothers come out to try to shoot 'em, but they was on horses and they's getting away, and her mammy had come to the door and said, "You North Carolina sons of bitches!" Shook her fist at 'em. And then he took the girl back home and married her and lived for eighty years.

Bobby missed recording that and the other stories told during the visit. "On the way back to the house," he says, "I looked down and realized that I hadn't turned the switch on." He never had another chance to go back and try again. Bobby can still remember much of what the man told but says that "there was some of it I would have *loved* to had. He had a sister that was real rough and nearly killed one of the brothers, and he had to save him. And oh, it was just wonderful what he told. It was something that I could never recapture again or get from any other person's perspective." He recalls another time after that when the same thing almost happened. Visiting in Tennessee, he asked his great-aunt Maw Maw Phillips about some of "the murder stories that happened up near Cosby." She gave him "just a wonderful narrative of her speaking without any interruptions, telling the whole story of how Mae Miller was killed by Johnny Phillips." After about forty-five minutes, Bobby realized he was not recording the story, got his machine working, and started over again. It had been "perfect" the first time, he says, but the second time he had to "dig it out more."[25]

Bobby has continued to learn current songs as a part of his everyday life. For example, for a number of years beginning in 1989 Bobby attended a Pentecostal church in Lenoir that had a biracial congregation and a repertory of largely oral choruses and gospel songs. His wife-to-be, Joyce, and her sister Marina grew up in this church and had known the songs since childhood. Bobby and Doug Trivette, whom Marina married, joined them in performing the music in services. These were songs Bobby absorbed as an adult. But as a self-conscious collector, Bobby made deliberate efforts to seek out people who knew older folksongs. Over the years he picked up songs and stories from many people, some widely known like the Hicks family of Beech Mountain and the Wallins in Madison County, others known only locally, like Wade Gilbert of Wilkes County, who played the fiddle and the fretless banjo, was related to the Dula family, and had many stories about Tom and the murder of Laura Foster. Bobby was probably most deeply influenced, however, by Maw Maw Phillips and by two other singers he knew and recorded as a teenager, Lou Brookshire and Rolf Ellison.

The fall before Bobby got his tape recorder, Maw Maw Phillips came to North Carolina to visit her daughter, Bobby's aunt by marriage. She learned of Bobby's love of songs, and "it just tickled her to death that there was somebody interested in that." Bobby calls her "the most open person that I was *ever* with" and says she "would willingly sing anything that she knew—and that's not common for most of the mountain people, even among your relatives." Their shared passion for song created a very deep bond between them, and from this visit till the day Maw Maw died, Bobby says, "she was just like my own grandmother."[26] (Reading this passage in my manuscript, Bobby felt he had not expressed himself strongly enough and wrote, "This bond transcended my description. Our spirits were atuned. . . . We were spiritual soul-mates.")

Mae Phillips, he says, "just really knew lots and lots of songs." From childhood she had loved all the music she heard. Many of her songs she had picked up from cousins as a young girl. Her stepfather, a Civil War veteran, was high strung. Mae said that "you couldn't turn a page of a

Mae ("Maw Maw") Shultz Phillips (1900–1980) at Maryville, Tennessee, in August 1979. Bobby's note: "From whom I learned a hundred songs." (Courtesy of Bobby McMillon)

book but what that would be too much noise for him. And you weren't allowed to sing love songs at his house. They . . . disapproved of it. So she said her and her cousins would have to go up in the hollows, and they'd just sing all day to entertain themselves." Mae learned other songs in her early teens from people in whose homes she worked as a hired girl. In big tent meetings down on the Pigeon River at Hartford, Tennessee, she picked up spirituals like "May the Lord Continue with Me." Bobby says she always continued to love all the music "in the world that she heard, . . . whether it was at church or on the radio. And she would sing 'The Window Up Above' by George Jones, you know, right in the midst of a bunch of ballads. And then she'd sing 'Where Shall I Shelter My Sheep Tonight?' or something like that." Like other mountain people, Bobby says, she "never distinguished much between the types of songs" she knew, "except to say that a religious song was a 'meeting-house song,' and a ballad was a 'love song,' unless you wrote it down on paper."[27] Bobby himself was most attracted to her older songs and their "minor"-sounding tunes. In childhood he had disliked these old modal melodies when they were used in Primitive Baptist congregational singing, but after Maw Maw sang him "Pretty Fair Maid in the Garden," he came to appreciate their beauty. Bobby says she knew over a hundred songs, and his notebooks hold more than sixty from her repertory. He sings still others that he learned from her but has never written down.

When he was a child, Bobby had heard "Aunt" Lou Brookshire sing "what we would call folksongs or ballads" without realizing what they were. As a teenager, he grew interested in her songs and began to tape-record them too. Aunt Lou and her husband Fred were neighbors and landlords from whom Bobby's parents rented a house near Lenoir. Bobby says that even as a little boy, he recognized that they were "quite colorful characters." They periodically drove across the country pulling "one of those little oval trailers behind them," looking for work on the West Coast as migrant laborers. Fred also cut hair. Aunt Lou always had a guitar around, and Bobby enjoyed her company. Eventually he came to realize that she had not learned her songs from recordings.

Aunt Lou was from a musical local family named Holsclaw. She told Bobby one reason she knew so many songs "was that when she was growing up she and her sisters had to stand guard on the Brushy Mountains to watch out for government agents, and they would pass the time of day by singing songs while the adults were making liquor."[28] She was the only person Bobby found who sang a version of the Child ballad "Edward," and she also knew a long and unusual version of "The Wreck of Old 97." Bobby wrote down and sings more than fifteen songs he learned from her.

When Bobby gained a name in the community as somebody interested in old songs, acquaintances began to put him in touch with other singers they knew. This is how he came to meet Rolf Ellison. Cliff Broyhill, whose father had persuaded Bobby's grandfather to come down to Caldwell County to run a store, loved music and invited local musicians to gather once a week in a little house at his fishpond on the Wilkesboro road. He brought one of the "regulars," a man named Rolf Ellison, to meet Bobby at his grandparents' house. Rolf, Bobby says, "would turn out to be one of the major people involved in my life that knew old music." He was the only person Bobby ever heard sing "The Lady Bright," a version of "The Wife of Usher's Well." Rolf remembered two verses of it and played it on the fiddle; his sister Lizzie remembered the whole ballad. They had learned it from their father.

Rolf came from a family of singers and storytellers who lived in sections of Watauga County known as Pottertown and Meat Camp, the latter of which got its name from a place where Daniel Boone camped before moving to Kentucky. The year after he had introduced them, Cliff

Broyhill drove Bobby and Rolf up Long Hope Mountain to see Rolf's father, W. T. "Bill" Ellison, who ran an antique shop high on the mountainside. W. T. was about sixty-nine, a "big tall man, heavy set, big frame, and he had rosy cheeks and wore a straw hat all the time and a forty-five." Rolf knew what would interest Bobby, so he said, "'Dad, Bobby wants to know if you ever knowed or heard tell of Birchie Potter.' 'Oh yeah,' said, 'I knowed him well.' So he sort of led him into that tale. He told two stories. One was about the death of little Boone Potter, who was a famous outlaw up there in the turn of the century, who was his father's half-brother. He told about how Boone Potter got killed, and then about Birchie Potter, what they were doing the day he got killed." In the course of the conversation Bill left the room and came back singing:

> Farewell to old Ireland and the place where I was born
> And the county of Limerick where the parish'ners still roam.
> It was there in old Ireland like a lily I stand;
> Now you see what I've come to by loving women.
>
> Oh it's oft times I've wondered why women love men.
> More than oft times I've wondered how men can love them.
> They will be the sure cause of some sudden downfall.
> They will cause you to labor behind the stone wall.

Bill Ellison said he "got to thinking about my people coming from Ireland, and some of his had come from there too and it made him think of that. Hadn't thought of it, said, in years and years. He wanted me to hear that." Bobby wrote down "Cold Mountain" and twenty-five more songs he heard from Rolf and Bill Ellison, and he learned others that he didn't write down, along with many tales.[29]

Long before Bobby McMillon began consciously to collect songs and tales, he had already begun to develop his skills as a performer. Up at Kona, he says, he and his Hopson cousins "would get together in the evenings" and "just tell everything in the world that we had heard."[30] He recalls beginning to sing in those same years:

> I was singing to myself along with those old records from my grand-daddy's talking machine. I knew some of those even earlier, but I never thought about ever singing anywhere else until Maw Maw got to singing all those old songs. What I'd do was—she'd only get to stay about a week; I wouldn't get to see her but about once or twice during that time—so when she'd sing, I set and make her stop and I'd write

the words down. . . . I think that's when it started spreading. I really got enjoying singing, 'cause seeing her do it inspired me to just sing more, and I began singing around the house quite a bit then.[31]

Within the next few years he began to play the guitar and to get together in the evenings after school or in summers with two or three high-school friends who lived in his community to "sing around for ourselves or our families." These gatherings put some constraints upon his choice of songs. His own favorites were the old songs in "minor keys" that he had learned from Maw Maw Phillips. He realized, however, that other people wouldn't appreciate them unless he gave them an instrumental accompaniment, and he had not yet learned how to chord this kind of melody. He also saw that he was "too far immersed" in older songs that the others would have no interest in, so he would "select certain things that, say, their parents knew something about and *they* enjoyed, like 'Takes a Worried Man to Sing a Worried Song' and 'Barbara Allen.' Families would know it, and so they would encourage it, and we would all get together and sing that."[32]

Bobby's first public performances came in his senior English class. When the students read *The Canterbury Tales*, the teacher let Bobby sing and talk about "The Jew's Daughter," "Lord Randall," and other ballads he had learned from people he knew. Cratis Williams, who was a popular speaker in the region, made other opportunities for Bobby to perform. When he could not accept an invitation to give programs on folklore for civic groups in Caldwell County, he began to offer Bobby's name as a substitute. Larger venues opened to Bobby through a chance meeting with Jean and Lee Schilling when he performed at the Union Grove Fiddler's Convention in 1973. There he learned that the Schillings lived in Cosby, Tennessee, and he told them about Maw Maw Phillips and the songs he had learned from her. In turn, they invited Bobby to come later that year to their Folk Festival of the Smokies. He says, "I thought I was just going to experience what a festival's like, and then they put my name up on the board. They wanted me to get up and tell the story of old Joe Dawson and sing the 'Cabbage Head' song or something like that. I've never been that shy around a crowd . . . so I got up there and done it, and that led into it—well, it was one of the things that led into it."[33]

Another thing was Bobby's visit the next year to my folksong class in Chapel Hill; George Holt, an undergraduate in that class, later asked

Bobby to appear in a folk festival he organized on the campus of Duke University in 1975. These public performances quickly led to many others, including invitations to the Festival for the Eno in Durham, North Carolina, the Festival of American Folklife in Washington, D.C., the National Storytelling Festival in Jonesboro, Tennessee, and storytelling workshops at the Augusta Heritage Center in Elkins, West Virginia; in some of these places, Bobby made repeat appearances across the years. Bobby also began to receive invitations to perform at other universities and for elder hostels, civic organizations, and public schools, and over the years built an impressive list of appearances and an outstanding reputation. Only between 1978 and 1989, however, was Bobby able to devote himself full-time to public performances. During that decade he was active in the Artists in the Schools and the Visiting Artists Programs, yearlong residencies in public schools and community colleges sponsored by the North Carolina Arts Council.

After the council unwisely ended those programs, Bobby McMillon continued to accept invitations to perform for a day or a week at public schools or at festivals and other events, but he once again had to rely on furniture factories in Lenoir and Spruce Pine for his livelihood. There his workday stretched from 6:45 in the morning to 3:15 in the afternoon, with breaks of fifteen minutes at 9:15, thirty minutes at 11:45, and ten minutes at 2:10. Bobby's normal job assignment was "utility": "That means that I do different things. Sometimes I put in bracer blocks behind dressers and chests. . . . Other times I'll nail the backs, or sometimes I put the drawers in. It's just different things. Somebody might be out— I'll take their place that day."

He describes the working conditions as bad. "You burn up in the summer, and freeze a lot of times in the winter, and . . . you're basically on your feet eight, nine, ten hours." You "just feel like a peon when you work in a place like that, because if you're just an employee, they treat you that way." One foreman said that

> it's a good thing that my brain's inside my head or it'd be floating all around the place. But of course he's for the company, and he thinks it's bad to be thinking about other things. He thinks you go to thinking about music and stories, you're going to let your job slack up or something. . . . He has some interest in things like that, but of course he can't let that get in the way of his business. So he doesn't. He wants you to leave that behind when you come in the door—which

you can't do. Or I can't. Never have been. And nobody else there—I mean, everybody daydreams. But some of them don't have daydreams toward anything that they can do something with, other than wishing that they were somewhere else. Of course, I'm always thinking where I could be singing, or studying about Frankie Silver or Tom Dula, or something like that. I guess I do daydream a whole lot. But of course I have hopes that someday I'll be able to leave that behind. Do better.

Although Bobby's work schedule was flexible enough to let him accept invitations to perform outside, he risked a reprimand if he sang on the job. If the department manager passed through and overheard him, he might say, "'It ain't break time!' or something like that. They can be hateful."

The response of fellow workers was also discouraging. There would be times on the job when workers could converse, and Bobby from time to time ran across "somebody that might know a piece of an old story or something and would tell it." Back in the 1970s Bobby worked with one friend who even knew a few ballads and played the banjo, and the two of them would occasionally do a duet together on the assembly line. Fellow workers would also "call on me to sing once in a while," Bobby says. "Of course I tell them riddles all the time, and jokes. They love to hear me sing them a bawdy song or something that I've heard—and they're amazed! They say, 'Where'd *that* come from?'" He thinks "they're not conscious" of what the material really is, "not hardly any of them."[34] Living in Spruce Pine, a town near Kona, when people found out, he says, "who I am and where my family go back to," they started to ask questions. "When they found out that I knew about maybe their grandfather—'Well now, what did my granddaddy do?'"[35] You're in "contact with people that live 'out in the field,'" he says. But "the field is becoming real barren." People in the younger generation "are just almost completely devoid of any knowledge of anything" except what they have heard on television.[36]

There is, however, one large exception to this lack of knowledge and interest in the old traditions: the story of Frankie Silver. Both locally at Kona, where Frankie murdered her husband Charlie in the winter of 1831, and more broadly in western North Carolina, the story still stirs keen interest. In Kona, Wayne Silver, a descendant of one of the half-brothers of the murder victim, has created a Silver family museum in a small, one-room building that formerly housed the Baptist church.

A sign in the former Baptist churchyard at Kona, near the grave of Charlie Silver. (Photograph by Dan Patterson)

It stands on the hillside above the old Silver family log house where Charlie Silver was raised. Charlie and many generations of Silvers are buried in the churchyard. Hung on the walls of the museum are a Silver coat of arms, photographs of early family members and homes, and many items related to the murder, including framed copies of a manuscript of the ballad and of newspaper articles about Frankie and Charlie. The museum is open daily to visitors, and Wayne Silver often meets both individuals and groups and gives them an informal presentation warmly sympathetic to Frankie. He also offers for sale a notebook of photocopied items about Frankie. Entitled *Frankie's Song,* the notebook includes a copy of a musical setting he himself composed for the text of the Frankie Silver ballad.[37]

Wayne Silver is also in charge of local arrangements for the annual Silver family reunion. The weekend is marked by a memorial service in the old graveyard and a family picnic at a newer and larger church on a knoll across the small valley. Some who attend the reunion are descendants of Frankie and Charlie's daughter Nancy, and the gathering naturally encourages the exchange of information and stories about the

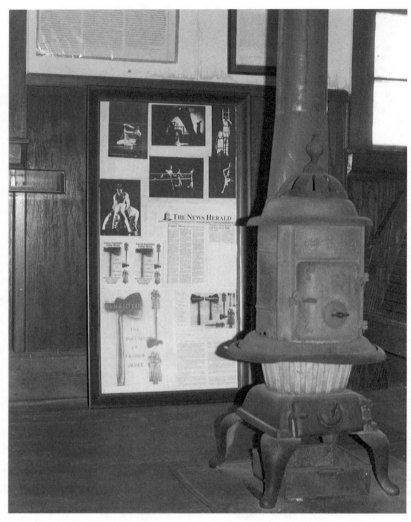

A display in the Silver family museum in the former Baptist Church at Kona, N.C. The poster shows a performance of Panaiotis's ballet about Frankie Silver by the Tanz Ensemble Cathy Sharp. (Photograph by Dan Patterson)

murder and other events in the family history. Wayne Silver also makes a point of keeping the family posted about outsiders' attention to the Frankie Silver story. In 1997, for example, he invited Sharyn McCrumb to read a portion of her novel *The Ballad of Frankie Silver* at the reunion. *Silver Notes,* a family newsletter, distributes information about Frankie materials along with its family items and genealogical data.

Although Wayne Silver and Bobby McMillon were not acquainted until the early 1990s, both spent their childhood years in Kona, are descendants of the early Silver settlers, and share a deep interest in the story of Charlie and Frankie. Both passionately want to know the truth of what happened that stormy night in December 1831 when Charlie Silver died. For both, the story offers a means, as Bobby puts it, of "trying to unify people that have grown apart in time and social conditions—have left their original homes—and give them something that they can look back at." In other ways, however, their approaches to the Frankie Silver story are markedly different. Wayne says that, especially when talking with schoolchildren, he uses it to argue and illustrate the case against capital punishment. Bobby could never bring himself to use a traditional story for a baldly didactic end. That would violate the aesthetic he absorbed from older traditional tale tellers. "To me," he says, "it has nothing to do with a cause." His storytelling is driven instead by his own "quest in life." He has always tried "to understand what life is."[38] And, Bobby McMillon adds, "that's why, I guess, I followed after stories and songs and ballads throughout my life."[39]

2

FRANKIE SILVER LORE AS PERFORMED BY BOBBY McMILLON

The following text is a transcription of Bobby McMillon's performance of the ballad "Frankie Silver" and the accompanying legends, as videotaped by Tom Davenport in October 1992.

(Singing):

    1 This dreadful dark and dismal day
        Has swept my glories all away.
        My sun goes down, my days are past,
        And I must leave this world at last.

    2 Oh, Lord what will become of me?
        I am condemned, you all now see.
        To Heaven or Hell my soul must fly
        All in one moment when I die.

3 For on a dark and dreary night
   I put his body out of sight.
   To see his soul and body part,
   It strikes with terror to my heart.

4 The jealous thought that first gave strife
   To make me take my husband's life.
   For days and months I spent my time
   Thinking how to commit this crime.

5 And on a dark and doleful night
   I put his body out of sight.
   With flames I tried to him consume,
   But time would not admit it done.

6 His chattering tongue fell gently down.
   His pitiful voice soon lost its sound.
   All ye that are of Adam's race
   Let not my fault this child disgrace.

7 Judge Daniels has my sentence passed.
These prison walls I leave at last.
Nothing to cheer my drooping head
Until I'm numbered with the dead.

8 Great God, how shall I be forgiven?—
Not fit for earth, not fit for heaven.
But little time to pray to God,
For now I try that awful road.[1]

(Speaking):

One of the strangest and most frightening stories, to me, in my lifetime that I remember, happened over in western North Carolina, in the Toe River country. That's where my mother was raised and her people. My folks came into that country back in the early 1800s, along about 1800 or 1 or 2. And they settled in there, and in those days it was like a wild wilderness, you might say. The woods was full of pant'ers and bears, and of course there was mink and beaver. And one of the children of the Silvers family that moved into the Mitchell and Yancey County sections of Toe River was a trapper. And his name was Charles Silvers. He was my third cousin. My grandfather, or my great-great-grandfather was his first cousin. And so it's been of course generations ago.

And it happened, the story that I'm about to tell, happened in the early 1830s, along about 1831 I believe, but the country was still fairly new. And Charles Silvers was the oldest son of preacher Jacob Silver. And Uncle Jake he was the son of old man George that had come down from Pennsylvania and Maryland back after the Revolutionary War, and the children had helped build a big cabin over there, and the cabin's still standing and in use by the family. But Charles was Jacob Silver's son by his first wife, Lizzie Wilson. She had took sick and had trouble in giving him birth and died just soon after he was born. And Charlie was raised by Uncle Jake Silvers and his second wife, whose name was Nancy Reed. And Nancy raised about eight or ten young'uns by preacher Jake, but she raised Charlie too. He was the oldest, and as Charles grew up he took to the woods, and he was a hunter and a trapper. And he would go out in the woods and get beaver and mink, and a big party of men sometimes would go and stay gone for months up back toward the—or weeks rather—back on the boundary, on the frontier then, I guess, of North Carolina and Tennessee.

And Charles when he was about eighteen he married a girl that's family had come into the Toe River section named Stewart. And her name was Frances Stewart. But the mountain people would call a girl named Frances Frankie, and Frankie they said was a girl that had charms. They said that she was a very pretty girl and a good dancer. And her folks, though, were real poor people. They didn't have much. They lived in a little shack of a cabin about a mile down the river below the Silvers. But Charlie married Frankie, and they built up a little pole cabin across the ridge behind the mountain where Charles's brothers and sisters and father and stepmother lived. And it was just a little one-room cabin that set over there in the holler. And they set up housekeeping there, and about a year later a baby come along. And he named the baby Nancy after his stepmother, that he thought a lot of.

Well, it was 'long about Christmas time. They said that Charlie was preparing to on a hunting trip with some friends back up on the Tennessee line, and he was going to be gone for about a week. And it was a cold time of year, and the snow was just a-pouring down, they said, that it just poured the snow all day long, and Charlie cut down an old sourwood tree. Said he chopped it up and said that, said after he'd split it, and he piled it up for wood that would do Frankie and the baby while he was gone a-trapping.

And when he come in that evening, they said that he sat down at the table and they ate. Well, according to my granny's uncle, her father was there too and ate supper with them, and when they got done, Charles said that "I'm beat, I think I'll lay down." And Frankie looked at him and said, "Well, I fixed a pallet for you by the fireplace." Said, "I thought you might want to take a nap till you got ready to go to bed." Well, I've wondered for years and years why in the world anybody would want to take a nap till they got ready to go to bed. And I can't figure it out, but that's the words that they claim that he said. So she had a sheepskin rug and had it laying there in front of the fireplace, and Charlie he just laid down on the rug with the little baby Nancy. It was just old enough to start walking. He went to sleep.

Well, after he seemed to be sound asleep, Frankie's daddy looked at her and said, "Now's your time, Frankie, now's your time." And so they went outside, and Charles had sharpened his ax, and come back in. And she stood over him, and she'd rear back with her ax and start to come down on him. And he's laying there—and he'd smile at her in his sleep. And said that she come back again, and he'd smile at her again. 'Bout the third time—he'd grin at her every time—the third time she finally said, "Well, I can't do it, I can't kill him a-smiling at me like that." And Charlie's—or Frankie's father—said, "Well, now, if you don't kill him," said, "I'll kill you." Said, "If you don't kill him, I'll kill you." So finally she come back and she come down on him and give him one lick to the side of the head. And they claim that she dropped the ax then. He jumped up and screamed, "God bless the child!" Well, she run over there and jumped in the bed and got under the covers with the—and laid hid there until she heard him hit the floor. And said that her daddy took the ax, when he fell, said he took the ax and come back, and he used such force to cut his head off that he split his head at the neck, and said his head bounced again' the rafters. And so the blood was just going everywhere. And said that when he fell, or after he cut his head off, he chopped him all to pieces right there where he lay. I guess it probably scared him a little bit too. And they said that the baby, Nancy, got to crawling. And said that it crawled through, through its dad's own blood, and where it was learning to walk, it tried to stand up at the table. It put its little hand prints on the table, and said that the mark was left there forever!

Well, anyway they burned him. Burned him all night long in that fireplace, with that wood that he had meant to keep Frankie and the baby warm while he was gone. And of course, naturally, all the parts of the body won't burn. It would take a awfully high heat to just about cremate anybody anyhow, so they took the parts that wouldn't burn—his guts, and his lungs, I guess, and the parts that, and liver, maybe—and put them in a sack. And she took his head, or her father did, one, and they said they went and hid it in a hollow stump off out at the edge of the yard.

It was still just a-snowing, a-snowing. And so, her daddy, now—and the reports over the years always said, now, that Frankie done this, 'cause she was the one that got into trouble for it, but now this is the way that they told it at home—said that her daddy put on his boots and took his lights that was in the sack and went down the holler toward the river— it's about, oh, not quite a half a mile, but right at it—and there's a little trail that went by a branch, and about halfway down the trail toward the river, they was a shelfing rock that stuck out, little stick-out point, and some rocks there around under it, and they claim that he hid that sack of lights underneath one of those rocks there, and that he marched on to the river, and he got down there and, when he got there, he found that the river was completely froze over. It was just, you know, right at Christmas, a cold time, and so he took a big log that he found close by, and he jabbed big holes in the ice. That way people would think that maybe Charlie had gotten drownded, had fallen through on his way across the river, maybe. So then he backtracked it home. And when he got back, they tried their best, I guess, to clean it up.

But anyway, the next morning, little after daylight, Charlie's step-mother and his sisters was a-washing over across the mountain at their house, outside—it was a real cold day—and had a big old wash pot and everything, and they said that Aunt Nancy, that was Charlie's step-mammy, she saw Frankie coming across the hill with her baby. Said she come down there. Frankie said to her mother-in-law, said, "Well, you'uns is hard at it early, hain't ye?" And she said, "Yeah, we're just getting ready for a rest. It's a holiday. We's trying to clean up." And said, "What have you done this morning?" She said, oh, she'd been hard at it a-washing and a-cleaning. She didn't tell what she'd been cleaning. And so they said, "Well, where's Charlie at?" And she said, "Well, he went to get some feed for the cow across the river, man that lived not too far away. Said he ought to be back the next day. Said he thought he might stay all night. And she was going to go and see her mother and dad and stay with them that night and wanted to know if some of the boys would care to feed the cow that evening. And she said, well she'd send some of them down there.

Well, they remarked that when they went to feed that evening the only tracks they saw leading to the barn was Frankie's. But anyway, the next day, some time up in the evening, after noon, Frankie come down to old man Jake's house and said, "Well, Charlie ain't got back yet," and said, "I just don't care if he don't come back." She said, "He didn't show up last night apparently, and he ain't been there all day." Said, "I'm just going back to Dad's and stay there." And so she acted real mad like, you know, and Charlie's daddy was getting pretty concerned about it then, so he put out word that Charlie was a-missing. And they got folks from all over the mountains to go to searching, and they hunted and looked, and covered ever track of ground, you know, in ten miles, I guess. Couldn't find a trace of him. They just didn't know what had happened.

And so after a few days old Uncle Jake Silvers, he started panicking. And he'd heard tell that there was a man over near Mountain City, Tennessee, up on, above Stony Creek, I guess, that had a slave who possessed what they called a conjure ball. It hung by a hair, and you could ask it questions, and it would give you some kind of answer. And he thought if they couldn't locate Charlie by any other means, maybe the, maybe the conjure ball could tell them where he was at. So he took some of the boys and made the trip over there. It was probably about a two-day trip, because it was along about forty miles, across the mountains. And when they got there, said the old man, he told the old man that owned the slave what they wanted and why they were there. And he said, "Well, he's gone off a-working somewhere today and won't be back." But said, "The conjure ball's here," and said, "I think I can probably work it for you." And so he went and got it out, and they started asking it questions. Used the ball itself would be like the house. And they'd say, "Well, what happened, which way did so-and-so go?" Well, it would just turn round and round, wouldn't move. And they couldn't seem to get any clear-cut answer out of it, and put it up. And so just as old Uncle Jake was fixing to leave, the man come out and said, "Well now, I've been thinking. Do you reckon if your son, that your son could have been murdered and done away with at the house?" Said Jake looked at him and said, "Well, his wife's not a big enough woman to take care of that kind of deed." Said, "I don't know, but uh, you know, guess anything could happen."

Well, before they got home, something had happened. They said that one of Charlie's buddies that would go with him a-trapping was a man named Jake Collis, and said that he was pretty good friends with him and knew him fairly well. And he got kindly suspicious about what was going on, because one day as he was a-walking over to old man Silvers' house, said that he noticed that Charlie's dog, that always went with him everywhere he went, would run up to the house and bark at it. And said it would just howl and bark and just go. And said then it would run down the trail out of sight, and he didn't know where it went. Well, he knew that Frankie was there then. But he kindly watched around the place till he seen her leave, and soon as she got out of sight, he went down there and investigated a little bit, and she'd boarded up the doors. So he went over to old Uncle Jake Silvers and told him that he was just suspicious — or no, he didn't tell Uncle Jake (he was gone), he told some of the boys that was there about being suspicious what was going on, and they got a magistrate that lived there in the area, and two or three of them went back to the house. And they pulled the boards off and they went in. Said when they went in there, said everything looked like it had been disturbed. Said it was pretty nice and neat in one way, but said they got over at the fireplaces and said that the ashes looked awful greasy. And they took some and poured water on them, and they went to making blubbers. And said that they got to looking, it looked like little chip marks on the wall. And they had puncheon floors back in them days—floors that had hooks, the planks had hooks on the end of them—and they raised that up, and said there was blood stains in the dirt, down underneath, and chips of bone.

And so they got to investigating further, and went out and that dog had come back, and it would go from place to place, and everywhere it would go they'd find a little something to remind them of Charlie. Found his head in that old hollow stump. And the reason it was a-going down the trail out of sight, it would go down there to that old stick-out rock where his lights was buried, and carry on. So they took his remains up, and buried them. Some people said they buried them a little bit at a time, instead of taking back up what they'd already buried, that they put him in three different graves. Now, I don't know whether that's the truth or not. I do know that the one gravestone that they used to have to mark him is gone now or else the wind and the rain has taken the name and dates off of it.

But anyway they arrested Frankie and her mother, whose name was Barbara Stewart, and her brother Blackstone Stewart. And they held them until they could investigate a little bit, and they finally brought it before the county prosecutor, and they filed a charge of murder against Frankie. Now that took place there, over in Morganton, which is about fifty miles away, east of the Blue Ridge, but in those days the counties were much bigger than they are now. And so they took them all to jail, but they only kept her mother and brother for a short time. And I don't know if there was just lack of evidence or what. But anyway the murder charge stuck for Frankie.

My great-great-great grandfather, he was a witness at the trial, and some of the other members of the family. It was a huge family, anyway. Charlie not only had eight or ten brothers and sisters, his father had eight or ten brothers and sisters, and they about all lived in that country by then. And so they put her in jail, and they had a trial. Well, for some reason—I don't know why—she kept pleading innocent and demanded proof. And they thought it strange that, you know, they figured that even if she hadn't killed him, that she must have known what was going on. It would just about be impossible that she wouldn't have, but that was the, her case. And so finally, since she wouldn't give any indi-cation that anybody else helped in the murder, they found her guilty on that evidence alone. And so they sentenced her to be hung.

Well, some time had passed, and of course they had appealed the case and was hoping for a stay of execution, but it didn't come for a while, but they did postpone the day of her hanging a couple of times. And in the meantime her father bribed the jailer at the jailhouse there in Mor-ganton to conveniently forget to lock the cell door. And so they spirited her out one night, and they got her out of town, and when they did, they cut her hair off short like a man's, and that was a wonderful disguise in those days, because women just didn't cut their hair then. It was thought to be just awful sinful for a woman to have her hair cut. So they cut her hair, and give her an old felt hat to wear, and dressed her up in men's clothing. And so they got her out of town, and they was a-going down the country towards South Carolina. And it was a day or two later, and the sheriff for some reason thought that—I don't know if he had a tip or what, but he was off a-looking in that direction, had him a posse. And they come across this great big open field, and over on the other side they was a party of people over there a-throwing a ball at each other. They said this one man kept catching it awful strange and missed the ball. 'Cause somebody'd throw it to him and he go, he'd sort of bend over and raise his hands up. And then the ball would hit the ground. And he got to thinking now—in that day and time women had aprons, and they would catch each side of the apron and catch a ball in the folds of it—so by the time that the sheriff and his men got across the field, those people over there had packed up and started on off, moving along, and that fellow that he saw was walking alongside the hay wagon, and it was Frankie's uncle a-driving the hay wagon. The sheriff rode up along-side where they was a-walking, and he looked down at Frankie, and he said, said, "Frankie, where you gwine?" Frankie looked around at him, tried to put on a voice, and said, "Thank you, sir, my name's Tom." Her uncle was up there in the wagon. He was trying to be real helpful, and he looked around and said, "Yes, sir, her name is Tom, her name is Tom." So the sheriff said, "Well, come on, Frankie, we got you now." And so they, uh, they took her back to jail.

And I don't know just how much time it was after that before the day of the hanging, but it finally got there. And they said there were people come from miles and miles around to see Frankie Silvers get hung. And they even had a ballad printed. Now the folklore goes that Frankie composed this ballad and sung it on the scaffold. And there's a lot of old-timers over around Wilkes and Caldwell and Burke County and up in the mountains around Mitchell and Yancey that sing that song and claim that Frankie wrote it and sung it before she died. Now whether she did or not, I don't know, but it is thought that the ballad was printed. I always figured that probably her daddy had it printed up and was trying to make money off of it because of greed. And that's probably what caused the murder anyway.

But, as she was waiting there behind the scaffold, and when the sheriff went to lead her up, they asked her if she had any request. And she said yes, she wanted a piece of cake. And so they said, "Well, we can do that for you, Frankie." So they had cake brought to her, and she eat her a piece of cake and went up on the scaffold. And they said, "Frankie, have you got anything you'd like to say?" And she said, "Well, yes, I do." And he said, "Well, we'd like for you to tell it." She went to open her mouth, and just as she did—that crowd was all assembled down there in front, and her dad and mother was standing down there—and he said that her daddy hollered out, "Die with it in you, Frankie. Die with it in you." And she closed her mouth and never said another word. Well, they put the cap over her face, as far as I know, and they hung her.

After they took her body down, they was afraid that—on account of in that day and time there were a lot of universities had medical schools and people were trying to find out the causes of diseases, and they would often dissect the bodies, and that was the time when the grave-robbing was going on—and they was afraid that since it was unheard of for a woman to be executed that her grave would be likely to get robbed. So they had several graves dug about that same day around about, so people would think that was where Frankie was going to be buried. Well, they covered her body up and put it under a load of sacks in that hay wagon. And they started back toward the mountains, and that night they stayed at a tavern, which was up near the head of Lake James in McDowell County, I guess now—it was probably Burke back then—and they stayed all night and the next day they decided that it was July, and they found out right quick that it was going to be hard to get the body back without an awful lot of discomfort to them, because of the body decomposing. So they buried a gra—they dug a grave, they claim, up near the head of Lake James and buried Frankie in it. Now there's some people that claim that she wasn't buried there, that they actually got to the head of the Blue Ridge near Gillespie Gap, which is near North Carolina Highway 226, and buried her up there. So the truth, you know, probably won't ever be known for sure about that, but they got on back home.

And they claim that the family was curst after that. They said that the old man was killed later on while he was trying to cut a rail, split a rail tree, and a limb fell, knocked his brains out. And they said eventually old lady Barbara Stewart got bit by a copperhead, and she was an old woman, died of the complications. And Blackstone Stewart apparently moved off to Kentucky, and he got caught horse thieving and they hung him. So that's the way people tend to think of getting paid back in communities like that.

As I began to look back and find out a little bit about that family, I found that that may have all happened, but it didn't happen real soon and all at once. That it was scattered out over maybe thirty years. But Frankie's grandmother Stewart was supposed to have gotten—Frankie's mother, Barbara Stewart, was supposed to have gotten the granddaughter Nancy and raised her until she was eighteen, at which time she would give her a suit of clothes and a cow or something, but according to the 1850 census Nancy was staying with her grandfather Silvers. I don't think they kept her very long. They was probably under threat of death anyway, by the family. But a feud never got started. I think the Stewarts sort of broke up. And there's still some Stewarts up in that part of the country. But after they had buried Charles up there in the graveyard, they just left his remains there, and the memory of him has sort of faded with time, because after about sixty or seventy years there were some other stories that took place out in the Midwest about a woman named Frankie Baker, who shot and killed her husband, and a song grew up called "Frankie Baker" or "Frankie and Albert" and then in the early 1900s the "Frankie and Johnny" song came about. So people's memory tend to confuse things, and now they say that "Frankie and Johnny" got started with Frankie Silvers.

But they still are a few people left that remember the old ballad that Frankie allegedly sang, and her descendants still live in that country and they've spread out. I found a granddaughter, or great-granddaughter, of Frankie Silvers that lived in Jackson County who made hominy, and she was down at the Eno River Festival in Durham, North Carolina, about fifteen years ago, and she heard me tell the story of Frankie Silvers and came and talked to me about it. And said that her mother, her grandmother was a sister to a woman that married my grandmother's uncle, and both of them were daughters of Nancy Silvers, who was Frankie and

Charlie's daughter, and so the family did spread on through the years, and through intermarriage you'll find that people are more or less kin to each other in a community like that. And by now they have spread out.

When I was growing up, my mother's, the house that my mother grew up in sat on the hill just above the mouth of the branch where Charlie was supposed to have fell through the ice. And we didn't have any inside bathroom facilities. We had an old privy outside on the side of the mountain in the woods. And at night until you went to bed, you had to go out of doors, and so as a child I didn't like to do that very well because the dirt road that come just up above our house was in plain sight, and I was always afraid that I would see Frankie's spirit come wandering around the road with an ax in her hand and blood in her eyes. And so I was real careful about how often I had to step outside till bedtime in those days. But, I could, especially at night in the summertime, when you could hear the katydids chattering, think about that story—I don't know why, since it took place in the winter.

But years have rolled on, and nobody I guess really knows for sure whether it was Frankie or her father that killed him, but his, Charles's nephew, old man Will Silvers, he died about thirty-five years ago, and he used to tell my grandfather that in his opinion the reason that Charles Silvers died was because her father, Frankie's father and family, wanted to move west. And back in those days, even people moving around had to have some source of exchange, money or barter or something, in order to do a lot of traveling, and so they needed him to sell his farm in order to raise funds for, I guess, the wagons that they would need to go west on. And Charlie didn't want to do it. He wanted to stay there, I guess, and raise his family near his own people, and at that time the hunting was great through there. And so it's said that that was the real reason that Charlie died, that they just coerced Frankie into it. You know, she probably was a product of her times, and was under the, you know, the bondage to her own family and still had that divided loyalty. And if she did have a hand in killing him, she was probably coerced into it.

And there was the other people, and maybe the Stewarts or some of their descendants or friends, that put out the word that Charlie was mean to Frankie, and that he was in a fit of passion and about to kill her when she struck him with the ax. I've always felt like if that were the case, it looks like Frankie could have claimed self-defense, and even if she had of been found guilty, she might have built time in prison rather than being hanged. So it's all been washed away like the river, waters of

Toe River, I guess, and we'll never know for sure. But I've always felt like the most sensible thing was the fact that her people wanted to leave. But it left a story that spread around in the western part of North Carolina for about 170 years, and of course as in all tales they get changed a little. Down in Caldwell County they used to claim that she killed him with a nail to the temple. While he was asleep, she just hammered a nail in. But there was nothing in the records that survived of the trial to ever indicate that, and there was nothing in the folklore of the family and the people of Toe River itself to say that.

But it's sort of a grim tale, because it was set at the background of the new world that people had come to, and in the mountains at that time you had people that still had certain family traditions that were in flux and joined together. The Silvers were of German stock, and many of their neighbors were of Scots and Irish and English background. And so you had a combination of this living in the new land and sort of being transplanted. A lot of people, I believe, thought at the beginning, that they would come to this country, gain their fortune, and eventually go home. But it never happened that way, and in the process of time and people changing and families coming together, many of these old stories were kept alive through people telling them to each other and to children as the years passed. And that's one from my family that used to fill me with pride in a way, because it was so bloody, and I could see in my mind that little cabin and hear those screams. And my grandmother that raised me, she said her brother, one of her brothers told me one time that he and another man were hunting up in that hollow where Charlie and Frankie lived, and said that all at once it sounded like somebody was just being killed. Their screams were just terrible. And so I think of that a lot, but it's a good story, and the song is being passed along, and I'll probably try to pass it on to my children some day.

3 *. . . the lawyer's advice to deny all*
and insist on proof.
—Henry Spainhour

THE STATE VERSUS FRANCES SILVER

Near the abandoned site of Frankie and Charlie's cabin grew a tree that, people told Bobby McMillon, had a curse on it and trapped anyone who climbed it. The tree is an emblem worthy of a Hawthorne tale, evocative of the long-lingering effects of crime and punishment, concealment and guilt. Many people have lived their lives in the cove, and passed away, and are forgotten, but this one tragedy still looms on the landscape. We, too, if we climb into this tree, find ourselves caught in a tangle of questions, looking for some clean line of descent to the firm ground of Truth.

For us, the story is weighted with both moral and social mysteries, but even the simplest—the factual—level presents gaps, contradictions, and ironies. Although we today can read public and private documents known to only a few of Frankie's contemporaries, the available information about the case leaves all too much room for conjecture. From the surviving legal records we can extract only the following outline of the actual events:[1]

1832

January 9—A warrant is issued for the arrest of Frances Silver
and her mother and younger brother, Barbara and Blackstone
Stewart, for the murder of Charles Silver.[2]

January 10—The three are committed to jail in Morganton.

January 13—Frankie's father, Isaiah Stewart, files a complaint
stating that the three have been jailed without an opportunity to
face their accusers.

January 17—Barbara and Blackstone Stewart plead not guilty at the
inquest and are recommended for discharge.

March 26—The Superior Court of Burke County convenes for its
regular spring session with the Honorable John R. Donnell as
presiding judge, W. C. Butler as high sheriff, Burgess S. Gaither
as clerk of the court, William J. Alexander as solicitor, and a
grand jury composed of eighteen men. A bill of indictment
charges that on December 22, 1831, Frances Silver and Barbara
and Blackstone Stuart [sic], "not having the fear of God before
their eyes but being moved and seduced by the instigation of the
devil, . . . feloneously wilfully and with malice aforethought did
make an assault . . . with a certain axe of the value of sixpence
. . . which the said Frances in both the hands of her . . . did cast
and throw . . . in and upon the head of . . . Charles Silver . . .
one mortal wound of the length of three inches and the depth
of one inch; of which he, the said Charles Silver, then and
there instantly died . . . and that the said Blackstone Stuart
and Barbara Stuart . . . were present aiding helping abetting
comforting and maintaining the said Frances Stuart." The grand
jury found a "True bill as to Frances Silver, not a true bill as to
the others."[3]

March 29—Frankie Silver is tried in the spring term of the superior
court. The prosecution presents circumstantial evidence to
support conviction; "about candlelight" the jury retires to
deliberate.

March 30—The jury reports its members have not yet come to
agreement, then asks and receives permission to question certain
witnesses further. The jury deliberates again and returns a verdict
of "guilty of the felony and murder . . . in the manner & form
charged." Judge Donnell sentences Frankie Silver to be hanged

John Robert Donnell (1789–1864), presiding judge at the trial of Frankie Silver. An outsider to the community, he resided in the eastern part of the state, in New Bern, and was a native of Scotland. (Courtesy of the North Carolina Collection, University of North Carolina Library at Chapel Hill)

William Julius Alexander (1797–1857), the solicitor who prosecuted Frankie Silver. He represented Mecklenburg County in the state legislature and was several times chosen speaker of the house. (Courtesy of the North Carolina Collection, University of North Carolina Library at Chapel Hill)

in July 1832. Her attorney appeals the verdict to the state supreme court on the grounds that the witnesses had had time to talk with each other overnight before their second questioning.[4]

Spring session of the supreme court—Frankie's appeal is denied, with Justice Thomas Ruffin writing that the thing to be avoided "is not that the witnesses should be together, but that they should be examined together," since separate questioning allows detection of falsehood.[5] The court in Burke is to set a new date for the execution.

Fourth Monday in September—David L. Swain, the judge scheduled for this session of the Superior Court of Burke County, fails to appear. After waiting for three days, the sheriff adjourns the session, thus postponing any appointment of a second date for the hanging.

1833

March—At this session of the superior court, Judge Henry Seawell sets the execution of Frankie Silver for June 28, between the hours of 1 and 4 P.M.

June 18—David L. Swain, now the governor, gives Frankie Silver a two-week respite, until the second Friday of July, to prepare for her death.

September term of the superior court—Isaiah Stewart, his brother-in-law Jessee Barnett, and probably a third party named William Powell are separately indicted as accessories in the escape of Frankie Silver and bound over to the March term of court.[6]

1834

March term of the superior court—Jessee Barnett fails to appear for trial and is bound over, with Isaiah Stewart, sheriff John Boone, and clerk of the court B. S. Gaither as security for his appearance.

September term of the superior court—Jessee Barnett is convicted "as an accessory after the fact to the Felony committed by Frances Sylvers in assisting her to escape after conviction," on the testimony of Isaiah Stewart, who had "turned states evidence" and was not prosecuted. Barnett is sentenced to ten months in jail.[7]

1835

March 25 — A few gentlemen in Burke County petition Governor Swain for a pardon for Jessee Barnett on the grounds that his "sympathy for a Brother in Law & niece" had "prevailed over his integrity" and that he had already been imprisoned for six months and had "suffered severely during the past winter."[8]

April 2 — Governor Swain issues a proclamation of pardon to Jessee Barnett.

To this outline, local historians and contemporary letters and news accounts can add a few more factual details: that Charles Silver died two months past his nineteenth birthday, that Judge Swain missed the September 1832 court session because of a driving accident near Hillsborough, and that Frankie's execution took place on July 12, 1833, in Morganton.[9] We gather a few additional facts from other documents such as letters, petitions to two governors (Montfort J. Stokes and David L. Swain), several newspaper accounts, and a memoir — materials with varying degrees of reliability, and none of them remarkable for completeness.

From this era, grand jury documents often provide the most detailed summary of the testimony of witnesses, but those for the Silver case are absent from the Burke County "criminal action papers" in the North Carolina State Archives. Concerning the trial itself, we have only fragments of information drawn from the trial summary, from petitions later written to the two governors, and in particular from a letter by one Henry Spainhour that appeared fifty years later in the *Lenoir News Topic* and the *Morganton Star*. This letter is the most informative document available about the trial.

Spainhour wrote from Garrard County, Kentucky, in response to the *Topic*'s publication of the Frankie Silver ballad in 1885. A respected Kentucky cabinetmaker, Spainhour had moved to that state about 1839. He had been born in North Carolina and, at the time of the murder and trial, was working in Morganton. Spainhour's obituary gives information with which we can evaluate the writer. Although he tended toward Quakerism in his later years, he never "attached himself to any creed," because he objected to "church turmoil, hypocrisy and priestcraft." He "was liberal enough to do his own thinking and allowed others all the privileges that he claimed for himself." Having voted for Lincoln and opposed slavery, he had to flee to Illinois during the Civil War, but after

Henry Spainhour (1809–1901), a cabinetmaker whose letter to the newspaper identified the author of the Frankie Silver ballad and gave information about her lost confession. (Reproduced from a clipping of Spainhour's obituary in the Neoga News)

the war he returned to Kentucky and "made friends of his enemys, for he loved all mankind, and for 25 years he had no thought of an enemy, and those who met him read him as if he was a book and respected him." Spainhour appears, then, to have been an intelligent, independent, religious, and principled man. I take his account, although written a half-century after the events, to be reasonably accurate.[10]

The case against Frances Silver was, the trial summary states, "one of circumstantial evidence."[11] The prosecutor had to prove that Charles Silver was in fact dead and a victim of homicide and that Frances Silver committed the crime. The bill of indictment shows that for evidence the prosecutor submitted testimony concerning a skull bearing marks of a wound. To this account, Spainhour adds information about other recoverable material evidence of the murder. It consisted, according to him, of testimony about blood that had run through a crack in the floor, "the heel irons" of Charlie's shoes discovered in ashes in the fireplace, and "some pieces of burned bones and the heart . . . found in a hole where a pine stump had been burned out." Witnesses appearing in the court, Spainhour says, included a smith who identified the heel irons as ones he had made for Charles Silver and doctors who swore that the pieces of bone and the heart were human.[12] The earliest newspaper account of the murder, based upon "particulars" related by "a gentleman who was lately near the place where the . . . deed was perpetrated," mentions speaks also a bench in the house where there was "a deep gash made with an axe, together with blood, where to appearance, the head of the victim had been chopped off."[13] The trial may have included testimony about this bench. The solicitor presumably convinced most people that Charles had been murdered.

Some who attended the trial, however, left unconvinced that the solicitor had proved Frankie Silver to be the murderer. Joseph McDowell Carson, himself an attorney, later signed a clemency petition to Governor Montfort Stokes, writing beside his name the words, "I was a disinterested spectator & thought the case doubtful." The jury also had difficulty agreeing on a verdict. It retired around dusk to begin its deliberations and returned the next morning to report a split decision, "nine for acquitting & three for convicting." The jury reached a unanimous verdict only after getting permission to further interrogate the witnesses, an examination that "ran into a Trane of Circumstances that were not related in the former examination."[14] What these circumstances were the account does not say, but the new testimony led the jurors to find Frankie Silver guilty and the judge to sentence her to death.

From this point on our certainty lessens. According to Henry Spainhour's account, Frankie at the trial "took the lawyer's advice to deny all and insist on proof." The situation seems actually to have been more complicated than this. On some points we can, however, still reach the truth, especially in matters concerning the general social circumstances and the system of legal practices within which the trial took place.

Frankie Silver's trial seems not to have conformed to the pattern that Lynwood Montell found along the western border of Kentucky and Tennessee ("an internal system for determining motives and therefore culpability for the killings") or that Altina Waller found in the nineteenth century deeper in Appalachia, along the Kentucky–West Virginia border, where "the justice meted out would approximate community consensus and parallel the informal authority structure of family and neighborhood."[15] The Frankie Silver case was tried a half-century earlier than the periods examined by these two scholars, and under very different conditions.

Present-day Burke County covers slightly more than five hundred square miles and is only a third as large as it was in the 1830s, before all or parts of five other counties were sliced from it. By twentieth-century standards it was thinly settled: the census of 1830 reported the county's population as 17,888 persons.[16] Its seat of justice was in the town of Morganton, forty miles to the east of the Silver house, beyond and below the first great ridge of mountains, in the western edge of the Piedmont. The two families affected by the crime were close neighbors, but the officers of the court were outsiders to them. The judge himself came from New Bern near the coast and had been born in Scotland. The others lived in the rolling Piedmont country. The solicitor, defense attorney, and clerk of the court not only held status as professional men but were active in state politics and were allied by marriage with well-to-do and socially prominent families. The jurors were mostly persons of a middle rank in the county. None of the county's twelve wealthiest men—those with property valued in 1830 at more than $10,000—served on the jury. Only three jurors came from among the 184 men with property of $1,000 or more, and only one juror owned no taxable property; the rest all held lands with a valuation that averaged $350. Two had already served as justices of the court of pleas and quarter sessions, and two more would be elected to the post in the 1830s.[17] Most were farming people, much like the Silvers and Stewarts though somewhat more prominent and better off than they.[18] None of the jurors came from their side of the mountains.[19]

The Stewarts had a marginal position in the social order. They had moved into Burke from Anson County less than a decade earlier and would scarcely have been known to the older, more established families living closer to town.[20] Frankie's attorney Thomas Worth Wilson was himself probably not acquainted with people like the Stewarts who were new arrivals in the remoter sections. Wilson was born in Randolph County in 1792. Although he must have moved to Morganton as a youngster—his father became a justice of the Burke County Court of Pleas and Quarter Sessions in 1811—as an adult Thomas Wilson spent some years in Wilkes County practicing law. He represented Wilkes in the state legislature from 1824 to 1826, moving back to Morganton only in 1830.[21]

A trial in Burke County in 1830 operated under what seems to us a peculiar set of circumstances. Court schedules created a difficult task for the defense, as they allowed little time for the conduct of a trial or the preparation of a case. Superior court judges came through only twice a year, traveling from great distances, and they had but one week in which to work through the entire docket before moving on to the next county in the circuit. Frankie Silver was arrested in early January 1832 and held until the next court session, in the last week of March. She went on trial on Thursday, three days after the grand jury returned a true bill against her. The trial lasted only a little over one day.

We do not know at what point Frankie's family engaged Thomas Worth Wilson to act as her counsel, but if he were retained late, local circumstances would have greatly handicapped him. He was probably unable—even if it occurred to him to do so—to find character witnesses and to sound out Frankie and Charlie's neighbors concerning their reputation in the community. The forty miles between Morganton and Kona were rugged terrain and the roads indirect.[22] It was late winter, the time for severe and unpredictable weather. These hindrances to an effective defense of Frankie Silver were unavoidable, given the condition of North Carolina in 1832—a large and poor state with bad roads, a thin population, and few trained jurists. But these conditions affected the prosecution as well as the defense. Solicitor William Julius Alexander lived in Mecklenburg County and had to work up the Silver case while also handling others on the week's docket.

As former North Carolina assistant attorney general Jeffrey Gray suggests, however, Frankie Silver's attorney encountered even greater obstacles imposed by legal tradition, which saw defendants as "incompetent" witnesses and did not allow them to testify either against or for themselves. If no one witnessed Frankie's crime, then her attorney could not present the jury with sworn testimony showing extenuating circumstances for her act. In 1831 Governor Montfort Stokes pardoned another prisoner named James Lea, who had been convicted in a trial illustrating the problem. Two persons present during the commission of the crime had been "indicted at the same time and in the same Indictment" as he, "whereby the said James Lea was deprived of the benefit of their testimony."[23]

British legal practices from the mid-eighteenth century underlay this North Carolina rule. At the beginning of the 1700s, attorneys had had little presence in criminal trials. Judges and even jurors interrogated the prisoner and the witnesses, and the prisoner also personally acted "as examiner, cross-examiner, and concluding orator." Courts admitted both hearsay and evidence of prior convictions. The procedures followed in the trial of Frankie Silver had developed in England during the 1730s, as lawyers began to take roles in prosecution and defense and courts began to develop more complex rules of evidence expounded by legal scholars such as Sir William Blackstone.[24]

The new standards of evidence bore directly upon the trial of Frankie Silver. As set forth in Blackstone's *Commentaries,* "all witnesses, of whatever religion or country, that have the use of their reason, are to be received and examined, except such as are *infamous,* or such as are *interested* in the event of the cause. All others are *competent* witnesses; though the jury from other circumstances will judge of their *credibility.*"[25] The rationale for this position was explained by the British barrister Thomas Starkie in *A Practical Treatise on the Law of Evidence.* The "rule of exclusion," he wrote, "is founded on the known infirmities of human nature, which is too weak to be generally restrained by religious or moral obligations, when tempted and solicited in a contrary direction by temporal interests."[26] If the exclusion of "interested" testimony strikes modern readers as unduly restricting the defendant, the procedure was a clear advance upon earlier British modes of proof: the ordeal, combat, and compurgation employed in the early medieval era, the torture introduced in the twelfth century to extract confessions, and the formal prosecution without counsel in the Tudor era. Frankie Silver benefited, at least theoretically, from the eighteenth-century British recourse to counsel and development of rules of evidence that replaced confession with circumstantial proofs.[27]

Long after Frankie Silver's trial, in any case, North Carolina courts continued to exclude a defendant's testimony. In 1873 *Battle's Revisal of the Public Statutes of North Carolina* stated that "nothing . . . shall render any person who, in any criminal proceeding, is charged with the commission of an indictable offense, competent or compellable to give evidence for or against himself."[28] Other states shared this rule but began in the 1860s to revise it by statute, and Congress followed suit in 1878.[29] But not until 1881 was the North Carolina statute revised to read: "In the trial of all indictments, complaints or other proceedings against persons charged with the commission of crimes, offenses and misdemeanors in the superior, inferior, criminal and justices of the peace courts of this state, the person so charged shall at his own request, but not otherwise, be a competent witness."[30]

That the exclusion of testimony from the defendant led to an unfair conviction of Frankie Silver was apparently the opinion of several contemporary attorneys. One was Nicholas Woodfin, who had read law under Judge David L. Swain, began to practice in 1832, and had some knowledge of Frankie's case. Two of the three copies of a petition dated June 3, 1833, appear to be in Woodfin's smooth, controlled handwriting, and in 1839 he married Eliza Grace McDowell, a Burke County lady who had signed the women's petition.[31] Kemp P. Battle reports Woodfin's opinion that Frankie was "unjustly hung" and that "if she could have told her story to the jury, the result would have been different."[32] The same view was held by Col. Burgess S. Gaither, according to Senator Sam J. Ervin Jr. Gaither, an attorney who went on to represent Burke County in the state legislature, was serving as clerk of the court during Frankie's trial. Senator Ervin was born in 1896, four years after the death of Gaither, but he learned the man's views from his own father, a friend of Gaither.[33] Ervin reports that Gaither "was familiar with the evidence, the gossip, and the rumors" and "maintained throughout life" that Frankie "would have been acquitted by the jury if she had been permitted to testify in her own behalf."[34]

Until 1866 the state of Vermont also excluded "interested" testimony of defendants, yet in the notorious Boorn-Colvin murder trial in 1819, a Vermont defense attorney found a way to introduce the words of Stephen Boorn. He brought in a confession Boorn had written and signed two months earlier.[35] A similar introduction of a prior written confession took place in 1831 in the North Carolina trial of "a certain negro Slave named Jerry," who was "convicted upon his own confession" of "conspiracy to raise an insurrection and was sentenced to be hanged."[36] The context of this trial was the panic that swept slaveholding counties following the Nat Turner revolt. Jerry's confession, however, was a ploy urged upon him by his master, James Wright, in order to save him from "the Severe and cruel torture to which other slaves had been subjected" to force self-incriminating statements from them. When the public hysteria had subsided, both the master and the trial judge, John R. Donnell (who would shortly preside also at Frankie Silver's trial), supported a petition to Governor Montfort Stokes for Jerry's pardon on the grounds that his confession was untrue. Stokes granted the pardon.

Frankie's defense attorney, Thomas W. Wilson, might possibly have saved his client's life by introducing a convincing prior sworn confession. But his statements show that at the time of the trial Wilson had not heard any account from Frankie about the events leading to the murder. He indicates that he did not learn her story until more than a year later. According to the petition he wrote on June 3, 1833, Frankie lost all hope following the rejection of her appeal by the state supreme court, her resentencing, and her recapture after the attempted escape in May. Then, "under the impending responsibility of passing from time into eternity

Nicholas W. Woodfin (1810–1876), who studied law with Judge David L. Swain and reportedly tried to get signatures for a petition on behalf of Frankie Silver and believed her confession showed her unaware of the legal distinctions between murder and manslaughter or self-defense. (Courtesy of the North Carolina Collection, University of North Carolina Library at Chapel Hill)

she made a free and full disclosure of all the facts." Her words were recorded in writing. This petition and its duplicate copies speak of "the undersigned having *seen* a statement of the confession" (italics mine). They refer to a verbal cross-examination of Frankie by persons suspicious that "the statement might have received a colouring from the individual who *wrote* it" (italics mine).[37] A newspaper account says that at Frankie's

Burgess S. Gaither (1807–1892), clerk of the court at the trial of Frankie Silver
and son-in-law of Matilda Sharpe Erwin, signed one petition to Governor Stokes.
Senator Sam J. Ervin Jr. recorded a family tradition that Gaither for the rest of
his life regarded Frankie as "unjustly hanged" (Courtesy of the North Carolina
Division of Archives and History)

execution she confirmed "under the [gallows]" the confession she had made before two lawyers and that it had "been published."[38] If the document survives in either manuscript or print, we do not know its present whereabouts, and no writer seems ever to have quoted directly from it.

Thomas Wilson, however, reported that the confession made a favorable impression on those who read it. He himself, on the basis of this confession, questioned the justice of her conviction. He now saw the crime as "clearly a case of manslaughter if not Justifiable Homacide," as did others closely tied to the case.[39] By the report of Senator Ervin, Burgess S. Gaither also believed "that Charlie Silver had mistreated Frankie" and "that she had killed him in self defense."[40]

The trial did include some testimony about the "brutal conduct of the husband toward the wife" ("as appeared in evidence," according to one petition).[41] The defense may have had to attack this testimony, for fear that it would feed a suspicion of guilt by implying a motive.[42] Moreover, in Frankie's day a North Carolina attorney would have had an even more difficult time than at present in using self-defense in the case of a wife charged with murdering her husband.[43] Newspaper reports of a trial in Fayetteville the year before the Silver murder show why:

> *Marital Rights.* — In our Court of Pleas and Quarter Sessions, which set last week, a man was indicted and tried for *whipping his wife.* The assault and battery were proven by the oath of the wife and another woman. — The Husband admitted the battery, but justified himself on the ground, that the wife habitually disobeyed his orders, and was in the violation of his commands when the battery, complained of was committed. The Jury acquitted the Defendant. — Wives, take warning![44]

In 1827 Judge Thomas Ruffin, soon to join the state supreme court and to review Frankie's appeal, had "laid it down as the law" in the trial of a defendant named Forkener "that the husband has a right to inflict moderate punishment on his wife."[45] In *State v. William Hussey* in 1852, the state supreme court upheld the argument of the defendant's counsel that the "husband had a right to give to the wife moderate chastisement, of which he is the judge; and he is not criminally responsible unless permanent injury is inflicted, or the chastisement is carried to such extent as to threaten permanent injury." The wife, moreover, was "judged to be not a competent witness to prove that she gave no provocation at the time of the alleged battery."[46] As late as 1867, in *State v. Rhodes,* a judge in the superior court of Wilkes County issued a ruling (overturned by the state supreme court on appeal) that a husband charged with assault for beating his wife "had a right to whip his wife with a switch no larger than his thumb," a common phrase recently demonstrated to derive more from legal folklore than from law.[47]

In these matters, North Carolina again followed earlier British law. A number of the citations in *State v. William Hussey* came from Sir William Blackstone's *Commentaries,* which aspiring American attorneys in the early nineteenth century studied as a standard textbook.[48] "The husband . . . (by the old law)," Blackstone says, "might give his wife moderate correction. For, as he is to answer for her misbehaviour, the law thought it reasonable to intrust him with this power of restraining her, by domestic chastisement, in the same moderation that a man is allowed to correct his apprentices or children."[49]

These last words suggest that the law rested not only on a pragmatic assignment of responsibility, but also on British allegiance to hierarchy. Blackstone's chapter "Of Treason" supports this inference. He writes that "for a wife to kill her lord or husband, a servant his lord or master, and an ecclesiastic his lord or ordinary; these, being breaches of the lower allegiance, of private and domestic faith, are denominated *petit* treasons. But when disloyalty so rears it's crest, as to attack even majesty itself, it is called by way of eminent distinction *high* treason."[50] Blackstone's exposition is based on a clause introduced into the statute of treason in 1352.[51] The penalty for petit treason was of greater severity than that for lesser crimes. Early in North Carolina history, several slave women convicted of poisoning their masters were sentenced "to be taken to the ground of the Court green" and "there to be burt [*sic*] to Death by a stake"; among those so punished were Jenny, "the Property of the late Lewis Bryan," in Johnston County in 1780 and another in Wayne County in 1805.[52] And in England, well into the eighteenth century, women who murdered their husbands, being guilty of petit treason, were executed by being burned at the stake — at least fourteen of them between 1722 and 1739 and others as late as 1773. A husband who murdered his wife had not committed a crime of treason and was only hanged.[53] North Carolina courts in the 1830s still perpetuated much of the law of the colonial fatherland, if not its full severity; the hierarchical British social assumptions that lay behind these laws also had a lingering life here.

Legal procedures of the era, then, made a defense of Frankie Silver difficult and, in the eyes of some of her informed contemporaries, caused her to suffer a heavier penalty than her crime warranted. A second tangle of problems in the case involves the conduct of her attorney, Thomas W. Wilson. One should concede at the outset that Frankie's mother, for one, appears not to have doubted his ability or commitment; she retained Wilson for at least one minor legal matter a few years after Frankie's death.[54] Nevertheless, a number of his actions raise questions about his competence.

The surviving documents, unfortunately, do not give us a clear view of Wilson's tactics. At the inquest hearing in January 1832, there were three witnesses for the defense. Under the heading "for the Deft" three names are scribbled on Isaiah Stewart's bond for the appearance of Blackstone and Barbara Stewart at the March session of the court. Frankie's brother Jackson was deputized to deliver summonses to three other people and reached two of them. However, a list of "Recognizances to March Term 1832" contains only seven names of witnesses for the state, plus Isaiah Stewart's recognizances for his wife and Blackstone.[55] There is no record that any witnesses appeared for the defense. At this remove, we cannot tell whether the documents are an incomplete record of the actions of the defense or whether Wilson's strategy was only to deny all and try to pick flaws in the prosecution's case. Such as it is, the record simply raises questions concerning the foresight or enterprise of the defense attorney.

More important, at the time of the trial, the public in Burke County regarded his client as infamous, yet Wilson did not ask for a change of venue. In 1824, when George Reves was accused of murdering Mary Stamper, the judge had moved the trial from Burke County to Wilkes. In 1831 the murder trial of Solomon Roper was moved to Lincolnton from Burke County, as was the trial of Aaron Norwood in 1835 for the murder of his wife Charity. Wilson never sought this protection for his client, although the Silver murder was quite recent and its circumstances, the newspaper reported, had "aroused the indignation of all classes of people."[56]

When the jury returned a verdict of guilty, the element on which Wilson chose to base an appeal was the possible contamination of testimony. The witnesses had been separated before their initial testimony but were dismissed when the jury retired at dusk to deliberate. In the morning the jury asked for and got permission to question the witnesses again. Wilson charged in his appeal that the witnesses had had a chance to talk with each other overnight. The state supreme court rejected the appeal. But might Wilson have succeeded if he had appealed on different grounds?

Judge Donnell had ruled that "no new witness should be examined at that stage of the trial nor remarks of counsel heard," despite the fact that the questioning ran into "a trane of Circumstances that were not related in the former examination."[57] Fairness would seem to have required that the defense be allowed to address the new issues.

Following the failure of the appeal on behalf of his client, Wilson seems to have lapsed into inactivity. Not so some of the other local citizens. Although we cannot know that Wilson had no hand in the business, the person who seems most to have bestirred himself was Col. David Newland, a legislator from the county. He addressed three letters on Frankie's behalf to Governor Montfort Stokes and personally called upon the governor in Raleigh to deliver a set of petitions.[58] Wilson first wrote Stokes in November 1832, following Newland's last letter, to let Stokes know that Newland had mistakenly given Frankie and others the impression that a pardon was forthcoming. Wilson probably wrote a now-lost letter to Governor David L. Swain in April 1833 requesting a postponement in the execution—the two-week "respite" granted by Swain. But it was the confession of Frankie Silver in late May or early June 1833 that seems finally to have jolted Wilson into action.

In any case, at the time of the trial Wilson had not elicited the actual circumstances of the murder from his client. More than a year later, hopeless and facing death, Frankie finally confided the truth—but to "some of her acquaintances" rather than to her counsel. Inspired by what they had heard, these people approached Wilson and Herman Gaither, asking them to sign a petition. Instead of signing it, Wilson says, "we proposed to see her ourselves" in order to interrogate her.[59] After grilling Frankie, Wilson finally concluded that she was guilty not of murder but of manslaughter. This change of attitude implies that even while representing her, he privately shared the initial public opinion of her infamy— and as a result he may have given her less than his best effort.

Nicholas Woodfin reportedly believed that Frankie's confession showed she herself "did not know the difference between murder and manslaughter or self-defence."[60] She was young. Census data indicate that at the time of the murder Frankie was between sixteen and twenty-one years of age; Burke County citizens who petitioned Governor Stokes in the fall of 1832 estimated her age as between twenty and twenty-two.[61] Frankie was also doubtless illiterate, like her mother, father, and brother Jackson.[62] They all presumably were, at that time, inexperienced with the law. Wilson may not be at fault for failing to learn Frankie's reasons for her act—defense attorneys are not generally eager to hear a client's confession of guilt, and she had her reasons for reticence—but as her counsel he certainly had the duty to give her timely clarification of the critical distinctions between murder and self-defense. Had she or her family seen reason to confide in him before the trial, he might have more successfully defended her.

When Frankie's confession circulated within the community, it had a demonstrable impact. One result was that the ladies of Morganton and Burke County now became strongly sympathetic to Frankie and were willing to petition Governor Swain on her behalf. But the cover letter for their petition—written by W. C. Bevens rather than by Wilson—states that "Mr. Stuard the father of the prisoner" was advised to "get up a petition among the Ladies" by "Col. John Carson . . . together with others of the Village."[63] It probably was not Wilson, then, who grasped the potential value of such a petition. More important, had the ladies' petition been posted to the governor at the time Wilson sent his own, rather than one month later, it would have arrived soon enough to enable Swain, if persuaded by it, to cancel the execution. The documents he received from Wilson led him only to postpone it for two weeks.

The petitions and letters Wilson undertook to send to Governor Swain do not create confidence in the attorney's judgment and tact. The letters are overlong and bombastic. They ramble. They hoist red flags better whisked out of sight. In the petition dated June 3, 1833, Wilson starts, for example, by reminding the governor that Frankie is indeed guilty of "a crime of the deepest dye, and which was aggravated by every circumstance which could give a darker colouring to the transaction and to your petitioner the most fiend like disposition." Worse, Wilson fails to offer any of the evidence that might have swayed Swain. Petition bearers showed Frankie's confession to the local community with considerable effect, but Wilson sends neither copy nor summary to the governor. He fails to tell why so many people trust Frankie's account. He thinks his best shot is the equivocal assertion that "many respectable and intelligent gentlemen who had before kept aloof" now step forward and say "if her confession was true, she ought not to be executed."[64]

Some see Thomas Wilson as a dark character in Frankie's story. Author Sharyn McCrumb told me in conversation that her suspicions were roused by his moving with all his family from Morganton to Seguin, Texas, in the 1850s. He and his wife, both by then in their sixties, were too old for pioneering on the frontier, and the move would have cost his

Col. John Carson (1752–1841), who signed a petition to Governor Stokes and advised Frankie's father "to get up a petition among the Ladies" to send to Governor Swain. His son, congressman Samuel Price Carson, killed Swain's close friend Robert B. Vance in a duel over Col. John Carson's reputation. (Courtesy of Elinor Henderson Swaim)

son prospects for education, his daughters their chance for marriage into propertied old families, and his wife the society of her friends. McCrumb wondered whether some unrecorded disgrace might have forced him to undertake such an unlikely move. Lloyd Bailey may offer some confirmation of this view in the form of a letter about an attorney named Thomas Wilson who was involved in a case in Yancey County in 1846, and who had "haponed to some misfortons and . . . left the contry."[65] The character of these misfortunes is unclear, and it is uncertain even that the letter refers to Thomas W. Wilson of Morganton, who was listed in the 1840 and 1850 censuses for Burke County and first appears in the records of Guadalupe County, Texas, in 1854, at which time he had twenty-two slaves, his taxables being valued at $11,570.[66]

Nor was Seguin a place of waste and desolation. Frederick Law Olmsted, who visited there in 1855, called it "the prettiest town in Texas."[67] It was also prosperous enough to support two weekly newspapers in years when Morganton had none. Guadalupe County tax records for 1855 show that Wilson, then sixty-five, gave his twenty-one-year-old son Joseph all his personal assets, setting him up in business as a stock raiser. The move was probably made just for that purpose, a family decision thought to offer Joseph a bright future in a recently formed state. Governor Swain had a nephew who also moved to Texas in the same decade to become a stock raiser; he lived in counties adjacent to Guadalupe, first Gonzales and later Travis.[68]

Once ensconced in Seguin, far from hiding from the public eye, Wilson wrote a long letter to the local newspaper offering himself as a Democratic candidate for the office of chief justice of the county court. This letter, however, like the one he sent Governor Swain with the petition of June 3, 1833, shows him deficient in tactical skills. He calls himself a "states-right Democrat of the old school" and declares his opposition "to any change in the laws pertaining to the naturalization of foreigners," but he offers no other substantive issues. The chief thrust of Wilson's campaign statement is his self-interest:

> It is not for love of the "dear people" (and perhaps I have as much as some who make greater pretensions,) that induces me to become a candidate but what, without inquiry or investigation, I suppose to be the emoluments of the office. . . . I cannot boast of strong solicitations to run; but the few friends, upon the advice of whom, I announced my candidacy, may perhaps be denominated a clique. If so, I care not.

. . . I am a much older man than either of my opponents, and can, I believe, plead necessity equally as strong; and I should, I think, be the recipient of your suffrages.[69]

This letter was no more persuasive with the Texas voters than his earlier letters had been with Governor Swain. Thomas Wilson was a man of comfortable standing in society, but clearly without distinction of mind. Frankie's prosecutor, Wilson's nephew-in-law William Julius Alexander, apparently had the gifts that Wilson lacked. He represented Mecklenburg County from 1826 to 1831 in the North Carolina House of Commons and again from 1833 to 1835. In three different sessions of the legislature—in 1829-30, 1833-34, and 1834-35—the House of Commons elected him its speaker.[70] I myself suspect, however, that Wilson's greatest disservice to his client Frankie Silver resulted less from his ineptitude than from an injury unintentionally inflicted. At a more appropriate point in the story—in Chapter 6—I will offer my speculation about what this injury may have been.

If Thomas Worth Wilson is a hazy figure in the contemporary documents, Frankie Silver herself we can scarcely see. She is either the bloody-minded butcher of public notoriety or a small figure we glimpse "in a ridged & severe confinement, a great Part of the time chained in a dungeon to the middle of the room."[71] Can oral tradition supplement the documents and bring Frankie Silver into any clearer view?

4

*Apparently it was just an echo
of the memory of something bad
that had happened there.*
— *Bobby McMillon*

A STORY THAT HAPPENED
THE LEGEND OF FRANKIE SILVER

For some months and years in his early childhood, often later on weekends and holidays, and during the summers, Bobby McMillon stayed with his grandparents Dewey and Rosa Woody in the tiny Blue Ridge settlement of Kona. One day when he was nine or ten, Bobby began listening to music on the family's "talking machine." When he put on a recording of Roba Stanley singing the ballad "Little Frankie," his grandmother remarked, "You know, that happened right here." "What do you mean *right here?*" Bobby asked. She answered, "Well, that song really talks about Frankie Silver, who lived up the hollow here."[1]

Bobby thinks that he had probably heard mention of Frankie by the time he was four or five, but the story had just "passed over" him until he was trying to learn this song. His grandmother Woody, Bobby says, was "never one that recalled a lot of stories"; she was, instead, "real sharp geared toward quilting and sewing and all kinds of housework and garden work and flowers—anything that grows or anything you do with your hands." The oral traditions most interesting to her were say-ings, "little protections for children or adults," or "what'd bring bad luck and what won't." Even many family stories, Bobby says, "went by her that one of her younger sisters would tell me about—things I guess that either didn't appeal or that just didn't stick with her." So when she told Bobby about Frankie Silver, she "sort of just glossed through it."[2] This, nevertheless, was the moment that awakened his interest in Frankie. He wanted to learn more.

What Bobby learned over the next decade was, in addition to a song, a set of local legends that he and other storytellers have sometimes woven into an unusual narrative cycle. He has told it publicly many times, and a form of the story he told when he was twenty-four was chosen for in-clusion in the 1982 anthology *A Celebration of American Family Folklore;* see Appendix A for this version.[3] The transcription in Chapter 2 is a very full version of this cycle that offers a story quite different from the one we might deduce from historical documents related to the case of Frankie Silver—a story with its own mysteries, its own powerful tradi-tional artistry, and its own evidence about the nature and uses of histori-cal legends.

By the 1960s, when Bobby became interested in the material, oral tra-dition and journalism had for a century and a quarter played interacting roles in perpetuating and spreading the memory of Frankie Silver. Con-temporary newspapers in the state had carried several short accounts of the murder, Frankie's escape and recapture, her confession, and her exe-cution. In the mid-1880s the *Morganton Star* and the *Lenoir News-Topic* had published a text of the ballad and a letter about the confession. But in working through stories later published about Frankie Silver in news-paper features, magazine articles, and chapters of books, one finds that virtually all of them lead back to one of two oral accounts by early mem-bers of the Silver family—Charlie's half-brother Alfred (1816–1905) and his half-sister Lucinda ("Aunt Cindy") Silver Norman (1826–1927).

Alfred Silver was interviewed in 1903 for a *Charlotte Daily Observer* feature written by a young journalist who would go on to become a pres-tigious member of the Washington press corps, H. E. C. ("Red Buck") Bryant. This account—the first publication of any of the legend material —has been reprinted and quoted numerous times, especially in local his-tories and newspaper articles.[4] Lucinda Norman's information served as the basis for part of a chapter in Muriel Earley Sheppard's book *Cabins in the Laurel,* published in 1935.[5] Her version has had greater influence on accounts written outside North Carolina, including those in Olive W. Burt's *American Murder Ballads*, Benjamin A. Botkin's *Treasury of Southern Folklore,* and similar books.[6] Arthur Palmer Hudson's lengthy headnote to the ballad in *The Frank C. Brown Collection of North Carolina Folklore* draws from both traditions.[7] (Appendix A holds the texts of these two accounts as preserved by Bryant and Sheppard.) Some episodes independently derived from oral sources have also cropped up in other publications.

Bobby's knowledge of the murder first came to him through oral tradition and developed slowly. Some people told him specific details in answer to his questions; he heard other episodes as they happened to come up in conversation. Bobby's grandfather told him some stories he had heard from Will Silver, a son of Charlie Silver's younger half-brother David. Bobby himself talked with one of Will's daughters, who confirmed things he had heard without adding anything fresh. His great-uncle Grady Thomas told him of an eerie experience he had while hunting that Bobby set down in a manuscript account:

> Me and another feller used to coon hunt up the holler around where the Frankie Silvers place was. One night in the fall of the year we 'as up in there with our guns, a-huntin'. The wind was a-sobbin' thru the dry leaves of the oaks and beeches with a cool lonesome edge, when my hair stood straight up! They was screams and groans commenced to peeling out in the dark that'd freeze your soul. We lit out a thair a-burning the wind as we went and never would hunt around in there no more.[8]

Bobby first heard the Frankie Silver ballad sung by "Granny Hopson" —Lou Hopson, the grandmother of his first cousins. After his father helped him get a portable recorder in 1968, he recorded her performance on his first tape. He learned a different tune for the ballad and other legends about Frankie from "Aunt" Lou Brookshire in Caldwell County. She had heard about Frankie as she grew up there in the Brushy Mountains.

Bobby is most indebted, however, to his grandmother's uncle Lattimore ("Uncle Latt") Hughes. This relative spoke to him about Frankie on several occasions, one of which Bobby recorded on tape; a transcription of Hughes's account is also included in Appendix A. Uncle Latt was not kin to the Silvers, but his family lived nearby in the Kona community. Bobby says Uncle Latt was born at the turn of the century and

H. E. C. ("Red Buck") Bryant (1873–1967), journalist who interviewed Charlie's half-brother Alfred Silver in 1903 and wrote the first printed version of the legend cycle. (Courtesy of the North Carolina Collection, University of North Carolina Library at Chapel Hill)

Muriel Earley Sheppard (d. 1951), whose *Cabins in the Laurel* in 1935 included a version of the legend cycle derived from Charlie's half-sister Lucinda Norman. (Courtesy of the University of North Carolina Press and the North Carolina Collection, University of North Carolina Library in Chapel Hill)

was "certainly very folksy." Bobby's description of the tale session during which he recorded Latt's story of Frankie Silver is a testimony to the man's immersion in the local traditions:

By the time that I got real good acquainted with Uncle Latt—he was my great-grandmother's brother—I was wanting the whole story. I mean I wanted to know what he'd heard. And I don't really know what made me—it was one of those days that I turned the tape recorder on, and he was telling me lots of different things not related to that either, about growing up and about witch tales he had heard. And he told me about the Civil War veteran whose name was Moses Fox that lived up on the Green Mountain. Said he burnt a hog in a brush pile, because he said it had been bewitched. He told me about this man that had trouble because the witches had bothered him, and he went to the witch doctor, and he told him to milk—his cow went dry's what happened—and the witch doctor told him to milk all the milk he could get in a pot and light a fire under it, and when it got hot, to go to switching it. Seem like it was willow switches, or something. And said he took his advice and done that, and when it got hot, he went to switching it. And said these two women started walking up on the mountain there where he was at. Said they got up there, and they stopped and they started using the bathroom—started peeing— and they peed a flood. And as long as he switched that hot milk, they

Lattimore ("Uncle Latt") Hughes (1895–1977) of Bowditch, N.C., Bobby McMillon's great-great-uncle "Latt," who told him stories of Frankie Silver and influenced his version of the legend cycle. (Courtesy of Clara Lee Hughes Riddle)

had to stand there and pee—much longer, of course, than would be natural for your bladder to empty. Anyway they had to promise never to bother his cows again. Anyway, he told stories about his daddy—my great-great-grandfather, who was a pretty wicked man—told how he mistreated my great-great-grandmother and had had an illegitimate child by this old woman who later killed him, and then the illegitimate child grew up to be an outlaw and was shot dead up in Spruce Pine. I need to look that up some time in the history books. Apparently it was after the railroad came in—he said he was killed on the railroad tracks. But Uncle Latt was the only one who really ever give me the full treatment of the [Frankie Silver] story.[9]

Bobby also gained knowledge of Frankie Silver from published sources. He heard a commercial recording of the ballad made in the 1920s by Clarence Green, Byrd Moore, and Clarence Ashley, and he also began to come upon printed versions of the song accompanied by accounts of the murder.[10] His Aunt Ona found a clipping with the text of the ballad at his grandmother's house. Granny Hopson showed him an article about Frankie Silver that came from a 1960 issue of the *Tri-County News,* a Spruce Pine weekly. Aunt Lou Brookshire had an article from the *Lenoir News-Topic* or the *Morganton News-Herald.* Somewhere along the line he came upon a reprinting of the Alfred Silver interview. When Bobby was about fifteen or sixteen, his mother's cousin Phil Thomas, an engineer with Harris Clay Company, introduced him to the account Muriel Sheppard had published in *Cabins in the Laurel.* About the same time Bobby found the material in *The Frank C. Brown Collection of North Carolina Folklore.* "Everything I would come across," he says, "I'd put up here in my noggin for future reference."[11]

The initial appeal of the story for Bobby was that it brought the local landscape to life around him. Across a ridge to the southeast, about a half-mile from his grandparents' house, lay the hollow where Frankie and Charlie Silver had lived. He saw the site of their cabin and climbed the tree that grew close by the ruins of the fireplace. Nearer, just over the crest of the ridge, was a churchyard where he could see fieldstones said to mark the three graves of Charles Silver. His grandparents' country store stood right across the road from this church, and the hill behind it sloped down to the old log house where Charlie Silver had grown up, still standing and, in Bobby's childhood, still lived in by members of the Silver family. Bobby's grandmother pointed out a rock they could see across a branch from the dirt road that ran by their own house; she told him that a sack holding Charlie Silver's "lights" (lungs) got hidden there. Bobby's mother told him that she and other children "used to be afraid to go by there at certain times, I guess toward dark or something, or when they'd ride the school bus out of the hollow to go to Bakersville to school. I'd always been able to see the rock, and so that was something I could *visually* picture. And so that incident had always stuck in my mind firmly. . . . The kids and everybody that went in and out always knew that that rock was supposed to either be haunted or had a legend behind it."[12] As a consequence, Bobby "always felt some kind of affinity with the story, because I lived here off and on with my grandparents as a child growing up and would walk these hollows and cross these ridges and look at the places where this story happened."[13]

The story gained an even stronger hold on Bobby in his teen years. He learned then that he was related to the Silver family and read materials by Monroe Thomas, a local teacher and genealogist, that filled in many of the blanks. Charlie Silver had an uncle named Greenberry Silver, who according to local lore had "forty children outside the home." "He was a rambler," says Bobby, "if not a rogue." Bobby learned that Greenberry's first child was by a girl named Sarah Woody, whom he would not marry. She raised the child, a son, as a Woody, but named him for his father. This Greenberry Woody was grandfather to Bobby's grandfather. Bobby learned of other family connections as well. His grandmother's uncle Mack Thomas married a granddaughter of Frankie and Charlie Silver. Through one of his grandmother's Wiseman relatives, he learned, he was related by marriage to David Baker, the acting justice who ordered the arrest of Frankie after the murder. "I would hear these stories," Bobby says, "and I would take them to heart. They meant something to me that I couldn't put into words at that time, but it was just a feeling of connection. I always had that need for some reason to feel a root system. And when I learned . . . that our family were really Silvers, although three generations went by the name of Woody, it became more interesting to me, . . . because I learned that many of these stories had happened to my kinfolk."[14] The Frankie Silver story, he says in the session transcribed in Chapter 2, was "one from my family that used to fill me with pride in a way, because it was so bloody"—that is, such a striking story.

Bobby McMillon's attraction to legends, then, was very different from that felt by a "folk-revival" storyteller, who may comfortably flit from a Russian to a Yiddish to a Yoruba tale. Bobby finds his main satisfaction in stories from his own world. Moreover, unlike the revivalist who gets material primarily from books, Bobby may consult books for information but feels a strong need to *hear* the story. When he got Stanley South's booklets *A Window to Times Gone By* and *I Never Killed a Man Didn't Need Killing!*, which include legends transcribed from recordings of interviews with Howard Woodring, Enoch Potter, Sam Trivette, and others in Watauga County, they appealed to him because he had been to places and known families that figured in the stories. Some of the characters were even kin to his brother-in-law, Doug Trivette.[15] But Bobby was especially eager to hear the original tapes. Far from sharing the fashionable distrust of oral tradition, he finds a story not fully compelling or authentic until he has experienced the telling of it. "To hear it told is a different world than reading it," he says. "I appreciate the printed word and I love to read anything about any of these things that I can. I love it! But it never has the same quality, being read, as it does being listened to."[16]

When he begins the Frankie Silver legend, Bobby uses a pointed phrase, calling it "a story that happened." He shortly uses this phrase again: "And it happened, the story that I'm about to tell, happened in the early 1830s." Again near the end of the session he returns to the phrase, saying that in the local community the Frankie Silver story got displaced by "some other stories that took place" there. This is Bobby's usual way of referring to historical legends in other interviews as well—including statements I have already quoted in this chapter. The phrase seems to fold together two assumptions: that the story deals with fact, and that we know the facts mainly through narrative art.

Concerning the story as fact, Bobby says in talking about the events, "I'd have to tell the way that I thought that must've happened."[17] Committed to the Silver legend as family and regional history, then, he is careful to situate the story in the historical past, with dates and names. He gives information he has learned about the social background—what animals men hunted, how women wore their hair, why people thought they needed to take protective measures against grave robbers. He even cites sources he has checked for facts: "But according to the 1850 census"; "But there was nothing in the records that survived of the trial to ever indicate that." As he moves from general background into traditional accounts, he marks the shift with the words "they said": "Well, it was 'long about Christmas time. *They said* that Charlie was preparing to go on a hunting trip." For a number of episodes from the Frankie Silver

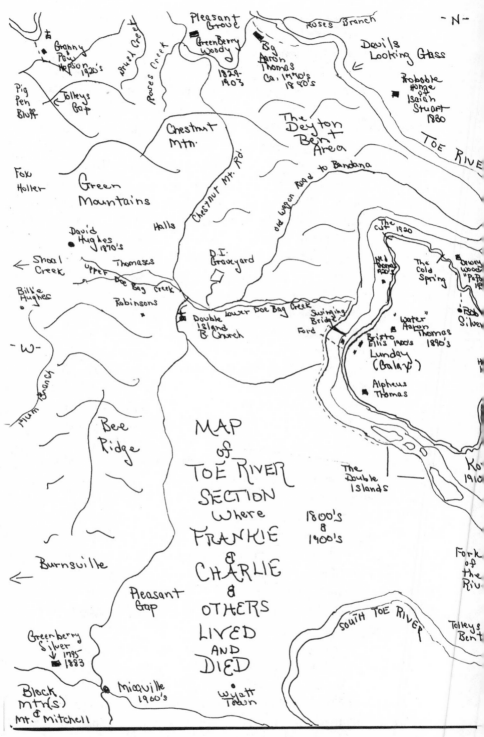

A map drawn by Bobby McMillon of the Toe River country, where the murder
took place in 1831 and where Bobby lived with his grandparents as a child.
(Courtesy of Bobby McMillon)

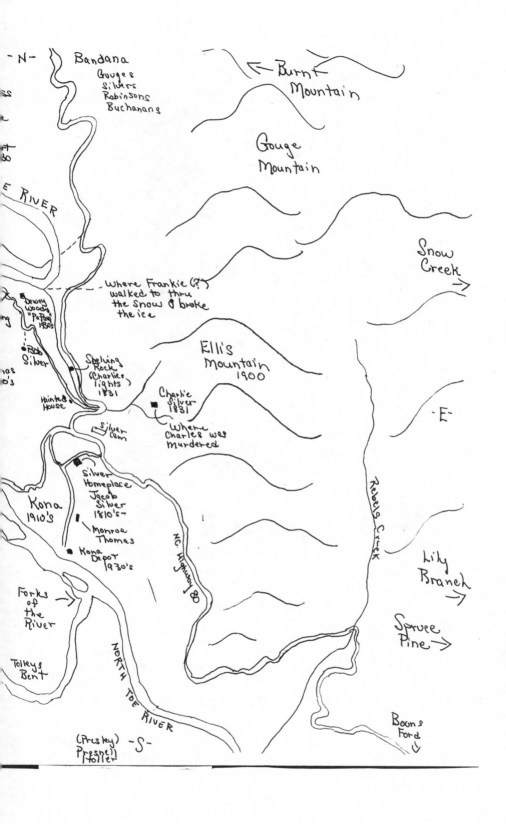

-N-

Bandana
Gouges
Silvers
Robinsons
Buchanans

← Burnt
Mountain

Gouge
Mountain

Snow
Creek →

E RIVER

Where Frankie (?)
walked to thru
the snow & broke
the ice

Ellis
Mountain
1900

Dewey
Woods
"Pa Palm"
1800s

Rob
Silver

Shelling
Rock
(Charlies
lights)
1831

Charlie
Silver
1831

Haunted
House

Where
Charles was
murdered

Silver
Cem

Kona
1910's

Silver
Homeplace
Jacob
Silver
1810's—

Monroe
Thomas

Kona
Depot
1930's

N.C. Highway 80

Rebels Creek

-E-

Lily
Branch →

Forks
of
the
River →

Spruce
Pine →

Tolleys
Bent

NORTH TOE RIVER

Boons
Ford

(Presley) -S-
Presnell
Holler

The log house of Jacob Silver, where Charlie was raised. The cabin of Charlie and Frankie was in a hollow beyond the ridge above this home. Governor David L. Swain reportedly grew up in a similar house; both were substantial ones for plain people in the backcountry. (Courtesy of Ann Parks Hawthorne)

story, then, Bobby nails down his family authorities: "But now this is the way that they told it at home"; "Well, according to my granny's uncle"; "Old Man Will Silvers, he died about thirty-five years ago, and he used to tell my grandfather that."

This citing of oral authority is characteristic of the telling of legends everywhere in society—and legends are a thriving form; Jan Brunvand's

Catherine and Greenberry Woody, Bobby McMillon's great-great-grandparents. Greenberry was an illegitimate son of Charlie Silver's uncle Greenberry Silver. Discovery of this family connection intensified Bobby's interest in the Frankie Silver lore. (Courtesy of Bobby McMillon)

popular collections of contemporary legends have made even the general public aware of that.[18] But to cite an oral authority is not necessarily to induce belief. Distrust of legends is also widespread and undermines the reputation of all oral tradition. "That's only folklore" is an all-too-common phrase, meaning that folklore is simply falsehood. Perry Deane Young has produced a book to "set the record straight" about errors in the lore and literature of Frankie Silver.[19] John Foster West, who wrote two similar books about the 1866 murder that gave rise to the North Carolina ballad "Tom Dooley," complained indignantly, "Folk tales about Tom Dula told over the decades have been woefully inaccurate." His purpose in writing the books was to dispose of the misconceptions "for anyone interested in learning the truth instead of believing old folk tales."[20]

But this is too simple a reading of historical legends. It is the nature of the legend to serve as contested terrain. "One might say that the question of belief-nonbelief," write Linda Dégh and Andrew Vázsonyi, "is an active problem in any community where legends are told." It is their observation that, during the telling of a legend, the "various types of participants—the proponent, the contributor, the expander, the stimulator, the critic and the challenger—play equally important roles, and often switch them."[21] A "true legend-telling session," they maintain, "is not therefore the solo performance of one accredited person to whom the others passively listen. It is a dispute—a dialectic duel of ideas, principles, beliefs, and passions."[22]

In Tom Davenport's video, we see this normal contesting of the legend when Wayne Silver uses the inquest description of the wound in Charlie's skull to challenge the story that Frankie Silver committed intentional murder. Watching the video, Jeffrey Gray challenged also the story that Frankie said to Charlie before the murder, "Well, I fixed a pallet for you by the fireplace. I thought you might want to take a nap till you got ready to go to bed." Gray's response was, "Why would people believe that? Nobody witnessed the murder."[23] The words had always puzzled Bobby, too, but he defends the account, saying, "That's the words that they claim that she said." To him it seems plausible that the dialogue would have become known by persons not present, because "people always blab." What puzzled him in the account was something different—the unlikelihood of Charlie's preparing for a night's sleep by taking a nap.

Bobby is fully aware, then, of the issue of credibility in oral traditions. The Silvers, he points out, "just like anybody else, they disagree amongst themselves and tell the same story different ways lots of times."[24] While he calls the multiplicity of variants one of the "glories" of balladry, that genre has a somewhat more relaxed standard for factual accuracy. In Bobby's mind, a historical legend requires at least plausibility. This standard casts Bobby in a role not unlike that of the jurors in a criminal trial. They learn a small body of undisputed facts and hear information and occasional stories from witnesses, all of which then get put together into the competing narrative constructions of the prosecutor and the defense attorney. The jurors weigh all this material and produce for themselves a narrative that conforms to their own sense of the plausible.[25]

The juror does not at first encounter an orderly body of information. Bobby too gathered his knowledge bit by bit. We get an erroneous impression when Bobby, in response to the filmmaker's request, sits and tells an entire cycle of Frankie Silver tales. An episode in the Davenport video that better captures the normally unpredictable exchange of tale materials is the scene in which Bobby and Tom Davenport accidentally encounter a local resident on Damon's Hill in Morganton, the site where Frankie Silver was hanged. This man tells them that, in earlier times, nursemaids passing the spot would frighten children by telling them that if they misbehaved, the booger on the hill would get them. Within minutes Bobby retells the story to the owner of the house now standing on the site of the hanging. Bobby himself picked up episodes from the Frankie Silver story in conversations like this, "in bits and pieces."[26] But Bobby McMillon is an experienced and gifted public performer who has sung and told stories on festival stages and in public schools. He can create a sense of fireside intimacy even when telling the tales to a camera in a motel room, and he can comfortably weave together the entire Frankie Silver legend cycle as if telling it to an outsider unfamiliar with the story.

It is even probable that the legend cycle itself crystallized only when insiders began to try to tell outsiders or members of later generations what had happened. In fashioning this story, the community created a repertory of sometimes competing episodes. Certain storytellers took a selection of these and, for outsiders, wove them into an aesthetically satisfying account. Print preserved their efforts for a later narrator like Bobby McMillon and, together with oral tradition, gave him models for both the form and the contents of the Frankie Silver legend. In stating this, I put a reverse spin on Charles Joyner's assertion that "legend formation is collective, but legend creation is individual."[27] Bobby has, in fact, selected elements from the collective repertory created by his community and formed them into his own powerful narrative.

Bobby McMillon himself can provide abundant evidence of how he formed his way of telling the legend cycle—and of how the oral aesthetic he had absorbed guided his choices. When Bobby began to encounter variants of the Frankie Silver legend, he often found them contradictory, a fact that challenged him to try to establish the truth. Was Charlie killed with an ax, as people said in Kona, or with a nail driven into his temple, as Aunt Lou Brookshire had heard in Caldwell County? When Frankie opened her mouth to speak on the scaffold, who called out, "Die with it in you, Frankie! Die with it in you!"? Was it Frankie's mother, as his grandmother told him, or her father, as he heard from Uncle Latt?[28]

For Bobby himself, the various stories of Frankie Silver, as he puts it, "all slowly came together." He recognizes that he has made some changes in the story unconsciously. "I'm beginning to see now after all these years," he says, "how those things in the old days came to be turned out the way they did, simply because with the passage of time" a certain part "fades, or blends into something."[29] Perhaps this fading happened with material Bobby probably saw in clippings from an issue of Spruce Pine's *Tri-County News*. These related that Wiley Woody saw Frankie, at the gallows, unwind her red ribbon waistband, cut it into small pieces, and toss them to the crowd; Wiley, according to this report, caught one, took it home, and placed it in the Woody family bible, where it still remains "fresh and bright red."[30] This episode, although associated with the Woody family, does not appear in any of Bobby's accounts of the execution. After reading of it in my manuscript, he wrote, "I can't at this point in time imagine why such an image (the band cutting) would have escaped my thought and attention at an age when such a poignant episode would have surely entered into my telling of the tale. . . . There was quite a bit of time between my knowing of the ribbon and the period in which I began to tell the story a lot. Most possibly it had slipped my mind by the time the version I told publicly took shape."[31] My own speculation is that the action may have seemed to him not in character for Frankie or not a plausible gesture for a woman in that circumstance, and hence the detail faded from his memory.

To a remarkable degree, however, Bobby has consciously weighed what he has heard and read, building his own version out of the details he finds the most convincing. He tells, for example, of being puzzled by what he saw as a contradiction between two accounts people gave him of the murder scene. Some said that after Charlie fell asleep on a rug by the fire, Frankie took the baby from beside him, put it in the bed, and then struck Charlie with the ax. At that point, they said, Charlie jumped up and screamed, "God bless the child!" But the baby, Uncle Latt said, then crawled to the table through its own father's blood, pulled itself up, and left its bloody handprints on the wood. Bobby thought it "wouldn't make sense for the child to got back out of the bed. *She* wouldn't let it up, I don't think, and if her mother or anybody else in the family'd been there, they'd have *held* it." Uncle Latt "didn't say anything about her picking up the child beforehand." This omission "opened up a little more sense" to the story than Bobby "had ever been able to make out from either the newspaper accounts or from what the people told me about it." Bobby says, "I interlaced my own thoughts about it here." He now saw that if the baby was actually near Charlie when he got struck, then Charlie, not grasping what was happening, would have thought the baby would be attacked too. That would explain why he screamed something like, "God save the child!" And it suggested further that the baby *might well* have crawled through its father's blood and left its prints upon the table. Bobby tests episode variants, then, for their logical consistency with other parts of the story cycle.[32]

In the passage just quoted we see him employing another criterion as well—his sense of how a person from this community would behave under specific circumstances. In such a horrific moment, Frankie would not have let the baby get back out of bed. Her mother, if she was there, would have held it. At another point in the story, Bobby explains that the dismemberment of Charlie's body would have required a sharp ax, and he always assumed Charlie had sharpened it when he got done chopping wood: "I think that's the way the mountain people would have thought, more to got it ready for the next time and had it ready, rather than put it off till then and do it. In light of what happened, it made more sense to me."[33]

In one book Bobby came across a detail that he had never heard from any storyteller. According to this account, when Frankie finally confessed the murder of Charlie to an acquaintance, the friend asked why she had buried rather than burned the heart, to which Frankie replied, "Because it were mine!"[34] Bobby thought this an interesting detail but never included it when he told the story. Partly he was distrustful of the episode because he had never heard anyone tell it when he was a youngster, but chiefly he felt that "in the heat of all that was going on"—the murder and the frantic efforts to conceal it—a person would be unlikely to be "giving thought for anything sentimental" like that.[35] To Bobby, plausibility in the light of local custom and of broader human behavior is an important test.

His quest for truth, then, prods Bobby to sort through the variants. His version changes as he learns more and ponders the material more deeply. He has made, for example, several substantive changes, including his interpretation of the motivation for the murder, since he recorded the tale for the Smithsonian Institution in 1976. But in calling the legend "a *story* that happened," Bobby is also acknowledging the place of artistic impulse in the process. This is a quality said not to be characteristic of the legend teller. Linda Dégh, the most thoughtful and experienced student of the form, found in Hungarian communities that "traditional Märchen-tellers conscious of their craft" were "careful to distinguish legends from tales" and seemed not to regard legends they told as part of their tale repertory.[36] After extensive fieldwork in the United States with "belief legends" about such things as UFOs, she stated unequivocally that "one thing is certain: the legend teller is no artist—he or she has no artistic aspirations, and claims only to tell a story that takes place in the real world."[37] This view, I think, is too colored by Dégh's work with belief legends. It is demonstrably not an accurate description of Bobby McMillon as a teller of historical legends.

Although he enjoys fantasy stories like Jack tales and tall tales and tells them superbly, Bobby seems to me more deeply engaged with local legends. Reading these words in my manuscript, he commented, "Personally I like to hear . . . the old wonder tales [i.e., Jack, Muncimeg, Nippy, etc.] most of all," but he also recognized that the legends are the core of his "performance repertory as it has unfolded thru the years."[38] His own assessment of Dégh's statement is that in everyday life "you'll hear enough things in that belief category that won't sound artistic," but if the talker is "actually artistic already, it's going to sound artistic."[39]

Bobby learned the legend material of his community. He relishes and likes to use the old words and pronunciations he heard in the speech of the most traditional talkers there. But more important, he absorbed the local style of storytelling, becoming himself a master of conscious artistry in this tradition. His artistry shows in many levels of his storytelling. His performances never sag with the filler phrases of the inexpert teenage talker: "Like, well, I mean, you know, there was this man that, uh. . . ." Bobby's discourse flows. He speaks with conciseness and with particularity. Charles cut down "a sourwood tree." Frankie's father hid the sack underneath "a shelving rock that stuck out" halfway down the trail toward the river. This attention to sharp details creates vivid pictures for the listener.

Bobby's style of delivery also shows the art of his regional tale tellers in another way. These speakers, like singers from their communities, do not much dramatize their performances. They prefer understatement and nuance. Since such performers virtually never gain air time on radio or television, most urban, middle-class audiences are inexperienced in listening to them. Trained to accept media hype, these audiences may respond more immediately to a professional tale teller who invents artful scenes and then gestures, mugs, and exaggerates changes in voice, volume, and pacing in order to reach and hold a restless audience.

Bobby McMillon's artistry is more subtle than that. For example, when he describes how Frankie tried three times to strike Charles with the ax and then said, "Well, I can't do it, I can't kill him, a-smiling at me like that," he makes his voice slightly lighter and a bit tentative, with a rising tone on the word *that*. In the episode relating the sheriff's recapture of Frankie, Bobby says the words of her numskull uncle with just a hint of puppylike eagerness: "Yes, sir, her name *is* Tom. Her name *is* Tom." As the sheriff on the scaffold, Bobby shades his words with a bit of the unction of a funeral director, "Frankie, have you got anything you'd like to say? . . . Well, we'd like for you to tell it."

Even when he inserts a word like *said* to authenticate the account, Bobby uses it for special narrative effect. In some stretches of the tale he does not say the word at all; in others he peppers a passage with it: "And *they said* that the baby, Nancy, got to crawling. *And said* that it crawled through, through its dad's own blood, and where it was learning to walk, it tried to stand up at the table. It put its little handprints on the table, *and said* that the mark was left there forever!" At the beginning of this passage, *said* turns the narrative flow choppy, heightening the tension of the scene. At the end, Bobby uses *said* to set off the final clause and give it weight: "and said that the mark was left there forever!" In another passage, he combines *said* with a subtly varied repetition of phrases to highlight key words. Frankie's father tells her, " 'Well, now, if you don't kill him,' *said*, 'I'll kill you.' *Said*, 'If you don't kill him, I'll kill you.' "

Bobby's artistry shows even more clearly in the materials of his legend. The regional tradition guides him. The mountain people, he says, whatever their story was,

> if it really happened to them, or if it was something they'd heard from somebody else, they would always tell it either in the first person or as if second hand. You never told it like, well, "Imagine this setting." You *never* put [in] anything—as soon as I hear that from a storyteller, they just might as well hush right then, 'cause they've not got anything that I can relate to enough to be interested in. I'll 'preciate them, but to me that's not what it was. The real storytelling was so intertwined that a bear tale or a fish tale or a witch tale or a tale of some history that'd really happened, a family tale, they were all equally believable. The tale tellers I grew up around sounded believable regardless of the type of tale they told.[40]

Bobby, then, does not invent or dress up scenes. His desire for truth would not permit him to do that, so the episodes and motifs in his stories are ones he has heard from older people. But Bobby himself has the gift of remembering the effective touches in stories he has encountered, especially those that seize the imagination. These are generally striking lines of speech such as Charles Silver's anguished cry, "God bless the child!" or images like the baby's bloody handprint. They are often charged with an emotion both unstated and indefinable, as in Frankie's stunning last request—for a piece of cake.

Bobby McMillon is probably the most self-conscious artist to have woven these various episodes into a legend cycle, but we have proof that he is not the only tradition bearer to have taken this step. Alfred Silver and Lucinda Norman each told an entire cycle, apparently in response to requests. Bobby recalls that his great-uncle Latt "sat down and just went through it all" when Bobby asked him to, telling him "parts I hadn't heard orally elsewhere."[41] It is not possible to get authoritative texts for these three early performances. Bobby's tape of Uncle Latt records an interview in which Latt Hughes tells extensive sections of the story, but in response to specific questions, although Bobby can describe in detail all the things Latt told him at one time or another. Alfred Silver's version is presented by H. E. C. Bryant as direct quotation, but in 1903 the journalist could not have made an actual sound recording of Silver for later transcription. We do not know whether he wrote up his account from notes taken as Silver talked or whether he reconstructed the story from memory.[42]

Lucinda Norman's narrative comes to us in an even more mediated form. Muriel Sheppard's account, published in 1935, summarizes the story as Lucinda told in it in 1914—her ninetieth year—to W. W. Bailey, a younger member of the local community. It has not been possible to recover either his papers or hers, so we do not know exactly what changes the story may have undergone in the hands of either Bailey or Sheppard. A second account claiming to be based on what Lucinda told in 1912 is less than a page long but includes material not in the Sheppard version, notably a reference to a "negro with a 'magic glass'" brought from Tennessee to help in the search for Charlie. As "the glass persisted in turning downward, the floor was removed and portions of the body found."[43] Bobby points out that Lucinda's ballad text, as printed in *Cabins in the Laurel,* is somewhat confused, a circumstance that leads him to think her advanced age may have affected her memory and hence her legend narrative too.

Bobby McMillon's accounts, then, are the only ones for which we have an actual transcription of a complete oral performance. The other versions are useful in corroborating the currency of Bobby McMillon's narrative and in highlighting his artistry and his personal view of the story. Although the four narrations differ in details, degree of fullness, and even interpretation, their story cycles are remarkably alike in content, structure, and narrative approach.

All four versions present the local community's view of the events, three of them even giving a Silver family member's perspective. Some additional tales have descended through the Stewart family. Lawrence E. Wood of Franklin, North Carolina, reported being told by Minnie Gregory Buchanon, a great-granddaughter of Frankie Silver, that she had often seen the table that bore the baby Nancy's handprint and that she had heard within the family that Barbara and Blackstone Stewart helped kill Charlie. But most stories reported from the Stewarts seem to concern family members other than Frankie. Wood had heard a story about the disappearance and probable murder of a male descendant of Nancy at a place called Red Rock.[44] The descendants of Frankie's brother Jackson Stewart tell stories about his actions as sheriff of Mitchell County during the Civil War, the enmity he aroused among Union sympathizers, and his murder at their hands.[45] Bobby McMillon and others among the Silvers with connections to both families also tell other tragic stories from the family's later history—as, for example, one about a black convict's rape of a granddaughter of Charlie and Frankie, an aunt by marriage of Bobby's grandmother Woody.[46] Except for Alfred Silver's mention of the death of Jackson Stewart, none of these additional incidents were incorporated into the Frankie Silver cycle as told by these four storytellers.

Linda Dégh describes the belief legend as generally having "an easily recognizable *frame*," that is, an introduction and a conclusion. The introduction, she writes, serves

> to strengthen the credit of the coming story. The importance of the message therein makes the detailed preliminaries indispensable. In this genre, which is marked by inconsistency of form, I cannot tell the precise sequence of elements in the introduction, but I certainly can tell what belongs to it. It contains first of all, the *reason* for the telling, the *essence,* the advice, the abstract or concrete warning. This is to attract attention, and to impress the listeners. Secondly comes the *identification* of the acting persons, to make certain that everybody knows them.[47]

We do not know whether Alfred Silver and Lucinda Norman opened their renditions with any framing sentences. Lattimore Hughes, when

Bobby recorded him, did not. Bobby McMillon, however, does frame the story. He annotated my manuscript draft of this passage with the words, "My introducing the tale with a brief history of the advent of the Silvers to N.C. slowly developed over the years as my knowledge of my family and their history grew into a more active interest and I began to suppose a little background might be of interest to audiences. Earlier I began it more in ballad style with the main action about to begin." His 1976 account corroborates this statement; it opens with only an attention-catching mention of a few lurid events in the tale and of Bobby's own relation to the protagonists.

Bobby's presentation of the Frankie Silver cycle to Tom Davenport's video camera begins with a framing introduction. But because this is a historical rather than a belief legend, its contents are in some ways different from what Dégh describes. The introduction offers no "message." Instead, Bobby attracts the listener's attention by calling the story that follows "one of the strangest and most frightening" that ever happened "over in western North Carolina, in the Toe River country." Bobby then gives background information about his own family's arrival in that region, about other settlers and the early wilderness, and about the Silvers and his relation to them. This provides an uninformed listener with helpful information and also grounds the story in its historical setting. Like the introduction to the belief legend, his account—and those of the two Silvers as well—then presents the key characters, Charlie and Frankie Silver.

Bobby's tale proper seems to unfold in fifteen segments:

1. *Charles's cutting of firewood.*
2. *Charles's supper and nap by the fireside.*
3. *The murder.*
4. *The disposition of the body.*
5. *Frankie's subsequent deceptive behavior.*
6. *The search for Charles.*
7. *Jake Collis's discovery of evidence.*
8. *Other searchers' discovery of evidence.*
9. The burial of Charles.
10. The arrest and trial of Frankie.
11. Frankie's jailbreak.
12. *The recapture of Frankie.*
13. *The execution.*

14. The burial of Frankie.
15. The curse on her family.

Bobby then closes the frame of his narrative with three additional sections:

16. The raising of the child Nancy.
17. The motives for the murder.
18. Recent experiences relating to the Silver story.

Bobby and the others present some of these steps as short summaries. The ones listed above in italics are episodes that he and other narrators develop as scenes with one or more motifs in the form of action, dialogue, or image.

In some small particulars Bobby McMillon's telling of the story differs from that given by the others. He knew their versions, but at times he appears guided by his own artistic sense. For example, in recounting the search episode, Lucinda Norman attributes the finding of the evidence of Charles's murder to Jake Collis. Alfred Silver follows this tradition, too, and develops Collis's detective skills through his series of discoveries: poking in the fireplace with his cane, Collis finds bones, greasy ashes, a heel iron from Charles's moccasins, and a stone that bubbles with grease when he drops it in water; in a mortar hole he finds other ashes. Bobby's account describes an equally long series of discoveries but attributes them to several searchers from the community. In his account, Jake merely initiates the search of the cabin when he notices the odd behavior of Charles's dog. Whatever the truth may have been, Bobby's version makes a more satisfying narrative structure. It does not give sudden importance to a new character who then, just as suddenly, drops forever out of the story.

But there are two much more important ways in which Bobby's version of the legend differs from the accounts of Alfred Silver and Lucinda Norman—and from other legendary reports and such facts as we can find in the sketchy records as well. In both, Bobby says he is following the traditions shared with him by Uncle Latt Hughes. Bobby's account consistently presents Frankie as less aggressive than most others do. He omits many motifs that suggest recklessness or coarseness of character in Frankie. For example, Lucinda Norman's account says that Frankie burst in upon the men searching her house, screeching like a wild woman, and that at her hanging she boldly pulled the black hood down over her face with her own hands. The Woody letter in the Spruce Pine newspaper described her as flamboyantly tossing pieces of her red waistband down from the scaffold to people in the mob. Bobby uses none of these touches in his picture of Frankie, and in his 1992 narration he does not repeat—as the other two Silver accounts do—the charge that Frankie acted in a fit of jealousy, believing that Charlie was having an affair with another woman. Bobby declined to incorporate this tradition into his story, despite saying in one interview that he does "recollect clearly that it was always told that she had a reason, that they thought maybe she was jealous" of another woman, somebody over toward Tennessee whom Charlie may have gone to see when he claimed to be away trapping.[48] He used this as the explanation of the crime when he told the story in the 1970s. But now he explains the murder with a motif that lays the responsibility upon Frankie's family.

Even more important, Bobby McMillon gives Frankie's father a key role in his story. Court records show that Frankie's mother and brother initially were arrested and charged with complicity but had to be freed for lack of evidence. Petitions and related letters show that her father made persistent but hapless efforts to save Frankie. Bobby's account of the murder, however, introduces and dwells on Frankie's father as the chief actor. This is not how he first heard the story. In the account his grandmother Woody gave him, Frankie committed the crime alone. Lucinda Norman and Alfred Silver also make Frankie the sole perpetrator. Only Latt Hughes's account has the father present during the murder. Of all the versions that Bobby McMillon knows, this is the one he chooses to follow. So he says that when Charlie falls asleep, Frankie's father tells her, "Now's your time, Frankie." When Frankie falters in the task, her father threatens, "If you don't kill him, I'll kill you." When Frankie, horror-stricken after she has wounded Charlie, hides under the bed covers, her father finishes the murder, striking Charlie's head from his body with such force that it bounces against the rafters. Bobby remembers very vividly that "Uncle Latt said her daddy finished it, every bit of it."[49] He, not Frankie, disposed of the body and walked in Charlie's boots to the riverside and punched holes in the ice to make people think Charlie had fallen in.

Bobby's later version includes other details to the same end. In the first account he ever heard—the one told him by his grandmother—when Frankie started to speak from the scaffold it was her mother who shouted out, "Die with it in you, Frankie!" Alfred Silver, Lucinda Norman, and Uncle Latt all attributed the words to Frankie's father instead, and Bobby recalls Latt's comment: "I guess he would've told her that. He didn't want her to tell on him."[50] Bobby accepts this version, and he intensifies the picture with the suggestion that if the "Frankie Silver" ballad was indeed sold at the hanging, he "always figured that probably her daddy had it printed up and was trying to make money off of it because of greed." And he adds, "that's probably what caused the murder anyway." Although Bobby does not exonerate Frankie, he has chosen to follow the somewhat less damning version he heard from Uncle Latt. This account carried special weight with him because he personally heard it from a relative; as a storyteller, Bobby probably was also attracted by its being different from what other people told. Across the years, too, he felt a growing sympathy for Frankie. In any case, Bobby now builds his narrative on the traditions that shift blame away from Frankie and toward her father.

Feminists who believe Frankie was a battered wife might not accept Bobby's portrait of her. They would perhaps even regard it as a stereotypical picture of an "acceptable" woman, one too passive to act. But some might also see, in this version told by Bobby and his great-great-uncle Lattimore Hughes, a suggestion of the role of fathers in the childhood experience of abused women. In her well-known book *The Battered Woman Syndrome*, Lenore E. Walker describes 67 percent of her subjects as reporting that they grew up in homes where battering occurred. Although the women claimed that they were "equally battered by their mothers and fathers," Walker also asserts in *Terrifying Love: Why Battered Women Kill and How Society Responds* that "a high percentage of battered women are incest survivors."[51] After reading these words in an early draft of this chapter, Bobby McMillon mentioned the matter to a woman descended from one of Frankie's brothers. She told him that there had been instances of male abusiveness, including incest, in her branch of the Stewart family, leading her to wonder if Frankie might have been abused by her father Isaiah.[52] Bobby also says that a fellow furniture worker recently warned one of his cousins "to not have anything to do with any of them Stewarts, that they were still as crazy as they used to be, and that they run the gamut from child molesters to witches to abusers."[53]

Bobby's singing partner Marina Trivette is inclined to think that Frankie indeed was avenging herself on Charlie: "I believe that's the only thing a woman'd get mad enough about: . . . if a man was running around on her or if he was abusing her in some way. And if she could catch him asleep she might get him. Like, you know, the women do nowadays, in 'The Burning Bed' and things like that. Maybe that was her only way to get him back, while he was a-napping."[54]

Bobby himself takes a different view of the marriage of Charlie and Frankie. Although he concedes the possibility that Charlie *might* have been "a rough character," he is not really convinced that Charles violently mistreated Frankie. To him this seems highly unlikely. He does feel some degree of family loyalty to Charlie, but he also argues a number of points in support of his view: that at nineteen Charlie was too young to have grown very abusive; that as Jacob's oldest son, Charlie would have been put to farm work quite young and thus would have had little time for shiftlessness; and that the family background was a good one. Bobby points out that Jacob Silver was more well-to-do than many of his neighbors—his substantial two-story double log house still stands, and tax records show that in 1830 he owned three hundred acres of land— and that the Silver family has had a long history of producing skilled woodworkers and preachers.[55] Jacob himself was a Baptist preacher and, Bobby says, "as far as I can tell, must have lived a *very* good life."[56]

Bobby further points out that the name given the child Nancy suggests that Charlie felt affection for the stepmother who raised him, Nancy Reed Silver. Moreover, the story as he heard it from Uncle Latt gives a generally favorable impression of Charlie. When it opens, Charlie is shown as a responsible provider, working all day in the snow to cut wood for his family. An affectionate father, he lies down with his baby in his arms. In his sleep, he smiles three times at Frankie. So Bobby does not see the murder as being motivated by Frankie's anger at any habitual abuse by Charlie.

The concluding frame that comes after the body of the narrative has a slot into which several of the storytellers place their theory concerning the motive for the crime. In his 1976 rendition of the story at the Smithsonian Bicentennial Festival of American Folklife, Bobby at this point attributed the crime to Frankie's jealousy, drawing on a line in the Frankie Silver ballad. Currently Bobby inserts here a different tradition concerning Frankie's motive, "old man Will Silver's" opinion that Frankie's father and family wanted to move west and needed Charlie to sell his farm in order to raise funds, and Charlie didn't want to do it. So Frankie's people "just coerced" Frankie into murdering him. Later, Bobby learned that "the farm wasn't Charlie's—it was his dad's, altho I suppose . . . his father might possibly have worked out something had Charlie wished to move away."[57]

Bobby separates this particular tradition, however, from the body of the story. He does not present it as dialogue in a scene. It remains an explanatory speculation, but one that probably has special plausibility for Bobby because of his own childhood experiences when his father moved the family from North Carolina to California. He felt almost unbearable homesickness in California and would sympathize with Charlie's reported reluctance to leave his home and kin. In the end Bobby says simply, "There's some element missing from the story, that we don't know, that [Frankie] must have carried to the grave with her and apparently her family carried to the grave with them. I don't have animosity like probably some of the closer relatives to Charles Silver would have had. It just seems sad that if she died for someone else's deed, that it never went avenged in this life."[58]

If Bobby and Marina take different readings of Frankie Silver's motives, and if Bobby feels abiding uncertainties about the case, this is wholly in keeping with the nature of the historical legend. In Bobby's own aesthetic, at least, the point of telling the story is not to preach a position. Other people who told him Frankie Silver stories, by his account, also did so not so much for didactic purposes as because they were struck by certain gestures in the story. He says, for example, that one "strong point of the story among the different people that told it" to him was the irony of the fact that Charlie "was burnt with the wood that he had cut that day." Another point he thought "the old timers" emphasized was that Frankie had sung her confession on the scaffold: "I think almost everybody that told me anything about it made a point to say that she sang that."[59] I believe there is, however, a further set of community meanings in the legend cycle, ones not openly stated but embedded in its structure. For the most remarkable thing about the "complete" tellings of the Frankie Silver legend is that all of them cover much the same story material and do so with the same narrative method.

Except for the version attributed to Lucinda Norman, recorded texts of the story open just before the climactic event, with Charles chopping wood in the snow on the day of his murder. Lucinda's opens with Frankie's arrival at the Silver home the morning after the murder but later reverts to the same initial scene in which Charles chops wood. This flashback is probably an artistic stratagem imposed on the material by Muriel Sheppard rather than by Lucinda Norman. Neither Bobby nor any of the other tale tellers offers any childhood incident that forecasts the character or fate of either Charles or Frankie. They may mention their cabin, their poverty, and their parenthood, but they have nothing to say about the condition of the couple's marriage. They tell no incident illustrative of either a happy courtship or the igniting of their conflict. They all elaborate on the murder, the dismemberment and concealment of the body, and Frankie's deceptive conversations to hide the murder. They detail the search for Charles and the discovery of evidence of the crime. Not one of them makes more than a passing mention of the trial, conviction, or appeal, and no account mentions the petitions circulated in the county and sent to two governors to request executive clemency for Frankie. Not one gives a detailed account of the jailbreak, but all dwell at length on Frankie's recapture and on the execution. All describe her family's frustrated efforts to protect her body for a decent burial, and all accounts follow this with a summary account of judgments that came upon members of Frankie's family.

Some of the events glossed over in this narrative cycle—such as the trial, the appeal of the sentence, and the submission of petitions to the governors—were important elements in the Frankie Silver case. Waiting to learn their outcomes would have been harrowing experiences for the Stewarts. Some of these steps may not have been widely known in the Kona community or would not have served well as scenes in a narrative. Nonetheless, the summary of the plot structure suggests that their absence is mainly owing to an approach to narrative that governs the cycle.

The storytellers focus on action and dialogue, not on psychology. Bobby, for example, draws Charles with a single broad stroke, saying that he was a hunter and a trapper. He also portrays Frankie in few words: she "had charms"; she was a pretty girl and a good dancer. Alfred Silver had sketched each in only slightly greater detail: Charlie was a woodsman, popular, and a good musician; Frankie had charms and was a hard worker.

All versions of the cycle open just before the murder, develop a few key scenes, leap from one to the next, and refrain from moralizing about the events. These features suggest narrative techniques long admired in traditional ballads. Gordon H. Gerould's description of the "classic" British ballad, for example, could be an analysis of the leaping and lingering in Bobby McMillon's treatment of scenes in his Frankie Silver cycle:

There is nothing irrelevant, but there is a good deal left unexplained. The events burst out in a series of flashes, each very sharp and each revealing one further step in the action. What lies before and after remains in darkness, and can be learned only by inference. There is unity because the flashes are all directed on what is essential to our imaginative and emotional grasp of a quite simple situation. No method of narration more direct and effective, within its limitations, could be desired.[60]

Although I do not think we can make a case for any direct influence of a ballad on the presentation of the Frankie Silver story, there are ballads that show not only general structural parallels but even similar solutions to similar narrative problems. The subordination of lengthy legal procedures to the moments of action or emotional intensity in the Frankie Silver story is, for example, very like the treatment of the trial in the much-admired Scottish ballad "Mary Hamilton." Longer versions of the ballad open with rumors of Mary's pregnancy speeding through the castle and reaching the old queen, who comes and interrogates Mary about the murder of her child and instructs her to dress for a trial in Edinburgh. The ballad finesses the trial and judgment:

When she gaed up the Parliament stair,
    The heel cam aff her shee;
And lang or she cam down again
    She was condemnd to dee.[61]

The scenes chosen for elaboration are Mary's interrogation by the old Queen, her public appearance in Edinburgh, and in particular Mary's subsequent lamentation on the day of her execution.

Bobby McMillon's prose narration of the Silver legend cycle is in fact much closer to the form and spirit of the traditional ballad than is the song "Frankie Silver." In balladry this narrative method seems partly a consequence of the story's being performed to a tune. One turn of the tune bounds the stanza; each stanza holds an utterance, or a question and answer, or an action, or an image. The stanzas develop the scenes, and the leaps across space and time take place between stanzas, with gaps between scenes doubtless sometimes being accentuated by the forgetting of a stanza. The song does not need a fully articulated plot in order to satisfy the singer and listener as unified and complete. The sense of completeness results from the juxtaposition of scenes. Both William McCarthy and David Buchan have offered elaborate demonstrations of this principle in the older Scottish balladry.[62] A remarkable feature of the Frankie Silver legend cycle is the application of this storytelling approach to a prose narrative.

What explains why Bobby McMillon and the other tellers of this legend linger on the particular chosen scenes? As in a traditional ballad, the elaborated scenes seem to be those most packed with emotion. The first part of the narrative, for example, emphasizes the murder of Charlie and the dismemberment of his body—the former a crime in law, the latter the breaking of a deeply felt taboo. Bobby in fact registers the intensity of these two scenes by deviating in each one from his normal delivery. In telling of the murder he actually enacts both Frankie's drawing back three times with an ax to strike and Charlie's smiling at her three times in his sleep. In only one other place in the entire narrative does Bobby do anything comparable, and that is when he follows the example of Uncle Latt Hughes in showing how Frankie betrayed her identity to the sheriff: "Uncle Latt made these gestures, putting his hands out as if a woman was a-trying to raise the folds of a apron to catch a ball in." But here he and Uncle Latt are simply trying to make sure that something unfamiliar will be clear to the listener. In Bobby's second emotionally charged scene—that in which the searchers begin to make their gruesome discoveries—he says that everywhere Charlie's dog led them "they'd find a little something to remind them of Charlie." This wry remark is one of his few touches of humor in the entire story. I take this to be Bobby's effort to make the horror of the episode bearable, for others and for himself. Both deviations reflect the emotional intensity of the episodes.

More important, in tragic traditional ballads the elaborated scenes have moral implications, but they dramatize the message or voice it indirectly. Mary Hamilton does not preach "Take warning by me." Instead, she simply laments,

> Last nicht there was four Maries,
>   The nicht there'l be but three;
> There was Marie Seton, and Marie Beton,
>   And Marie Carmichael, and me.

Ballad singers and their audiences feel intensely the moral implications of such a passage, but the direct expression of these judgments comes, if at all, outside the song. Cecilia Costello, a British singer, recalled her father's comments on "The Cruel Mother," a ballad about infanticide: "When you get married and you have any children, . . . don't do what this woman's done what I'm going to sing to you."[63] Ozark singer Almeda Riddle, even as a child of seven, strongly responded to the implied moral of another ballad, "The House Carpenter," in which a woman deserts her husband and baby to cross the sea with a lover: "I thought that was a terrible thing, this mother leaving that baby. That was the thing that struck me the worst, you know, the mother deserting the child. . . . And when she drowned, I remembered getting great satisfaction out of the thought that she got her just deserts. Even a child can have thoughts like that."[64]

All four versions of the Frankie Silver legend cycle present their moral statements indirectly, but hearers unaware of the guiding aesthetic may respond as if the story were simply an unreliable report of historical facts, instead of a narrative form akin to the ballad in seriousness, if not in apparent fictionality. I see implied lessons in the scenes on which Bobby lingers. As in the ballads, the moral attitudes disclose themselves in a series of juxtaposed episodes. One pair of early scenes (those showing the concealment of evidence of the crime and Frankie's bravado the next morning at the Silvers' house) elaborates on Frankie's attempt to mislead the community; answering scenes unfold the community's discovery of the truth (through the conjure ball's answers to Jacob Silver's questions and the search conducted at Charlie and Frankie's cabin). Another early scene dwells on the murder Frankie commits; the answering scene elaborates upon her punishment for that crime.

A third early scene lingers on the shocking desecration of Charles's body and its consequent burial in three different graves. The answering episode has the Stewarts dig several false graves to mislead people who might steal Frankie's body for medical dissection, a detail that carries a good deal of force. People in Burke County may no longer have remembered the insults that authorities in the British Isles for centuries inflicted on the bodies of felons (beheading, drawing, quartering, disemboweling, displaying, or burning them, or turning them over to the Worshipful Company of Barbers and Surgeons for dissection).[65] As the county lacked a newspaper, they may also not have known of the sensational 1828 trial in Edinburgh of the notorious "resurrectionists" or body-snatchers William Burke and William Hare, or of the elaborate measures being taken in Scotland to protect the recently buried.[66] But much evidence shows that in North Carolina insults to dead bodies continued to rouse horror and dread. The maiming of a criminal's body by flogging or branding remained in the legal code as a form of punishment until after the Civil War. Lynch mobs developed ritual forms of assault upon the corpses of their victims. And horrifying tales still circulate today concerning bodies once stolen in nearby Cleveland County for use by physicians.[67] So the Frankie Silver legend reports that the Stewarts tried frantically to protect her body from men who might insult it, only to have the summer heat force them to huddle Frankie into a dishonored grave far from home. Nature itself avenges the desecration of Charles's body.

None of us can say to what degree the various episodes in the cycle are historically accurate. They do, however, accurately dramatize the community's sense of morality. Bobby McMillon says as much when he tells about the violent ends believed to have come upon Isaiah, Barbara, and Blackstone Stewart. Acknowledging with a slight wink that the stories may not be entirely true, he says, "That's the way people tend to think of getting paid back in communities like that."[68] Perry Deane Young points out that six of the thirteen children of Jacob Silver "met untimely deaths" without bringing the Silver family under suspicion of a curse.[69] Tales about the Stewarts, however, clearly served to redress wrongs the community suspected them of committing.

Stories similar to the ones about Frankie Silver cluster around several other North Carolina ballads. The murder of Patsy Beasly in Anson County in 1844 begot legends as well as the ballad that bears her name. According to one story, a local Primitive Baptist preacher "opened his Sunday service by laying a large flint rock on the pulpit. He announced the murder of Patsy Beasly as his text and during the course of the sermon said, 'The man who killed Patsy Beasly is in this church house and I am going to smash his head with this rock.'" Startled, a man named Tom Nash "jumped through an open window and ran like a jack rabbit," thus betraying his guilt.[70] Associated with the song "Tom Dooley" is a legend that Ann Melton, widely regarded as Tom Dula's unindicted co-conspirator in the murder of Laura Foster in 1866, got her punishment on her deathbed. "I can remember one of the horror tales of my childhood," the journalist Maude Minish Sutton wrote, "was how the devil came after Ann Melton when she died. An old lady told me that she saw her and that blue flames crackled around her bed, and that she screamed in agony to her friends to 'take him away, the big black man in the corner, the one with the pitchfork!'"[71] It is typical for these historical legends to assert the reality of moral order. The tale tellers may not preach, but they want moral clarity, a useful past.

Bobby's own comment on these words, when he read them in my manuscript, was:

This is true, altho' I wonder if later generations of tellers tend to assert these moralistic wonders, especially if one of *their* ancestors was witness to the tragedy. Uncle Wade Gilbert, himself a fine singer, banjoist and fiddler, told a very interesting, straight-forward version of Tom Dula in which his grandmother and other relatives were involved. However, in telling his granny's and other women's nursing of Ann Melton on her deathbed till the point of death itself, he made no mention of the frying meat and black cat incident which he surely would have had it been told him, as he and the people around him at that time easily believed in signs and wonders, especially ones with such colour, drama and lessons that would embellish the story to a satisfying end.

The Frankie Silver legend cycle, in any case, came over the years to be composed of sets of paired scenes that in effect dramatize proverbial teachings: Truth will out. Justice prevails. Respect the dead. To me these messages seem implicit in the structure of the narrative, but I do not know that Bobby McMillon would be comfortable with this interpretation, for he is quite clear about his dislike for stories told to preach a point. "I don't see stories," he says, "as always being put out with the object of having a moral lesson, but I think the lesson is in the person. . . . There's a moral. You got to figure it out yourself."[72]

If the messages I see are in fact implicit in the Frankie Silver legend cycle, they are sufficiently submerged not to violate the standards of the storytelling tradition Bobby represents. It prefers understatement and implication. This aesthetic, however, is more than an artistic strategy; it reflects an outlook on the world. As Bobby formulates it, "You don't have these people here that you say, 'Well, these are the good ones, and these over here are the bad ones.' Because there's good and bad in everybody. And in the most colorful characters, you see some awful cruelty, and then again you see some acts of just uncommon kindness. And that's the way all of them that I grew up around were."[73] When Bobby heard the lingering gossip about the Stewart family, he was inclined to credit it, "still believing the old adage that 'blood [traits] will out' in succeeding generations." Nevertheless, he added the comment, "Sometimes you have to accept people whatever they're like."[74]

Bobby's view rests on his own experiences in his region, but he also grounds it in his religious faith: "We're sort of like Paul said. What he wants to do, he can't. And what he don't want to do, he does it a whole lot. And I think every human being's like that. . . . To me it's perfectly all right to make mistakes, because you can't help it. It's right to feel remorse for mistakes that might hurt other people, but yet as long as we're living, we're faced with contradictions within ourselves that we don't understand."[75] It follows, then, that Bobby and the narrative aesthetic he serves would assert moral standards without becoming openly judgmental about persons.

Bobby McMillon's legend cycle also carries another kind of implicit truth. It reveals not only the community's values, but also issues that trouble it. Two episodes that Bobby added to the end of the story suggest the lingering wound this murder left in the community.[76] He says his grandmother's brother told him that one time "he and another man were hunting up in that hollow where Charlie and Frankie lived, and said that all at once it sounded like somebody was just being killed. Their screams were just terrible." The men ran "like scalded dogs."[77] Bobby also tells of his own anxiety as a child when he had to go outdoors at night—his fear that he would "see Frankie's spirit come wandering around the road with an ax in her hand and blood in her eyes."

Bobby openly explains what this kind of material means to him. He could just imagine, Bobby says, "that anything so tragic as that story would leave behind some residue of where you'd have a haunt, or what we called a 'haint,' a ghost." He recognizes the same thing in the story about the nursemaids who passed Frankie's execution site on Damon's Hill and threatened their charges with words like, "Now if you don't be quiet and mind, that booger that lives up there on the hill is going to come after you." A terrible event had taken place on the hill. The nursemaids' words—like the newspaper articles and novels and plays and the ballet, like the historical studies, and like Bobby's song and stories—are "just an echo of the memory" of it.[78]

5

We've got some ballads we can't sing,
because we can't get to the end of them
for crying!
    —Marina Trivette

THE BALLAD "FRANKIE SILVER"

Frankie Silver was not the only regional candidate for notoriety in the 1830s. Within a month of Frankie's execution, newspapers in the state reported another family tragedy:

Danville, Va. July 20
Horrid Murder. — George Craft of this County was murdered on Thursday week last by his brother Armistead Craft. We are informed that they disputed at table, about some matter of little moment, and finally in defiance of the interposition of their father who was present came to blows; when Armistead drew a dirk & stabbed his brother in the left side. He died instantly and Armistead fled and is yet going at large.[1]

And three years earlier another lurid report had circulated:

Melancholy. — We learn, that *Joseph Wilson*, who lived on Clark's creek, Montgomery county, while under the influence of mental derangement, *hung his wife* to a sapling, in the woods, near his house;

when found by the neighbors she was entirely dead. Wilson made off with himself; and at last advices, had not been taken. Mrs. Wilson was about 50 years old, and has left a number of children. We learn that she had left her husband several times, during his crazy fits; but in this fatal instance it would seem that he was more self-possessed than usual on such occasions: it is thought that he must have decoyed his wife into the woods, and knocked her down before hanging her up to the tree. — *Western Carolinian.*[2]

And in that same year newspapers carried yet a third sensational story:

A most atrocious murder was perpetrated in Davidson county, on Monday, the 11th inst. by a man named *Osborn.* — He had been separated from his wife for some months, and on the day above mentioned, he went to the house of his mother-in-law, with whom she resided; his conduct being very outrageous, his wife became alarmed and ran off to the neighbors. On this, he gave vent to his passion by throwing a pair of shoes into the fire; and on his mother-in-law, an old lady 80 years of age, attempting to take them out, he assaulted her, and with an axe split her head across the temples, and chopped her body to pieces in such a manner as to render it impossible for the jury of inquest to join together the separated and mangled parts; he then murdered one of his children, by dividing its body into two parts with his axe. After completing this most unnatural and diabolical butchery, he commenced piling up the chairs and other furniture in the centre of the room, with the intention of setting fire to them and consuming the victims of his ferocity; but the arrival of the neighbors prevented the execution of his design. He was secured and is now confined in the jail at Lexington. We cannot learn that the wretch was insane; though the plea of insanity will doubtless be set up, as few will be willing to believe that such a monster could exist in civilized society, who could deliberately and in the full possession of his rational faculties commit a deed so savage, bloody and unnatural. — *Yadkin Journal.*[3]

From none of these shocking contemporaneous incidents do we have a legacy of story or song. Why did Frankie Silver's act alone engender a vigorous cycle of legends and a ballad still sung today?

Setting them against the body of folk songs that originated in America, one would not have expected any of these four events to beget a ballad. The violence most commonly commemorated in song in this country is the murder of an unmarried girl by a lover who is jealous or finds her pregnancy inconvenient. Early settlers brought many ballads on this theme from the British Isles, and when events recalled the stereotype, American singers poured new songs into the old mold.[4] From North Carolina alone, one can cite "Poor Omie" or "Naomi Wise" (Randolph County, 1807), "Patsy Beasly" (Anson County, 1844), "Tom Dooley" (four different ballads, Wilkes County, 1866), "Ellen Smith" (two different ballads, Forsyth County, 1893), and "Nell Cropsie" (Pasquotank County, 1901). Perhaps Frankie Silver's notoriety came from her very reversal of the stereotype: she was a married woman who murdered her husband.

But one legend about Frankie Silver suggests a better explanation for this ballad. Although Bobby McMillon questions the story's accuracy, people in the community, he says, made a special point of telling that on the day of her hanging, Frankie stood at the scaffold and sang the words of the ballad that bears her name. A rather lurid and inventive retelling of the murder, published in *True Detective Mysteries*, even elaborated this legend into a scene in which Frankie "reached into the folds of her homespun dress and brought out a long sheet of folded paper" inscribed with the song and sang it in "a voice clear and unwavering."[5]

This story may have gotten much of its currency from H. E. C. Bryant's often reprinted 1903 interview with Alfred Silver, half-brother of the murder victim. The journalist quotes Silver as calling the song "her confession" and "a printed ballad that she made." Bryant himself further describes it as "printed on a strip of paper and sold to people who were assembled at Morganton to see Franky Silver executed."[6] No such broadside of the song has ever been found, nor is any song broadside known to have been printed in North Carolina that early. The earliest known copy of the Frankie Silver song is a manuscript dated 1865, and the verses seem first to have appeared in print in 1885 in a local newspaper, under the title "Francis Silvers' Confession":

1 This dreadful, dark, and dismal day
  Has swept my glories all away,
  My sun goes down, my days are past,
  And I must leave this world at last.

2 Oh! Lord, what will become of me?
  I am condemned you all now see,

To heaven or hell my soul must fly
All in a moment when I die.

3 Judge Daniel has my sentence pass'd,
Those prison walls I leave at last,
Nothing to cheer my drooping head
Until I'm numbered with the dead.

4 But oh! that Dreadful Judge I fear;
Shall I that awful sentence hear:
"Depart ye cursed down to hell
And forever there to dwell"?

5 I know that frightful ghosts I'll see
Gnawing their flesh in misery,
And then and their attended be
For murder in the first degree.

6 There shall I meet that mournful face
Whose blood I spilled upon this place;
With flaming eyes to me he'll say,
"Why did you take my life away?"

7 His feeble hands fell gently down,
His chattering tongue soon lost its sound,
To see his soul and body part
It strikes with terror to my heart.

8 I took his blooming days away,
Left him no time to God to pray,
And if his sins fall on his head
Must I not bear them in his stead?

9 The jealous thought that first gave strife
To make me take my husband's life,
For months and days I spent my time
Thinking how to commit this crime.

10 And on a dark and doleful night
I put his body out of sight,

With flames I tried him to consume,
But time would not admit it done.

11 You all see me and on me gaze,
   Be careful how you spend your days,
   And never commit this awful crime,
   But try to serve your God in time.

12 My mind on solemn subjects roll;
   My little child, God bless its soul!
   All you that are of Adams race
   Let not my faults this child disgrace.

13 Farewell good people, you all now see
   What my bad conduct's brought on me—
   To die of shame and disgrace
   Before this world of human race.[7]

The title "Frances Silver's Confession," however, drew a sharp letter
from Henry Spainhour in Kentucky. He had been living in Morganton
at the time of the murder, trial, and execution, Spainhour said, and knew
the circumstances of

how this piece that is now published in THE TOPIC was gotten up.
Many years ago there was a man by the name of Beacham who killed
another man by the name of Sharp, in Frankfort, this State, (Ky.) He
was condemned to be hanged. He composed a song that was called
"Beacham's address." There was a young man who came to Morganton from Lincoln county, by the name of Wycough. He worked
one year in the shop where I worked. He had learned the song that
Beacham had composed and frequently sang it, so that I learned it but
have forgotten part of it. . . . Thomas W. Scott, then living in Morganton, got of Wycough a copy of the forenamed Beacham's song,
and from it composed the piece now in THE TOPIC copied from the
Morganton paper. . . . Now, after nearly 53 years, some person has
gotten hold of Scott's piece, composed from Beacham's song, many
verses and lines the very same as taken from Beacham's, with others
commingled and other additions to make the thing look as dark as
the ingenuity of man could devise, when there is not the slightest evidence that it was a premeditated murder, but a matter of an instant.

If Scott is yet living he will certainly know that these statements are true, but I am persuaded that it could not have been him that had this put in the papers. Some person not acquainted with the facts must have done it. I consider it wrong to brand the dead with greater crimes than we believe they were guilty of.[8]

The earlier event to which Spainhour referred was the murder of Col. Solomon P. Sharpe by Jereboam Beauchamp in 1824, given notoriety in the twentieth century by Robert Penn Warren's novel *World Enough and Time*. The flamboyant Beauchamp wrote a prose confession and even composed verses about his impending death—and on his way through the streets acknowledged the weeping ladies of Frankfort with gestures "peculiarly affecting and manly." Then, before "5 or 6 thousand spectators," Beauchamp "ordered the Musick" to strike up the fiddle tune "Bonaparte's Retreat from Moscow" as he stood beside his coffin in a cart beneath the gallows, awaiting Eternity.[9]

"Beacham's Address" was apparently not one of Beauchamp's own compositions, but other details in Spainhour's account are verifiable. Spainhour was twenty-four when Frankie died, and he was born in Burke County.[10] The U.S. census for 1830 lists two men named Wycough (father and son) in Lincoln County. Thomas W. Scott was a lad of seventeen at the time of the execution, lived in Burke County, served as clerk and master-in-equity in 1841–42, and was later a schoolteacher there.[11] And there was, in fact, a song entitled "Beacham's Address" or "Beauchamp's Confession," occasioned by the execution of Jereboam Beauchamp in 1826.

A second song dealing with that murder, "The Ballad of Colonel Sharp," gained some circulation; ballad singer Doug Wallin of Madison County sang it for Mike Yates, who published it on a cassette recording.[12] "Beauchamp's Confession," in contrast, apparently has not survived in oral tradition. The text, however, was described in 1911 in a checklist of Kentucky folksongs compiled by Hubert G. Shearin and Josiah Combs: "BEAUCHAMP'S CONFESSION, 4aabb, 7: Under sentence of death by Judge Davidge, for the murder of Sharpe . . . , Beauchamp pictures the meeting of himself and his victim in hell."[13] Combs did not include the text of this piece in his subsequently published collection of Kentucky folksongs, and it is not among his papers now at Berea College; Shearin's papers disappeared after his death in 1919.[14] But from the description above, we know that the seven-stanza "Beauchamp's

Confession" was, like "Frances Silver's Confession," in quatrain form, rhymed in couplets, included lines about the judge passing the sentence, and presented a scene in which the murderer meets the victim in hell. All this corroborates Spainhour's account of the making of the ballad. Six lines of verse in an 1835 manuscript that Perry Deane Young found in McDowell County, North Carolina, seem also to support Spainhour's report:

1st o dredfull dark and fearefull Day
How heas my glory fled away
my sun goes Down to rise no more
Who will my Dismal fate Deplore

2d O lord what will Bee Com of mee
Fore Deth must sun my potion bee

These words roughly parallel the opening of the "Frankie Silver" ballad, but they also differ significantly. Here "fearefull" appears where the "Frankie Silver" text says "dismal," and "fled" instead of "swept." The second half of the third line reads "to rise no more" rather than "my days are past." The last line of the first stanza is "Who will my Dismal fate Deplore" rather than "And I must leave this world at last." The second stanza opens with the same line as in "Frances Silver's Confession," but the second line is "Fore Deth must sun my potion bee," not "I am condemned, you all now see." These alternate readings occur in no other reported variant of "Frankie Silver." This, then, may well be a surviving fragment of "Beauchamp's Address."[15]

The significance of these details is not simply that they exonerate Frankie of the authorship of rather weak verse, but that both songs follow the venerable tradition of the journalistic "criminal's farewell" or "criminal's goodnight" ballads.[16] These began to appear in England during the sixteenth century, soon after publishers discovered the market for news stories printed on single sheets of paper, or "broadsides."[17] Though an ancestor of modern print journalism, the broadside news story was routinely composed in verse, and vendors hawked it by singing it loudly in the streets. For three hundred years, one of the staples of the trade was the broadside occasioned by an actual crime. V. A. C. Gatrell describes the "standard sequence" generated for a major crime: first, a quarter sheet with a "Sorrowful Lamentation" on the death of the victim; next, a half sheet with the particulars of the crime; then, on the day of the execution, a full broadsheet telling of the trial, confession, and execution, with verses and one or more woodcuts.[18] These broadsides were immensely popular, with sales reaching a peak during the century following 1750. In the 1840s, "farewells" issued for two British executions are said to have sold two-and-a-half-million copies each.[19]

The printing of broadsides carried over to colonial New England, but in North Carolina this form of publication developed late and served chiefly for political, legal, and commercial announcements.[20] Nevertheless, the influence of broadside verse is evident in many songs collected from oral tradition in the state. In the British Isles, many orally composed folksongs got printed on broadsides, and in turn many broadside poems struck the fancy of traditional singers and entered their repertories. Whatever their origin, a high proportion of the British ballads surviving in the Appalachians had appeared in the seventeenth and eighteenth centuries on British broadsides.[21] And a number of these are execution ballads.

Songs that originated as broadside texts are usually fairly easy to spot. Their texts lack the qualities for which folk verse has been justly admired: simple and vivid diction, naturalness of syntax, and economy of statement. Narrative songs that originated in oral tradition or that circulated orally for a long enough period usually focus on a few crucial scenes and develop them with dialogue and action. To survive long in oral tradition, a ballad had to be easily caught by ear. To be memorable, it also had to touch the heart and hence is often about tragic love. Broadside verse, the product of hack poets, has the opposite qualities. The writers typically used high-flown diction and complex sentences. They regularly inverted word order to achieve their rhymes and singsong meter. Their "stories" substituted moralizing for scene, character, and action, or, alternatively, had diffuse plots of many episodes. Like modern journalists, broadside authors panted after disasters and crimes (and found them financially rewarding).[22] All of these traits of broadside verse appear in the "Frankie Silver" ballad.

But some broadsides had enough appeal to be long and widely sung, and when this happened, the broadside text often underwent dramatic change. Its plot tightened. Its syntax simplified. Its fancy diction fell away. The eighteenth-century English broadside "The Gosport Tragedy," for example, which told of the murder of a girl by her sweetheart, became the Appalachian ballad "Pretty Polly." The original broadside is thirty-four stanzas long, and its plot is composed of many episodes: the seduction; the murder and concealment of the body; the murderer's enlistment as a ship's carpenter; the appearance on the ship of the ghost of the murdered girl; the captain's investigation; the murderer's denial, subsequent confession, and death; and the discovery and burial of the girl's body. In most Appalachian variants, the song has only six to a dozen stanzas and closes with the murder of the girl, the concealment of her body, and the flight of the murderer, leaving behind "nothing but the wild birds to mourn." Oral transmission has worn it to a smooth and classic shape. It has also made remarkable improvements in the diction and syntax. Originally the song opened,

> In Gosport of late there a damsel did dwell,
> For riches and beauty did many excell;
> A young man did court her to be his dear,
> And he by his trade was a Ship-Carpenter.

But in floating across time to Appalachia, the lines underwent a wondrous sea change. The original rhymed couplets still survive, and the bouncy anapestic meter has been only partially roughened into the accentual verse of traditional balladry. But the abstract nouns have turned into images. The word order is relaxed and normal. The lines sing well, because a syntactical unit in the text exactly fits one musical phrase:

> When I was a young man all in yonder's town,
> When I was a young man all in yonder's town,
> I courted pretty Polly, the lady of the town.

> O'er yonder's Pretty Polly, over yonder she stands,
> O'er yonder's Pretty Polly, over yonder she stands,
> With gold diamond rings on her lily-white hands.[23]

The local composition of ballads imitating the broadside model continued in western North Carolina well into the twentieth century. Bobby McMillon himself met some of the ballad makers. One was Henry Holsclaw, the brother of Aunt Lou Brookshire, a neighbor from whom Bobby collected the Frankie Silver ballad. Between 1915 and 1925, Henry composed a number of ballads and had them printed at a shop in Lenoir to sell for two or three cents apiece. One, "The Blockader's Trail," dealt with a time when Henry had gotten in trouble making liquor. Most of his ballads, however, were about disasters and violent crimes in the region, such as "The Landslide," about a flood in 1916 that took the lives of several people in Alexander County, and "Gladys Kincaid," about a girl murdered in Morganton by a black man named Broadus Miller.[24]

W. T. Ellison, from whom Bobby collected both stories and songs, was responsible for a ballad about the murder of Birchie Potter, a piece that Bobby knew from *The Frank C. Brown Collection of North Carolina Folklore.*[25] Ellison also told Bobby stories about the murder of a girl named Lily Shaw near Mountain City, Tennessee, and said his own cousin Edmund Miller wrote a song about it, "The Ballad of Finley Preston," which began:

> A great crowd now has gathered round this jailhouse today
> To see my execution and to hear what I do say.
> I must hang for the murder of Lily Shaw, you've learned,
> Who lies so cruelly murdered and her body shamefully burned.[26]

A century earlier, the authors of the ballads about Jereboam Beauchamp and Frankie Silver also modeled their songs, as Miller did, upon broadside-style verse, and "Frankie Silver" itself was reworked for another farewell, "Pennington's Lament," associated with the hanging of a Kentucky fiddler, that opened with the stanza:

> Oh, dreadful, dark and dismal day,
> How have my joys all passed away!
> My sun's gone down, my days are done,
> My race on earth has now been run.[27]

"Frankie Silver," however, circulated primarily in western North Carolina, and singers there made only modest attempts to rework it. The song generally has fifteen stanzas of monotonous iambic verse, rhyming in couplets; in diction, sentiment, and form it closely resembles both broadsides and common-meter hymns. The lines are clogged with inversions such as "that Dreadful Judge I fear" and "left him no time to God to pray." It makes reference to the sentencing, a commonplace in the criminal's farewell broadside genre. Although the narrative is a bit more focussed than in some farewells (which may survey the prisoner's progress from small sins to major crimes), it has only two passages of dialogue, and but one vaguely realized scene, an anticipated meeting with Charles's ghost.[28] The rest is lamenting and exhortation. Variation from text to text is minimal. The words have been sung, however, to at least four different traditional tunes. Two are associated with the ballads "Barbara Allen" and "Lord Bateman."[29] For a third tune, which

Bobby learned from Aunt Lou Brookshire, we have found no specific antecedent, although it has a traditional cast. The most common tune—the one that Bobby prefers and the one he sang in the session transcribed in Chapter 2—is closely related to the shape-note hymn tune "Devotion."[30] The minimal variation in the collected texts and their pairing with several unrelated tunes are two sure signs that many of the singers were learning the words from manuscript or print.

Those changes that do occur in the text are of several sorts. Four stanzas appear that are not in the 1885 newspaper text. Two normally come as a pair at the end of the song:

> 14 Awful indeed to think of death,
>   In perfect health to lose my breath.
>   Farewell my friends, I bid adieu,
>   Vengeance on me you must now pursue.
>
> 15 Great God! how shall I be forgiven?
>   Not fit for earth, not fit for Heaven,
>   But little time to pray to God,
>   For now I try that awful road.

The first of these stanzas may have been part of Thomas Scott's original song; it is in a manuscript copy that Perry Young dates to 1883. The second appears for the first time in the 1903 news story based on the interview with Alfred Silver. In 1923 James A. Turpin added two other stanzas when he "adapted" the Frankie Silver ballad "to the admission which, if she ever wrote the lines (a matter of doubt), she evidently intended to make"; in his book they come at the end of the song, but they appear separately at other points in the poem as Bobby McMillon likes to sing it.[31]

> 6a In that last calm sleep I see him now,
> The beautiful peace on his handsome brow.
> Our winsome babe on his heaving chest.
> The crimson blade, and the dreamless rest.

> 14a Now that I may no longer live,
> Oh pitying Lord, my crime forgive.
> When I hear the call of Judgement roll,
> May I appear with a blood-washed soul.[32]

The usual variations in the song text, however, are the dropping of stanzas or the scrambling of their order. Several traditional musicians who recorded "Frankie Silver" commercially—Clarence Ashley and Gwen Foster, for example, and Byrd Moore and His Hot Shots—clearly had to shorten the song to four or five stanzas to make it fit on a ten-inch 78-rpm disk.[33] In those variants, the limitations of the recording technology, rather than taste, brought improvements to the piece. Other verbal changes are numerous but small. They as often distort the meaning as improve the song:

> 5 I know that frightful ghosts I'll see
> Gnawing their flesh in misery,
> And then and there attended be
> For murder in the first degree.

Attended makes little sense here, although *tormented* would—and that is, in fact, the wording preserved in the earliest manuscript copy of the stanza, one written about 1883.[34]

For all its indebtedness to broadside verse, however, the "Frankie Silver" song is more than a bit of conventional doggerel. Its very conventionality is significant. The song presents itself as the first-person confession of a remorseful criminal. Hundreds of earlier broadsides also took this stance. And like "Frankie Silver," many of these other songs were said to have been performed by the condemned at the scaffold. Perhaps the most elaborate story is one associated with a farewell ballad for the execution of James McPherson, a half-gypsy Scottish freebooter, in 1701. The legend says that he made up verses and sang them to the accompaniment of his own fiddling beneath the gallows, with a "rant" tune ever since called "McPherson's Lament." When he finished, according to the story, he broke the fiddle; the broken remains of an instrument said to be his are on display now in the Macpherson Clan House Museum at Newtonmore, Inverness-shire. Robert Burns took the tune, one stanza, and the chorus of this confessional broadside and created a dashing, defiant ballad, but the original was tamely contrite and moralistic.[35] The criminal's farewell broadside, then, long had an expected place at executions.

Living in an era that holds a different perspective on executions, we forget that, until the second third of the nineteenth century, both trials and punishments were popular public events everywhere in the United States.[36] To residents of a sleepy North Carolina county seat, the court week was as good as a fair. In a fictional sketch, journalist Maude Minish Sutton embedded her recollection of the start of court week in Lenoir—Bobby McMillon's home town—at the turn of the twentieth century:

> The back lots of all the stores were full of covered wagons, surreys, buggies, carts, and all varieties of wheeled vehicles. Little camp fires still smoldered in these lots, for it was soon in the morning. A few belated campers were frying meat in iron skillets on these low fires. Others were hanging the skillets and coffee pots, in which they had cooked breakfast, on the high green sides of the covered wagons. The courthouse square swarmed with folks. . . . "Hoss traders" led their wares around in the crowd, or galloped them at full speed around the congested square and up and down the streets leading from it. . . . On the outskirts of the crowd an itinerant peddlar of "Ruteena" cried his wares. One red-coated Negro danced on the medicine wagon to the jig that another one played on a banjo.[37]

An attorney from Asheville left us glimpses of earlier court-day festivities in the mountain counties. In 1853, when he attended the fall term of court in Madison County, there was "a goodeal of noise kept up round a liquor wagon," and the "Crowd in attendance were 'getting in a weaving way' about night." Scores of women attended the court "for the sole purpose of drinking and pandering to the lustful passions of dirty men." In Yancey County the next year, he reported, there was "quite a crowd in attendance," and they "tried to see how badly they could behave themselves." Groups in the yard of the courthouse gathered about "a large gauky looking fellow with a fiddle" who would "saw off some silly ditty," while "two or three drunken fools would dance to the same."[38]

Court week in Morganton during Frankie Silver's lifetime would have drawn just such a crowd—but the people would have encountered solemn reminders of forms of public punishment that had vanished by Mrs. Sutton's day. One resident described the town square as he saw it when he first entered Morganton in 1816. The public buildings were a shabby, unpainted courthouse and a jail that was "a mere weatherboarded pen built of hewed logs with a door and two windows like portholes, and secured with iron bars." But "hard by" stood "a splended two story whipping post and pillory."[39] Many persons in Burke County must have been exhilarated by the spectacle of punishment—like one woman who heard a rumor that the governor had pardoned Frankie and, in disappointment, "went home crying, a pardon had been granted to a poor culprit & she had missed seeing a great sight."[40]

But the purpose of pillory, whipping post, and gallows was not spectacle for spectacle's sake. Public punishment, a legacy of British justice and the colonial era, was social drama: "Whipping, branding, and pillory were public displays of the fruits of crime designed to warn the immoral. In a face-to-face society, public rituals of this nature" were felt to strengthen "the legitimacy of criminal proceedings."[41] As one New England minister declared in his sermon to a criminal, "In about three hours you must die—must be hanged as a spectacle to the world, a warning to the vicious."[42]

North Carolina justice, until ratification of the constitution of 1868, perpetuated many varieties of public punishment as example.[43] For a number of crimes, the punishment was thirty-nine lashes on the bare back, "well laid on." At the beginning of the nineteenth century, a person convicted of perjury was to "stand in the pillory for one hour" and, at the end of that time, was to have both ears cut off and "nailed to the pillory by the officer, and there remain until the setting of the sun."[44] In 1837 this punishment was mitigated so that only the right ear was cut off. But even these milder statutes still decreed that for counterfeiting the malefactor should receive, in addition to a fine, thirty-nine lashes, imprisonment, and a branding "in the right cheek with the letter C." Many other felonies were punished with a brand "upon the brawn of the left thumb," with "these marks to be made by the sheriff openly in the court."[45] And they were carried out with an insistence on proper form. According to a tradition in Burke County, Samuel McDowell Tate, sheriff from 1824 to 1829, had the duty of branding one man convicted of a clergyable felony. Tate was to apply a red-hot iron to the felon's thumb while he said "God save the State" three times. The man "cried 'God save the State' twice and then added 'God damn Sam Tate.' Being a stickler for decorum, Sheriff Tate reapplied the branding iron until the felon repeated the proper phrase thrice."[46]

Executions remained, of course, the most dramatic of the public punishments. They had customary settings, actors, costumes, plots, speeches, and audiences.[47] An editorial account of an execution in Raleigh in 1830 exclaims, "Such a multitude never before assembled in this City. . . . During the morning, every avenue leading to town, was literally blocked up with human beings of both sexes and of all colors, and ages." Authorities heightened the drama of the event by the way they clothed the criminals. One of the condemned men, Elijah W. Kimbrough, "was habited in a long white shroud which entirely concealed his person"; the other, "negro Carey," wore "a similar garment, except that it was black."[48] Five years earlier in Warrenton, Oliver Lewis, a man hanged for murder, was first taken "under a strong guard" to the Episcopal Church, where, like the New England minister quoted above, the Rev. Mr. Brainerd delivered "a most eloquent and touching discourse on the occasion."[49] A similar instructive purpose was recognized by those obliged to make decisions in Frankie Silver's case. An acquaintance writing to Governor Montfort Stokes recalled a conversation in which he advised the governor that he thought her a "fit subject for Example"— that is, that she should be executed as an example to the public.[50]

The early nineteenth century, however, was an era of transition in criminal punishment. As late as 1827, a crowd of between thirty and forty thousand had attended the hanging of one Jesse Strang in Albany, New York, but by 1835, two years after Frankie Silver's death, a New York law would order that executions be "inflicted within the walls of the prison . . . or within a yard or enclosure adjoining."[51] New Jersey and Massachusetts passed similar acts in 1835. Pennsylvania had already held its first private execution the year before, and by 1845 all the other states in New England and the Middle Atlantic region had abandoned public hangings.[52]

We find evidence of a similar transition even in Morganton. At Frankie's execution, according to local report, authorities erected a wooden wall to shield her from public view. But tradition says that large crowds flocked to Morganton to see the hanging on Damons Hill and that the screen was not entirely successful. At least one person reportedly used a knife to dig a peephole in the cracks between the boards.[53] The Erwin family has an oral tradition of sights seen at the hanging by an ancestor who was then a boy of fourteen.[54]

So, in Frankie's time, an execution still generated behavior that had been commonplace in the British Isles and in colonial America, when "Theatrical elements came out with special force at hangings. The condemned were expected to play the role of the penitent sinner; it was best of all if they offered a final confession, a prayer, and affirmed their faith, in the very shadow of the gallows."[55]

In some recorded cases prisoners fulfilled the expectations of penitence. When the Rev. Mr. Brainerd delivered his sermon to Oliver Lewis in Warrenton, the prisoner did not speak but did exhibit "apparent piety." The condemned, however, was not always so compliant. Joseph Sollis, at his execution in Duplin County in 1827 for the murder of Abraham Kornegay, refused to play his part:

> After the clerical gentlemen had done what they conceived to be their duty, the Sheriff told the criminal that he had but a few moments to live, and that if he had any thing to say to his friends or the public, now was the time. He observed, in a strong tone of voice, that "he had nothing to say more, than he would not be in this fix but for Kornegay." He was admonished by a humane gentleman present, not to die with malice in his breast; to which he replied, "Kornegay was in fault, he began the affray, he was to blame for all." He then with a firm step mounted the scaffold; the sheriff tied the rope, pulled the cap over his eyes, and cut away the scaffold.[56]

On occasions when the criminal did not confess or act remorseful, the "criminal's farewell" song may have served the community as surrogate confession to round out the ritual. The hanging of Levi Ames for the crime of burglary in Boston in 1773 actually called forth at least four broadsides—three in verse and one in prose—all purporting to present his dying words. They offer four differing confessional texts on the same conventional theme.[57]

The "Frankie Silver" ballad fits squarely within this tradition. We should not be surprised, then, when legends tell us that Frankie Silver wrote the confession ballad herself and sang it beneath the gallows.[58] Nor should we wonder that the song offers a conventional and over-simple motive for the crime — jealousy — or be surprised that the song, awkward as it is, still gives satisfaction. We, too, long for justice and order. Celebrated trials of our own day have left the public exasperated with defendants who "deny all."

But we also sense in these criminals' confession songs an undercurrent of ambivalence. Early justice was harsh, and in the British Isles, from which many new Americans emigrated, crimes carrying the death penalty leapt from about fifty in 1688 to more than two hundred by 1820.[59] Property rights were ascendant, and the propertied protected their privileges with sanctions of utmost severity. The Irishman or Scot, the farm laborer or street vendor or London poor, too often felt the weight of the law. They resented its abuse by the wealthy and powerful. They might attend the spectacle of a punishment at the pillory, whipping post, or gallows, but often they sympathized with the criminals, particularly those who had committed no heinous crime and bore their part with courage. In London in 1717, for example, a mob broke up one procession to the gallows at Tyburn, pounced upon the hangman, beat him unconscious, and then almost killed a bricklayer who had volunteered to take the hangman's place and carry out the execution.[60] A number of old songs about executions show this sympathy for the condemned, especially those ballads that survived long in oral tradition, such as "Geordie," "Mary Hamilton," "The Maid Freed from the Gallows," and "Hughie Graeme."

In North Carolina, as in the British Isles, a public execution might on occasion fail to produce the officially intended effect. The newspaper account of the execution of Oliver Lewis in Warrenton complained that the feelings of the public were not "roused against the enormity of the crime, for which the criminal suffers." Instead, during the discourse of the Rev. Mr. Brainerd, the demeanor of the prisoner "created universal sympathy." And oddly enough, the Frankie Silver ballad also undercut the intention of the Execution for Example.

Admittedly, the song falsely presents itself as Frankie's voice pointing out the official moral of the public drama of her own hanging:

The Dying Groans of
LEVI AMES,

Who was Executed at Boston, the 21ſt of October, 1773,

for BURGLARY.

I.

YE youth! who throng this fatal plain,
   And croud th' accurſed Tree:
O! ſhun the paths that lead to ſhame,
   Nor fall like wretched me.

II.

On the dark confines of the Grave,
   With trembling haſte I tread;
No Eye to chear, no Hand to ſave,
   I'm hurri'd to the dead.

III.

Juſtice forbids a longer Day,
   My dying Hour is come,
When my poor Soul muſt haſte away,
   To her Eternal home.

IV.

Methinks I ſee your pitying Tears,
   You mourn my wretched State;
To ſhun my Crimes, avoid the Snares,
   If you would ſhun my Fate.

V.

Tho' young in Years, I'm old in Crimes,
   To lawleſs Rapine bred;
The Scourge and Scandal of theſe Crimes,
   When living and when dead.

VI.

Is there a Man thro'out this Throng,
   To ſinful Robbery prone?
Forbear to do thy Neighbour wrong,
   And mourn the Crimes You've done.

VII.

See angry Juſtice ſhakes her rod,
   And points to Guilt's black ſcroll;
The terrors of a frowning God,
   Diſtract my ſinking Soul.

VIII.

Unleſs kind Mercy interpoſe,
   And deepRepentance rain,
To change theſe momentary Throws,
   For Hell's Eternal pain.

IX.

O! for a beam of Love divine,
   To chear this gloomy Day;
To make me chearfully reſign,
   To give my Life away.

X.

Thou who did'ſt ſuffer Death and Shame,
   Such Rebels to reſtore:
O! for thy great and glorious Name,
   Accept one Rebel more.

XI.

Inſpir'd by thee, I fix my Truſt,
   On thine atoning Blood,
To join th'Aſſembly of the Juſt,
   And praiſe my Saviour GOD.

XII.

Farewell to Earth, farewell to Sin,
   One Pang will ſet me free;
Support me, O! thou Rock divine,
   And ſnatch my Soul to Thee.

A "criminal's farewell" broadside printed for the execution of Levi Ames in Boston in 1773. (Courtesy of The Historical Society of Pennsylvania)

You all see me and on me gaze,
Be careful how you spend your days.
And ne'er commit this awful crime,
But try to serve your God in time.

Great God, how shall I be forgiven—
Not fit for earth, not fit for heaven.
But little time to pray to God,
For now I try that awful road.

These lines would seem to corroborate Stuart A. Kane's theoretical, political interpretation of the function of ballads and chapbooks about "wives with knives": that authorities allowed their printing and circulation because they had "an instructional effect," stimulating "a consensual self-regulation by the lower classes, men and women alike."[61] In this reading, "The Ballad of Frankie Silver" would be simply a ventriloquist's performance, with Frankie speaking words plagiarized from the ballad confession of Jereboam Beauchamp, who is himself only a puppet mouthing the conventional "criminal's goodnight."[62]

The song seems one last outrageous indignity inflicted upon Frankie Silver. Her real voice had been silenced by circumstances: her illiteracy, rules of evidence that stopped the mouth of a defendant, laws that discounted a woman's claim to have acted in self-defense. She was silenced, too, by her backcountry, subsistence-farming family's lack of political leverage; a lady of the polite class would have had at least her family's position to speak for her. Time itself stole the confession Frankie dictated to friends in her final weeks of life; we cannot find either the manuscript or the printed form of the document.

Nevertheless, we must be cautious about this reading of the ballad. Community responses to other ballads about local crimes should serve as a warning. It has been reported, for example, that when Edmund Miller wrote his ballad "The Triplett Tragedy," about murders in Watauga County in 1909, the song had local repercussions. Columbus ("Lum") Triplett had killed his brother Marshall in a fracas and then confessed his crime to Marshall's son Granville. Although he was a deputy sheriff, Granville flew into a rage and beat his uncle to death. Edmund Miller's song outraged him, and he threatened to kill anyone who sang it. The only person in the community who dared to defy him was Lum's widow, Sophronie Miller Greer. She took her revenge upon Granville by standing on her porch and singing the ballad as he stalked past her house, with his face stony and his fists clinched. She was able to make her protest a permanent one by recording the song for inclusion on the *The Doc Watson Family Album*.[63] Further evidence of local sensitivity to murder ballads is found in accounts of a song about the murder of Birchie Potter by his cousin Glenn Brown in Watauga County in 1937. Uncle Bill Ellison told Bobby McMillon that he himself wrote the ballad about the murder and first sang it for some of the Potters. As Ellison told Bobby, he

> asked if they minded that—'cause he didn't want to get no trouble started. They said, "No, they didn't." So he give it to Jim Brown, who was a brother or cousin to Glenn Brown, the murderer of Birchie Potter. He was sort of a—preached a little, timbered a little—a jack of all trades. And he doctored it up. He added a verse or two of it, and he turned it over to a man named Presnell, who left it in the office of the Watauga Democrat in Boone [to be printed].[64]

According to information printed with the song in *The Frank C. Brown Collection of North Carolina Folklore*, Jim Brown wanted the song circulating in public but asked Presnell to deliver it to the paper without mentioning his name, to avoid personal repercussions.[65] Topical ballads, then, were not just songs. Within a community, they took on significant and sometimes differing roles in people's lives.

What evidence is there of how people in the region responded to the ballad about Frankie Silver? No early record preserves information about the community's reaction to the song, but—although both Alfred Silver and Lucinda Silver Norman appear to have known and shared the ballad—Muriel Sheppard's account says that decorum required that it "be sung only when no members of either family were present, lest they be reminded of the tragedy." The widespread tradition that Frankie herself wrote the piece and sang it at the scaffold implies that people felt its sentiments of fear and remorse were appropriate for Frankie. But one piece of specific evidence suggests an additional response to the song. The earliest known text is a manuscript found by the late Lawrence Wood in Macon County. It is inscribed "Written Feb. 15th, 1865 Song Ballad for Margaret A. Henry copied by James T. Henry." James would not have copied it for her if he thought it would merely horrify her. Margaret may even have asked for a copy. Why would she have wanted it?

The comments of Bobby McMillon and Marina Trivette give us an answer. The apparent moral of the ballad does not, for them, hold the song's entire meaning. It is certainly not the reason why they and others

Bobby McMillon and Marina Trivette, his sister-in-law and singing partner, in 1992. (Courtesy of Bobby McMillon)

still sing it. The first-person stance of "Frankie Silver's Confession" in fact compels identification with Frankie:

This dreadful dark and dismal day
Has swept my glories all away.
My sun goes down, my days are passed,
And I must leave this world at last.

Oh Lord! what will become of me?
I am condemned, you all now see
To Heaven or hell my soul must fly
All in a moment when I die.

My mind on solemn subjects roll,
My little child, God bless its soul.
All ye that are of Adams race
Let not my faults this child disgrace.

Singers and listeners alike must in some degree take these words as their own and genuinely share Frankie's feelings of remorse, fear, and despair. Bobby McMillon says this is the reason why he himself sings the two stanzas not found in most printed versions:

In that last calm sleep I see him now,
The beautiful peace on his handsome brow.
Our winsome babe on his heaving chest.
The crimson blade, and the dreamless rest.

Now that I may no longer live,
Oh pitying Lord, my crime forgive.
When I hear the call of Judgement roll,
May I appear with a blood-washed soul.

"In singing that song," he says, "that makes all the difference in the world to me personally, as far as identifying with a repentant sinner, facing eternity. I thought about that more than anything else I've ever thought about in that song."[66] The human suffering that the song presents—its poignancy heightened by a moving old melody—transfigures the awkward verse, then, and undercuts the intended moral. Marina Trivette says as much. The history of the "criminal's farewell" genre may explain why the song "Frankie Silver" came to be written, but Marina's comments show the literary theorist why people cared to keep it alive in memory: "I sort of put myself in her place and imagine how I'd feel, knowing that I was facing death and was going to be hanged. I mean, that would be a scary thought for anybody." And she added, as her own child clambered into her lap, "To know you're going to leave your child for other people to raise would be scary. It gets to me sometimes. We've got some ballads we can't sing, because we can't get to the end of them for crying!"

6

Tell her to prize above all things, "the
adornment of a meek and quiet spirit."
— Governor David Lowry Swain

A TALE OF A GOVERNOR

Court records concerning Frankie Silver compose only half of the official documents relating to her case. Six petitions sent from Burke County to Raleigh in the fall of 1832 and in June 1833 entered the records of the executive branch. These all requested a pardon for Frankie Silver and required decisions by two governors. The people who petitioned Governor Montfort Stokes in the fall did not think the case against Frankie had been proved. Those who drafted petitions to Governor David L. Swain half a year later knew from her confession that she was guilty of the murder but believed there were mitigating circumstances. The communications carried weight with neither official. Since these two men had the power to decide Frankie's fate, her case becomes a test of their judgment and character and her story, in effect, the story of what shaped each man. The documentary evidence is rather thin for Governor Stokes, but it is full and highly complex for Governor Swain.

A short account of Stokes will provide at least a background for the portrait of his successor, Swain. Stokes was in his second one-year term as governor of North Carolina at the time of the murder and the trial.

David Lowry Swain (1801–1868), the governor who failed to grant a proclamation
of pardon to Frankie Silver. (Courtesy of the North Carolina Collection,
University of North Carolina Library at Chapel Hill)

The legislature would probably have elected him for a customary third term had not a friend of his youth, President Andrew Jackson, asked him to serve as Commissioner of Indian Affairs in Oklahoma. Stokes accepted. He vacated the governor's office in December 1832, leaving his successor to act upon the petitions he had received on behalf of Frankie Silver. These bore the signatures of 152 persons, including four members of the jury that convicted her and two people from the grand jury that returned a true bill.[1]

Stokes's failure to respond seems, on the surface, out of character. In his two years as governor, he pardoned fifty-four criminals and gave a period of respite to two others. Most of the crimes were minor offenses such as trespass, affray, or assault and battery, but some were the capital offenses of murder, rape, burglary, and barn burning. He pardoned one woman—Sally Barnicastle—convicted and condemned to be hanged for infanticide.[2] Only in the case of Frankie Silver did he fail to act favorably on a petition.

Governor Stokes clearly felt greater uneasiness about this case than about the others for which he received petitions, but perhaps he was in the end guided less by his scruples than by his temperament. Stokes's letterbooks, which consist almost exclusively of pardons and other perfunctory documents, suggest that he acquiesced in the limitations of his office, sardonically characterized by Judge William Gaston in the comment that a North Carolina governor "has no share in the making of laws, he has no share in the appointment of officers. Except the right of granting reprieves and pardons, all that is required of him is, that he should be a gentleman in character and manners, and exercise a liberal hospitality."[3]

The governorship may have been the post most suited to Stokes in his long career of public service. He had been a United States Senator, and within the state he had served in the legislature both in the senate and the commons. But one observer—Professor Elisha Mitchell—wondered "why he was so often put forward." Mitchell thought Stokes's main qualification for office was his being "a very pleasant man of good sense."[4] Chief Justice Thomas Ruffin, a longtime acquaintance, in a private letter to his daughter described Stokes less charitably as "an *Old Politician*." That character, Ruffin explained, seldom "exhibits any anxiety but for popular favor."[5] William O. Foster, a student of Stokes's career in North Carolina politics, assessed him as dutiful and well meaning but undistinguished. "Like most of our governors," Foster wrote, "Stokes made nice speeches, kept his ear to the ground, and played safe. He gave most of his attention to routine matters." Governor Stokes, he concluded, "is conspicuous chiefly for what he failed to do."[6] In leaving office, Stokes presumably could have acted on Frankie Silver's behalf without fear of political consequences; but since the case troubled him, he seems simply to have acted in character. He left the hard decision to the man who followed him.

David Lowry Swain, who succeeded Stokes in December 1832 and was governor at the time of Frankie's execution, had a very different personality. He had worked hard to amass factual knowledge of the state, had a serious interest in "internal improvements," and tried to serve his native region, the North Carolina mountains. As governor, he did not let lack of real power prevent him from showing leadership. He worked to mobilize public opinion in order to accomplish several aims, particularly building railroads and revising the legal code. A number of his efforts failed, but through no fault of his own; they foundered on competing sectional interests within the state. Swain, too, received letters and petitions about Frankie Silver. He was in possession of greater knowledge of the case—the report of her confession—than was available to Stokes, but he granted her only a two-week respite to prepare for death. He refused to issue a pardon.

Swain's motivation is considerably more opaque than that of Stokes. On May 3, 1833, he wrote Thomas W. Wilson a discouraging letter. No copy is known to survive—an unusual fact. Swain's surviving correspondence is copious, and this was a letter about an official matter and should normally have been copied into the governor's letterbook, as his secretary did the lengthy and emphatic letters in which Swain denied executive clemency in three other cases. Thomas Wilson had the impression that Swain intended the letter to be "confidential & private," so Swain may deliberately have kept it out of the record.[7] But for what reason? Whatever his motive, the letter probably conveyed what W. C. Bevens later described as the governor's "peremptory refusal to pardon without a different character on the nature of the affair could be produced."[8]

Many people felt that Frankie Silver's confession actually *had* given a different character to the affair. Certainly the confession produced a considerable change of views in Burke County—shown both by statements made in letters to Governor Swain and by the number and weight of the eighty-three signatures on the four petitions that came to him.

The petition that perhaps would have had the best chance of swaying Governor Swain was sent by ladies of Burke County, who raised the issue of wife abuse. Thirty-five women signed the document, and collectively their names are more socially impressive than those of men who signed the petitions.[9] Those names would have recommended the petitioners to Swain as gentlewomen of the highest respectability in Morganton and Burke County. They included Goodwin and Elinor M. Bouchelle from the family of a prominent local physician; Catherine Wilson Carson, wife of congressman Samuel Price Carson and daughter-in-law of Col. John Carson, a major landowner and horse and cattle producer; Matilda Sharpe Erwin, whose husband, William Willoughby Erwin, was one of the county's wealthiest citizens, owner of Belvidere Plantation and a bank in Morganton; Matilda's daughters Elizabeth Sharpe Gaither and Catherine Reese Gaither, wife and sister-in-law of clerk of the court Burgess S. Gaither; Eliza Grace McDowell, daughter of Col. Charles McDowell of Quaker Meadows and granddaughter of Revolutionary War general Charles McDowell, soon to marry attorney Nicholas W. Woodfin; Jane S. Tate, daughter of Maj. David Tate, who had represented Burke County in the state House of Commons and senate; Martha Matilda Walton, daughter of a local merchant and political leader; and Catherine Caldwell Wilson, who was a daughter of Col. Andrew Caldwell (a political leader in Iredell County), granddaughter of William Sharpe (a delegate to the Continental Congress), and wife of Frankie's attorney, Thomas W. Wilson.[10] We know that Swain had high personal regard for the leading figure in this list, Matilda Sharpe Erwin. In a letter to his father in 1822, Swain spoke of her as a "lady I conjecture, to be one of the most interesting with whom I have had the good fortune to meet in the course of my acquaintance."[11]

But it is unclear what weight even this petition carried with the governor. The document is dated Saturday, June 29, 1833, and bears a postmark of Wednesday, July 3. In his answer dated Tuesday, July 9, Swain sent his appreciation to "the fair Petitioners, with the most of whom, I have the pleasure of an acquaintance." But in regard to Mrs. Silver, he said, "All that it is now in my power to do is to unite in the anxious wish, which doubtless pervades the whole community to which she belongs, that she may find that mercy in Heaven, which seemed to be necessarily denied upon earth, a free pardon for all the offences of her life."[12]

With the words *now in my power to do* and *mercy necessarily denied upon earth*, Swain equivocates. He may mean that he believes it physi-

Matilda Sharpe Erwin (1769–1843), the leading matron of Burke County to sign the ladies' petition to Governor Swain on behalf of Frankie Silver. (Courtesy of Anne A. Connelly and The Burke County Historical Society)

cally impossible to send a pardon from Raleigh on Tuesday and have it travel the 199 miles to Morganton in time to halt an execution scheduled for early afternoon on the following Friday, July 12.[13] Traveling the same road in the 1820s, Swain recorded a day's journey of 58 miles. A letter written in 1833 says that a traveler going by stagecoach could leave Morganton on Thursday, arrive in Salem on Friday night, leave there the next morning, and reach Raleigh on Sunday night or Monday morning. A rider on horseback might not have made the trip much faster, since the stage, with, presumably, one or more changes of horses and driver, covered portions of the trip without overnight rest stops.[14] The return trip presumably took the same length of time. By stage or by horse, every element of scheduling and weather would have had to be favorable to enable an emissary of the governor to reach Morganton in time to halt the execution.

On the other hand, Swain's wording may mean that Frankie's abhorrent crime and character ("all the offences of her life") necessitate her execution. But there is a third possible implication in his words. Could Swain have received the petition on Monday, July 8—in time, perhaps, to send a proclamation of executive clemency to Morganton before the

Eliza Grace McDowell Woodfin (1816–1876), who was seventeen when she signed the ladies' petition on behalf of Frankie Silver and who later married Nicholas W. Woodfin. (Courtesy of the North Carolina Collection, Pack Memorial Public Library, Asheville, North Carolina)

execution—and chosen to delay his response to the petition for a day, clothing his executive decision in the robes of necessity? We do not know the answer to these questions. We have only, from oral tradition, two reports of criticism of Swain's decision by responsible contemporaries— views attributed to Burgess S. Gaither and to Swain's student, business associate, and friend Nicholas Woodfin. I have not found any record of a contemporary attempt to explain Swain's action.

Some persons have suggested that political considerations may have influenced Swain's stand. If so, it was not elective politics that affected his decision, but what one might call more broadly the state's political culture. Neither Swain nor Stokes ran for any elective office after holding the post of governor, to which they had been elected by a vote in the legislature. And the two came from opposing ends of the political spectrum in the state—Stokes being a Democratic supporter of Jackson and Swain one of the nominal Democrats who turned Whig. At most, conflicting political allegiances could have discouraged some who had signed petitions to Stokes from making an effort to contact the new governor—for example, two former legislators from Burke County, Col. John Carson and his son Joseph McDowell Carson.[15]

In the 1820s Swain and Samuel Price Carson, son of Col. John and brother to Joseph, were in opposing political camps. Swain implies dislike for Samuel in an 1822 letter, noting wryly that Carson has arrived in Raleigh "'to thunder thrice in the capitol' & is not without his admirers."[16] Carson was shortly to wage a successful congressional campaign against Swain's close friend Robert B. Vance. Subsequently, in 1827, Congressman Carson killed Vance in a duel. Swain, in Raleigh at the time, received speedy notification from a friend who was present with Vance at the scene.[17] "The poor fellow," Swain later learned, "at the moment he had finished undressing in order to take his position pulled out his watch and requested young Patton to take care of it for me." When he next went to Asheville, Swain was overwhelmed by memories of the last time Vance had visited in his home; he wrote his wife that his grief over Vance's death kept him sleepless till daylight.[18] The Carsons, at any rate, made no attempt to intervene on Frankie Silver's behalf with this new governor.

Fran Farlow, a novelist and researcher from Gastonia, has suggested a more personal tie that may have colored Governor Swain's attitude toward Frankie: Jacob Silver, Charlie's father, served in the War of 1812 in a company commanded by Swain's older half-brother, Capt. James

Lowry.[19] Although James was a married man heading his own household by the time David was three years old, the two took a trip to Georgia together in the early 1820s, and when James ran for the state legislature in 1823 David helped in the campaign. But we have no documentary evidence that James Lowry communicated with his half-brother in the interest of the Silver family, although Swain preserved a number of letters from Lowry.[20]

Moreover, it seems unlikely that Jacob Silver could have made use of his personal connection to the Swain family. His house in Kona was some seventy miles from Lowry's home in the Sandy Mush Valley of present-day Macon County, and both Jacob and his wife apparently were illiterate. Both used their marks to sign applications for a pension for his service in the War of 1812.[21] Furthermore, even assuming that Jacob wished to see Frankie hanged, he may have felt no need to take personal action. He could not have had full knowledge of the various petitions gotten up on her behalf. Nevertheless, when Swain went west to Morganton and on to Asheville in the fall of 1832 after missing the court appointment at which he would have sentenced Frankie, he may have heard in family circles that James was acquainted with Charlie's father.

A tight network of personal relations characterized North Carolina political life in the era. James Lowry, despite describing himself as a farmer with an inadequate education, served in the House of Commons in 1815, 1816, and 1823, in the state senate in 1834, and in the Governor's Council of State for two terms in the mid-1840s. He knew both Judge Donnell, who presided at the trial, and Judge Ruffin, who rejected Frankie's appeal to the state supreme court; Lowry introduced a stranger to the two of them in a hotel lobby in 1846.[22] Governor Swain was also well acquainted with both Judge Ruffin and Judge Donnell. In March 1827, Swain and Donnell had boarded together in Winton during court week, and Swain wrote his wife that he spent most of his leisure hours with Donnell and found him "a very sociable and agreeable man," wanting nothing "but the familiar and intimate." Swain had "seldom met with company so entirely agreeable" as Judge Donnell and two other companions on this trip.[23]

Upon his election as governor in December 1832, Swain also received a letter of congratulations from William Julius Alexander, who had prosecuted Frankie earlier in the year.[24] The two men had served together in the House of Commons in 1829, and Alexander was speaker of the house in 1833, the year when Swain was receiving petitions on Frankie's behalf.

Swain is quite likely to have had undocumented conversations about the case with some of these people.

Impressions formed in personal contacts with such key players in the case may have darkened Swain's view of Frankie Silver. But one contact might as easily have worked to Frankie's advantage, for Thomas W. Wilson, Frankie's defense attorney, was not only the uncle of William Julius Alexander's wife, but he was also personally acquainted with Governor Swain. The two had known each other in Raleigh while representing their counties—Wilkes and Buncombe—in the legislature in 1824, 1825, and 1826. They were more than nodding acquaintances. Thomas W. Wilson, by Governor Swain's own account, was the "only groomsman" at Swain's wedding with Eleanor White in 1826. Their intimacy must have continued, for Swain clearly followed Wilson's subsequent career and knew of his death in Texas in 1863.[25] One could well ask why the June 3, 1833, petition from the hand of his groomsman Wilson carried so little weight with Swain.

The answer, I suspect, is that Swain and Wilson met and discussed this recent lurid case when Swain passed through Morganton in the fall of 1832. Swain would have wanted to tell officers of the court that a carriage accident was to blame for his failure to reach Morganton in time to preside at the September session, at which he was to have set the date for Frankie's execution. The two friends could have spoken freely about the matter because neither had any reason to anticipate that Swain would soon become governor or have further involvement with the case. At this point Wilson, as we have seen, had not heard Frankie's confession or conceived that she might have acted in self-defense, and he probably shared the common view that her crime was infamous. Wilson's greatest disservice to his client Frankie Silver, then, may have been to unintentionally plant in Swain's mind a view of her that no later circumstances could dislodge.

Such personal ties, however, were not the only things that may have affected Swain's decision about Frankie's petition for clemency. The governor was struggling with what he must have regarded as larger issues. At the time when citizens of Burke County were sending petitions on Frankie's behalf, Swain was deeply engaged in building public support for internal improvements in the state. In June, the month before Frankie's execution, he was writing individuals and newspapers, trying to attract attention to a conference scheduled for July 4–6 in Hillsborough, which he hoped would develop plans for establishing state-wide railroads. It was such pragmatic activities that chiefly engaged Swain's mind. Other persons in the state—such as his friends Joseph and Weston Gales, editors of the *Raleigh Register*—might urge changes in the legal code to end slavery, to abolish the death penalty for burglary, or to end public executions and corporal punishments like flogging and branding.[26] But when Swain pushed for a revision of the state constitution in 1835, the two issues that most concerned him were to secure equal representation for the people of the western part of the state and to remove orthodox Protestantism as a qualification for holding public office. His motivation for pushing the former was the hope of increasing votes for the internal improvements he sought for the state, particularly those benefiting the west. His support for religious toleration was probably motivated at least in part by his debt to his old mentor, former chief justice John L. Taylor, whose distinguished brother-in-law Judge William Gaston was a Roman Catholic. Swain also felt a personal debt to Gaston, who from their earliest acquaintance in the 1820s had treated him, he said, "with the kindness of a father."[27]

Swain was intelligent and public-spirited, but his was a practical and political rather than a probing, humanistic bent of mind. He exhibited these qualities both as governor and later in his life as president of the university, where his leadership was more evident in his efforts to build enrollment and facilities than in his encouragement of intellectual interests. Cornelia Phillips Spencer wrote revealingly that Swain "set very little value on accumulations of books. He called them 'dead capital,' and would neither amass them himself, nor encourage the University to do so."[28]

The record of Governor Swain's action upon other petitions for pardon gives further insight into the outlook he would have brought to a consideration of Frankie Silver's case. In his first two years in office, he issued seven fewer pardons than Stokes had in the same period of time, and unlike Stokes, he rejected four petitions outright. Stokes occasionally waxed philosophical. In releasing one prisoner, he declared himself "fixed upon the principle, that to a mind of sensibility & honorable feeling the degradation of one days imprisonment has the same effect as that of one or more years." He believed that "no possible good can arise from a protracted confinement in Jail."[29] Swain, by contrast, seems to have been a by-the-book administrator. He pardoned Catherine Bostian, whom he himself had sentenced to be hanged for the crime of infanticide, but his reason for the pardon was technical: he had doubts as to "whether she was convicted upon competent testimony."[30] And he could show severity. Of one man sentenced to death for burglary he wrote, "The law under which he is to suffer, is in my opinion a severe one, but this consideration is proper for the Legislature only."[31] He dealt harshly with Benjamin F. Seaborn, a white man convicted of concealing evidence that a slave had committed arson. "No case has in my opinion occurred for years," Swain wrote, in "which a pardon would so clearly prove the truth of the maxim that mercy to the guilty is cruelty to the commonwealth."[32] Swain let stand the sentence of execution.

In all these cases what seems most to have provoked his severity is any suggestion of defiance of law and authority. One example of this may throw direct light on his view of Frankie Silver. Swain had inherited from Governor Stokes the case of Washington Taburn, "a free man of colour," condemned to death for the crime of burglary. Petitioners argued that Taburn was feeble-minded and deserved to be spared. Swain was on the point of granting a pardon, reluctantly (and solely to honor Governor Stokes's promise to pardon the convict on condition that he be transported to Haiti), when Taburn escaped, causing considerable outcry. After the felon's recapture, Swain rejected any further consideration of mercy, since Taburn had "persevered in the commission of crimes."[33] Frankie Silver's escape from jail, despite the apparent absence of public protest, may well have provoked a similar reaction in Swain.

This reading of Swain's character is made problematic, however, by the fact that his contemporaries during his later presidency of the university regarded his dealings with the "wild boys" at Chapel Hill as charitable to a fault. A trustee of the university once publicly chastised him for his leniency. A streak of the authoritarian in Swain does not seem to provide a completely convincing explanation of why he did not respond favorably to appeals based on Frankie's confession.

The intellectual ambiance of the late twentieth century makes us immediately assume that the gender biases of Frankie Silver's era determined her fate, shaping her husband's behavior, the verdict of the jurors, and especially the governors' perception of her case. This view holds some truth, but we need to explore the circumstances with care. Bias can operate with insidious indirection.

In some ways, the gender assumptions of the era actually worked *for* Frankie. When she was indicted for murdering Charles and destroying his body, some people in the community refused to believe she could be guilty. To them it seemed "that the greatest exertion of female fortitude could not possibly have accomplished the horrid deed."[34] One petition begged clemency from Governor Montfort Stokes for "a poor woman whose very name tis frailty."[35] Stokes himself reportedly said that he did not know "of there ever haveing been a Female Executed in N. Carolina" and that he felt himself "delicately situated."[36] The ladies of Burke County who sent Governor Swain a petition on Frankie's behalf justified their act "by claiming as a duty peculiar to the Sex to be allways on the side of mercy towards their fellow beings and to the female more particularly." They hoped the governor would "wipe from the character of the female in this community the Stigma of a womans being hung under the Gallows."[37] Frankie's own attorney, Thomas Wilson, grandly urged the governor to "save to North Carolina the disgrace of seeing a woman under the gallows."[38] These efforts were premised on the assumed delicacy of woman, an article of faith among the gentry—and it failed to bring any benefit whatever to Frankie Silver.

In other ways, the gender patterns of the era did work to Frankie's disadvantage. From early in the case there had been suggestions that Frankie had much to bear in the marriage. The initial news account reported simply that the "deceased is represented to have been a man of rather vagrant and intemperate habits."[39] Ladies of the county later mounted a defense of Frankie by declaring that Charles had a reputation for failing to fulfill his own expected role of protector and provider. They portrayed Charles as

> one of that cast of mankind who are wholly destitute of any of the feeling that is necesary to make a good Husband or parent—the neighbourhood people are concured that his treatment to her was both unbecoming and cruell verry often and at the time too when female Delicacy would most forbid it. he treated her with personal violence he was said by all the Neighbourhood to have been a man who never made use of any exertions to support Either his wife or child which terminated as is frequently the case that those Dutys nature ordered and intended the husband to perform were thrown on her—his own relations admit of his haveing been a lasy trifling man it is also admitted by them also that she was an industrious woman.

The women may even have injured Frankie's case with Governor Swain by declaring her to have "contrary to the Law of God & the country but so consistant with our nature been her own avenger."[40] These are powerful words. One assumes that, for some among the women, the words were charged with a sense of private grievance. Perry D. Young, however, discovered another circumstance that may explain the intensity of their indignation. Just two months before Frankie's murder of her husband, he found, a Matilda Southard (or Sudderth) died in Morganton. Witnesses testified that they had watched her abusive husband, Reuben, strike her, that they had seen wounds upon her body (including broken ribs), and that they had heard him threaten to beat, shoot, or kill her.[41] Reuben Southard was tried in the same week as Frankie Silver, with two of the same jurors (Robert McElrath and David Beedle). The jury found "the Prisoner Reuben Southards," who in 1831 had been a justice of the court of pleas and quarter sessions, "not guilty of the felony & murder whereof he stands charged in the manner & form as charged."[42] This event was probably rankling in the minds of the women of Morganton when they petitioned Governor Swain in June 1833, as it had been in the minds of persons who petitioned Governor Stokes on Frankie's behalf the year before. One earlier petition directly questioned the fairness of executing a woman for killing her husband, when "it has so frequently happened that husbands have murdered their wives and escaped Punishment."[43]

And Burke County husbands may have continued to escape punishment for murdering their wives. In the fall of 1835 the body of Charity Norwood was found beaten, cut, and burned in the furnace of her husband Aaron's blacksmith shop. Although the grand jury charged the husband with the murder and local opinion was inflamed against him, the jury in this trial also found "the prisoner at the Bar not guilty of the felony & murder in the manner & form as charged."[44]

The assumption that Frankie Silver suffered abuse from her husband and acted as "her own avenger" creates problems even within modern legal constructions. Jeffrey Gray, former North Carolina assistant attorney general, points out that it raises the issue of whether her presumed act of self-defense was "perfect" or "imperfect"—that is, in response to an immediate threat to her life or taken in anticipation of mortal danger.[45] In such a case, the circumstances of the murder become crucial.

Later accounts of the murder by Alfred Silver and his sister Lucinda, and the newspaper stories based on them, have said that Frankie struck Charlie while he was asleep—an imperfect defense, even assuming that Charles had abused and threatened her. If no witness to the murder testified at the trial, though, where did this theory originate? Bobby McMillon assumes that if Frankie's father or other family members witnessed or were implicated in the murder, they may have yielded to the human impulse to "blab." The only early documentary record for the theory, however, is a letter sent to Governor Swain from defense attorney Thomas W. Wilson, who says that, at the trial, the solicitor offered the hypothesis that Frankie must have killed Charlie while he was "lying a sleep by the fire." Wilson presumably disputed this assumption in court, as he did in the letter, arguing that Charlie "went from his fathers near dark perfectly cool & sober in the dead of winter—the house very open—I say it is not probable that he would have lain down to sleep by the fire."[46] The prosecutor's supposition—his narrative reconstruction of the events—may, however, have thrown a lasting shadow over the case. It is the account most often followed in both oral tradition and writings about the case.

In his letter to Swain, Thomas Wilson added that Frankie "must have killed him by some unlikely blow not premeditated." Frankie's missing confession, according to four different accounts of it, did describe the murder of her husband as occurring during an altercation, but just what she said happened is unclear. A newspaper notice written shortly after her execution says her confession stated that "at the time of the murder" Charlie was "loading his gun to shoot" Frankie, "whose life he had threatened."[47] Henry Spainhour's recollection of the confession was that Frankie said "that Silvers was loading his gun to kill her and she took the ax and struck him on the head and knocked him down."[48] Kemp Plummer Battle heard a somewhat different version of the confession from attorney Nicholas Woodfin: "Her husband came home drunk and began to beat her with a stick; she struck back and killed him. She did not intend to kill him, but only to keep him from beating her."[49] William F. Thomas, a local physician, wrote the governor shortly after she confessed that "now the belief is prevalent that she killed him in a fracus, that part of her confession is not doubted."[50]

Those who questioned Frankie about her confession reportedly regarded it "as reasonable and told with every evidence of sincerity."[51] It gains credibility, too, from having apparently been made in ignorance of the legal distinctions between murder and manslaughter or self-defense. The murder, then, may have been an instance of perfect self-defense. Members of the Silver family doubtless would not have accepted this argument. Bobby McMillon still does not. Nevertheless, this was the view held by many prominent local people, including the groomsman from Swain's own wedding. But it is not an interpretation that Governor Swain was willing to accept. One is left wondering if anything else in the general culture of the time or in his individual temperament and experience may have colored his opinion of the case.

The most troubling issue must have been the violence that surrounded the case. Accounts from several different sources give the impression that both Frankie and Charlie were immature, fiery, and quarrelsome. Their stability may have been impaired by individual early wounds: Charlie's loss of his mother in the first year of his life, and the abuse Frankie possibly suffered at the hands of her father. For whatever reason, Frankie appears to have been willing to give as good as she got. Her older brother, Jackson Stewart, "often bragged that he 'would not stand down from nor step aside for any man.'"[52] Standing something over six feet three inches and weighing more than two hundred pounds, Jackson was better equipped than Frankie to assert himself, but his sister may have shared something of his spirit. If the first news report of the murder is accurate, she "had often declared to her husband and others, that she would kill him."[53]

The Stewarts were Ulster Scots, and the question arises whether Swain, who came from English stock out of eastern North Carolina and New England, would have viewed Frankie stereotypically as one of the "most wretchedly ignorant and uncivilized" Scotch-Irish.[54] From commentators both early and late, the Scotch-Irish in the South have had a decidedly mixed review, regarded at best as proud and combative and at worst as violent. The colonial Anglican minister Charles Woodmason called them "Ignorant, mean, worthless, beggarly Irish Presbyterians, the Scum of the Earth, and Refuse of Mankind."[55] David Hackett Fischer, a leading recent historian of the settlement era, wrote that "even in their poverty they carried themselves with a fierce and stubborn pride that warned others to treat them with respect."[56]

Moreover, early accounts by the Scotch-Irish themselves do suggest boldness in their women. Writing in 1854 of the experience of Scotch-Irish Presbyterians in central North Carolina during the American Revolution, the Rev. Eli W. Caruthers presented a catalog of spirited women celebrated in local historical legends, including Elizabeth Wiley Forbis, who wielded her hoe to drive off Tory marauders trying to steal her horse and plow; Margaret Gillespie Caruthers, who beat two Tory thieves with an ax handle as they crawled out of her corn crib; and Martha Bell, who used an ax to drive off a band of Tories threatening to kill her father.[57] These were among the more socially prominent women in the region, but Caruthers gives a glimpse of the working-class Scotch-Irish woman too. Margaret, a servant employed by the Rev. David Caldwell, "exerted herself greatly" to get food for his family from the British troops occupying the house, "passing fearlessly and resolutely among the officers and soldiers, and returning them curse for curse."[58] Similar legends appear in other sources.[59]

But these women lived during wartime and were of the pioneer generation of European settlers in the region. And Swain had close associations with many of the Scotch-Irish who had become political and professional leaders in the state, men such as solicitor William Julius Alexander. Swain even wrote short historical treatises on the Mecklenburg Declaration of Independence and the local resistance to Lord Cornwallis's invasion of the state, events in which the Scotch-Irish settlers played prominent roles. Far from writing about the Scotch-Irish in pejorative terms, he described the participants simply as of "the revolutionary stock" and took no notice whatever of their ethnic background or character.[60]

And if Swain probably would not have looked down upon the Stewarts for being Scotch-Irish, he might well have disliked the Silvers if he knew them to be of German stock. His early letters contain several satirical comments on Germans of the Piedmont. Passing through Salem on his way to Raleigh in 1822, he was given a tour of the village by the Rev. P. M. Sholer and rewarded the kindness by writing his father that Sholer was "one of the ugliest, & bluntest dutchmen, by whom my vision was ever cursed." On the east side of Greensboro, he stopped in the home of a Mr. Albright, "a wealthy dutchman . . . as stupid as a mule." Albright's daughter ("likewise a Dutchman") was "a female, wanting in every thing calculated to excite, esteem & respect, but C-a-s-h."[61]

Another possibility is that Swain would have seen people like the Stewarts as embodiments of a different stereotype: the rough individualists bred by hard-scrabble conditions in the backcountry. One Briton traveling through southern Ohio in 1816 described the backwoodsmen he met there as "coarse, large, and strong, vulgar, sturdy, and impudent." These "vulgar Democrats," he wrote, "are attached to liberty and understand it. they hold in supreme contempt everything like, refinement, or neatness." If they gathered at a tavern, he reported, they spent the day shooting at marks and drinking whiskey. "These meetings are now and then enlivened by a fight in the backwoods fashion. But gouging and biting are now almost at an end, the laws of the state punishing such offenses by ten years imprisonment."[62]

The southern educated class recoiled from such behavior in the backcountry, and the meeting of the two cultures precipitated a whole school of southern comic journalism in the 1830s and 1840s, in which gentlemen described and satirized the fights, talk, chicanery, and ignorance of the backwoodsman. And the tough backwoodswoman also appeared in these comic writings. In his autobiography, the Methodist circuit rider Peter Cartwright, himself both a colorful product of the backwoods and a teller of backwoods tales, gave an account purporting to describe one such woman. She was "high-tempered, overbearing, quarrelsome, and a violent opposer of religion." When her husband "would attempt to pray, she would not conform, but tear around and make all the noise and disturbance in her power. She would turn the chairs over while he was reading, singing, or praying, and if she could not stop him any other way, she would catch a cat and throw it in his face while he was kneeling and trying to pray." In desperation the husband brought home Peter Cartwright to see if he could not "moderate her." When Cartwright tried to offer a prayer, she boiled over, declaring, "I will have none of your praying about me." When he threatened to put her out of doors while they prayed, she "clinched her fist" and launched into a "brag talk" tirade, swearing "she was one half alligator, and the other half snapping-turtle, and that it would take a better man than I was to put her out."[63] Cartwright closed with a triumphant account of how her conversion to Methodism led to wifely submission.

In North Carolina, however, David L. Swain and his circle seem not to have written about such people as representing a regional culture any more than an ethnic one. Swain himself mentions only his own "romantic notions about mountain scenery, and the interesting simplicity of highland life."[64] Rather than holding stereotypes of the mountaineer, he and others seem to see all across the state a white population divided into "the polite class" and "the people." (I draw the terms from the usage of Swain's student, devoted friend, and fellow mountain man Governor Zebulon B. Vance; writing in 1864 about the Civil War, Vance says that "the great popular heart is not now and never has been in this war. It was a revolution of the polite class, not the people.")[65] The polite class is distinguished by some combination of family connections, social and political leadership, wealth, education, and knowledge of appropriate behav-

Quaker Meadows, the seat of the McDowells, one of the leading polite families of Burke County, and childhood home of Eliza Grace McDowell Woodfin. (Photograph by Bayard Wootten, from Old Homes and Gardens of North Carolina [1939]; courtesy of the University of North Carolina Press)

ior. How members of the polite class should behave in marriage appears to have concerned these people greatly.

In the early 1830s newspapers that circulated within their households contained numerous articles on marital roles and relations. The *Greensborough Patriot* alone printed almost a half-dozen pieces on the subject in 1830 and 1832: "Countryman and His Wife," "A Good Wife," "Rules for Ladies," "Husbands and Wives," and "The Female Heart."[66] Most of these newspaper pieces on gender roles are clearly directed toward a genteel reader.[67] They show this in both diction and sentiment. The effusion entitled "The Female Heart," for example, exclaims rapturously, "More priceless than the gems of Galconda is the female heart: more devoted than the idoletry of Mecca, is woman's love. There is no sordid view, or gratifying self-interest in the feeling. It is a principle and a character of her nature, a faculty and infatuation which absorbs and concentrates all the fervor of her soul, and all the depths of her bosom."

Most of the other pieces are more soberly stated, explicitly didactic, and directed toward improving both parties in a marriage. "Husbands and Wives" admonishes the man that "a good husband will always regard his wife as his equal, treat her with kindness, respect, and attention, and never address her with an air of authority, as if she were, as some husbands appear to regard their wives, a mere housekeeper." It continues with advice that he "never interfere with her domestic concerns," cheerfully comply with all her "reasonable requests," never allow himself to lose his temper because of "indifferent cookery" or other "mismanagement of her servants," and consult her on business matters, "if she has prudence and good sense." The same essay tells females that a "good wife will always receive her husband with smiles," try to "discover means to gratify his inclinations, in regard to food and cookery," never "attempt to rule, or appear to rule her husband," avoid "all altercations or arguments leading to ill-humor," and "never attempt to interfere in his business." It recommends that, rather than try to show who can "display the most spirit," the husband should "treat his wife, and the wife treat her husband with as much respect and attention as he would a strange lady, & as she would a strange gentleman."[68]

The references in this piece to "lady," "gentleman," and the "mismanagement of servants" reveal the social standing of the intended readers, or at least their social aspirations, for this was an era of social fluidity. In an unpublished manuscript on his life in Burke County, Silas McDowell (who was married to the daughter of Governor Swain's half-sister) purports to give his recollections of similar instruction that a wise and benevolent elderly lady in Morganton offered when he arrived in 1816.[69] He came as a "mechanic" with the trade of tailoring. The old lady told him his social footing was precarious and warned him that the first families of the county would look askance at him as an unmarried mechanic until he proved his character and sense of propriety.[70]

The articles in the *Greensborough Patriot,* too, were giving instruction on the deportment appropriate to social superiors. The advice to husbands and wives came, in fact, from a Philadelphia newspaper, the *United States Gazette;* the Greensboro editor was trying to educate local readers in national, urban, polite norms for acceptable behavior. In the eyes of such readers, the marital strife of the Silvers could only appear ignorant and abhorrent. The butchery of Charles's body would have seemed to them, even more than to others, a "horrible outrage."

Because of his own origins, Governor Swain may have felt a particular sensitivity to the prevailing social distinctions. One friend wrote that Swain had "arisen to positions of power and usefulness" in the state "without the advantages of high birth or fortune."[71] He was raised near Asheville in, according to a sketch written by Zebulon B. Vance, "an old-fashioned log-house of the kind familiarly known to our mountain people as a 'double-cabin.'" Born in 1801, Swain remembered vividly his childhood experience of seeing what he believed to be the first wagon to cross the Blue Ridge. "There being no road for such vehicles, this wagon had approached the house . . . in the washed-out channel of the creek," and it frightened him so badly that he "incontinently took to his heels, and only rallied when safely entrenched behind his father's house."[72]

To compound Swain's problem, his Massachusetts-born father, George Swain, had lacked social advantages, having been apprenticed at the age of fourteen to learn "the art or mystery" of a hatter. George Swain, however, had some education (mostly self-acquired) and considerable enterprise. In the mid-1780s he undertook a business venture, sailing for Charleston with a shipment of apples, cider, and cheese, but lost his goods in a storm. He nevertheless persisted in seeking his fortune in the South. Moving to the rough Georgia country beyond Augusta, he married a widow with good family connections in North Carolina. George Swain prospered and gained some local prominence in politics, but in 1796, for health reasons, he resettled his family near present-day Asheville.[73] During David's childhood there, his father farmed, made hats, traded in real estate, took a role in civic affairs, and in 1807 secured an appointment as postmaster. George Swain had achieved a competence, but a modest one. His older son, George Jr., later wrote that his father was "a mechanick & he had a large & helpless family . . . & father you know was no farmer"; "myself and one negro woman," he said, "were all the help my father had to tend his plantation."[74]

The elder Swain recognized the gifts of his younger son, David, and managed to send him out into the world with schooling from a Latin academy, the best education available in his section of the state. In 1822 David gained admittance to the university in Chapel Hill, but after a short time there, he moved to Raleigh, where he hoped to advance himself more cheaply and speedily. He shrewdly read law with North Carolina's first chief justice, John L. Taylor, formed a friendship with the family of Joseph Gales, editor of the *Raleigh Register,* and made himself useful to the legislators from his county. Although Swain impressed one traveler as "one of the most ungainly, awkward, homely looking men I ever saw" and "decidedly the awkwardest man I ever saw in any public station," he advanced himself through marriage in 1826 to Eleanor H. White, daughter of former secretary of state William White and grand-daughter of Governor Richard Caswell.[75] By this time Swain had already begun his law practice and become active in politics. Beginning in 1824 he served five years in the General Assembly, which then made him solicitor of the Edenton circuit and later judge of the superior court. In the latter post, he served for two years before the legislature selected him as a compromise candidate for governor in 1832. At the conclusion of his third one-year term as governor, he leveraged his appointment as president of the University of North Carolina, which he headed until after the Civil War. Throughout his adult life Swain was an active and canny businessman and managed at his death in 1868 to leave an estate valued at some $68,000.

David L. Swain's social ascent has implications for his view of Frankie Silver. Swain's father had bought modestly into the slaveholding system, and Swain himself began to acquire slaves in 1826. Identifying with men of property and standing, Swain aligned himself with the Whig Party in the 1830s. Swain, in fact, seems in some ways to have overcompensated for his rather plain beginnings. Genealogy became a passion with him—the genealogy of those with higher social standing. Governor Zebulon B. Vance wrote that at the university during Swain's presidency, "almost the first question he would ask a student on meeting him, if indeed he did not already know, was, 'Who is your father?' On being told, by a few quick questions he would possess himself of the boy's lineage, and would never forget it. . . . It was equally so with all strangers whom he met, and frequently ludicrous scenes resulted from his insatiable desire to trace pedigree."[76]

The obverse of this concern was Swain's adoption of some of the racial and class stances of the slaveholder. Writing his wife from a town in northeastern North Carolina, Swain describes the "morals of the contiguous country" as "depraved, oweing to the great proportion of free negroes and mulattoes in the County who not only grow up in vice and wretchedness themselves but spread a moral pestilence around them."[77] He reveals his view even more explicitly in comments on the "free man of colour" Washington Taburn: "His intellect was naturally feeble, he belonged to a degraded caste and had enjoyed little opportunity either of mental or moral culture."[78]

Nevertheless, the social world into which Swain had moved was not that of the polite class of South Carolina or Virginia, but a cruder North Carolina society filled with many self-made men. Governor Montfort Stokes, by contrast, had ties to old Virginia families with pretensions to descent from such figures as Sir Simon de Montfort and Sir Adam de Stokes. He gained a military record in the Revolution and was reportedly a profane, hot-tempered, witty fellow with an inordinate love of poker, who had taken his wound in a duel. One contemporary called him "a type of chivalry of those days . . . quick to resent an insult."[79]

When Swain encountered people of Stokes's background in the North Carolina lowlands, he did not react with entire admiration. Newly arrived in Raleigh in 1822, he made contact with the family of his mother's uncle, Joel Lane, and wrote his father that "the whole race are as proud, as pompous, as generous & as dissipated as any family in the State." He determined to "have little intercourse" with them.[80] As a judge traveling the eastern circuit of the superior court, he had occasion to stop with the Collins family at Somerset Plantation. "They live well," he wrote in his diary, "if good living consists in luxury."[81]

Swain's account of the Collins women is very revealing of his own mind. He records first their pedigrees (their ties to male relatives of high status), then their appearance, then their mental traits, and lastly the degree of public regard he thinks they would command in polite society. Collins's wife and her sister, he says, are the daughters of a solicitor, the nieces of a judge and senator from Ohio, and sisters of the wife of a son of Chancellor James Kent of New York. Mrs. Collins is twenty, pretty, and has "flaxen hair & a mild blue eye"; her sister is "a red haired lady" with "the best turned & the most highly polished forehead, I have ever seen." They are not strikingly beautiful but "mild, interesting and amiable," and they possess "much more than ordinary southern intelligence." His assessment is that "if they do not command general admiration," they are "entitled to universal esteem."[82] His own mother's cousin in Raleigh Swain describes, tellingly, as "a widow lady of intelligence, & I suspect, respectability."[83]

Swain's actions and attitudes suggest a man striving hard to rise above his own social background, but one who also brings some of its attitudes with him. His mother was an aggressive Southern Methodist, his father a New England Presbyterian who, all his life, strictly opposed dancing and "ardent spirits."[84] David Swain also became a lifelong Presbyterian. If not as prudish as his parents, he was sufficiently conforming and pious to send a statement for inclusion in an American Bible Society publication, *Testimony of Distinguished Laymen to the Value of the Sacred Scriptures, Particularly in Their Bearing on Civil and Social Life.*[85]

What Swain valued in young women, he revealed in a letter sent to his wife in 1840 regarding the conduct of his daughter:

> Tell Anna, if she loves her father, and is anxious, that he should love her, she must improve her time while he is absent, must learn to govern her temper, and avoid evil speaking, and over hasty and petulant replies. She will never be very pretty, nor is it very important that she should be. I neither expect, nor desire, my children to be rich. But I am very anxious that they should be respectable and useful here, and happy hereafter. This result cannot be secured without diligent cultivation of the mind and the heart. Tell her to prize above all things, "the adornment of a meek and quiet spirit."[86]

To a man of Governor Swain's piety, aspiration to polite society, and regard for female respectability, Frankie Silver must have seemed beyond pardon. Some of Frankie Silver's petitioners, however, saw her lack of social advantages as an extenuating circumstance. They described her as "of Low and humble Parentage who have ever been incapable of administering either to the mind or body, such comfort as nature and Childhood may have required."[87] Swain had once hearkened to such an argument and used a legal loophole to pardon the infanticide of Catherine Bostian, whom one correspondent had defended on the grounds that "the public good—public Justice surely does not demand the execution of so degraded and debased a being—Humanity and moral feeling, I think, oppose the idea of hurling into the presence of her God, one so, totally unprepared for the awful change."[88] If Swain would not find a comparable way to pardon Frances Silver—whom others believed to have committed her murder without premeditation, in a "fracas" or even in self-defense—he must have regarded her as even more "degraded and debased." Did he find her infamous because she murdered a husband, the crime for which she was convicted, or was it rather that he accepted the charge that Frankie dismembered and burned the body?

People in the local community, as elsewhere, had originally seen as this act as "an occurrence which for turpitude can scarcely find an equal in the pages of fiction."[89] Frankie herself, according to Thomas Wilson, made her confession "not doubting but what it would in the estimation of the world greatly aggravate her guilt and forever consign her character to disgrace and infamy."[90] The horror of the act is one of the reasons why this long-ago case still rouses uneasy wonder.

Of all the issues in the case, this is the one least susceptible of explanation. Frankie's confession, according to Spainhour, said that after she killed Charles, "she was struck with terror, knowing that she would be hung unless she could conceal him, upon which she concluded to burn him up." We now debate whether she performed this action out of panic or out of rage. We question whether she did the deed alone, had help, or took no part in it at all. Her mother and brother Blackstone were originally arrested for complicity in the events, only to be released for lack of evidence. Many local people at the time thought the parents "very instrumental in the Perpetration of that horrid Deed."[91]

Frankie may have accepted the blame out of loyalty to kin who had tried to help her, as she did when she refused to give evidence against those who helped her escape from jail. By what means she effected the escape, wrote Thomas Wilson to Governor Swain, "she will never disclose."[92] Her claim of self-defense and the suspicion of family involvement in the destruction of the body moved many in the local community to compassion. The ladies of Burke County saw her as an injured woman who "for the want of Grace Religion and Refinement . . . committed an act that she herself would have Given a world to have been able to call back."[93] One is left, then, with the puzzle of why the confession did not also move Swain. Was there a reason beyond the influence of his conventional piety, his social aspiration, and his attachment to female respectability?

Perhaps we find a darker clue in his wish that his daughter Anne should seek "the adornment of a meek and quiet spirit." These words of fatherly counsel did not have their intended effect. Cornelia Spencer, a chronicler of antebellum Chapel Hill, wrote years later, "I cannot now think of Anne Swain, the playmate of my childhood, without a pang of regret and of sorrow for her fate." She remembered Anne as "always affectionate, generous, charitable, humble," and as one who loved "her humblest neighbors, and loved to sit in their cabins and hear their simple annals." But from childhood Anne had also shown "a tendency towards abberration of mind." She was "sometimes partially, sometimes wholly deranged, and sometimes brighter than the best of us, yet suffering the agony of knowing that she was smitten." "Her days were passed," the account continues, "how sadly, how painfully, how hopelessly, none can now say."[94]

Her illness may possibly have had a genetic component. Her grandfather Swain had developed a mental derangement "of the most melancholy cast," and a disorder also affected Anne's brother Richard. Cornelia Spencer discreetly stated that he was "in no respect a source of comfort to his father."[95] A physician who met Richard in 1861 wrote the father in alarm, "It is unfortunately too true that your son is quite wayward in his habits, and the whole arises from his habit of indulging too freely in spirituous liquors. I had not made his acquaintance five minutes before I discovered this."[96] A letter from one student at the university further reports that Richard deserted to the Yankees from the Confederate army during the Civil War.[97] Still, whatever predisposition her family may have had toward mental problems, it is hard not to see Anne Swain as another nineteenth-century "madwoman in the attic," living out an "aimless, beclouded life" within narrow social conventions.[98]

Two other Swain women struggled more aggressively against confining expectations. One, the Swains' younger daughter Eleanor (Ellie), was courted by Smith B. Atkins, the Union general commanding the four thousand Michigan troops who occupied Chapel Hill in April 1865. On a May evening a month later, Ellie "handed her parents a note in which she formally notified them she had accepted an offer of marriage from the General, and nothing could change her resolve. She would regret to disoblige them, but she was twenty-one years old and must judge for herself."[99] This action outraged many in the community and the state and helped cost Swain the presidency of the university and, indirectly, even his life three years later, when a horse Ellie's suitor had given him bolted, overturning his buggy and mortally injuring him.[100]

Even more than her daughters Anne and Ellie, David Swain's wife Eleanor struggled with the roles defined for her. Raised in polite social circles in Raleigh, she grew into a woman with what others saw as troubling eccentricities. Cornelia Spencer, a friend of the Swains but a clear-eyed observer nonetheless, tells five things about Eleanor that show her rebellion against conventions for women of her station. Spencer says that on the Swains' wedding day, as soon as they were alone after the ceremony, Eleanor told her husband she was secretly addicted to snuff dipping "and had hitherto concealed the habit from her mother, and he must not betray her, nor must he prevent her from the indulgence," which he hated.[101] Spencer also says that Eleanor Swain was a good housekeeper—but only "when she chose to exert the gift." Even more tellingly, her account points out that Mrs. Swain "very seldom ever attended public worship," never joined any church, and died without "any explicit profession of any faith."[102] Spencer was struck, too, by Eleanor's refusal to discipline her slaves, who were "a by-word for wickedness." Mrs. Swain's most "signal" failure, however, lay in the training of her children. She spoiled them "systematically," being "unable to see any faults in them, or to allow the least criticism of them from others," and standing between them and their father "in every attempt on his part to bring them to account."[103] Perhaps marriage to a self-made and singularly awkward mountain lad of New England ancestry was yet another expression of Eleanor White's rebellion against the conventions of her social class.

We do not know to what degree Mrs. Swain's attitudes were formed by her own wealthy, slaveholding family. Her father died in 1811, when Eleanor was a child. There is no indication that she shared the motives of South Carolinian Mary Boykin Chesnut, who wrote in disgust, "Any lady is ready to tell you who is the father of all the mulatto children in everybody's household but her own."[104] Chesnut quoted a South Carolina plantation overseer as saying, "In all my life I have only met one or two womenfolk who were not abolitionists in their hearts, and hot ones too." This may not have been the case with Eleanor Swain.

Ironic parallels between the misfortunes of the Stewart and Swain families, however, are not entirely the work of chance. The dilemmas of gender were heightened for both families by their social circumstances. The Stewarts were hampered by the roughness of life in their community and by their poverty, illiteracy, ignorance of the law, and lack of social leverage. The Swains, by contrast, were successful enough to be caught in the dilemmas of polite society, intensified by the social insecurity and the strain of piety David Swain brought with him in his climb. David wanted respectability—the esteem of people of high status—and had bought into the very stereotypes of female propriety that his wife resisted.

When Governor Swain had the Frankie Silver case thrust upon him, he seems to have seen Frankie very differently than many people in Burke County, who had come to feel compassion for her. An eyewitness reported that Sheriff John Boone carried out the hanging of Frankie Silver with tears flowing "freely down his cheeks on both sides."[105] But at his distance in Raleigh, Swain probably felt only abhorrence for a woman who could murder her husband and desecrate his body. David Swain was singularly ill equipped to deal with such a convention-defying act. He was then less than a decade married, a young father, and surely already struggling to resolve the painful contradictions between realities emerging within his own marriage and his personal aspiration to social success—a success whose defining symbols were possession of slaves and wealth, the holding of public office, and marriage to a woman of such pedigree and "respectability" as to merit not only "universal esteem" but "general admiration."

Six months after his wedding, he was already writing from Asheville to complain that Eleanor seemed "to have forgotten what I have always deemed the leading article of the female catechism—'Whither thou goest I will goe and whither thou lodgest, I will lodge and thy people shall be my people and thy God my God.'"[106] He would soon have to accept not only that Eleanor neglected his family in Asheville, but that she had an "utter aversion to the mountains" and refused to live there. Her "predilection for Raleigh" was so strong that she was unwilling to follow her husband even to a town in the east when he was appointed solicitor of the Edenton circuit. Her refusal threatened to cost the newlyweds six months of separation a year. David Swain's "prospects" in the eastern region—"professionally and politically"—were, he wrote her in January 1828, "becoming daily more flattering and should not be abandoned rashly."[107] But two days later, he did abandon them rather than endure separation from his wife.[108] The solution he eventually found, according to Cornelia Spencer, was to convince himself that Eleanor White Swain was "perfection, a model wife and mother," and never to oppose "a motion of hers in his life."[109] David Swain, too, had climbed a tree under a curse and was struggling in its branches. His inability to deal with his wife's rebelliousness was costly to his own family. Frankie Silver, another seemingly rebellious woman, may also have had to pay part of the price.

As I grew up, I realized that a lot
of the tales were . . . based on the
dark side of things.
—*Bobby McMillon*

CONCLUSION

Bobby McMillon presented a hard saying when he spoke of the murder of Charlie Silver as "a story that happened." His phrase sent us searching along two paths. One of these—the one that asks "What happened?"—forced us to see how imperfectly we were able to reconstruct the actual events from the surviving documents. They leave us with many uncertainties about Frankie Silver's motives and actions.

In contemporaneous records, moreover, once Frankie has struck her husband she is only a small figure, mute and powerless, acted upon by others. The leading players in the trial—the great scene of this drama —were the solicitor, defense attorney, witnesses, jurors, and judge. We know what rules governed their legal rituals and what decision the courtroom produced, but very little about the stories the men told each other as they tried to explain the crime and determine guilt and punishment. This story of Frankie Silver began with her arrest, dwelt moderately on the trial itself and the appeal to the state supreme court, and gave only glimpses of her escape, recapture, appeals for executive clemency, and execution. The main actor was Frankie's attorney, Thomas Worth Wilson, and the events were a test of his dedication and professional skill. He seemed wanting.

What happened also intersected with other happenings that had their own story lines. A second tale helpful in unlocking one puzzle in Frankie's case was that of David L. Swain, for petitions from Burke County and his own unexpected elevation to the office of governor forced Swain to decide whether Frankie would hang. The fullness of Swain's surviving documents made him, in fact, the most clearly perceived actor in the entire Frankie Silver case. His decision was a test of his character and values. Swain did not pass it with distinction.

Other figures also move about in the background, with implied stories of their own—in particular Frankie's father and mother. We see Isaiah Stewart, an unlettered man who signed documents with his *X*, trying to get his wife and son released from jail. We hear that he traveled to Morganton, hoping for news of a governor's response to petitions on behalf of his daughter. We discover that Col. John Carson told Isaiah the fine ladies had been moved by Frankie's confession and would sign a petition on her behalf. We learn from a letter written to Swain in 1835 that it was Isaiah Stewart who arranged Frankie's jailbreak—that he confessed to having gone to Jessee Barnett, his wife's brother, in Anson County, "& by makeing strong appeals to his sympathy induced him to leave home & come in to Burke" to receive Frankie "in disguise some twelve miles from Morganton."[1] Barnett, according to a news account, posed as a peddler selling wares in Burke, received Frankie "dressed in man's apparel" with her hair cut short, and carried her as far as "Sandy-Run, in the Southeastern part" of Rutherford County, before they were apprehended.[2]

Both Isaiah Stewart and Jessee Barnett were arrested, arraigned at the fall court term after Frankie's execution, and bound over for trial at the March 1834 term. Jessee Barnett, however, failed to appear. The judge raised Jessee's recognizance fee to $1,000 for his appearance at the September 1834 court term and made Isaiah pledge $500 as security for his appearance. Since the value of Isaiah's taxable property in 1830 (before the beginning of his legal expenses) totaled only $50, this was an amount beyond his resources.[3] Probably out of sympathy for him, Sheriff John Boone and Clerk of the Court Burgess Gaither took the extraordinary step of pledging $500 each as security for Jessee's appearance.[4] In return for this generous gesture or because he was under threat of prosecution or out of exhaustion from the distress his daughter's act had brought upon him, Isaiah turned state's evidence for the trial that convicted Jessee. The court sentenced Barnett to ten months in jail, of which he served seven before being pardoned by Governor Swain.[5] The court dropped the charges against Isaiah, who died a year later in February 1836, probably in his late fifties. Whether he was an anguished father doing for his daughter all that he knew to do, or whether he had a guilty role in the murder itself—as Latt Hughes told Bobby—or in her early life, we cannot determine. We learn little more of his story.

Barbara Stewart's story is even sketchier. She was probably fifty-three at the time of the murder and the mother of most or all of Isaiah's eight known children. She outlived Isaiah by some years, dying after 1850.[6] We do not know what caused magistrate David Baker to arrest Barbara and her son Blackstone along with Frankie in January 1832. Novelist Sharyn McCrumb's reconstruction of the events places Isaiah and his older son Jackson away on a hunt at the time of the murder, a theory that plausibly explains why neither of these seasoned men came under investigation. The grand jury did not find sufficient evidence to indict Barbara Stewart or Blackstone, but Thomas Wilson later reported to Governor Stokes that many people in the county thought Frankie's family "very instrumental in the Perpetration of that horrid Deed."[7]

What actually happened in the Silver cabin has been, from the first, a matter of debate. According to Henry Spainhour, Frankie's confession stated that, having killed Charlie, "she was struck with terror, knowing that she would be hung unless she could conceal him, upon which she concluded to burn him up."[8] Many in the community seem not to have found this statement very convincing. William F. Thomas, a local physician, wrote Governor Swain that although many thought she must indeed have killed Charlie in a quarrel, "the maner in which she disposed of him is not fully believed."[9] Tom Davenport's speculation is that Frankie would have snatched up her baby and rushed to her mother after striking and killing Charles and that Barbara, overwhelmed by a frantic, ill-considered impulse to protect her child, thought only of hiding the evidence. But the ground was hard and the river frozen over. She could not bury the body or drop it in the stream. Burning it would have been the only way to conceal the crime. She and Blackstone, rather than Frankie, may even have carried out this deed. This reading of the event is also substantially shared by Sharyn McCrumb and Wayne Silver.[10] If the supposition is true, then between them Frankie's mother and father actually ensured her execution. Governor Swain would have viewed the destruction of Charlie's body as infamous and the jailbreak as evidence of incorrigible criminality.

This Stewart story holds a deeper lesson about the culture, for all members of the family followed the same code. Frankie would "never disclose," wrote Thomas Wilson, the means by which "she effected" her escape.[11] And, as Bobby McMillon says, she took to her grave any other secrets that could implicate her family. Sharyn McCrumb also accepts the legendary accounts of this part of the story. Bobby reconstructs the murder itself differently, but his story dramatizes the same underlying allegiances in the characters. Frankie strikes Charlie in obedience to her father's command. Her father successfully stops her scaffold confession by shouting, "Die with it in you, Frankie! Die with it in you!" And Bobby follows the tradition that she sided with her family rather than Charlie in a dispute over selling land to get money for moving west. History, fiction, and legend, then, all identify the tragic flaw of the Stewarts as their overriding loyalty to blood kin.

Governor Swain's story discloses a different social code, for it shows a shift of allegiance from family to broader social connections and standards. Swain still felt the powerful claims of kinship and throughout his life repeatedly gave financial help to his brother George, his half-brother James Lowry, and his various nephews. But within the Swain family, loyalty had begun to fail. To make his fortune in the world, George Swain Sr., David's father, had left his kin in New England, embarked for the South, and never returned. Toward the end of his life, George fell into insanity and became estranged even from the remainder of his family. "My cup of bitterness is full," David wrote his wife in 1828. "At Haywood Court I met with father. . . . He now seems bereft of every ray of reason. He knew me at sight and for a moment his eye seemed to sparkle with pleasure, but he never checked his bridle, or seemed to be conscious that I had been absent from him. He has become very troublesome and his wife"—a Miss Brittain whom he married after the death of David's mother in the mid-1820s—"is odious to him."[12]

David L. Swain's own mother, scarcely literate despite her ties with good families in Raleigh, gave her allegiance to Methodism. Her letters to David have a sharp edge, as if she has quite taken to heart the scriptural pronouncement, "I am come to set a man at variance against his father, and the daughter against her mother. . . . He that loveth son or daughter more than me is not worthy of me" (Matt. 10:35, 37). She could scarcely reconcile herself to David's choice of profession and wrote him cuttingly, "I should never have chosen the law for you but . . . Christ came to fulfill the law & He did it & made it honorable but can anything be meaner than a wicked lawyer."[13] On hearing that David has been attending parties in the best social circles in Raleigh, she writes, "david what have you to do with partes have you any time to spair then think what you are a poor blind naked rebel an enemy to god and hair of hell."[14]

Swain did not follow his mother into her abrasive Methodist piety but labored instead to enter the polite class. Since he was not born to a family of high standing, he could best gain entrée to that world through his education, offices, associates, marriage, and financial success and by adopting the social codes of those he sought to join. He accepted the polite ideal of womanhood, the female whose refinement inspired respect, universal esteem, and general admiration. This must have framed —in ways already discussed—his view of Frankie Silver.

But Swain's executive decision in the Frankie Silver case, when set against actions in other cases of the period, illustrates contradictions and inequalities inherent in that social code. In the polite class the men, at least, wanted the female to wear the adornment of a meek and quiet spirit, but they respected spirited behavior in the male. By law they granted the husband authority, as we have seen, to administer moderate chastisement to his wife, and both juries and jurists were reluctant to believe that he might exceed moderation. Further, they admired the male who boldly defended his own honor as a husband.

Swain, in fact, was less committed to this view than many others. In 1831 Robert Potter, a congressman from Granville County, believing his wife to have betrayed him both with her cousin, a minister in his fifties, and with her stepmother's nephew, a lad of seventeen, assaulted and castrated both men. Swain sardonically commented that, in comparison to this case, the recent lurid murder of Solomon Sharp by Jereboam Beauchamp in Kentucky was "characterized in its leading features, by good faith, gentleness, and amiability."[15] Potter suffered a fine of $1,000 and a six months' jail term. Governor Swain remitted the fine in response to the prisoner's claim of insolvency, and on Potter's release from jail, his admiring constituents elected him to a term in the state House of Commons.[16] He did in 1835 have to leave the legislature and state in disgrace after pulling a weapon to reclaim his losses at the gaming table. Nevertheless, he went on to political prominence in Texas, where he was serving in the senate when a political opponent murdered him in 1842.

Men of the polite class also expected a gentleman to defend his honor physically in appropriate circumstances outside the marital sphere. In her novel, Sharyn McCrumb uses well-known instances of this approved male aggression from Burke County history to create a counterpoint to Frankie's story. The most flamboyant example she chooses is William Waightstill Avery's fatal shooting of Samuel Fleming in open court in 1851. Two weeks earlier, Fleming had whipped Avery with a cowhide in a public street and ridiculed him. Both law and public opinion exonerated Avery of murdering Fleming, on the grounds of "extreme provocation leading to temporary insanity." The jury deliberated a full ten minutes.[17]

The attitudes dramatized in these incidents, of course, were not strictly local but were shared by many polite males across the state and throughout much of the South.[18] Governor Stokes acted favorably, for example, upon petitions on behalf of young Claiborn Carroll in the eastern North Carolina town of Clinton. Carroll had stabbed the buttocks of a bully named James Jordan for "repeatedly running his backside on him & in his face." One petitioner declared emphatically, "if a child of mine under such circumstances, did not resent such insults, *with any means which nature or art* furnished him, I would cease to acknowledge him, & give him 39 lashes, to boot."[19]

Another—and more serious—contemporaneous North Carolina case makes the polite assumptions about male violence even more clear. A fiery nineteen-year-old named Logan Henderson returned to Lincolnton in 1837 after serving in the Texas Rangers. He learned that one Marcus Hoke had called Henderson's father a "damned liar," a "damned old scoundrel," and a "damned old grayheaded rascal." Henderson could perhaps have borne a thousand injuries, but when Hoke ventured upon insult to his family, he vowed revenge. He sought out Hoke and beat him with a cane that shattered, revealing that it sheathed a sword blade. Hoke drew a pistol and Henderson his Bowie knife, the two grappled, and as they tussled, Henderson stabbed the other man. Hoke died from the wound nine hours later. A court found Henderson guilty of manslaughter and sentenced him to six months in jail and to be "burned on the hand."[20]

Marcus Hoke's widow thought the court outrageously lenient. Logan Henderson deserved to be hanged. Henderson, she charged in a letter to Governor Edward Dudley, "came into Our house and Murdered my dear husband in his own house where his family that was devoted to him were." She blamed the verdict on the change of venue for the trial from

Lincoln to Rutherford County, "where there are so manny of the Allen Twitty friends." She thought that if the case had been tried "at anny other court but Rutherford . . . he could not posibly get clear."[21]

Mrs. Hoke's analysis was probably wrong. To a certainty it was incomplete, as we learn from the flood of petitions that swept away her lone letter to the governor. These petitions, which included the signatures of some sixty-seven gentlemen in neighboring Burke County, argued that the sentence of branding was too severe.[22] Only seven of these men had signed a petition on behalf of Frankie Silver. The approximately 175 persons who supported Frankie included five who had been justices of the Burke court of pleas and quarter sessions, three who had held other county offices, two who had served in the state legislature, and fifteen with property valued at $1,000 or more.

Logan Henderson's supporters clearly had much greater social luster. They included Averys, Erwins, and McDowells who had not signed a petition for Frankie. Although they were far fewer, these sixty-seven men included seven justices of the court of pleas and quarter sessions, five other county officers, six state legislators, and sixteen landowners with property valued at $1,000 or more.[23] Isaac T. Avery of Burke, who appears to have directly declined to sign a petition on behalf of Frankie Silver, urged Governor Dudley to take account of "the Family, to which the young man belongs, their bravery (for they have been prodigal of their blood whenever their Country claimed it.) the high sense of honor, and regard for Character, which they have ever manifested. Principles, which have been instilled into the mind of this youth, and no doubt had their influence, in producing the affray." Avery went on to declare that Logan Henderson considered branding to be "ignomenious, and ignominy, to a mind, peculiarly sensitive, on the subject of Character, as I believe his to be, is worse than Death."[24] The governor concurred, pardoning Henderson on the grounds of his youth and "the honorable feeling which seems to have urged him to the commission of the deed."[25]

The jury found Logan Henderson's crime to be manslaughter, the judge sentenced him to less jail time than Jessee Barnett received for helping Frankie Silver after her escape, and the governor, responding to the opinion of influential men, waived the remaining part of Logan's sentence. These actions seem to confirm Bertram Wyatt-Brown's thesis that, "above all else," white southerners of the antebellum era "adhered to a moral code that may be summarized as the rule of honor."[26] In overgeneralizing the code of the polite male to white southerners in the aggregate, Wyatt-Brown gives a distorted picture of the Old South, but his brilliant exposition of the code of honor does clarify the assumption made in these legal cases: a gentleman's reputation had more value than a life. What the law would punish, jurors would reconstrue as a lesser crime. When jurors would punish, gentlemen of the community would seek mitigation of the sentence in petitions to the governor. And governors found the petitioners' arguments convincing and were willing to act favorably upon them.

These cases show that the administration of the law in antebellum North Carolina protected males of the polite class from sanctions it would impose on a woman like Frankie Silver. But these practices were not local inventions. They, like the rules of evidence, were an inheritance from earlier British legal and social traditions, which had come to define some "provocations" and not others as mitigating circumstances in murder cases. Early modern English society, writes Lawrence Stone, was "at least five times more violence-prone than contemporary English society," and "most of this pre-modern violence was outside the family rather than within it."[27] Murders typically were "acts of sudden, unpremeditated aggression"—that is, they often occurred during quarrels and brawls. They were a mainly male behavior.[28]

Courts developed distinctions between premeditated murder, manslaughter, and self-defense chiefly in order to deal with varying degrees of culpability in male violence. The duel of honor imported into the British Isles from the European continent in the late sixteenth century served "to limit violence and regulate its expression."[29] But it also provided a framework for mitigating legal and social penalties for upper-class male aggression. The man of honor, according to Bernard Mandeville, could "suffer no affront, which is a term of Art for every Action designedly done to undervalue him."[30] Twentieth-century feminists argue that these social and legal developments not only had the consequence of facilitating male violence, but also failed to address with equal concern the kinds of provocations suffered by women.[31] Spousal abuse was chief among these. Insofar, then, as abusive treatment by Charlie Silver or by her father may have provoked Frankie to act, the cultural and legal accommodation to male but not female violence exposed her to harsher treatment in the courts of both law and public opinion.

Bobby McMillon's phrase "a story that happened," however, also pointed to a second direction for exploration. It made us not only look at events and their legal and social implications but also consider the stories as *story*. What shaped the narratives embedded in the Frankie Silver ballad and legend cycle? Here, too, we wandered amid complexities. British popular culture provided conventions of syntax, diction, verse form, narrative point of view, plot, and theme for the ballad. The conventions explain why the ballad offers a stereotyped expression of guilt and self-condemnation, but they could not control people's response to the material.

Like its British prototypes, "Frankie Silver's Confession" could make people feel the criminal's plight. The legend cycle drew both from local oral tradition and from published accounts. It was influenced by the aims of journalists but also by the concerns and aesthetic of local storytellers. Bobby McMillon's own temperament, experience, and judgment, his aesthetic sense, even his loyalty as a member of the Silver family, have played their roles too. We have seen that he selected some episodes to include in his version, ignored others, and changed his way of telling the story across the years. But we have not yet explored questions about narrative as far as they can take us.

The Frankie Silver legend cycle raises feminist issues for Bobby Mc-Millon's friend Charlotte Ross, a teacher and folklorist.[32] Charlotte has recently come to think that she, like Bobby, is a distant descendant of Charles's uncle Greenberry Silver, by his illegitimate son Greenberry Woody. Like Bobby, she grew up immersed in Appalachian traditional culture and is also both a storyteller and a collector of tales, with a passion for regional legends. She, however, is a woman from the region and is particularly engaged with stories of women's lives. The Frankie Silver story is one she too has often heard, but she says she will not tell it.

In Charlotte Ross's experience, it is the men who tell the Frankie legend. Their wives listen uncomfortably. Afterward, the women do not counter with a woman's narrative of the murder but do, if given space in the conversation, undercut the legend with a few pained comments. They may remark that they have heard Frankie was a small woman or a hard worker or that Charlie was not a good husband. Charlotte sees the legend cycle as the Silver version of events—maybe even predominantly Alfred Silver's version, with a male as well as a family bias.

Counterarguments are possible. For one thing, some women do tell these stories. One early version of the legend came from Alfred's sister Lucinda, and Bobby himself first heard the story from his grandmother, learned other episodes from "Aunt" Lou Brookshire in Caldwell County, and recorded the "Frankie Silver" song from Granny Hopson. Bobby's grandmother did not know at the time that she was related to the Silvers; the other two women were unrelated, as was Bobby's principal male source, Latt Hughes. The inference I draw from his sources is that the murder and the horrifying manner in which it was concealed disturbed many people—women as well as men—in the region. The legend and the song must have served these people, too, and therefore had uses other than simply projecting the bitterness of the Silver family or the prejudices of males.

Brutal crimes elsewhere provoked a similar need for the telling of stories. They called into print, in fact, not only the confession ballad but three other forms of early British and American gallows literature: the execution sermon, the "flash" ballad, and the prose chapbook confession. At least thirty sermons surviving in print were preached in New England between 1674 and 1750 to the condemned and the public on the day of execution.[33] These sermons frame the crimes with familiar theology: God controls the universe and man. Man can freely choose between good and evil and is thus a responsible creature. The evil man is condemned to hell in the future life unless he shows contrition.[34] The preachers directed these set pieces less to the condemned than to the community at large. Daniel Boorstin sees the sermons as the "ritual application of theology to community-building." In that theocratic society, the sermons spoke with the voice of God—and that of the social authorities. And the condemned themselves sometimes repeated the same themes in sermons they gave beneath the gallows. James Morgan, executed in Boston in 1686, expostulated, "O, take warning by me, and beg of God to keep you from this sin, which has been my ruine!"[35]

Chapbook "confessions"—which were published throughout several centuries in the British Isles and still survive in enormous numbers—offer even stronger evidence of a need to repair a rent torn in beliefs, feelings, and the social fabric. They drew on a broad confessional tradition that took on many colorations across the centuries. Tudor aristocrats sentenced to death for treason had offered, even when they were innocent, abject but apparently sincere confessions before their executions, holding "themselves up as examples of the frightful fate in store for those who dared to sin against God and their king."[36] They also exhibited an effort to "die well"—sharing in a long and evolving Christian tradition that remained still powerful in the nineteenth century.

The popular deathbed farewell of a fictional Little Eva or Little Nell had real-life parallels even in North Carolina. The family papers of Governor David Lowry Swain include lengthy letters describing deathbed testimonies of his sister Mary, of the Swains' aged slave Phebe, and of the wife of his half-brother James Lowry.[37] Mary's death, Swain reported to his wife, was "impressive," "consolitary," and "interesting." Phebe exclaimed to him with tears streaming from her eyes, "I want to see you in Heaven Mas. David, I pray for you on my knees every night." James Lowry's "Dear Companion" gave "a suitable talk to all her Children & then to Every one of the black family" and "with out the least flattery to one individual." Afterward, when she appeared nearly insensible, Brother Robeson (the local preacher) "spake out Sister Lowry if you still feal that the Lord is with you pleas rais your hand and then she Raisd up her hand & arm strait in an instant it seamd to Effect Everyone in the Room as quick as litening and then she left this world died quite Easy without a struggle."[38]

The dying testimonies of criminals through the centuries might be less edifying. Jack K. Williams reports a tradition that one woman in nineteenth-century Charleston shouted to the mob gathered for her execution, "If you have a message you want to send to hell, give it to me, I'll carry it."[39] Her remark echoes a "scaffold culture" of "knowing, reality-facing fatalism": "the knowledge that, if life was a joke, its ending was not the worst of outcomes; that among survivors life must continue; and that contrition was the last thing to be displayed."[40] The flash ballads—often in the cant language of the criminal underclass—captured this spirit, as one can see in "Jack Sheppard's Last Epistle":

Oh! then to the tree I must go;
    The judge he has ordered that sentence.
And then comes a gownsman you know,
    And tells a dull tale of repentance.
By the gullet we're ty'd very tight;
    We beg all spectators, pray for us.
Our peepers are hid from the light,
    The tumbril shoves off and we morrice.[41]

The press, however, particularly in Great Britain, turned the execution into an occasion for selling chapbooks that put a more widely acceptable message into the criminal's mouth. Although chapbook confessions did not directly influence the Frankie Silver legends, both bodies of material shape "the facts of actuality" into socially helpful patterns—

taking the executed criminal's life, in Lincoln Faller's phrase, "twice over."[42] The way in which chapbook confessions did this highlights the contrasting artistic stratagems of the traditional legends.

One of the two main categories of chapbook confessions in the seventeenth and eighteenth centuries, according to Faller, is that of persons who murdered members of their own households. These accounts give little attention to the criminals' motivations; the consequence of the crime is their central focus. The Frankie Silver legend cycle shares with them the theme of "radical rebellion against the discipline of the family" and the emphasis on consequence rather than motive. The legend cycle also shares the thrust of the chapbook confessions. Both try "to counterbalance and so control" all that the acts "so unsettlingly suggested of the human condition."[43]

But in other ways, the Frankie Silver legends are very different from the chapbook narratives. The chapbook authors choose a first-person rather than a third-person voice, and they close the account with a religious exhortation. In the chapbooks, the reassurance for the community "came with the criminal's readiness to confess and accept responsibility for his crime, to convert and die an enthusiastic Christian, to close out his life in a peculiar mixture of self-abasement and self-glorification."[44] With art superior to this, the Frankie Silver legend ignores Frankie's actual confession. Instead, it dramatizes her inability to "tell all" and thus avoids preaching. The legend affirms moral law through its narrative structure, its powerful balancing scenes of violation and retribution. But the story is clouded with mysteries.

This does not mean that the Frankie Silver legend cycle reflects the new consciousness that Karen Halttunen sees in the crime writing of nineteenth-century print culture. Whereas in the eighteenth century, she writes, "the classic execution sermon had assumed the guilt of the convicted murderer," now "trial reports and other legal accounts made the guilt of the accused murderer their central problematic."[45] Enlightenment ideas, she argues, focused attention upon motive, with the consequence that "the new crime narrative focused on a question that had not been necessary within the sacred masterplot: What went wrong?"[46] Thus it was the "discourse of the law" that "led to the cultural construction of murder as mystery, which spilled over from formally legal narratives of the crime into the larger popular literature."[47]

The mysteries in the Frankie Silver crime story, however, derive not from popular accounts of crime but from older, deeper sources. Debate and uncertainty, as we have seen, mark the traditional use of the legend form. And narrative reticence lies at the core of the aesthetic strategy of Bobby McMillon and the storytellers who influenced him. As Bobby says, "There's a moral. You got to figure it out yourself."[48]

This reticence is, in fact, one secret of the force of the legend cycle. It does not insist on its interpretation. Bobby McMillon, to offer an additional instance of his method, opens his tale session with a description of how early settlers came into the country and found it a "wild wilderness" full of panthers and bears. At the end of the story he closes this frame. He reminds us that the background of the story was "the new world that people had come to" and says, "A lot of people, I believe, thought at the beginning, that they would come to this country, gain their fortune, and eventually go home. But it never happened that way." Without at all insisting, these words seem to place the Frankie Silver story inside one of the overarching narratives of his culture, the story of mankind's long exile in the wilderness of the world. I sent Bobby a draft of this passage with a note, "This is what I feel when I hear your words—am I pushing it too far?" Bobby's reply was, "No. You hit the nail on the head."

Another secret of the power of the Frankie Silver legend cycle is that it is neither "true" nor "pure fiction." The craving for factual truth seems to drive our interest in such historical legends, and two things keep this interest alive. One is that the story does not tell all but holds its mysteries. Our minds gnaw at the narrative. We want to crack it open. If we succeed, we may leave the story a dry and empty shell, something to drop or bury. But to stay alive, the legend also needs to have at least the potential of being factually true. And yet historical legends as a group fall under suspicion. People see discrepancies in the tales. How can the tale teller really know that the wounded Charlie cried out, "God bless the child"? So they dismiss the stories as "only folklore," something unreliable and therefore trivial.

This is too simple a reading of the legends. We do not even have to defend them on the grounds that they preserve, if not facts, then attitudes, and hence are a window through which we can peer into the culture in which they circulate. We do not have to argue that they are valuable because they provoke the writing of a play or a novel or a historical study, works that try to fill in the gaps between the provable facts and to disclose structures and forces in the social world of the events. In their own right, historical legends are narratives with demonstrated staying power. Something about a legend episode catches attention, both in the traditional community and outside it. It sticks in the memory. It becomes the subject of debate in the telling—and then of continued private reflection. To the extent that historians or folklorists or even novelists succeed in establishing the facts of the case, they may do so, to paraphrase Poe, at the risk of "overturning a fiction."

Nathaniel Hawthorne, who has some repute for loving history and for using it in his fiction, wrote sensitively about the issue. After moving into the Old Manse in Concord, Massachusetts, Hawthorne heard a legend from James Russell Lowell about two graves behind the house. On the April morning in 1776 when British troops and local farmers confronted each other in a field just across the stream below the house, Lowell told him, a youth was chopping wood at the rear of the Manse. Tradition, according to Lowell, said that the lad

> left his task, and hurried to the battle-field, with the axe still in his hand. The British had by this time retreated—the Americans were in pursuit—and the late scene of strife was thus deserted by both parties. Two soldiers lay on the ground; one was a corpse; but, as the young New-Englander drew nigh, the other Briton raised himself painfully upon his hands and knees, and gave a ghastly stare into his face. The boy—it must have been a nervous impulse, without purpose, without thought, and betokening a sensitive and impressionable nature, rather than a hardened one—the boy uplifted his axe and dealt the wounded soldier a fierce and fatal blow upon the head.

Hawthorne comments, "I could wish that the grave might be opened; for I would fain know whether either of the skeleton soldiers have the mark of an axe in his skull." The story has been useful to him, he says, "as an intellectual and moral exercise." He has often "sought to follow that poor youth through his subsequent career, and observe how his soul was tortured by the blood-stain." The story, he feels, "has something deeply impressive," and he adds, "This one circumstance has borne more fruit for me, than all that history tells us of the fight." Although its circumstances "cannot altogether be reconciled with probability," Hawthorne says the legend "comes home to me like truth."[49]

Perhaps Bobby McMillon's legend cycle about Frankie Silver cannot altogether be reconciled with probability, but it too comes home to us like truth. Particular episodes, images, and phrases are charged with unexplainable power: Frankie's last request for a piece of cake; the baby's bloody handprint; the cry "Die with it in you, Frankie! Die with it in you!"; the tree under a curse that grew near the ruins of the Silver cabin. The truth in the story is less historical than existential. A story, as Roger Abrahams says, is our "way of translating the transformations and calamities of the past into records of meaning and interest to those of the present."[50] Whether told by an academic historian or by a traditional historian like Bobby McMillon, the story is what Henry Glassie calls a way of "making the past useful to the future." But as Glassie points out, "The welter of dull detail and fine webs of qualification that make written arguments seem complex and convincing do not belong in good tales. Oral history cannot be boring."[51] Whether we accept the account or debate it, Bobby's Frankie Silver legend cycle makes us feel the human experience of crime to a degree that the court records, historical studies, and, to my mind, even the novels, plays, and ballet do not equal.

The historical Frankie Silver may have been a victim of the accident of her petitioners' timing, of her husband's unfaithfulness or brutality, of abuse by her father, of misguided family loyalty, of the ineptitude of her lawyer or the personal dilemmas of a governor, of the law's procedural inadequacies, or of inequities weighing upon women, the illiterate, backwoods people, or the subsistence-farming class. The enigmatic Frankie of legend looms larger than this—particularly in the versions least sympathetic to her. She is less victim than doer. She terrifies us with her measureless rage or with the huge and devastating consequences of a moment's mindless act. The legend brings us face to face with "ancient and immitigable" facts of character and fate. And the Frankie Silver ballad compounds this by compelling us for a moment not merely to contemplate but to become the remorseful and terrified murderer.

And so it was for Bobby McMillon. Little that was dramatic happened in the tiny community of Kona while he was growing up there. But he was a sensitive and thoughtful youngster, and the old songs and stories he heard gave richness to the landscape about him and to his imaginative life. He came to realize that they were "based on the dark side of things."[52] They helped awaken him to an adult awareness of the recalcitrant mixture of good and evil in all people and to "the still, sad music of humanity."

APPENDIX A

Variants of the Frankie Silver Legend Cycle

ALFRED SILVER

[From H. E. C. Bryant, "The Horrible Deed of a Wife,"
Charlotte Daily Observer, March 22, 1903, p. 10.]

Mr. Alfred Silver, half-brother of the murdered man, is living to-day, on Curtis creek, four miles northwest of the town of Old Fort, McDowell county. He will be 87 years old the 15th of November, if the Great Master allows him to live to see his next birthday. I went out to see Mr. Silver one morning last week. He is the finest type of the best class of mountaineer that I ever saw, being large, strong-featured and manly. His face looks like the pictures of the old patriarchs as they appear in the histories. He has a large head, a fine mouth and silken hair. As he lay in bed and conversed with me I could see nothing but his long, bony hands, his soft, white beard, his brilliant eyes and the general outline of his face, for he wore a fur cap and had the cover pulled up around him.

I found him willing and able to talk about the murder, the trial and the hanging. His mind is sound and clear. He remembers the details of the case as well as if the crime had been perpetrated last month. At the time of the deed he was just at the tender age when a bright mind takes and retains most.

The Story of the Crime

In giving the story of the affair I shall let him tell it in his vigorous, forceful way. He uses plain but eloquent English.

He began: "Charles Silver, killed and destroyed by his wife, Franky Silver, about the year 1832 was my half-brother. He was strong, healthy, good-looking and agreeable. He had lots of friends. Everybody liked him. He was a favorite at all the parties for he could make merry by talking, laughing and playing musical instruments. I think he was the best fifer that I ever heard. He had been married long enough to have one heir before he died. He lived in a cabin across a ridge, a quarter of a mile from my father's home on Toe river.

Cut the Wood Used in Burning His Body

"Charles was pretty much of a gunner, a hunter, and it was Christmas, just his time for hunting. The ground was all covered with snow and the river frozen hard. His wife, contending that he would be off soon on a hunt, urged him to cut enough wood to do all week. He fell in with his axe and cut up a whole hickory tree, and shocked it so that it would keep dry and clean.

"Being tired and sleepy after the labor of chopping, my brother lay down on the floor, close by the fire with his little girl in his arms, and went to sleep. His head rested on an inverted stool for a pillow. Franky gently took the baby from his breast, put it in the bed, picked up the axe from the door, where she had placed it for the purpose, and whacked his head half off at a single blow. She intended to cut it clean off but miscalculated and either stood too close or too far back. The first lick did not kill him instantly for he sprang to his feet and cried: 'God bless the child.' His wife fled to the bed, by the child, and covered herself up, till she heard Charles fall and then jumped out, and finished the job, with a second blow. But the most inhuman part of the atrocious deed was to come. The woman went to work, cut the body into small pieces and burned it bit by bit. The entire night and all the wood available were consumed in burning the body. The hickory tree, a dog house and the door steps went up in the effort. It is believed that her mother and youngest brother helped to dispose of the body. In fact, she confessed as much to a woman who called on her in jail. I believe the killing was a conspiracy entered into by the whole Stewart family.

The Search for the Missing Man

"Of course we knew nothing of the crime at my father's house. Franky came early the next morning, stopped where my mother and the girls were washing for Christmas and remarked: 'You are hard at it early.' My mother answered: 'Yes, we are trying to get ready for a rest.' 'Yes,' said Franky, 'I've been at it myself ever since before day.' She told mother that Charles had gone up the river to George Young's.

"That same afternoon Franky came over and reported that Charles had not returned. She expected him back earlier. Mother noticed that she was a bit nervous, but thought it was on account of the prolonged absence of Charles. She said she would go down to her father's home, three-quarters of a mile away, if some of the boys would attend to the feeding of her cow; explaining that Charles had fed her that morning, but, when we went there that night we saw none but women tracks.

"Charles didn't show up the next day, nor the one following. Franky told mother that as he had remained away so long she did not care whether he ever came or not, and went back to her father's.

A Conjure Ball Consulted

"After several days had passed and nothing was heard of Charles the alarm was given. The word was put out all through the mountains. No track or trace of him could be found. The river was searched, for some thought that he might have gone through the ice. He had not been to George Young's. My father was greatly stirred up about it. He was ready to do anything. So when he heard of an old guinea negro over in Tennessee, 40 miles away, who had a kind of conjure ball that told things, he set out on horseback, to see him. The negro was not at home, but the man, a Mr. Williams, for whom he worked, said he could interpret the behavior of the ball. He hung the ball up like a pendulum and marked off the points of the compass. Father told Williams all about the location of the house where Charles lived and drew a map of the section round about. The ball didn't seem to point away from the house and Williams asked, 'Wasn't it possible that the man was done away with at home?'

"Father said that was impossible for if Franky had desired to do so she couldn't have killed Charles and hid his body. Williams finally said: 'Well, his kindred.' That was towards his own house, from ours. Later in the day Williams tried his ball and told my father that it indicated that the body had been found. Sure enough it was.

The First Evidences of the Crime and What Followed

"On the very day that father started for Tennessee the mystery was partially solved. Some one of the searching party suggested that the cabin and the premises be examined. An old man by the name of Jack Collis thought it wise to look around in the house. He went about the yard and cabin probing with his walking cane. In stirring the ashes in the fireplace he found several pieces of bone, which caused him to say, 'There's too many bits of bone in this fireplace and the ashes are too greasy.' A small rock taken from the ashes was put into water to see if any grease bubbles would rise. They did, in great plenty. It was discovered that fresh ashes had been poured in a mortar hole near the spring. Pieces of bone and flesh were found there: also, a heel-iron, such as Charles wore on his hunting moccasins. After all this evidence, strong and convincing, was found, a jury was summoned and an inquest held. As an immediate result, Franky her mother and youngest brother were arrested. All were bound over to court.

The Trial and Execution

"A more thorough investigation about the place revealed substantial proof. On the ground, under the house, beneath a dark spot on the floor a circle of blood as large as a hog's liver was found and the walls were specked. There could be no doubt. Charles had been murdered and his body burned.

"Franky was tried at Morganton at about the third court after she killed Charles. She got out of jail, dressed in a man's clothing and escaped into the country, following the wagon of her uncle. The sheriff of the county, discovering that his prisoner had fled, hurried on her trail and overtook her several miles out of town. He rode up close and said: 'Franky.' She turned and answered: 'I thank you, sir, my name is Tommy.' 'Yes,' her uncle put in, 'her name is Tommy.' He gave himself and the woman away by saying 'her.' She was returned to her prison cell and on the appointed day, the 12th of July, 1833, in the presence of a great throng of people, hanged. It was hoped that she would make a public confession on the scaffold, and she seemed prepared and ready to do so, but her father yelled out from the midst of the crowd: 'Die with it in you, Franky.' There was a sight of folks there to see her hanged.

Franky Stewart (that was her maiden name) was a mighty likely little woman. She had fair skin, bright eyes and was counted very pretty. She had charms. I never saw a smarter little woman. She could card and spin her three yards of cotton a day on a big wheel.

"The motive for the crime will never be known. Jealousy, she claimed, in a printed ballad that she made, gave rise to the first thought. No one could ever imagine any one that she had cause to be jealous of, for Charles was true to her. He laughed and talked with the women of his acquaintance, but that was all.

The Fate of the Stewarts

"The surviving members of the Stewart family met violent deaths, in one form or another. The old man, Franky's father, lost his life while cutting a rail-tree; a limb struck him on the head and crushed out his brains. The mother died from the effects of a snake-bite, and was in great agony the last hours of her life. Jack, one of the brothers, was killed during the civil war. Joe met a sudden death, but I have forgotten the facts concerning it. Blackstone, the brother charged with helping her burn my brother, went to Kentucky, stole a horse and was hung for it. All went. It looks like God made way with them on purpose. I believe that they all conspired to kill Charles. It was a horrible deed. He was such a fine fellow. We loved him."

Thus ends the story of the old man. It was told with the directness and power that inspires a truthful man.

LUCINDA SILVER NORMAN

[As summarized in Muriel E. Sheppard, *Cabins in the Laurel* (Chapel Hill: University of North Carolina Press, 1935), pp. 31–39.]

In her ninetieth year Aunt Cindy Norman, sister of the murdered man, gave W. W. Bailey, of Spruce Pine, the following account of the killing.

In the winter of 1831 Charles Silvers was living in the Deyton Bend with his wife, Frankie, and their baby daughter. Very early on the morning of December 23rd Frankie dropped in at her father-in-law's and found the family preparing to wash. "My washing is done and I've scoured too," she boasted, and her mother-in-law marvelled at her smartness to do a day's work before dawn. Frankie went on to tell the reason for her visit. Charlie had gone over the river on the ice the day before for his Christmas liquor, and had not returned. She was worried and begged his people to took at the crossings to see if he had fallen through. They searched the river for a considerable distance, but there was neither trail nor break in the ice. When he was still absent after several days, other families joined in the search. Frankie shook the valley with her lamentations. Word of the strange disappearance seeped into the country around Bear Creek and Art'ur's Knob.

An old man named Jakie Collis determined to go and walk over the ground himself to satisfy his curiosity on certain points. He went first to the father's house, where Cindy Silvers, the eight-year-old sister of the lost man, offered to take him to Charlie's empty cabin. Frankie had by now given up his return and refused to stay there alone with her grief. At the deserted cabin Jakie and Cindy and others who had joined them scrutinized closely the mantel and sides of the fireplace. There were fresh irregular chippings at intervals over the whole surface where someone had hewn lightly with an axe. It gave Jakie an idea.

"Help me lift the puncheons," he said to one of the men.

The upper surface of the slabs was neatly scoured, but the rounded sides underneath were streaked at the cracks with old blood stains. There was a fresh layer of ashes between the puncheons and the earth. Old Jakie thrust his hand into them and found them clotted with what appeared to be dried blood. Just then Frankie, who had watched from a distance, pushed her way among the men like a mad woman and ordered them off. The men stood still, looking at her with horror in their eyes that told her what they suspected. They went on with their work. In a frenzy of despair she wept and swore and made wild protestations while she saw the men sift the ashes in the fireplace and find human teeth and the remains of bones showing hack marks. Somebody realized that the big pile of hickory wood that had stood by the door was gone. When they looked at the axe, its edge was dulled with chopping something other than wood. The facts were plain enough without Frankie's extraordinary behavior. They sent for the sheriff to take charge of her.

More evidence came to light as the weather grew warmer. The investigation of a hollow sourwood where a dog sniffed suspiciously revealed the intestines and other parts of the body that did not burn readily. The horror of the tragedy shook the Valley from end to end.

Judge Donnell sentenced Frankie to death at the June term, 1832. She appealed, but Judge Ruffin sustained the conviction. When there was no hope through the regular channels of the law, her kinfolks took a hand in the affair. They spirited her out of jail and took her through the streets in a load of hay. As soon as they were out of town, Frankie climbed off the wagon. Dressed in a man's clothes and carrying a gun, she tramped behind the hay. The sheriff's posse overtook the suspicious load too quickly for her to crawl back out of sight. She tried to brazen it out.

"Want to buy some hay?" she asked in the deepest possible voice.

"No. We don't want hay," answered the sheriff, helping himself to the gun. "But we do want you, Frankie."

It was no use. She went back to jail. In the beginning she had protested her innocence. Now when there was no hope she made full confession.

According to her story she had been goaded by jealousy to kill her husband, and was awaiting the first opportunity to do it. On the night of December 22nd, he came into the house tired and cold from a day spent chopping wood to last over Christmas. He had a big pile of hickory chunks laid by to show for his labor. After supper he took the baby in his arms and lay down on a sheepskin in front of the fire to get the chill out of his bones. The axe lay handy, and in her anger she longed to seize the chance to kill him. In case she should find courage to go through with it, she gently slid the sleeping baby out of his arms. He did not waken.

At last, to end the torment of indecision, she seized the axe and tried to sever his head from his body in one mighty stroke. The blow glanced, and Charlie, horribly mutilated, sprang up and thrashed about making noises that frightened her half to death. She jumped into bed and covered her head to shut out the sound until he commenced to grow quieter from loss of blood. There was no way but to go on with it now. When she could muster courage, she got out of bed and struck the blows that quieted him forever. The rest of the night she spent dismembering and burning the body. It took a hot fire, and in a single night she used the whole of the Christmas hickory. Then in that blazing, suffocating cabin she carefully whittled away the spatters of blood and grease from the mantel and sides of the fireplace and scoured every stain from the floor that had been generously smirched as the body thrashed about. She washed the spattered bedding. That was the washing of which she boasted to her mother-in-law a few hours later.

Frankie Silvers must have had some feeling, because in the last days of her imprisonment she contrived a long, gloomy poem which she recited from the scaffold before her execution, July 12, 1833.

The Frankie Silvers Song

On one dark and dreary night
I put his body out of sight.
To see his soul and body part
It strikes with terror to my heart

[14 more stanzas]

Throughout her trial and imprisonment Frankie maintained a philosophic indifference. People whispered that she had not told all she knew; that some of her kinfolks helped her murder her husband and she was shielding them; that even as she mounted the scaffold, she expected a pardon. Everyone looked forward to a spectacular last moment develop-ment. At the top of the gallows steps Frankie indicated to the hangman that she wanted to say something. Now it was coming.

"Die with it in you, Frankie!" called her father from the crowd.

But Frankie was not going to tell anything more than everyone knew already. She wanted to read her poem. One story says that she had a piece of cake in her hand as she ascended the gallows platform. When the hangman asked if she were ready, she said that she would be when she finished eating her cake. Then Frankie Silvers pulled the black cap down over her face herself and shut out the daylight forever.

At that period it was the custom of the state to turn over a hanged man's body to medical students for dissection. There were many peti-tions for Frankie's body because a woman's corpse was hard to obtain. The father, harassed with the fear of such ignominy for his daughter, caused several graves to be dug before the execution, all of which were made into mounds by the following morning. Meanwhile he spirited the body away. The night after the execution it lay hidden under sacks in the barn of the Buck Horne Tavern ten miles from Morganton. Then it was secretly buried in a private burying ground nearby.

The words of the poem were eagerly seized upon by a countryside familiar with the dramatic story. It became a song, but it could be sung only when no members of either family were present, lest they be re-minded of the tragedy. This is not a feud country, and while neither family took up the grudge, everyone felt that it was better not to meddle with fresh wounds. The song survives today in an eerie, mournful tune whose urgent minor beat is the restless scurrying of unlaid ghosts in lonely places.

LATTIMORE HUGHES

[Interview by Bobby McMillon, Bowditch, North Carolina, 1975. Transcribed by Daniel W. Patterson.]

BM: Did you ever hear anybody talk about Frankie Silvers and Charlie?

LH: Unh-hunh.

BM: Who was the first 'un you ever heard tell that story, do you guess?

LH: (Laughs). I don't know. Frankie Silvers—that there was the woman that killed her husband.

BM: Well, where did they live at? Didn't they live up there at Kona?

LH: Yes—lived right up there at Kona.

BM: What did her man do for a living?—Charles, wasn't that his name?

LH: Yeah. I don't reckon he done anything but farm. They wasn't no public work back in them days, I don't reckon. Just lived kind of like the Indians.

BM: I wonder if he done any hunting or was a trapper?

LH: Yeah, he trapped all the time. That's the reason that, they claimed, after she killed him, her daddy backtracked hisself from there to the river, where he went trapping around the riverbank. Big snow, you see. Backtracked hisself, and the people thought he'd went down there, and got drownded and never come back. His tracks just—he backtracked hisself—walked backwards.

BM: Well, was her daddy the reason they done it?

LH: Yeah. Her daddy was cause of 'em a-killing him. He made her to do it, they said.

BM: How did that come about? What had he been a-doing?

LH: Well, I don't lie. I don't reckon her daddy liked him, something, going to get rid of him, and made her kill him. He had one kid.

BM: Well, how did she kill him, do you reckon? What led up to it? What he'd been a-doing?

LH: He cut wood all that day. And it a-pouring down with snow. Said he chopped and hauled wood in all day and piled the porch house full. Then he was tired after supper and she made him a pallet down before the fireplace, so he could lay down and rest, take a nap. He laid down there and this old man had the ax there and just as sharp as a razor, her daddy. And he went and got the ax and brought it to her, told her, said, "Now's your time." She drawed back to hit him, and he'd smile at her, and him a-sleep. She said, "Dad, I can't." "Yeah, now's the time. If you don't, I'll kill you. If you don't, I'll kill you." She kept right on, she hit him one lick. Then he grabbed the ax and finished it. And said the head bounced and hit the ceiling. Now I don't—the blood splattered all over the ceiling up there and on the floor. And that little kid was laying in his arms asleep, and it waked up and crawled on its hands in the blood and walked to the table and took ahold of the table—and found its fingers and hands on the table, with that blood. They couldn't wash or scour it off. That's people's talk. I used to hear old people talk about it.

BM: How come them to find her out, do you reckon?

LH: Well, they missed him, and everybody worried the snow to the river and claimed he got around it. Had no way of searching the river, I don't reckon, for him. And the dog got barking and taking on and howling. They kept watching the dog—he'd go down the road where they took his head and part of his insides and buried them in a rock, and howl and bark and take on. They watched the dog till they found out, and then he'd try to get under the floor where they'd buried so much of him under the floor, and howl and bark and take on, and they got under there, dug under there and found it. And they know'd some of 'em killed him.

BM: Well, wasn't there something about her playing ball?

LH: Yeah, she, she put on men's clothes and got out, passing ball with other men, and she'd grab down to her apron and jerk it up every time they'd throw the ball at her. They say a woman'll do that. I don't know. Try to catch the ball in their apron. Kept on watching her that way. She had her hair cut, and everything, like a man. And they pulled her off a wagonload of hay, when they got regular truth on her. She's a-riding on a wagonload of hay with another man, where they hauled hay. And the law pulled her off the wagonload of hay. Took her to jail. Then when they hung her, they took her to the gallows, I reckon that's what you call it, put her on the scaffold. Her daddy stood right by her. "Die with it in you, Frankie, die with it in you." That's all he would say to her. Then I think she sung some kind of old song on the scaffold, before they hung her.

BM: Did you ever hear it sung?

LH: Yeah. Somebody used to have it down there, somebody that printed it.

BOBBY McMILLON

[From "Die with It in You, Frankie." In *A Celebration of American Family Folklore: Tales and Traditions from the Smithsonian Collection*, edited by Steven J. Zeitlin, Amy J. Kotkin, and Holly Cutting Baker, pp. 104-8 (New York: Pantheon Books, 1982).]

Well, my great-great-grandfather was a first cousin to Charlie Silvers that got his head cut off. Charlie's wife, Frankie, cut his head off, cut his body up, and burned it all night. Hid part of his remains in a log—his lights, the guts, the parts that won't burn, under a rock. He was buried in a little family cemetery up on the ridge above where she killed him, what was left of him, what they could find. And she was the first woman ever hanged in North Carolina, or legally anyway. My mother was raised just about a half a mile from where that happened. Oh Lordy, I've heard that all my life. Well, I tell you, it's even been put in books.

I tell it to you like my uncle Latt told me because he told it different than anybody else. He said it wasn't Frankie that started it, it was her daddy. I don't know what they had against Charlie, but he was a trapper. This was way back before the Civil War, a long time ago. It was nearly Christmas and Charlie had been out cutting wood all that day to burn all during Christmas. There was a big snow on the ground. They lived in a little shantylike cabin that just had two rooms, a kitchen-livingroom where the fireplace was, and a back bedroom. And they had a daughter — she couldn't have been more than a year old; she was still crawling.

So anyway, my great-great-uncle Latt told me that her daddy was down to supper that night and Charlie had got through cutting that tree down. He had piled up the wood and come in and eaten supper. And they said that when Charlie got in, he said, "I'm beat, I think I'll lay down." And Frankie said, "Well, I fixed a pallet for you by the fireplace. I thought you might want to take a nap before you got ready to go to bed." [Laughs] I don't know why he wanted to take a nap before he got ready to go to bed to sleep again. But anyway, he got the baby and laid down there in front of the fireplace and went to sleep. And when he got to sleep, my great-uncle said that her daddy said, "Now's your chance, Frankie."

And they said she went and laid the baby in the back room. Then she took the ax that Charlie had brought in and come back in there. Charlie was laying on his back, and they said everytime she'd come back to take a swing at him, he would smile at her in his sleep. And she swung about three times and her arm about give out. "Well," she said, "I just can't do it. I can't kill him like this." And her pap said, "If you don't kill him, I'll kill you and him both." So I reckon she figured she better go ahead. And they said that finally she come down and give one hit in the head. They claim that he jumped up and screamed, "God bless the child." And she run back there in the bedroom and jumped under the covers and hid. She was so scared. Well, according to my uncle Latt, when she went in there her daddy took the ax and he come back and cut Charlie's head square off. They said he hit him so hard that his head bounced against the rafters of the cabin.

And they said about that time the baby got up and was crawling, and they said it crawled in its own dad's blood. And they said it got over there to the table where it tried to stand itself up with its hands, and it left blood prints on the table. They said you couldn't wash them off or nothing. You couldn't get them off.

So Uncle Latt said Frankie's daddy cut him up and done all that dirty work hisself. And he used all that wood Charlie had cut up to last through Christmas and burned his body all night long. And they said he took Charlie's head and put it under a stump, an old hollow stump, and that he put on his boots to carry the rest of him and put it under a rock. I've seen that rock a hundred times. And then he went down to the river, the Toe River that runs by the foot of that holler, about half a mile down the road there. And he walked in the snow down there and then backtracked up. And of course it was put out that Frankie claimed that Charlie had went across the river for his Christmas liquor and hadn't come back.

It got to be two or three days, and everybody was wondering what had happened to him. They said this old man, I forget his name—I think they called him Dickie Collins—lived over cross the mountain somewhere and had been a' noticing Charlie's dog. It had always been with Charlie, and he said the dog would go up to the house and holler and just bark and go on. And Dickie just got suspicious, so one day when Frankie was out he went down there to the house and got to looking around. And he found some bloody chips and things around the fireplace, and he lifted up the floor boards and found blood down under there. So word got out that he had been killed. I mean that was evidence enough to know.

And they always told something about how his daddy had went over to Tennessee where they had this New Guinea slave that had what they called a conjure ball, or something. You'd ask it a question and it would swing. And however it was that they was asking it, they said it would swing right toward the house. When they come back they arrested Frankie. I reckon they got her to confess to killing him.

At that time the county seat was in Morganton, North Carolina, almost fifty miles away on the east side of the Blue Ridge Mountains. You had to go plum over there to the courthouse. They took her over there where they had her trial and they found her guilty and sentenced her to be hung.

I don't know if she bribed the jailer or who it was, but anyway, her family slipped her out and was trying to get back over the mountains. They had her hair cut off short like a man's and she was wearing a big old hat and walking alongside a haywagon. Her uncle was up in the hay-wagon driving. The sheriff comes up and says, "Where are you going, Frankie?" And she turned around and tried to put on a man's voice and said, "Thank you, sir, but my name is Tom." And they said her uncle turned around and said, "Yes sir *her* name is Tom." And so they knew right then who it was and took her back in to jail.

Before they hung her she was supposed to have sung this song, an old ballad that they sing back up there now. They just call it "Frankie Silvers' Ballad." I don't know whether she did sing it or not. They claim up there that that's how the Frankie and Johnny story got started. Course the Frankie and Johnny song ain't nothing like the song that she sung. But I reckon it just rolled over.

According to the best I ever heard, when they were taking her body back across the mountains to bury her—you know, they didn't have no embalming in them days—that she just got to stinking so bad that finally they had to bury her on the way, somewhere close to where Lake James is now. And they got her husband Charlie's remains and buried him in the graveyard up on the hill with the Silvers family.

People never could figure out why she done it, unless it was jealousy. In the song there's a rhyme that says "the jealous thought that first gave strife." They don't know why she was jealous. One of [Charlie's] brothers who lived to be way up in his nineties told years and years later that there wasn't never nothing bad come out on him. And in communities like that nothing happened that wasn't found out and told, you know. My grandmammy's uncle was the only one that I ever heard say that her daddy was there eating supper with them that evening, and that he done it. He's way up in his eighties, or close to eighty anyway now, and its not been a year ago since he told me that.

But they did always say that before she hung she was about to tell something and her mother or her daddy either one hollered out, "Die with it in you, Frankie." They say she just didn't say anything.

Frankie's daughter, the little baby, I think her mother kept it for a while, but most of them moved off. But her girl married somebody from Madison County, I think. And then *her* daughter, Frankie's granddaughter, married my grandmother's uncle. Anyway that's about all I know about it.

APPENDIX B

Variants of the Ballad "Frankie Silver" (Laws E 13)

CHECKLIST OF RECORDINGS

Clarence Ashley and Gwen Foster, "Frankie Silvers." Vocal with guitar
and harmonica. 4 stanzas. 78 rpm disc. Recorded September 8, 1933.
Vocalion 02647.

Clarence Ashley and Tex Isley, "Frankie Silvers." Vocal with guitar.
5 stanzas. On *Clarence Ashley and Tex Isley*, recorded by Ralph
Rinzler, edited by Peter Seigel, notes by Jon Pankake, 1966. 33⅓
rpm disc. Folkways Records FA-2350.

Clarence Green and Byrd Moore, "Frankie Silvers' Confession." Vocal
with fiddle and guitar. 78 rpm disc. Recorded February 14, 1930.
Gennett 16267-A. [Never released, and presumed to be lost.]

Isaac G. Greer, "Frankie Silver." 5 stanzas. 78 rpm disc, Arthur P.
Hudson Collection. NCU-SFC, FD-100.

Bascom L. Lunsford, "Frankie Silvers." 5 stanzas. 78 rpm disc, Jan P.
Schinhan Collection. NCU-SFC, FD-250.

Bobby McMillon, "Frankie Silvers' Confession." Tape of tunes of
songs in Bobby McMillon Song Collection notebooks, recorded by
Jim McGee. NCU-SFC, tape #4. [Two tunes, one learned from Lou
Brookshire, the other from Lou Hopson.]

Bobby McMillon, "Frankie Silvers' Confession." 8 stanzas. Videotaped
by Tom Davenport, October 1992.

Bobby McMillon and Marina Trivette, "Frankie Silvers' Confession."
In *The Ballad of Frankie Silver*, with epilogue "The Making of a
Ballad Singer." VHS videocassette, color, 55 minutes. Delaplane, Va.:
Tom Davenport Films, 1999.

Byrd Moore and His Hotshots, "Frankie Silvers." Vocal with fiddle,
guitar, and banjo. 5 stanzas. 78 rpm disc. Recorded October 23,
1929. Columbia 15536-D. Reissued on *Old Time Southern Ballads and
Songs*. 33⅓ rpm disc. Old Timey LP-102.

New Lost City Ramblers, "Frankie Silvers." On *The New Lost City Ramblers,* vol. 4, 1962. Folkways FA-2399.

Toe River Valley Boys, "Frankie Silvers." 5 stanzas. On *Toe River Country,* 1968. 33⅓ rmp disc. Rite Record GHP-903.

Hedy West, "Frankie Silvers." 7 stanzas. On *Pretty Saro and Other Appalachian Ballads.* 33⅓ rpm disc. Topic Record 12T146.

Note: A recording listed as "Frankie Silver" in *Time Stands Still* and various other recordings by the "heavy-metal" band The Divine Horsemen is actually a version of "Frankie and Johnny."

CHECKLIST OF TEXTS

Unpublished

"Ballad of Frances Silver." 15 stanzas. "This copy made for W. C. Silver by Monroe Thomas from copy owned by Bryan Robinson, of Bandana, N.C."; currently displayed in the Silver Family Museum, Kona, N.C. Facsimile reproduction in Silver, *Frankie's Song,* 72–74.

"Francisco Silver (Execution Song)." 1 stanza, with tune. "Mr. Macdonald Franklin at Berea, KY, May 26, 1917." D. K. Wilgus Papers, No. 20003, NCU-SFC.

"Frankie Silvers Confession." 17 stanzas. Bobby McMillon Ballad Notebooks, Book 4, no. 15, NCU-SFC.

"Song Ballad." 8 stanzas, fragment. "Written Feb. 15th 1865 Song Ballad for Margaret A. Henry Copied By James T. Henry." Manuscript in the possession of the late Lawrence Wood of Macon County, N.C.; 2 stanzas printed in Young, *Untold Story,* 115.

"Song Ballate." 11 stanzas. Manuscript (ca. 1883) in the possession of the late Lawrence Wood, Macon County, N.C.; 2 stanzas printed in Young, *Untold Story,* 115.

"Song Ballet." 17 stanzas. Collected from "E. N. Caldwell, N.C., 1913," E. C. Perrow Collection, Western Kentucky University Folklore Archive.

Published

"Frances Silvers." 15 stanzas. "Obtained from Miss Ronnie Johnson, Crossnore, Avery County, N.C., July 12th, 1929." In Henry, *Songs Sung in the Southern Appalachians,* 48–50.

———. 4 stanzas. "Collected from Marie Wilbur of Pineville, Mo., in 1934." In Randolph, *Ozark Folksongs*, 2:125.

"Frances Silver's Confession." 13 stanzas. "We publish, by request, the following confession." *Morganton Star*, March 27, 1885, [3]. Very widely reprinted in later articles and in books.

"Francis Silvers." 15 stanzas. "Contributed by M. I. Pickens, a student in Trinity College, Sept. 22, 1922." In Belden and Hudson, *Folk Ballads from North Carolina*, 701–3.

"Frankie Silver." 2 tunes with the first stanza, without attribution. In McCall, *They Won't Hang a Woman*, 46–47.

"Susie Silvers." 12 stanzas. Not dated or attributed; like Pickens's text but lacking the last three stanzas. Cited but not printed in Belden and Hudson, *Folk Ballads from North Carolina*, 703.

[Untitled]. In Bryant, "Horrible Deed of a Wife." 15 stanzas. From Bryant's interview with Alfred Silver but not presented as learned from him: "The following verses were printed on a strip of paper and sold to people who assembled at Morganton to see Franky Silver executed. It is claimed that she composed it and gave it out as her confession." Very widely reprinted in later articles and in books.

APPENDIX C

Artistic Treatments of the Frankie Silver Story

BALLET

The Ballad of Frankie Silver. Choreographed by Cathy Sharp,
    performed by Tanz Ensemble Cathy Sharp, with musical score by
    Panaiotis. Premiered in Basel, Switzerland, 1992.

CLASSICAL MUSIC

Panaiotis. *The Ballad of Frankie Silver.* Kingston, N.Y.: PanDigital
    Corporation and Maverick Music Projects, Inc., 1994.

DRAMAS

Erwin, Susan Graham. *The Ballad of Frankie Silver.* Unpublished,
    premiered at Mars Hill College, 1977.
McCall, Maxine. *They Won't Hang a Woman.* Adapted by Cheryl
    Oxford. Unpublished, produced in Morganton, 1977 and
    subsequent years.
Williams, Howard. *The Legend of Frankie Silver.* Unpublished,
    premiered at Parker-Brewton College, Mount Vernon, Ga., 1993.

FICTION

Farlow, Fran. "Frankie." Unpublished manuscript of a completed novel
    about Frankie Silver.
McCall, Maxine. *They Won't Hang a Woman.* Burke County Cultural
    Project. N.p.: Burke County Public Schools, 1972.
McCrumb, Sharyn. *The Ballad of Frankie Silver.* New York: E. P.
    Dutton, 1998.
Rhyne, Nancy. "Poetry on the Gallows." In *Murder in the Carolinas,*
    pp. 14–22. Winston-Salem: John F. Blair, 1988. Fictional recreation
    of Frankie's story.

POEMS

Sheppard, Muriel Earley. "The Quiltin'." In *Cabins in the Laurel*, pp. 25–31. Chapel Hill: University of North Carolina Press, 1935.

VIDEOS

Davenport, Tom. *The Ballad of Frankie Silver, with The Making of a Ballad Singer,* featuring Bobby McMillon and Marina Trivette. VHS videocassette, color, 46 min. Delaplane, Va.: Tom Davenport Films, 1997.

Eller, Richard. *Frankie Silver's Deed: Crime and Punishment in the 1830s.* "Back Then . . ." Series. VHS videocassette, color, 30 min. Hickory, N.C.: Charter Communications, 1997.

Mull, David S. *The Frankie Silvers Story as Told by Geoff Wood.* VHS videocassette, color, 34 min. Morganton, N.C.: Crossroads Video Production, 1997.

Phillips, Theresa. *The Ballad of Frankie Silver.* Dramatization of screenplay. Mars Hill, N.C.: Legacy Films, in progress.

NOTES

ABBREVIATIONS

Archives
GLB   Governors' Letterbooks
GP   Governors' Papers
NcAr   North Carolina State Archives, Raleigh, North Carolina
NcU-NCC   North Carolina Collection, University of North Carolina
              Library at Chapel Hill
NcU-SFC   Southern Folklife Collection, University of North Carolina
              Library at Chapel Hill
PC   Personal Collection, David L. Swain Papers
SC   North Carolina Supreme Court Records
Tx   Texas State Library, Austin, Texas

Interviews with Bobby McMillon
Interview P/M   Interview by Beverly B. Patterson and Wayne Martin
Interview DP   Interview by Daniel W. Patterson
Interview TD   Interview by Tom Davenport

INTRODUCTION

1 Davenport gives an account of the filming and editing of his video in "Remarks on the Making of *The Ballad of Frankie Silver*."
2 Writings about Bobby include Wise, "About This Here Tom Dooley"; Kenkel, "Constant Aesthetic of Bobby McMillon" and "Frank Proffitt, Jr., and Bobby McMillon"; Dirlam, "Bobby McMillon." Bobby's performances can be heard on *Carolina Sampler* and *A Deeper Feeling*.
3 Bobby McMillon placed the originals of his notebooks in the Southern Folklife Collection at the University of North Carolina at Chapel Hill. For the collection, Jim McGee tape-recorded Bobby singing the melodies of the songs in his notebooks, and Beverly Patterson has transcribed all these tunes.
4 The American Traditional Culture Series—jointly produced by Tom Davenport Films and the Curriculum in Folklore at UNC–Chapel Hill—contains the following titles: *The Shakers* (1972), *Born for Hard Luck* (1976), *Being a Joines* (1980), *A Singing Stream* (1986), *The Ballad of Frankie Silver* (1999), and *When My Work*

Is Over: The Life and Stories of Louise Anderson (1999). Study guides are available for all of these but *The Shakers* and *When My Work Is Over*. Videos and guides can be ordered directly from the website of Davenport Films: http://www.davenportfilms.com/orderform.html.

5 In 1924 Ervin read a paper on Frankie Silver at a meeting of the Morganton Kiwanis Club. It was published a few days later in the local newspaper and again in his *Burke County Courthouses*, 27–31.

6 Sheppard, *Cabins in the Laurel*, 25–39.

7 B. Patterson, "Give Me the Truth!" The Davenport video is reviewed in the same issue; Patterson's essay, ones by Bobby McMillon, Tom Davenport, and several others, along with photographs not reproduced in this book, also appear in a special Frankie Silver issue of the *North Carolina Folklore Journal* (Baldwin and Patterson, *Bobby McMillon and "The Ballad of Frankie Silver"*).

8 Rountree, "Folk Music at WFDD and WUNC."

9 Interview TD, tape 5, p. 4.

CHAPTER ONE

1 Interview P/M, November 20, 1992, 12–13.
2 Interview DP, November 18, 1998, 18.
3 Interview TD, tape 5, p. 4.
4 Interview DP, May 27, 1997, 41–42.
5 Interview P/M, November 20, 1992, 5.
6 Interview TD, tape 1, 11.
7 Interview P/M, November 20, 1992, 5.
8 Interview TD, tape 1, 9.
9 Interview P/M, November 20, 1992, 4.
10 Ibid.
11 Ibid., 7, 5.
12 Interview DP, May 27, 1997, 27–29.
13 Interview P/M, November 20, 1992, 6.
14 Interview TD, tape 1, 8.
15 Interview DP, May 27, 1997, 30.
16 Ibid., 29. Maude Minish Sutton found that mountain singers she collected songs from in the Blue Ridge had a very similar response to the songs. See my essay "A Woman of the Hills."
17 Interview P/M, November 20, 1992, 6.
18 On Primitive Baptist singing traditions, see Beverly B. Patterson, *Sound of the Dove*.
19 Interview DP, May 27, 1997, 24–26.
20 Interview TD, tape 1, 8.
21 Interview P/M, November 20, 1992, 1–2.
22 Interview DP, November 18, 1998, 14.

23 Interview P/M, November 20, 1992, 8.
24 Ibid., 14–15.
25 Ibid., 8–9.
26 Ibid., 11, 14.
27 Ibid., 11–13.
28 Ibid., 20–21.
29 Ibid., 16–19.
30 Ibid., 6.
31 Interview DP, May 27, 1997, 32.
32 Ibid.
33 Ibid., November 18, 1998, 14.
34 Ibid., May 27, 1997, 43–45.
35 Ibid., November 18, 1998, 14.
36 Ibid., May 27, 1997, 43–45.
37 W. Silver, *Frankie's Song,* 94–97.
38 Interview DP, November 18, 1998, 10, 18.
39 Interview TD, tape 5, p. 4.

CHAPTER TWO

1 Bobby McMillon learned this tune, a variant of the shape-note hymn tune "Devotion," from "Granny" Lou Hopson of Green Mountain, N.C. The tune was transcribed by Beverly B. Patterson.

CHAPTER THREE

1 Transcriptions of many of the court records have been published; the occasional illegibility of some of the documents and the carelessness of the copyists, however, keep most of the transcriptions from being entirely reliable. For Burke County holdings, see Avery, *Official Court Record,* and Young, *Untold Story,* 131–38. A microfilm of the original documents is in NcAr, "Burke County Clerk." For official records preserved in NcAr, see Young, "Documents . . . of the N.C. Supreme Court," "Documents . . . in the Governor's Letterbooks," and *Untold Story,* 139–61. Young is also the author of examinations of the documents; see his essay "Frankie Silver and the Laws of God" and *Untold Story,* passim. Additional documents in NcAr not reprinted or cited in these sources are: Governor Swain's proclamation of respite to Frankie Silver (GLB 30:78–79), D. F. Caldwell's letter to Governor Swain on behalf of Jessee Barnett (GP 71:904–5), Governor Swain's proclamation of pardon to Jessee Barnett (GLB 30:341), and entries regarding the various cases in the Burke County Superior Court State Docket (CR 014.321.1, pp. 32, 61, 87, 88, 96, 97, 113, 125) and Minute Docket (CR 014.311.1, pp. 67, 69, 73, 84). There is a gap in the Minute Docket from the fall term of

1833 until 1851. NcAr also holds repetitive Supreme Court records relating to the case: Original Cases, 1800–1909, box 114, case 3018; "Common Law Cases Argued and Determined," SC 39:389–94, and "Minute Docket," SC 255:190. See also "The State v. Frances Silver," in Devereux, *Cases Argued*, 14:358–360.

2 A number of early documents spell this name "Blackston," presumably reflecting the local pronunciation; as in the case of the name Silver, I follow the spelling currently preferred by the family (see Olds, "Stewart Line").

3 "The State of No. Caro. v. Francis Silver," NcAr, SC, Box 114, Case 3018, 1–2.

4 Ibid., 3.

5 Ibid., 4; Devereux, *Cases Argued*, 14:359.

6 Court records do not make Powell's role clear, but Isaiah Stewart was to appear as a witness in his case. Different documents record the brother-in-law's name variously as "Barnett" or "Barnet."

7 Petition to Swain, March 25, 1835, NcAr, GP 71:904–5.

8 Ibid.

9 Charles Silver was born in October 1812 (see John Silver Harris, "Jacob Silver," in Bailey, *Heritage of the Toe*, 1:407). Judge Swain missed the court session after he overturned his sulky just west of Hillsborough, dislocating a shoulder, fracturing an arm, and giving one of his short ribs "rather a rude shock." He was laid up there for several weeks, not reaching Morganton until September 30 (see Wallace, "David Lowry Swain," 235, based on accounts in two of Swain's letters and an issue of the *Greensborough Patriot*). Frankie's execution was reported in "Frances Silver," *The Star*, August 2, 1833, 3.

10 See Jinnette, "Henry Spainhour"; Spainhower, "Obituary"; and Brown, "He Fashioned Beauty."

11 "The State of No. Caro. v. Frances Silver," NcAr, SC, Box 114, Case 3018, p. 3.

12 Spainhour, "Frances Silvers' Confession." A Howell family tradition offers corroboration and correction of one detail. It says that Thomas Howell, a neighbor and friend of Charlie, had made shoe buckles for him in his blacksmith shop and that at the trial he identified scorched buckles found at the house as the ones he made. See Larry Howell, "Thomas Howell."

13 "Horrible Outrage."

14 Petition to Stokes, NcAr, GP 65:339–40, 342–43.

15 Montell, *Killings*, 151; Waller, *Feud*, 86.

16 *Fifth Census*, 91.

17 My figures are based on the Burke County tax rolls for 1830, which may be incomplete—they do not include, for example, Col. John Carson and others of his family. But all the jurors do appear in the lists. William L. Baird's property was valued at $5,700, Robert McElrath's at $2,200, and Oscar Willis's at $1,200; Joseph Tipps was the one who had no land (NCAr, CR 014.703.3).

18 Cyrus P. Connelly served as a justice in 1811, Baird in 1831, Lafayette P. Collins in 1835, and Henry Paine in 1839. See Phifer, *Burke*, 416–21.

19 The jurors' property lay in six of the fifteen or more "companies" that divided the county for census, tax, and militia purposes. None of the jurors lived in the town

of Morganton (Smyth's Company) or in the bounds of Captain Cox's Company, where the Silvers and the Stewarts lived, or of Captain Burcheld's Company to the north of it, where magistrate David Baker and witness John Collis lived.

20 According to Dan W. Olds, Isaiah Stewart sold property in Anson County on November 15, 1825, and "must have soon left for the mountains"; he appears in the 1830 census for Burke County ("Stewart Line," 2–3).

21 Kemp P. Battle states that the attorney was Nicholas Washington Woodfin. Woodfin had told him of riding the mountains to secure signatures for petitions on Frankie's behalf (*Memories*, 90–91). Many other accounts have followed Battle's version. Contemporaneous legal documents, though, name only Thomas Worth Wilson as filling that role. He was a former legislator and a seasoned attorney; Woodfin had but recently been admitted to the bar. Information about Wilson's life comes from Ervin, "Thomas Worth Wilson" and "William Wilson."

22 David D. Baker, the magistrate who ordered the arrest of Frankie Silver, estimated the distance from Kona to the courthouse as "at least forty miles" in the Revolutionary War pension application he prepared for George Silver in 1833. See Bailey, *Heritage of the Toe*, 1:97.

23 Proclamation of pardon to James Lea, NcAr, GLB 29:123.

24 Langbein, "Criminal Trial," 312 and passim.

25 Blackstone, *Commentaries*, book 3, p. 369.

26 Starkie, *Practical Treatise*, vol. 1, pt. 1, sec. 58, p. 83.

27 Welsh, *Strong Representations*, 10–12.

28 Battle, *Battle's Revisal*, 389.

29 Grant, *Our Common Law*, 39.

30 *Laws and Resolutions*, 167.

31 Petitions to Swain, NcAr, GP 67:209–10, 211–12. Swain's papers (NcAr, PC 84) contain numerous specimens of the handwriting of Woodfin, who acted for years as an agent in Swain's business dealings in western North Carolina.

32 Battle, *Memories*, 91.

33 Young quotes a personal letter in which Ervin states this in "Why Frankie Silver Swung," 122.

34 Ervin, *Burke County Courthouses*, 30–31.

35 McFarland, *"Counterfeit" Man*, 93–99.

36 Proclamation by Stokes, December 5, 1831, NcAr, GLB 29:95.

37 Petition to Swain from Frances Silver through her lawyer Thomas Wilson, June 3, 1833, NcAr, GP 67:207, 208.

38 *Miners' and Farmers' Journal*, July 27, 1833, [3]. My own speculation is that Frankie's confession probably appeared in one of the lost issues of the Rutherfordton newspaper.

39 Wilson to Swain, June 12, 1833, NcAr, GP 65:231–32.

40 Ervin, *Burke County Courthouses*, 30–31.

41 Petition to Stokes, n.d., NcAr, GP 65:339–40.

42 It is a tactic that defense attorneys avoided in a later murder trial in a community

in Iowa where for years the husband had a reputation for abusing his wife. The strategy has the ironic consequence of suppressing the truth of an abused wife's experience. See Bryan, "Stories in Fiction and in Fact."

43 See also Gray, "Was the First Woman?" Gray discusses the case in the light of the "battered spouse syndrome" and recent North Carolina court cases.

44 Reprinted from the *Fayetteville Journal* in the *Raleigh Star*.

45 *Raleigh Register*, May 1, 1827, [3].

46 "State v. William Hussey," in Busbee, *Cases at Law*, 44:124.

47 This case and others, as well as the phrase "rule of thumb," are discussed in Kelly, "Rule of Thumb and the Folklaw."

48 Friedman, *History of American Law*, 88–89, 98, 278–80, 285.

49 Blackstone, *Commentaries* (1807), book 1, chap. 15, pp. 443–44.

50 Blackstone, *Commentaries* (1800), book 1, chap. 6, p. 75.

51 *Statutes of the Realm*, Stat. 320; PR, 2:239. See also Hanawalt, "Violence in the Domestic Milieu."

52 Record of the trial of Jenny, Johnston County, N.C., November 8, 1780, NcAr, CR 056.928.3, 1764–80, pp. 1–2; Johnson, *Ante-Bellum North Carolina*, 513.

53 Faller, *Turned to Account*, 49; see also Doody, "'Those Eyes,'" 59–62.

54 Petition of Barbary Stewart to the Court of Pleas and Quarter Session, signed "Th W Wilson attorney for Petitioner," Isaiah Stewart Estate Record, 1836, Burke County Estate Records, NcAr, CR 014.508.51.

55 Burke County Superior Court, State Docket, 1830–41, NcAr, CR 014.321.1, p. 61.

56 "Horrible Outrage."

57 Petition to Stokes, October 8, [1832], NcAr, GP 65:342–43.

58 Newland's letters suggest an enthusiastic and generous, if not entirely judicious, temperament. He was a surveyor and postmaster and represented Burke in the House of Commons from 1826 to 1828 and in the North Carolina senate in 1830. He ran unsuccessfully for the U.S. Congress in 1832, following which he got appointed surveyor general of the Northwest Territories and moved to Wisconsin, where he several times was elected to the legislature and served even as speaker of the house in the 1840s. He later fruitlessly sought appointments in Washington and died there in 1857, a suicide by drowning, according to Wheeler, *Reminiscences and Memoirs*, 93–94. See also White, "History of Alexander County," 14.

59 Wilson to Swain, June 12, 1833, NcAr, GP 67:231.

60 Battle, *Memories*, 90–91.

61 Petition to Stokes, n.d., NcAr, GP 65:339–40. The 1820 census of Anson County indicates that Isaiah's household held two females, one aged 26–45 (Barbara) and one aged 0–10 (Frankie). The 1830 census of Burke County lists in his household a daughter 15–20, who would be Frankie.

62 Barbara Stewart, as administrator of his estate, signed with her mark the "Inventory of the Property of Isaiah Steward Decd" (Isaiah Stewart Estate Record, Burke County Estate Records, NcAr, CR 014.508.51). Isaiah used his mark to sign the January 13, 1832, complaint against the improper jailing of Frankie, Barbara, and Blackstone, and Jackson used his mark to sign "State vs Franky Sil-

vers summons for deft Edward Wilson & others To March Term 1832" (Burke County Clerk of the Court Papers, Burke County Superior Court, C 014.30023).

63 Bevens to Swain, June 30, 1833, NcAr, GLB 30:83.

64 Petition to Swain from Frances Silver through her lawyer Thomas Wilson, June 3, 1833, NcAr, GP 67:207.

65 Bailey, *Heritage of the Toe*, 1:456.

66 Guadalupe County Tax Rolls, 1846-88, Texas State Library, Austin.

67 Olmsted, *Journey through Texas*, 231.

68 J. H. Coleman to "Dear Uncle David," Travis County, Texas, January 21, 1861, NcAr, PC 84:6.

69 Wilson, "To the FREEMEN and Voters."

70 Bennett, *Chronology*, 123-24; Kirkman, "William Julius Alexander."

71 Wilson to Swain, June 12, 1833, NcAr, GP 65:232.

CHAPTER FOUR

1 Roba Stanley's 1925 recording—reissued on *Country and Western Classics: The Women*—is actually a variant of "Frankie and Johnny," a different song, which local people confused with the ballad "Frankie Silver."

2 Interview DP, May 28, 1997, 1-3, 16.

3 McMillon, "Die with It in You, Frankie."

4 Bryant, "Horrible Deed of a Wife." Reprintings include, among others, Turpin, *Serpent Slips into a Modern Eden*, 49-59; *Watauga Democrat*, March 20, 1969; McCall, *They Won't Hang a Woman*, 55-58; Phillips, *One of God's Children*, 95-102.

5 Sheppard, *Cabins in the Laurel*, 25-39; John P. Arthur describes Lucinda Norman as eighty-eight years old in 1912 and gives what seems to be a short summary of an account by her that differs in some details from that given in *Cabins in the Laurel* (*Western North Carolina*, 294).

6 Botkin, *Treasury of Southern Folklore*, 323-27; Burt, *American Murder Ballads*, 16-18; Crissman, *Death and Dying*, 176.

7 Belden and Hudson, *Folk Ballads*, 699-703.

8 As presented by Bobby McMillon in his manuscript "A Fly in Amber," NcU-SFC, Bobby McMillon Papers).

9 Interview DP, May 27, 1997, 17.

10 "Frankie Silver," sung by Byrd Moore and His Hot Shots, reissued on *Old Time Southern Ballads and Southern Songs*, Old Timey LP-102.

11 Interview DP, May 27, 1997, 6.

12 Ibid., 13.

13 Interview TD, tape 5, p. 11. Bobby's account of these childhood years in his manuscript "A Fly in Amber" is included in Baldwin and Patterson, *Bobby McMillon and "The Ballad of Frankie Silver."*

14 Ibid., tape 2, pp. 11, 12.

15 South, ed., *"Window to Times Gone By"* and *"I Never Killed a Man."* Bobby's

brother-in-law Doug Trivette is from an old Watauga family. Like several generations of his ancestors, he makes and plays musical instruments.

16 Interview DP, November 18, 1998, 8.

17 Ibid., May 27, 1997, 16.

18 Brunvand, *Vanishing Hitchhiker* and four subsequent collections.

19 Young, *Untold Story*, preface. In a one-page letter that covered many of Young's points, Fran Farlow had earlier expostulated against an article on the case, writing, "You do your readers a disservice by perpetuating folk tales regarding the trial and hanging of Frankie Silver" ("Gastonia Reader").

20 West, *Lift Up Your Head, Tom Dooley*, xviii.

21 Dégh and Vázsonyi, "Legend and Belief," 293–94.

22 Dégh and Vázsonyi, "The Crack on the Red Goblet," 253. Additional insightful comments occur in an early, longer version of this essay published as "The Dialectics of the Legend."

23 A reaction Gray reported in a telephone conversation. His father's response was to tease him for having a lawyer's mind—and to remind him that he disrupted a Sunday school lesson as a small boy by asking how Mark knew what Jesus prayed in the Garden of Gethsemane, when he had just said Jesus was alone.

24 Interview DP, May 27, 1997, 16.

25 The law court as a storytelling venue has been a topic of considerable discussion in legal circles. See, for example, Abrams, "Hearing the Call of Stories" and "Narrative and the Normative"; Bennett and Feldman, *Reconstructing Reality*; Brooks and Gewirtz, *Law's Stories*; Papke, *Narrative and the Legal Discourse*; Thomas, "Narratives of Responsibility and Blame"; and West, *Narrative, Authority, and Law*.

26 Interview DP, May 27, 1997, 16.

27 Joyner, " 'Alice of the Hermitage,' " 253.

28 Interview DP, May 27, 1997, 8, 2, 15.

29 Ibid., 6, 16.

30 Woody, "Red Ribbon Marker."

31 From Bobby McMillon's annotation on a draft of the manuscript of this book. His note continues, "The epilogue to that is my recent discovery of a student at Burnsville Elementary School who borrowed his grandmother's alleged piece of the band and used it or a photograph of it with a written project which was displayed a year or two ago at the History Museum in Raleigh."

32 Interview DP, May 27, 1997, 12–13.

33 Ibid., 12.

34 Bolté, *Dark and Bloodied Ground*, 102.

35 Interview DP, November 18, 1998, 25–26.

36 Dégh, "The Legend Teller," in *Narratives in Society*, 82.

37 Dégh, "Processes of Legend Formation," in *Narratives in Society*, 234.

38 "Part of me," Bobby's annotation continued, "has always been grounded in the present world while my ears and spirit are ever listening to the sounds and watching the scenes from *Tir Nan Og*."

39 Interview DP, November 18, 1998, 15.

40 Ibid., May 27, 1997, 28–29. I have amended this quotation in two places with annotations Bobby made in the statement in my manuscript draft.

41 From Bobby's annotation on my draft manuscript of this chapter.

42 Bryant's family placed his papers in the North Carolina State Archives, but the collection holds nothing dating from so early in his career.

43 Arthur, *Western North Carolina*, 294.

44 Related to me in a telephone conversation in 1997 and in a letter dated December 27 of that year.

45 Knight, "Sheriff Jackson ('Jack') Stewart."

46 Interview TD, tape 1, p. 9.

47 Dégh, "Processes of Legend Formation," 234.

48 Interview DP, May 27, 1997, 3.

49 Ibid., 13.

50 Ibid., 15. In *The Village That Disappeared*, published in 1996, Susan G. Erwin reports that her grandfather Joseph J. Erwin, as a boy of fourteen, was in the crowd at Frankie's hanging and came home saying that Frankie "appeared about to speak and then fell silent after being ordered to do so by her father." The boy "repeated to his family what Frankie's father had said to her," which Susan Erwin describes as "the same words I have read in printed accounts written by different persons" (p. 9).

51 Walker, *Battered Woman Syndrome*, 19, and *Terrifying Love*, 152.

52 Interview DP, November 18, 1998, 1–2, 6, and telephone interviews for corroboration.

53 Interview DP, November 18, 1998, 1.

54 Marina Trivette makes this statement in the "The Making of a Ballad Singer," the epilogue to the Davenport video *The Ballad of Frankie Silver*. Marina's allusion is to the made-for-television movie *The Burning Bed*, starring Farrah Fawcett, broadcast on NBC, October 8, 1984.

55 "Return of the List of taxables of Capt Coxes Company taken in 1830 By Wm Dickson Esqr," p. [2] (NcAr, CR 014.703.3, 1830).

56 Interview DP, May 27, 1997, 18.

57 Charles is not listed among property holders in the Burke County tax lists for 1830, and there is no Burke County record of his holding a deed to property. Bobby's words are from his annotation on a manuscript draft of this chapter.

58 Interview TD, tape 4, p. 10.

59 Ibid., 2, 5.

60 Gerould, *Ballad of Tradition*, 89.

61 Child, *English and Scottish Popular Ballads*, 3:384–85 (Child 173).

62 See Buchan, *Ballad and the Folk*, chaps. 9–11; McCarthy, *Ballad Matrix*, 13–21, 57–82.

63 *Cecilia Costello: Recordings*, album notes, [2].

64 Abrahams, *Singer and Her Songs*, 9–10.

65 See Bleackley, *Hangmen of England*, 64.

66 Ritchie, "Account of the Watch-Houses."

67 Joseph Sobol allowed me to read a manuscript entitled "The Singing Bones,"

which he based on a Cleveland County oral tradition about a hanged man exhumed and boiled down to make a skeleton for a physician; for a second and similar case from the same county, see DePriest, "Chill of the Grave."

68 No one has so far been able to authenticate the accounts of any of these deaths. Alfred Silver's list of the family's misfortunes adds the violent death of Frankie's older brother, Jackson Stewart. The cause of that death seems well established. Jackson, who had a minor role in Frankie's legal proceedings, went on to serve in the Mexican War, become a lieutenant in the Confederate Army, and get elected sheriff of Mitchell County. He was shot and killed in the road by a group of Union soldiers. His death seems owing to both his political allegiance and his assertive personal character. See Knight, "Sheriff Jackson ('Jack') Stewart."

69 Young, *Untold Story*, 93.

70 Helms, "Murder of Patsy Beasly," 52. Helms's informant performs the song on the LP album *Hand-Me-Down Music*.

71 I quote from a manuscript notebook, one of three that in 1922 Sutton (then Maude Pennell Minish) sent to Professor George Lyman Kittredge at Harvard University. They survive in the university library manuscript collection (with a later typescript copy in the manuscript collection at Duke University). The Tom Dula songs and legends occur on pp. [42–52] of one of these unnumbered, untitled volumes. A typescript formerly in the possession of her daughter, Mrs. Robert A. Nelson, bears the title "Ballads Collected in Avery County, 1917–1918." This and other materials related to Sutton are now in the Southern Historical Collection at the University of North Carolina at Chapel Hill.

72 Interview DP, November 18, 1998, 19.

73 Interview P/M, November 20, 1992, 14–18.

74 From Bobby's annotation on a manuscript draft of this chapter.

75 Interview DP, November 18, 1998, 18.

76 Another piece of evidence of this wound is the account of S. C. Jones, who as a child during the Civil War years "used to lie awake at night in the Silvers home and see the ghosts of the murdered man and his executed wife come back to frighten the wits out of those who dared to live in the haunted cabin." He told a reporter in 1931 that "he could not dismiss it from his consciousness for years." See "Recalls Ghosts."

77 A motif commonly associated with murder sites. For a very similar example, see Montell, *Killings*, 18–19.

78 Interview TD, tape 5, p. 4, and tape 4, p. 6.

CHAPTER FIVE

1 *Raleigh Star*, August 2, 1833, 3.

2 Ibid., June 10, 1830, [3].

3 *Raleigh Register*, October 28, 1830, [3].

4 Cohen, *Poor Pearl, Poor Girl!*, 4–5.

5 Menzies and Smith, "Scarlet Enigma," 73.

6 Bryant, "Horrible Deed," 10.

7 "Francis Silvers' Confession," *Lenoir Topic*, March 24, 1885, 3, and "Frances Sivers' Confession," *Morganton Star*, March 27, 1885, 3. The 1865 manuscript copy was owned by the late Lawrence Wood of Macon County, N.C.; Young quotes the first two stanzas in *Untold Story*, 115.

8 "Frances Silver's Confession," *Lenoir Topic*, May 5, 1886, 4. Senator Sam J. Ervin Jr. reported that a Squire Waits A. Cook of Burke County told him "that the verses Frankie had allegedly written were composed by a Methodist minister whose surname was Stacy" (see *Burke County Courthouses*, 28). Spainhour writes with greater authority.

9 "Execution of Beauchamp," undated clipping from an unidentified contemporary newspaper, tipped inside the cover of a copy of *Beauchamp's Trial* in the Rare Book Collection of the Library of Congress.

10 *Heritage of Burke County*, 401.

11 Phifer, *Burke*, 85, 424, and Population Schedules, U.S. censuses of 1840 and 1850. Scott's name does not appear in the census of Burke County after the latter year.

12 See Laws, *Native American Balladry*, 268, no. dF38. Wallin's version is "The Murder of Colonel Sharp," on *"Crazy about a Song."*

13 Shearin and Combs, *Syllabus of Kentucky Folk-Songs*, 16.

14 In correspondence with a librarian at Transylvania College in Lexington, Ky., Shearin's widow referred to his papers' having been stored in a college vault. They have not been found at either Transylvania College or Occidental College in Los Angeles, where Shearin was teaching when he died.

15 Young, *Untold Story*, 114.

16 Frankie's authorship of the lines is unlikely also on another score: she doubtless could neither read nor write. Her father, mother, and older brother Jackson all signed court documents with an "X."

17 Palmer cites examples from 1569, 1576, 1594, and 1598 in *Sound of History*, 122.

18 Gatrell, *Hanging Tree*, 159.

19 Hindley, *Catnach Press*, 92.

20 See Hummel, *Southern Broadsides*.

21 Many of the broadside poems also were gathered, published, and widely circulated in small books like *The Forget-Me-Not Songster*, a highly popular one issued in American cities.

22 "A street hawker," writes Leslie Shepard, "could live for four to six weeks off an important murder. Often the ballad printers beat the conventional newspapers with the news, since they had no hesitation in describing the final scenes before they happened!" (*John Pitts*, 62).

23 From a version sung by Doug Wallin in Madison County, N.C., and recorded by Wayne Martin and Beverly Patterson (NcU-SFC, N.C. Arts Council Collection).

24 Interview P/M, November 20, 1992, 21.

25 "The Death of Birchie Potter," in Belden and Hudson, *Folk Ballads*, 683–84.

26 Interview P/M, November 20, 1992, 19. The text is printed, without this information, in Belden and Hudson, *Folk Ballads*, 721–22.

27 Otto A. Rothert, *A History of Muhlenberg County* (Louisville, 1913), 147, quoted in Wilgus, "Fiddler's Farewell," 203.

28 For an example of a farewell that dwells on the condemned person's crimes, see "Luke Huttons lamentation," in Collmann, *Ballads and Broadsides*, no. 54.

29 I. G. Greer sings "Frankie Silver" to the "Barbara Allen" tune in NcU-SFC, Arthur Palmer Hudson Collection, FD-100, Side B. The tune used by Clarence Green and the Toe River Boys in their commercial recordings is a distant variant of "Lord Bateman," in Sharp, *English Folk Songs*, 1:71.

30 The "Devotion" tune probably comes from ballad-tune stock, but it appeared early (1818) and often in shape-note tunebooks and gained wide circulation in the South. See Walker, *Southern Harmony*, 13, and White, *Sacred Harp*, 48. Bobby learned the "Devotion" melody for "Frankie Silver" from Granny Hopson.

31 Turpin, *Serpent Slips into a Modern Eden*, 59-60, 79. Turpin's eight-stanza revision of the ballad also omits stanzas common in other variants and revises many lines to make them more pious.

32 Bobby McMillon never heard these stanzas sung but was struck by them when he read them in Belden and Hudson, *Folk Ballads*, 2:701. He often uses them when he sings the song.

33 The recordings by Tom Ashley and Gwen Foster are on Vocalion 02647-B, those by Byrd Moore and His Hot Shots on *Old-Time Southern Ballads*, and those by the Toe River Valley Boys on *Toe River Country*. Clarence Green Sr. performed on the latter two recordings and copyrighted the arrangement.

34 One earlier text, dated 1865, is fragmentary. The stanza in which these lines occur is among the ones lost from that copy.

35 Collinson, *Traditional and National Music*, 210-11 and plate 18. Burns's poem has also entered oral tradition. The Scottish traveler singer Davy Stewart gives a stirring performance of it on *Heather and Glen*. For Stewart's text and tune, see Kennedy, *Folksongs of Britain and Ireland*, 776. For a comprehensive account of "McPherson's Lament," broadsides related to it, and American parallels, see Wilgus, "Fiddler's Farewell."

36 Jack K. Williams gives informative accounts of the public conduct of both trials and punishments in neighboring South Carolina (*Vogues in Villainy*, chaps. 4, 5).

37 Quoted in Patterson, "Woman of the Hills," 110.

38 Newsome, "Merrimon Journal," 311, 328, 329.

39 "Morganton and Its Surroundings," 4, in Silas McDowell Papers, NcU-SHC, no. 1554, ser. 2, no. 11.

40 Wilson to Swain, June 12, 1833, NcAr, GP 65:232.

41 Hoffer and Scott, *Criminal Proceedings*, xx.

42 Quoted in Masur, "Design of Public Executions," 25.

43 Battle, *Battle's Revisal*, 298, citing 1868-69 statute, chap. 167, sec. 9. The new state constitution of 1868 also redefined the object of punishments as "being not only to satisfy justice, but also to reform the offender, and thus prevent crime" (Art. 11, sec. 2).

44 Iredell, *Public Acts*, 1:9-10.

45 Iredell and Battle, *Revised Statutes*, 196, 204.

46 Simpson and Ervin, "David Tate," 415.

47 See John Lofland's analysis in "Dramaturgy of State Executions," 285–321.

48 *Raleigh Register,* November 8, 1830, [3]. For an eighteenth-century English precedent for clothing the condemned in a shroud, see the engraving of the 1724 execution of Stephen Gardener at Tyburn, in Bleackley, *Hangmen of England,* 46.

49 *Raleigh Register,* July 1, 1825, [3].

50 Newland to Stokes, September 6, 1832, NcAr, GP 65:203.

51 Friedman, *Crime and Punishment,* 76.

52 Masur, *Rites of Execution,* 94.

53 Hiergesell, "Here's More."

54 Erwin, *Village That Disappeared,* 9.

55 Friedman, *Crime and Punishment,* 26.

56 "Execution," *Raleigh Register,* May 4, 1827, [3].

57 Two of these texts—"The Dying Groans of Levi Ames" and "An Exhortation to young and old to be cautious of small Crimes, lest they become habitual . . . Occasioned by the unhappy Case of Levi Ames"—are reproduced in Winslow, *American Broadside Verse,* 100–103. The American Antiquarian Society has two others: "A Prospective View of Death: Being A solemn Warning to inconsiderate Youth, occasioned by the Trial and Condemnation of Levi Ames" and "The last Words and Dying Speech of Levi Ames."

58 In his *Southeastern Broadsides,* Ray O. Hummel does not report any printing of "Frankie Silver"—or, in fact, of any southern broadsides of criminals' farewells; newspapers were possible outlets for this kind of verse in the South, but they typically printed either comic poems or sentimental effusions, not topical verse.

59 Hay, "Property, Authority, and the Criminal Law," 18.

60 Bleackley, *Hangmen of England,* 30. The book contains numerous other accounts of threats and violence against hangmen.

61 Kane, "Wives with Knives," 232. This jargon-ridden essay and a somewhat more felicitous one by Dolan, "Home-Rebels and House-Traitors," grow from Michel Foucault, *Discipline and Punish.*

62 I echo one incisive word in Kane's awkward passage: "the ballads, consistently written in the voice of the condemned, not only present a ventriloquized and confessional feminine subject, but also carefully display the legal discourses, court apparatus, and punitive technologies which formulated, maintained, and ultimately claimed a prerogative to disrupt that subject" ("Wives with Knives," 219).

63 Smithsonian/Folkways CD SF 40012.

64 Interview P/M, November 20, 1992, 16.

65 Belden and Hudson, *Folk Ballads,* 683–84.

66 Interview DP, November 18, 1998, 23.

CHAPTER SIX

1 Newland to Stokes, September 22, 1832, NcAr, GP 65:216–17. Newland reports being told that seven of the signers were jurors; the only members of the jury to sign, however, were Richard Bean, Robert Garrison, John Hall, and Robert

McElrath, although two others—Joseph Scott and William Walker—were on the grand jury that presented a true bill. An additional juror, Oscar Willis, later signed the petition of June 3, 1833. Two witnesses for the defense in the original inquest—Isaac Grindstaff and William James Howell—signed one petition to Stokes, along with three other neighbors from the Kona community. Officers of the court who signed petitions included constable John H. Pearson (later sheriff), jailor John McGuire, and clerk of the court Burgess S. Gaither.

2 See Stokes's proclamations in NcAr, GLB 29. The pardon to Sally Barnicastle is no. 115.

3 Quoted in Wallace, "David Lowry Swain," 255.

4 Quoted in Foster, "Career of Montfort Stokes," 270–71.

5 Ibid., 272. See also Ruffin to Catherine, January 21, 1831, p. 1, NcU-SHC, no. 641, ser. 1.5, box 17, folder 239.

6 Foster, "Career of Montford Stokes," 269–70. Stokes's finest hour came later, in Oklahoma, where he felt a serious obligation to serve Native Americans and labored hard, if ineffectually, on their behalf. See Foreman, "Life of Montfort Stokes."

7 Wilson to Swain, June 12, 1833, NcAr, GP 67:231.

8 Bevens to Swain, June 30, 1833, NcAr, GLB 30:262.

9 With the exception of the Carsons, very few men of the wealthiest families signed any of the petitions.

10 For family backgrounds, see *Heritage of Burke County*, passim.

11 David L. Swain to George Swain, April 15, 1822, p. 1, NcU-NcC, Swain Epistolary Correspondence, vol. 2.

12 Swain to W. C. Bevens, July 9, 1833, NcAr, GLB 30:83–84.

13 This is the mileage given in *Table of the Post Offices*, [138–39].

14 David L. Swain to George Swain, April 24, 1822, NcU-NcC, Swain Epistolary Correspondence, vol. 2; James Martin Jr. to Swain, May 31, 1833, p. [2], ibid., vol. 4.

15 Only three persons signed petitions to both Stokes and Swain. It is possible that most saw no need, realizing that petitions sent to Stokes would remain on file and available to the new governor.

16 David L. Swain to George Swain, December 11, 1822, NcU-NcC, Swain Epistolary Correspondence, vol. 2.

17 George D. Philips to Swain, November 8, 1827, p. 1, ibid., vol. 3.

18 Swain to Eleanor W. Swain, January 4, 1828, pp. 2–3, ibid., vol. 5.

19 Fran Farlow to John S. Harris, February 15, 1992, in Silver, *Frankie's Stories*, 237. The name of James Lowry does not appear in the published *Muster Rolls* of 1812, which list Jacob Silver in the Third Regiment of Buncombe County (p. 137), nor is James's name in the State Archives' index to the pay vouchers from that war. But Jacob Silver's "Declaration for a Pension under Act of February 14, 1871, War of 1812," dated January 24, 1872, and signed by him with "his X mark" states that he volunteered in Captain Lowry's company (reproduced in facsimile in Harris, *Silver*, 51).

20 They are scattered through NcAr, PC 84.

21 Harris, *Silver*, 45, 51.

22 James Lowry to Swain, March 24, 1846, NcAr, PC 84:3).

23 Swain to Eleanor W. Swain, March 18 and 30, 1827, NcU-NcC, Swain Epistolary Correspondence, vol. 5.

24 William J. Alexander to Swain, Charlotte, December 21, 1832, ibid., vol. 4.

25 Account of the marriage of David Swain and Eleanor H. White, January 12, 1826, ibid., vol. 3.

26 See, for example, the account of the execution of John Sampson, *Hillsborough Recorder*, June 26, 1822, [2–3]; "Public Executions," *Raleigh Register*, May 11, 1839, [3]; the discussion of the sentences passed on slaves Green and Dick, *Hillsborough Recorder*, March 21, 1844, [3], and of the public whipping of two white men, *Raleigh Register*, April 7, 1846, [3]; and "The Death Penalty,—Public Executions," *Raleigh Register*, November 2, 1853, [3].

27 Swain, "Early Times in Raleigh," 262.

28 Spencer, "Old Times," no. 7, p. 102. Another early account says not one book was purchased for the university library during Swain's first twenty years as president (see Snider, *Light on the Hill*, 63).

29 Proclamation of pardon to John Malpass, NcAr, GLB 29:105.

30 Proclamation regarding Catherine Bostian, ibid., 30:28.

31 Swain to James M. Wiggins, April 7, 1834, ibid., 30:192.

32 Swain to Henry Potter, May 1834, ibid., 30:204.

33 Swain to Wiggins, April 7, 1834, ibid., 30:192. See also the discussion of the case in Wallace, "David Lowry Swain," 263–64.

34 Petition to Stokes, [October 8, 1832], NcAr, GP 65:342–43.

35 Petition to Stokes, n.d., ibid., 339–40.

36 David Newland to Stokes, September 6, 1832, ibid., no. 203. Frankie Silver has often been described as "the only woman ever hanged in North Carolina." While the execution of women had clearly been rare, there is evidence of others. In a letter dated October 29, 1832, Hugh M. Stokes wrote Governor Stokes that he had heard of one white woman executed in North Carolina "since the formation of our present government," but he does not give a name (ibid., nos. 256–57). Edward W. Phifer Jr. states that Frankie "is believed to have been the second in Burke County, the other being a slave named Betsey, hanged in the summer of 1813 for the murder of her master" (see *Burke*, 344). Young assembles evidence of a half-dozen others (*Untold Story*, 18–21). Records show additional executions of women in the state. The colonial Executive Council denied the "Petition of Eleoner Russel setting forth that she was under Sentence of death and praying to be reprieved." The entry is marked "Ordered for Execution," referring presumably to the sentence rather than a reprieve (see Cain, *Records of the Executive Council*, 131). In two earlier cases, those of "Jane Fenix alias Anderson" in 1715 and "Magdalen Collar alias Dictus Collard alias Colliar" in 1720, women were condemned to be hanged; there is no indication whether the sentences got carried out (see Price, *North Carolina Higher-Court Minutes*, 78, 212).

37 Petition to Swain from ladies of Burke and Buncombe counties, June 29, 1833, NcAr, GP 67:261.

38 Petition to Swain from Frances Silver through her lawyer Thomas Wilson, June 3, 1833, ibid., 67:208.

39 *North Carolina Spectator,* January 28, 1832, 3.

40 Petition to Swain from ladies of Burke and Buncombe counties, June 29, 1833, NcAr, GP 67:261.

41 Young, *Untold Story,* 36–37. Young relies on the inquest documents, which present a true bill and indicate fees billed against the husband for the costs of the inquest. Young mistakenly reports these fees as his sentence in the trial itself.

42 Burke County Superior Court, Minute Docket, p, 73, NcAr, CR 014.311.1; Burke County Superior Court, State Docket, 1830–41, p. 32, no. 24, NcAr, CR 014.321.1.

43 Petition to Stokes, n.d., NcAr, GP 65:339–40.

44 "State v. Aaron Norwood," Lincoln County Superior Court, State Docket, 1823–42, NcAr, CR 060.321.1, no. 8. Solicitor William Julius Alexander's bill of indictment is preserved in CR 014.326.3, 1835, Norwood folder.

45 Gray, "Was the First Woman?"

46 Petition to Swain, June 3, 1833, NcAr, GP 67:207.

47 *Miners' and Farmers' Journal,* July 27, 1833, [3].

48 Spainhour, "Frances Silver's Confession."

49 Battle, *Memories,* 90.

50 William F. Thomas to Swain, June 3, 1833, NcAr, GLB 30:213.

51 Battle, *Memories,* 90.

52 Knight, "Sheriff Jackson ('Jack') Stewart," 418.

53 *North Carolina Spectator,* January 28, 1832, 3.

54 The description of Scotch-Irish people encountered in the North Carolina Piedmont comes from Smyth, *Tour in the United States,* 1:236.

55 Hooker, *Carolina Backcountry,* 60.

56 Fischer, *Albion's Seed,* 606.

57 Caruthers, *Interesting Revolutionary Incidents.*

58 Caruthers, *Sketch of the Life,* 220–21.

59 One example is the legend that Mrs. Sarah Erwin defied and was mortally wounded by a British soldier attempting to kill an injured Whig she had sheltered (W. C. Erwin, "Sarah Robinson Erwin").

60 See Swain, *Declaration of Independence,* vi, and "British Invasion."

61 David L. Swain to George Swain, April 24, 1822, [1], [3], NcU-NcC, Swain Epistolary Correspondence, vol. 2.

62 G. Flower Diary, vol. 2, October 6, 1816, Chicago Historical Society.

63 Cartwright, *Autobiography,* 304–7.

64 Swain to Eleanor W. Swain, August 25, 1826, NcU-NcC, Swain Epistolary Correspondence, vol. 5.

65 Chamberlain, *Old Days in Chapel Hill,* 105.

66 *Greensborough Patriot,* April 14, 1830, p. 3, May 12, 1830, p. 3, October 24, 1832, p. 4, April 7, 1830, pp. 1–2, October 24, 1832, p. 4.

67 A Jacksonian paper from Salisbury, by contrast, printed one in praise of wives "in the middle ranks of life" (see "Mechanics' Wives," *Western Carolinian*, February 7, 1831, 1).

68 *Greensborough Patriot*, April 7, 1830, 1–2.

69 On McDowell's family connection to Swain, see Sutton, *Heritage of Macon County*, entry 438.

70 "Morganton and Its Surroundings," Silas McDowell Papers, NcU-SHC, no. 1554, ser. 2, no. 11, undated.

71 Quoted in Bennett, *Chronology*, 45.

72 Vance, "David Lowry Swain," 230, 232.

73 Wallace, "David Lowry Swain," 5. An account surprisingly detailed for a man so obscure occurs in Bennett, *Chronology*, 25–27.

74 George Swain Jr. to David L. Swain, n.d., quoted in Wallace, "David Lowry Swain," 8.

75 The description of Swain is quoted in Steiner, "South Atlantic States," 322–23.

76 Vance, "David Lowry Swain," 246.

77 Swain to Eleanor W. Swain, March 30, 1827, [2], NcU-NcC, Swain Epistolary Correspondence, vol. 5.

78 Swain to Gentlemen, May 29, 1834, NcAr, GLB 30:209.

79 Foster, "Career of Montfort Stokes," 237–39, 270–72.

80 Quoted in Wallace, "David Lowry Swain," 21.

81 David L. Swain, [Diary], p. 24, NcAr, PC 84.

82 Ibid., 21–24.

83 Wallace, "David Lowry Swain," 21.

84 Ibid., 7.

85 Swain, [Testimony], 56–58.

86 Swain to Eleanor W. Swain, June 12, 1840, [3], NcAr, PC 84:2.

87 Petition to Stokes, n.d., NcAr, GP 65:339.

88 John Giles to Swain, January 25, 1833, NcAr, GP 66:42.

89 "Horrible Outrage."

90 Petition to Swain from Frances Silver through her lawyer Thomas Wilson, June 3, 1833, NcAr, GP 67:207.

91 Wilson to Stokes, November 19, 1832, NcAr, GP 65:284.

92 Petition to Swain from Frances Silver, June 3, 1933, NcAr, GP 67:207.

93 Petition to Swain from ladies of Burke and Buncombe counties, June 29, 1833, NcAr, GP 67:261.

94 Spencer, "Old Times," no. 8, 157–58.

95 Swain to Eleanor W. Swain, January 4, 1832, 1, NcU-NcC, Swain Epistolary Correspondence, vol. 5.

96 James Philips to Swain, September 8, 1861, [1–2], NcAr, PC 84:6.

97 Millard Stancell to Dear Brother, March 16, 1867, [4], NcU-SHC, Benjamin D. Stancell Papers, no. 2845Z. I am indebted to Professor Erika Lindemann for this citation.

98 This image has been explored by Sandra M. Gilbert and Susan Gubar, who find it pervading nineteenth-century women's writing and reflecting "the woman

writer's own discomfort, her sense of powerlessness, her fear that she inhabits alien and incomprehensible places. Indeed, it reflects her growing suspicion that what the nineteenth century called 'woman's place' is itself irrational and strange" (Gilbert and Gubar, *Madwoman in the Attic*, 84).

99 Spencer, "Old Times," no. 9, 217–18.

100 It was rumored with indignation that this horse and one that General Atkins gave Ellen Swain had been "swept from southern stables" (Chamberlain, *Old Days in Chapel Hill*, 95).

101 Spencer, "Old Times," no. 7, 104.

102 Ibid., no. 8, 157.

103 Ibid, 103.

104 Chesnut, *Diary from Dixie*, 21, 169.

105 Kincaid, *History of the Kincaid Family*, 15.

106 Swain to Eleanor W. Swain, September 8, 1826, [2], NcU-NcC, Swain Epistolary Correspondence, vol. 5.

107 Ibid., January 18, 1828, [2].

108 Ibid., January 20, 1828.

109 Spencer, "Old Times," no. 7, 104.

CONCLUSION

1 Petition to Swain from D. F. Caldwell and six others, March 25, 1835, NcAr, GP 71:904.

2 "Felon Apprehended," *Miners' and Farmers' Journal*, June 1, 1833, [3].

3 The auction of Isaiah's estate after his death in 1836 brought $86.87 for the support of his widow (NcAr, Burke County Estate Records, Isaiah Stewart Estate, CR 014.508.51)

4 Burke County Superior Court, State Docket, 1830–41, State Docket to March 1834, no. 24, "State vs. Jesse Barnett," NcAr, CR 014.321.1, p. 113.

5 Burke County Superior Court, State Docket, 1830–41, pp. [88, 97, 125], ibid.; Proclamation of pardon to Jessee Barnet, April 2, 1835, NcAr, GLB 30:341.

6 Olds, "Stewart Line," 3, 6–8.

7 Thomas W. Wilson to Stokes, November 19, 1832, NcAr, GP 65:284.

8 Spainhour, "Frances Silvers' Confession."

9 William F. Thomas to Swain, June 3, 1833, [1–2], NcAr, GLB 67:213.

10 McCrumb's novel depicts Charlie as provoking Frankie to action by his drunken threats to harm the crying baby. Frankie strikes to stop him and then leaves the baby in the warm cabin while she hurries out into the bitter-cold and snowy night to get help at her parents' home (*Ballad of Frankie Silver*, 344–50).

11 Petition to Governor Swain from Frankie Silver through Thomas W. Wilson, June 3, 1833, [2], NcAr, GP 67:207–8.

12 Swain to Eleanor W. Swain, January 4, 1828, 1, NcU-NcC, Swain Epistolary Correspondence, vol. 5.

13 Unsigned and undated letter from Caroline Swain to David Swain, the second

of five letters he preserved from her. This one he transcribed, silently correcting it. Three others are in her own scrawl, punctuation, and spelling (ibid., vol. 2).

14 Unsigned and undated letter from Caroline Swain to David Swain, the fourth of five letters, this one in her own hand (ibid.).

15 Swain to Eleanor W. Swain, September 6, 1831, [2], ibid., vol. 5.

16 Proclamation of pardon to Robert Potter, April 17, 1834, NcAr, GLB 30:193. See also Carolyn A. Wallace's entry on Potter in Powell, *Dictionary of North Carolina Biography*, 5:132–34.

17 Watson, "William Waightstill Avery," 71.

18 A number of writers have explored these attitudes, among them Bruce (*Violence and Culture*), Wyatt-Brown (*Southern Honor*), and Ayers (*Vengeance and Justice*).

19 Petition to Stokes from Edward C. Gavin and fifteen others, May 31, 1831, NcAr, GP 61:173; William B. Meares to Stokes, May 17, 1831, ibid., 171.

20 Petition to Dudley from Joseph MDowell and fifty-one other persons, n.d., NcAr, GP 81:1170–71; Leon Henderson to Swain, November 13, 1837, [1–3], NcAr, PC 841:1.

21 M. L. Hoke to Dudley, November 20, 1837, NcAr, GP 81:1042.

22 See, for example, NcAr, GP 81:1170–72.

23 The figures are based on a comparison of the names on the petitions with those in the 1830 tax rolls for Burke County (NcAr, CR 014.703.3) and the lists of officeholders in Phifer, *Burke*, 410–30.

24 Avery to Dudley, November 30, 1837, NcAr, GP 81:1065.

25 Proclamation of pardon to Logan Henderson, February 15, 1838, NcAr, GLB 32:146.

26 Wyatt-Brown, *Southern Honor*, 3. To take contrary evidence emerging only from this study of the Frankie Silver case, one could call into question such statements as "startlingly few antebellum Southern murders occurred among people closely related by blood or matrimony" (381), "white society was small, homogeneous, and cohesive about fundamental values" (370), and that the criminal justice system "sustained local autonomy" (365).

27 Stone, "Interpersonal Violence," 32.

28 Quoted from J. S. Cockburn in Gurr, "Historical Trends," 308.

29 Andrew, "Code of Honour," 410.

30 Quoted from Mandeville, *Enquiry into the Origins*, in ibid., 411. See also the account of the place of honor in the development of legal doctrines of provocation in Horder, *Provocation and Responsibility*.

31 See, in particular, the review of the history of the theory of provocation in Bandalli, "Women, Spousal Homicide, and the Doctrine of Provocation," 55–75.

32 Charlotte Ross outlined her view of the Frankie Silver material in introducing a panel at the 1998 annual meeting of the Appalachian Studies Association in Boone, N.C.

33 Bosco, "Lectures at the Pillory," 157–58.

34 Minnick, "New England Execution Sermon," 82.

35 Boorstin, *The Americans: The Colonial Experience*, 12, 14.

36 Smith, "English Treason Trials and Confessions," 476. An extensive literature

explores the criminal confession in the early British Isles. See also Langston, "Essex and the Art of Dying," and Sharpe, " 'Last Dying Speeches' " and "Elite Perceptions and Popular Images."

37 Swain to Eleanor W. Swain, March 21, July 4, 1828, NcU-NcC, Swain Epistolary Correspondence, vol. 5; James Lowry to Swain, April 5, 1849, NcAr, PC 84:4.

38 James Lowry to Swain, April 5, 1848, NcAr, PC 84:3.

39 Williams cites a variety of gallows speeches in *Vogues in Villainy,* 35, 103.

40 Gatrell, *Hanging Tree,* 138. Gatrell's chap. 4 explores this rebellious subculture of the poor.

41 Ibid., 140.

42 Ibid., 2, 3. Faller echoes, perhaps, the line about prisoners executed twice—"At the Gallowes first, and after in a Ballad Sung to some villanous tune"—in Massinger, *Bondman,* Act 5, scene 3.

43 Faller, *Turned to Account,* 22, 67.

44 Ibid., 68.

45 Halttunen, "Divine Providence," 7–8.

46 Halttunen, *Murder Most Foul,* 43–45.

47 Halttunen, "Divine Providence," 11.

48 Interview DP, November 18, 1998, 19.

49 Hawthorne, *Mosses,* 9–10.

50 Abrahams, "Story and History," 2.

51 Glassie, "Folklore and History," 190.

52 Interview DP, May 27, 1997, 22.

WORKS CITED

MANUSCRIPTS

Austin, Texas
Texas State Library
    Guadalupe County Tax Rolls, Reel 109401, 1846–88

Chapel Hill, North Carolina
North Carolina Collection, University of North Carolina Library
    David L. Swain Epistolary Correspondence, 5 vols., Vault Collection,
        Cobb Loan
Southern Folklife Collection, University of North Carolina Library
    Tom Davenport Papers
    Arthur Palmer Hudson Collection
    Bobby McMillon Papers
        Ballad Collection (11 notebooks of song texts collected from relatives and
            acquaintances)
        "Like a Fly in Amber" (manuscript, 30 pp.)
    Rountree, Sage. "Folk Music at WFDD and WUNC."
Southern Historical Collection, University of North Carolina Library
    Silas McDowell Papers
    Thomas Ruffin Papers
    Benjamin D. Stancell Papers
    Maude Minish Sutton, "Ballads Collected in Avery County, 1917–1918"
    David L. Swain Papers

Chicago, Illinois
Chicago Historical Society
    G. Flowers Diary

Raleigh, North Carolina
North Carolina State Archives
    Alexander County Records
        "A History of Alexander County . . . by William E. White," Alexander,
            Box 003, Folder 1
    Burke County Court of Pleas and Quarter Sessions
        Records, CR 014.508.51
    Burke County Estate Records
        Isaiah Stewart Estate Record, CR 014.508.51

Burke County Superior Court
  Clerk of the Court Papers Concerning the Trial of Frances Silvers
    (microfilm, C 014.30023)
  Minute Docket, CR 014.311.1
  State Docket, CR 014.321.1 and CR 014.326.3
Burke County Tax Records, 1782–1894, CR 014.703.3
Edward B. Dudley Papers
  Governors' Papers
Lincoln County Superior Court
  State Docket, 1823–48, CR 060.321.1
North Carolina Supreme Court Records
  Original Cases, 1800–1909
  Volume 39, "Common Law Cases Argued and Determined"
  Volume 255, "Minute Docket"
Montfort Stokes Papers
  Governors' Letterbook
  Governors' Papers
David L. Swain Papers
  Governors' Letterbooks
  Governors' Papers
  Personal Collection

Wise, Virginia
Clinch Valley College Library
  James Taylor Adams, "The Silvers Murder Case," WPA Box 8, Folder 10

INTERVIEWS AND FIELD RECORDINGS
All of the interviews and recordings listed below are located in the Southern Folklife
Collection, University of North Carolina Library.

Lattimore Hughes. Interview by Bobby McMillon, Bowditch, N.C., 1975.
  1 audiocassette copy. Logged and partially transcribed by Daniel W. Patterson.
Bobby McMillon. Interviews by Tom Davenport, 1994, 1995. Hi-8mm video
  recording, 8 tapes. Transcribed by Bruce E. Baker.
———. Interview by Beverly B. Patterson and Wayne Martin, November 20,
  1992. 2 audiocassettes. Logged and partially transcribed by Beverly B.
  Patterson, with additional transcriptions by Daniel W. Patterson.
———. Interview by Beverly B. Patterson and Wayne Martin, February 4, 1993.
  3 audiocassettes. Logged and partially transcribed by Beverly Patterson.
———. Interview by Daniel W. Patterson, May 27–28, 1997. 4 audiocassettes.
  Logged and partially transcribed by Daniel W. Patterson.
———. Recordings by Jim McGee. 11 reels. DAT tape recordings of Bobby
  McMillon singing the melodies of the song texts in his 11 notebooks. Recorded
  as a project of the North Carolina Folklife Office.

Accounts are listed below in chronological order.

"Horrible Outrage." *North Carolina Spectator and Western Advertiser* (Rutherfordton), January 28, 1832, [3].
"Horrible Outrage." *Miners' and Farmers' Journal* (Charlotte), February 8, 1832, [2]. [Reprinted with small changes from the Rutherfordton *Spectator.*]
[On "Mrs. Sylvers"'s escape from jail.] *Carolina Watchman* (Salisbury), May 25, 1833, [3].
"Felon Apprehended." *Miners' and Farmers' Journal*, June 1, 1833, [3].
[On the escape and recapture.] *Star and North Carolina Gazette* (Raleigh), June 7, 1833, [3].
[On the escape and recapture.] *Raleigh Constitutionalist, People's Advocate and State Gazette*, June 11, 1833, [2]. Reprinted with no changes from the *Star.*
[On the execution.] *Miners' and Farmers' Journal*, July 27, 1833, [3].
[On the execution.] *Star and North Carolina Gazette*, August 2, 1833, [3].
"Francis Silvers' Confession." *Lenoir Topic*, March 24, 1885, [3].
"Frances Sivers' Confession." *Morganton Star*, March 27, 1885, [3].
Spainhour, Henry. "Frances Silvers' Confession." *Lenoir Topic*, May 5, 1886, 4.
Spainhour, N. P. "Obituary" [of Henry Spainhour]. *Neoga News* (Illinois), ca. February 1901. [From clipping without date or page number.]
Bryant, H. E. C. "The Horrible Deed of a Wife." *Charlotte Daily Observer*, March 22, 1903, 10.

"Countryman and His Wife." *Greensborough Patriot*, April 14, 1830, 3. [Prose variant of "The Old Woman of Slapsadam" ballad on marital conflict.]
"Death Penalty—Public Executions, The." *Raleigh Register*, November 2, 1853, [3].
"Execution" [of Sollis]. *Raleigh Register*, May 4, 1827, [3].
"Execution!" [of Kimbrough and Carey]. *Raleigh Register*, November 8, 1830, [3].
[Execution of Lewis]. *Raleigh Register*, July 1, 1825, [3].
[Execution of Sampson]. *Hillsborough Recorder*, June 26, 1822, [2-3].
"Female Heart, The." *Greensborough Patriot*, October 24, 1832, 4.
[Forkener case]. *Raleigh Register*, May 1, 1827, [2].
"Good Wife, A." *Greensborough Patriot*, May 12, 1830, 3, "Variety" column. [On husband tried and acquitted for whipping wife.]
"Horrid Murder" [by Craft]. *Star and North Carolina Gazette*, August 2, 1833, 3.
"Husband and Wife." *Raleigh Register*, August 26, 1825, [3].
"Husbands and Wives." *Greensborough Patriot*, April 7, 1830, 1. [On S.C. supreme court's ruling against wife beating.]
"Mechanics' Wives." *Western Carolinian*, February 7, 1831, 1.
[Murders by Osborn]. *Raleigh Register*, October 28, 1830, [3].

[Murders by Wilson]. *Raleigh Star,* October 28, 1830, [3].
"Public Executions." *Raleigh Register,* May 11, 1839, [3].
"Rules for Husbands." *Greensborough Patriot,* April 7, 1830, 1.
"Rules for Ladies." *Greensborough Patriot,* October 24, 1832, 4.
"Rules for Wives." *Greensborough Patriot,* April 7, 1830, 1.
[Slaves Green and Dick]. *Hillsborough Recorder,* March 21, 1844, [3].
[White men whipped]. *Raleigh Register,* April 7, 1846, [3].
Wilson, Thomas Worth. "To the FREEMEN and Voters of Guadalupe County."
    Seguin Mercury (Texas), July 14, 1858, [3].

BOOKS AND ARTICLES

Abrahams, Roger D., ed. *A Singer and Her Songs: Almeda Riddle's Book of Ballads.*
    Baton Rouge: Louisiana State University Press, 1970.
———. "Story and History: A Folklorist's View." *Oral History Review* 9 (1981):
    1–11.
Abrams, Kathryn. "Hearing the Call of Stories." *California Law Review* 79 (1991):
    971–1052.
———. "The Narrative and the Normative in Legal Scholarship." In *Representing*
    Women: Law, Literature, and Feminism, edited by Susan S. Heinzelman and
    Zipporah B. Wiseman, 44–56. Durham: Duke University Press, 1994.
Anglin, Mary K. "Lives on the Margin: Rediscovering the Women of Antebellum
    Western North Carolina." In *Appalachia in the Making: The Mountain South in*
    the Nineteenth Century, edited by Mary B. Pudup, Dwight B. Billings, and
    Altina L. Waller, 185–209. Chapel Hill: University of North Carolina Press,
    1995.
Andrew, Donna T. "The Code of Honour and Its Critics: The Opposition to
    Duelling in England, 1700–1850." *Social History* 5 (1980): 409–34.
Arthur, John P. *Western North Carolina: A History (from 1730 to 1913).* Raleigh:
    Edwards and Broughton, 1914.
Avery, Clifton K., ed. *Official Court Record of the Trial, Conviction and Execution of*
    Francis Silvers, First Woman Hanged in North Carolina: From the Minutes of the
    Burke County Superior Court, Morganton, N.C. Morganton, N.C.: The
    News-Herald, 1969.
Ayers, Edward L. *Vengeance and Justice: Crime and Punishment in the*
    Nineteenth-Century American South. New York: Oxford University Press, 1984.
Bailey, Lloyd R. Sr., ed. *The Heritage of the Toe River Valley.* 2 vols. Durham, N.C.:
    privately printed, 1994, 1997.
Baldwin, Karen, and Daniel W. Patterson, eds. *Bobby McMillon and "The Ballad of*
    Frankie Silver." Special issue, *North Carolina Folklore Journal* 47, no. 1
    (Winter/Spring 2000).
Bandalli, Susan L. "Women, Spousal Homicide, and the Doctrine of Provocation
    in English Criminal Law." M.L. thesis, University of York, 1993.

Battle, Kemp P. *Memories of an Old-Time Tarheel.* Edited by William J. Battle. Chapel Hill: University of North Carolina Press, 1945.

Battle, William H. *Battle's Revisal of the Public Statutes of North Carolina, Adopted by the General Assembly at the Session of 1872–'3.* Raleigh: n.p., 1873.

Beauchamp's Trial. A Report of the Trial of Jereboam O. Beauchamp, before the Franklin Circuit Court, in May, 1826, upon an Indictment for the Murder of Col. Solomon P. Sharp. Frankfort, Ky.: n.p., 1826.

Belden, Henry M., and Arthur P. Hudson, eds. *Folk Ballads from North Carolina.* Vol. 2 of *The Frank C. Brown Collection of North Carolina Folklore,* edited by Newman Ivey White et al. Durham: Duke University Press, 1952.

Bennett, D. K. *Chronology of North Carolina.* New York: n.p., 1858.

Bennett, Gillian. " 'Belief Stories': The Forgotten Genre." *Western Folklore* 48 (1989): 289–311.

Bennett, W. Lance, and Martha S. Feldman. *Reconstructing Reality in the Courtroom: Justice and Judgment in American Culture.* New Brunswick, N.J.: Rutgers University Press, 1981.

Blackstone, William. *Commentaries on the Laws of England.* 13th ed. London: n.p., 1800.

———. *Commentaries on the Laws of England, in Four Books.* Portland, Maine: n.p., 1807.

Bleackley, Horace. *The Hangmen of England.* In *State Executions Viewed Historically and Sociologically,* 1–272. Montclair, N.J.: Patterson Smith, 1977.

Bolté, Mary. *Dark and Bloodied Ground.* Riverside, Conn.: Chatham Press, 1973.

Boorstin, Daniel. *The Americans: The Colonial Experience.* New York: Vintage, 1964.

Bosco, Ronald A. "Lectures at the Pillory: The Early American Execution Sermon." *American Quarterly* 30 (1978): 156–76.

Botkin, B. A., ed. *A Treasury of Southern Folklore: Stories, Ballads, Traditions, and Folkways of the People of the South.* New York: Crown, 1949.

Brooks, Peter, and Paul Gewirtz. *Law's Stories: Narrative and Rhetoric in the Law.* New Haven, Conn.: Yale University Press, 1996.

Brown, Anne B. "He Fashioned Beauty out of Wood." *Louisville Courier-Journal Magazine,* January 8, 1950, 26–28.

Bruce, Dickson D., Jr. *Violence and Culture in the Antebellum South.* Austin: University of Texas Press, 1979.

Brunvand, Jan. *The Vanishing Hitchhiker: American Urban Legends and Their Meanings.* New York: W. W. Norton, 1981.

Bryan, Patricia. "Stories in Fiction and in Fact: Susan Glaspell's *A Jury of Her Peers* and the 1901 Murder Trial of Margaret Hossack." *Stanford Law Review* 49 (1997): 401–70.

Buchan, David. *The Ballad and the Folk.* London: Routledge and Kegan Paul, 1972.

Burt, Olive W. *American Murder Ballads and Their Stories.* New York: Oxford University Press, 1958.

Busbee, Perrin, ed. *Cases at Law Argued and Determined in the Supreme Court of*

North Carolina, from December Term, 1852, to August Term, 1853, Both Inclusive.
Vol. 44 of *North Carolina Reports.* Richmond, Va.: n.p., 1899.

Cain, Robert J., Jr., ed. *Records of the Executive Council, 1735–1754.* Vol. 8 of *The Colonial Records of North Carolina.* 2d ser. Raleigh: North Carolina Division of Archives and History, 1988.

Cannon, Charles Dale, ed. *A Warning for Fair Women.* The Hague: Mouton, 1975.

Cartwright, Peter. *Autobiography of Peter Cartwright, the Backwoods Preacher.* Edited by William P. Strickland. New York, 1856.

Caruthers, Eli W. *Interesting Revolutionary Incidents: And Sketches of Character, Chiefly in the "Old North State."* 2d ser. Philadelphia: n.p., 1854.

——. *A Sketch of the Life and Character of the Rev. David Caldwell, D.D.* Greensboro, N.C.: n.p., 1842.

Chamberlain, Hope S. *Old Days in Chapel Hill: Being the Life and Letters of Cornelia Phillips Spencer.* Chapel Hill: University of North Carolina Press, 1926.

Chesnut, Mary B. *A Diary from Dixie.* Edited by Ben Ames Williams. Cambridge: Houghton Mifflin, 1961.

Child, Francis James, ed. *The English and Scottish Popular Ballads.* 5 vols. Boston: n.p., 1888–89.

Cohen, Anne B. *Poor Pearl, Poor Girl!: The Murdered-Girl Stereotype in Ballad and Newspaper.* Publications of the American Folklore Society Memoir Series, vol. 58. Austin: University of Texas Press, 1973.

Collinson, Francis M. *The Traditional and National Music of Scotland.* Nashville, Tenn.: Vanderbilt University Press, 1966.

Collmann, Herbert L., ed. *Ballads and Broadsides Chiefly of the Elizabethan Period and Printed in Black-Letter.* 1912. Reprint. New York: Burt Franklin, 1971.

Common Times: Written and Pictorial History of Yancey County. Burnsville, N.C.: Yancey Graphics, 1981.

Constitution of North Carolina, Established the 16th Day of March, 1868. Raleigh: n.p., 1868.

Crissman, James K. *Death and Dying in Central Appalachia: Changing Attitudes and Practices.* Urbana: University of Illinois Press, 1994.

Davenport, Tom. "Remarks on the Making of *The Ballad of Frankie Silver.*" In Baldwin and Patterson, *Bobby McMillon and "The Ballad of Frankie Silver."*

Dégh, Linda. *Narratives in Society: A Performer-Centered Study of Narration.* FF Communications No. 255. Helsinki: Academia Scientiarum Fennica, 1995.

——. "The Variant and the Folklorization Process in the Basic Forms of Narration: Märchen and Legend." In *American Folklore and the Mass Media,* 12–22. Bloomington: Indiana University Press, 1994.

Dégh, Linda, and Andrew Vázsonyi. "The Crack on the Red Goblet, or Truth and Modern Legend." In *Folklore in the Modern World,* edited by Richard Dorson, 253–72. The Hague: Mouton, 1978.

——. "The Dialectics of the Legend." *Folklore Preprint Series,* vol. 1, no. 6. Bloomington: Folklore Institute, 1973.

——. "Legend and Belief." *Genre* 4 (1971): 281–304.

Delgado, Richard. "Storytelling for Oppositionists and Others: A Plea for

Narrative." In *Narrative and the Legal Discourse: A Reader in Storytelling and the Law*, edited by David R. Papke, 289–97. Liverpool: Deborah Charles Publications, 1991.

DePriest, Joe. "Chill of the Grave." *Charlotte Observer*, April 21, 1996, 1L.

Devereux, Thomas P., ed. *Cases Argued and Determined in the Supreme Court of North Carolina, from June Term, 1831, to December Term, 1832*. Vol. 14 of *North Carolina Reports*. [Raleigh]: Edwards and Broughton, 1908.

Dirlam, Hilary. "Bobby McMillon: Blue Ridge Story Teller." *Old-Time Herald* 2 (1990): 12–14, 43–44.

Dolan, Frances E. "Home-Rebels and House-Traitors: Murderous Wives in Early Modern England." *Yale Journal of Law and the Humanities* 4 (1992): 1–31.

Doody, Margaret A. " 'Those Eyes Are Made So Killing': Eighteenth-Century Murderesses and the Law." *Princeton University Library Chronicle* 46 (1984): 49–80.

Ervin, Sam J., Jr. *Burke County Courthouses and Related Matters*. Morganton, N.C.: Historic Burke Foundation, 1985.

———. "Frankie Silver." *Morganton News-Herald*, April 3, 1924.

———. "Thomas Worth Wilson and Catherine Calhoun Caldwell" and "William Wilson." In *The Heritage of Burke County*, 476–78. Morganton, N.C.: Burke County Historical Society, 1981.

Erwin, Susan G. *The Village That Disappeared*. Charlotte, N.C.: Laney-Smith, 1996.

Erwin, W. Clark. "Sarah Robinson Erwin." In *The Heritage of Burke County*, 178. Morganton, N.C.: Burke County Historical Society, 1981.

Ewing, Charles P. *Battered Women Who Kill: Psychological Self-Defense as Legal Justification*. Lexington, Mass.: Lexington Books, 1987.

Faller, Lincoln B. *Turned to Account: The Forms and Functions of Criminal Biography in Late Seventeenth- and Early Eighteenth-Century England*. Cambridge: Cambridge University Press, 1987.

Farlow, Fran. "Gastonia Reader Trumpets Frankie Silver's Innocence." *The State*, 60 (December 1992): 6.

Fifth Census, or Enumeration of the Inhabitants of the United States as Corrected at the Department of State. Washington, D.C.: Duff Green, 1832.

Fischer, David H. *Albion's Seed: Four British Folkways in America*. New York: Oxford University Press, 1989.

Foreman, Grant. "The Life of Montfort Stokes in the Indian Territory." *North Carolina Historical Review* 16 (1939): 373–403.

Foster, William O. "The Career of Montfort Stokes in North Carolina." *North Carolina Historical Review* 16 (1939): 237–72.

Foucault, Michel. *Discipline and Punish: The Birth of the Prison*. Translated by Alan Sheridan. New York: Vintage, 1977.

Friedman, Albert B., ed. *The Viking Book of Folk Ballads*. New York: Viking Press, 1956.

Friedman, Lawrence M. *Crime and Punishment in American History*. New York: Basic Books, 1993.

—————. *A History of American Law*. New York: Simon and Schuster, 1973.

Gatrell, V. A. C. *The Hanging Tree: Execution and the English People, 1770–1868*. Oxford: Oxford University Press, 1994.

Gerould, Gordon H. *The Ballad of Tradition*. New York: Oxford University Press, 1957.

Gilbert, Sandra M., and Susan Gubar. *The Madwoman in the Attic: The Woman Writer and the Nineteenth-Century Literary Imagination*. New Haven, Conn.: Yale University Press, 1979.

Gilmore, Leigh. *Autobiographics: A Feminist Theory of Women's Self-Representation*. Ithaca, N.Y.: Cornell University Press, 1994.

Glassie, Henry. "Folklore and History." *Minnesota History* 50 (1987): 188–92.

Gorn, Elliott J. " 'Gouge and Bite, Pull Hair and Scratch': The Social Significance of Fighting in the Southern Backcountry." *American Historical Review* 90 (1985): 18–43.

Grant, J. A. C. *Our Common Law Constitution*. Boston: Boston University Press, 1960.

Gray, Jeffrey P. "Was the First Woman Hanged in North Carolina a 'Battered Spouse'?" *Campbell Law Review* 19 (1997): 311–31.

Gurr, Ted R. "Historical Trends in Violent Crime: A Critical Review of the Evidence." In *Crime and Justice: An Annual Review of Research*, edited by Michael Tonry and Norval Morris. 3:295–353. Chicago: University of Chicago Press, 1981.

Halttunen, Karen. "Divine Providence and Dr. Parkman's Jawbone: The Cultural Construction of Murder as Mystery." *Ideas from the National Humanities Center* 4 (1996): 4–21.

—————. *Murder Most Foul: The Killer and the American Gothic Imagination*. Cambridge, Mass.: Harvard University Press, 1998.

Hanawalt, Barbara. "Violence in the Domestic Milieu of Late Medieval England." In *Violence in Medieval Society*, edited by Richard W. Kaeuper. Rochester: Boydell and Brewer, forthcoming.

Harbin, Jim. *Nancy's Story: To Right the Legend of Frankie Silver*. Maggie Valley, N.C.: Ravenscroft Publishing, 1999.

Harris, John S. *Silver: Our Pioneer Ancestors*. Rev. ed. N.p.: privately printed, 1997.

Haun, Weynette P., ed. *Morgan District, North Carolina, Superior Court of Law and Equity, Pt. 1: "Criminal Action Papers" [no date] to 1789*. Book 4. Durham, N.C.: privately printed, 1995.

Hawthorne, Nathaniel. *Mosses from an Old Manse*. Columbus: Ohio State University Press, 1974.

Hay, Douglas. "Property, Authority, and the Criminal Law." In *Albion's Fatal Tree: Crime and Society in Eighteenth-Century England*, edited by Douglas Hay, 17–63. New York: Pantheon, 1975.

Helms, Douglas. "The Murder of Patsy Beasly: The Story behind the Folksong." *North Carolina Folklore* 15 (1967): 51–55.

Henry, Mellinger E. *Songs Sung in the Southern Appalachians, Many of Them Illustrating Ballads in the Making*. London: Mitre Press, 1934.

Heritage of Burke County, The. Morganton, N.C.: Burke County Historical
Society, 1981.

Hiergesell, Geneva. "Here's More about Poor Frankie Silvers." *Morganton News-
Herald*, February 13, 1968; reprinted in McCall, *They Won't Hang a
Woman*.

Hindley, Charles. *The History of the Catnach Press*. London: Charles Hindley, 1886.

Hoffer, Peter C., and William B. Scott, eds. *Criminal Proceedings in Colonial
Virginia*. American Legal Records Series. Athens: Published for the American
Historical Association by the University of Georgia Press, 1984.

Hooker, Richard J., ed. *The Carolina Backcountry on the Eve of the Revolution: The
Journal and Other Writings of Charles Woodmason, Anglican Itinerant*. Chapel
Hill: University of North Carolina Press, 1953.

Horder, Jeremy. *Provocation and Responsibility*. Oxford: Clarendon Press, 1992.

Howell, Larry. "Thomas Howell." In *The Heritage of the Toe River Valley*, edited
by Lloyd R. Bailey Sr., 2:285–86. Durham, N.C.: privately printed, 1997.

Hummel, Ray O. *Southern Broadsides before 1877: A Bibliography*. Richmond:
Virginia State Library, 1971.

Hunter, Elizabeth. "Remarkable History of the Silver Family." In *Common Times:
Written and Pictorial History of Yancey County*, 13–18. Burnsville, N.C.: Yancey
Graphics, 1981.

Iredell, James, ed. *The Public Acts of the General Assembly of North-Carolina from
1715–1790*. Revised by François-Xavier Martin. Vol. 1. New Bern: n.p., 1804.

Iredell, James, and William H. Battle, eds. *The Revised Statutes of the State of
North Carolina Passed by the General Assembly at the Session of 1836-7*. Raleigh:
n.p., 1837.

Jackson, Bernard S. "Narrative Models in Legal Proof." In *Narrative and the Legal
Discourse: A Reader in Storytelling and the Law*, edited David R. Papke, 158–78.
Liverpool: Deborah Charles Publications, 1991.

Jinnette, Janet S. "Henry Spainhour." In *The Heritage of Burke County*, 401–2.
Morganton, N.C.: Burke County Historical Society, 1981.

Johnson, Guion G. *Ante-Bellum North Carolina: A Social History*. Chapel Hill:
University of North Carolina Press, 1937.

Joyner, Charles W. "'Alice of the Hermitage': A Study in Legend, Belief, and
History." In *Shared Traditions: Southern History and Folk Culture*, 243–53.
Urbana: University of Illinois Press, 1999.

Kane, Stuart A. "Wives with Knives: Early Modern Murder Ballads and the
Transgressive Commodity." *Criticism* 38 (1996): 219–37.

Kelly, Henry A. "Rule of Thumb and the Folklaw of the Husband's Stick."
Journal of Legal Education 44 (1994): 341–65.

Kenkel, Kenneth R. "The Constant Aesthetic of Bobby McMillon: 'I've Just
Always Tried to Find Any Old Song or Story That I Could.'" *North Carolina
Folklore Journal* 32 (1984): 18–29.

———. "Frank Proffitt, Jr., and Bobby McMillon: Traditional Artists in the
Public Eye." M.A. thesis, University of North Carolina, 1986.

Kennedy, Peter. *Folksongs of Britain and Ireland*. London: Cassell, 1975.

Kincaid, James M. *History of the Kincaid Family.* La Veta, Colo.: Joe K. Kincaid, 1918.

Kirkman, Roger N. "William Julius Alexander." In *Dictionary of North Carolina Biography,* edited by William S. Powell, 1:19. Chapel Hill: University of North Carolina Press, 1979.

Knight, William C. "Sheriff Jackson ('Jack') Stewart." In *The Heritage of the Toe River Valley,* edited by Lloyd R. Bailey Sr., 1:418–19 (with Bailey's additional note). N.p., 1994.

Langbein, John H. "The Criminal Trial before the Lawyers." *University of Chicago Law Review* 45 (1978): 263–316.

Langston, Beach. "Essex and the Art of Dying." *Huntington Library Quarterly* 13 (1950): 109–29.

Laws, G. Malcolm. *Native American Balladry: A Descriptive Study and a Bibliographical Syllabus.* Rev. ed. Philadelphia: American Folklore Society, 1964.

Laws and Resolutions of the State of North Carolina, Passed by the General Assembly at Its Session of 1881. Raleigh: n.p., 1881.

Linebaugh, Peter. "The Tyburn Riot against the Surgeons." In *Albion's Fatal Tree: Crime and Society in Eighteenth-Century England,* edited by Douglas Hay, 65–117. New York: Pantheon, 1975.

Lofland, John. "The Dramaturgy of State Executions." In *State Executions Viewed Historically and Sociologically,* 273–325. Montclair, N.J.: Patterson Smith, 1977.

McCarthy, William B. *The Ballad Matrix: Personality, Milieu, and the Oral Tradition.* Bloomington: Indiana University Press, 1990.

McFarland, Gerald W. *The "Counterfeit" Man: The True Story of the Boorn-Colvin Murder Case.* New York: Pantheon, 1990.

McMillon, Bobby. "Die with It in You, Frankie." In *A Celebration of American Family Folklore: Tales and Traditions from the Smithsonian Collection,* edited by Steven J. Zeitlin, Amy J. Kotkin, and Holly C. Baker, 104–8. New York: Pantheon, 1982.

———. "Excerpt from 'A Fly in Amber: Faded Leaves of Time.'" In Baldwin and Patterson, *Bobby McMillon and "The Ballad of Frankie Silver."*

Mandeville, Bernard. *An Enquiry into the Origins of Honour and the Usefulness of Christianity in War.* London: n.p., 1732.

Massinger, Philip. *The Bondman: An Antient Storie.* Edited by Benjamin Townley Spencer. Princeton, N.J.: Princeton University Press, 1932.

Masur, Louis P. "The Design of Public Executions in the Early American Republic." In *Rites of Execution,* 25–49.

———. *Rites of Execution: Capital Punishment and the Transformation of American Culture, 1776–1865.* New York: Oxford University Press, 1989.

Menzies, Robert, and Edmond Smith Jr. "The Scarlet Enigma of Toe River." *True Detective Mysteries,* July 1935, 14–19, 72–73.

Minnick, Wayne C. "The New England Execution Sermon, 1639–1800." *Speech Monographs* 35 (1968): 77–89.

Montell, W. Lynwood. *Killings: Folk Justice in the Upper South.* Lexington: University Press of Kentucky, 1986.

Mull, J. Alexander. *Mountain Yarns, Legends, and Lore.* Banner Elk, N.C.: Pudding Stone Press, 1972.

Mullen, Patrick B. "Modern Legend and Rumor Theory." *Journal of the Folklore Institute* 9 (1972): 95–109.

Muster Rolls of Soldiers of the War of 1812. Raleigh: n.p., 1851.

Newsome, Alfred R., ed. "The A. S. Merrimon Journal, 1853–1854." *North Carolina Historical Review* 8 (1931): 300–330.

Nicolaisen, W. F. H. "Legends as Narrative Response." In *Perspectives on Contemporary Legend,* edited by Paul Smith, 167–78. CECTAL Conference Papers Series No. 4. Sheffield: Centre for English Cultural Tradition and Language, 1984.

———. "The Linguistic Structure of Legends." In *Perspectives on Contemporary Legend, Vol. 2,* edited by Gillian Bennett, Paul Smith, and J. D. A. Widdowson, 61–76. CECTAL Conference Papers Series No. 5. Sheffield: Sheffield Academic Press, 1987.

Old Homes and Gardens of North Carolina. Edited by Mrs. Charles A. Cannon et al. Chapel Hill: University of North Carolina Press, 1939.

Olds, Dan W. "Stewart Line, Tentative Research Notes." Spartanburg, S.C.: privately printed, 1998.

Olmsted, Frederick L. *A Journey through Texas; or, A Saddle-Trip on the Southwestern Frontier.* New York: n.p., 1857.

Palmer, Roy. *The Sound of History: Songs and Social Comment.* Oxford: Oxford University Press, 1988.

Papke, David R., ed. *Narrative and the Legal Discourse: A Reader in Storytelling and the Law.* Liverpool: Deborah Charles Publications, 1991.

Parramore, Tom. "Gouging in Early North Carolina." *North Carolina Folklore Journal* 22 (1974): 55–62.

Patterson, Beverly B. " 'Give Me the Truth!': The Frankie Silver Story in Contemporary North Carolina." *Journal of American Folklore,* forthcoming. Reprinted, with changes, in Baldwin and Patterson, *Bobby McMillon and "The Ballad of Frankie Silver."*

———. *The Sound of the Dove: Singing in Appalachian Primitive Baptist Churches.* Urbana: University of Illinois Press, 1995.

Patterson, Daniel W. "A Woman of the Hills: The Work of Maude Minish Sutton." *Southern Exposure* 5, nos. 2–3 (1977): 105–13.

Phifer, Edward W., Jr. *Burke: The History of a North Carolina County, 1777–1920.* Rev. ed. Morganton, N.C.: privately printed, 1982.

Phillips, Robert B. *One of God's Children in Toe River Valley.* Bakersville, N.C.: privately printed, 1982.

Powell, William S., ed. *Dictionary of North Carolina Biography.* 6 vols. Chapel Hill: University of North Carolina Press, 1979–96.

Price, William S., Jr., ed. *North Carolina Higher-Court Minutes.* Vol. 5 in *The Colonial Records of North Carolina,* 2d ser. Raleigh: North Carolina Division of Archives and History, 1974.

Randolph, Vance, and Floyd C. Shoemaker, eds. *Ozark Folksongs*. 4 vols. Columbia: State Historical Society of Missouri, 1946–50.

"Recalls Ghosts of Two in Old Tragedy: S. C. Jones as a Child Lived in Silvers' Burke County Home." *Morganton News-Herald*, February 5, 1931, 3.

Ritchie, James. "An Account of the Watch-Houses, Mortsafes, and Public Vaults in Aberdeenshire Churchyards, Formerly Used for the Protection of the Dead from the Resurrectionists." *Proceedings of the Society of Antiquaries of Scotland*, 4th ser., vol. 10 (1911–12): 285–326.

Rhyne, Nancy. *Murder in the Carolinas*. Winston-Salem: John F. Blair, 1988.

Sakowski, Carolyn. "The Life and Death of Frankie Silver." M.L.A. thesis, Appalachian State University, 1972.

Schaeffer, Susan F. *The Madness of a Seduced Woman*. New York: E. P. Dutton, 1983.

Sharp, Cecil, ed. *English Folk Songs from the Southern Appalachians*. 2 vols. New York: Oxford University Press, 1933.

Sharpe, J. A. "Elite Perceptions and Popular Images." In *Crime in Early Modern England, 1550–1750*, 143–67. London: Longman, 1984.

———. " 'Last Dying Speeches': Religion, Ideology, and Public Execution in Seventeenth-Century England." *Past and Present* 107 (1985): 144–67.

Shearin, Hubert G., and Josiah H. Combs. *A Syllabus of Kentucky Folk-Songs*. Lexington, Ky.: Transylvania Printing Co., 1911.

Shepard, Leslie. *John Pitts: Ballad Printer of Seven Dials, London, 1765–1844, with a Short Account of His Predecessors in the Ballad and Chapbook Trade*. London: Private Libraries Association, 1969.

Sheppard, Muriel E. *Cabins in the Laurel*. Chapel Hill: University of North Carolina Press, 1935.

Silver, James D. ("John"), ed. *Frankie's Stories*. N.p.: privately printed, 1996.

Silver, Wayne. *Frankie's Song: A Collection from the Kona Baptist Church Library with Notes and Comments by Wayne Silver*. Kona, N.C.: privately printed, 1989.

Simpson, Robert F., Jr, and Sam J. Ervin Jr. "David Tate and Nancy Ann Elizabeth McCall and Christiana Wakefield." In *The Heritage of Burke County*, 414–15. Morganton, N.C.: Burke County Historical Society, 1981.

Smith, Lacey B. "English Treason Trials and Confessions in the Sixteenth Century." *Journal of the History of Ideas* 15 (1954): 471–98.

Smyth, J. F. D. *A Tour in the United States of America*. 2 vols. London: n.p., 1784.

Snedaker, Kathryn H. "Storytelling in Opening Statements: Framing the Argumentation of the Trial." In *Narrative and the Legal Discourse: A Reader in Storytelling and the Law*, edited by David R. Papke, 132–57. Liverpool: Deborah Charles Publications, 1991.

Snider, William D. *Light on the Hill: A History of the University of North Carolina at Chapel Hill*. Chapel Hill: University of North Carolina Press, 1992.

South, Stanley E., ed. *"I Never Killed a Man Didn't Need Killing!": Clarence Potter*. Columbia, S.C.: privately printed, 1996.

———. *"A Window to Times Gone By": Tales and Songs by Howard Woodring*. Columbia, S.C.: privately printed, 1996.

Spainhower, N. P. "Obituary [of Henry Spainhour]." *Neoga News* (Illinois), ca. February 1901.

Spencer, Cornelia P. "Old Times in Chapel Hill. No. VII. Governor Swain." *North Carolina University Magazine*, old ser. 20 (1888): 98–104.

———. "Old Times in Chapel Hill. No. VIII. Governor Swain." *North Carolina University Magazine*, old ser. 20 (1888): 151–59.

———. "Old Times in Chapel Hill. No. IX. Governor Swain." *North Carolina University Magazine*, old ser. 20 (1888): 214–21.

Spierenburg, Petrus. "The Watchers: Spectators at the Scaffold." In *The Spectacle of Suffering: Executions and the Evolution of Repression*, 81–109. Cambridge: Cambridge University Press, 1984).

Starkie, Thomas. *A Practical Treatise on the Law of Evidence, and Digests of Proofs, in Civil and Criminal Proceedings*. 3d American ed. Philadelphia: n.p., 1830.

Statutes of the Realm. Printed by Command of His Majesty King George the Third. 9 vols. London, 1810–22.

Steiner, Bernard C., ed. "The South Atlantic States in 1833, as Seen by a New Englander. Being a Narrative of a Tour Taken by Henry Barnard, Principal of St. John's College, Annapolis (1860–1867)." *Maryland Historical Magazine* 13 (1918): 295–386.

Stone, Lawrence. "Interpersonal Violence in English Society, 1300–1980." *Past and Present* 101 (1983): 22–33.

Sutton, Jessie, ed. *The Heritage of Macon County, North Carolina*. Franklin, N.C.: Macon County Historical Society, 1987.

Swain, David L. "British Invasion of North Carolina in 1776. A Lecture, Delivered before the Historical Society of North Carolina, Friday, April 1st, 1853." N.p., n.d.

———. *The Declaration of Independence by the Citizens of Mecklenburg County on the Twentieth Day of May, 1775*. Raleigh: n.p., 1831.

———. "Early Times in Raleigh." In *Lives of Distinguished North Carolinians, with Illustrations and Speeches*, edited by W. J. Peele, 256–78. Raleigh: n.p., 1897.

———. [Testimony]. In *Testimony of Distinguished Laymen to the Value of the Sacred Scriptures, Particularly in Their Bearing on Civil and Social Life*. New York: American Bible Society, 1859.

Table of the Post Offices in the United States Arranged by States and Counties. Washington, D.C.: n.p., 1831.

Thomas, Brook. "Narratives of Responsibility and Blame in Nineteenth-Century United States Law and Literature." *Narrative* 5 (1997): 3–19.

Turpin, James A. *The Serpent Slips into a Modern Eden, or Nancy Kerlee and Her Crime*. Raleigh: Edwards and Broughton, 1923.

Vance, Zebulon B. "David Lowry Swain." In *Lives of Distinguished North Carolinians*, edited by W. J. Peele, 229–55. Raleigh: n.p., 1898.

Walker, Lenore E. *The Battered Woman Syndrome*. New York: Springer Publishing Co., 1984.

———. *Terrifying Love: Why Battered Women Kill and How Society Responds*. New York: Harper and Row, 1989.

Walker, William. *The Southern Harmony.* 1854. Reprint, edited by Glenn C. Wilcox. Los Angeles: Pro Musicamericana, 1966.

[Wallace], Carolyn A. Daniel. "David Lowry Swain, 1801–1835." Ph.D. diss., University of North Carolina at Chapel Hill, 1954.

———. "Robert Potter." In *Dictionary of North Carolina Biography,* edited by William S. Powell, 3:132–34. Chapel Hill: University of North Carolina Press, 1988.

Waller, Altina L. *Feud: Hatfields, McCoys, and Social Change in Appalachia, 1860–1900.* Chapel Hill: University of North Carolina Press, 1988.

Ward, Donald. "On the Genre Morphology of Legendry: Belief Story versus Belief Legend." *Western Folklore* 50 (1991): 296–303.

Watson, Elgiva D. "William Waightstill Avery." In *Dictionary of North Carolina Biography,* edited by William S. Powell, 1:71–72. Chapel Hill: University of North Carolina Press, 1979.

Watt, Tessa. *Cheap Print and Popular Piety, 1550–1640.* Cambridge: Cambridge University Press, 1991.

Wellman, Manly W. *Dead and Gone: Classic Crimes of North Carolina.* Chapel Hill: University of North Carolina Press, 1954.

Welsh, Alexander. *Strong Representations: Narrative and Circumstantial Evidence in England.* Baltimore, Md.: Johns Hopkins University Press, 1992.

West, John F. *The Ballad of Tom Dula; The Documented Story behind the Murder of Laura Foster and the Trials and Execution of Tom Dula.* Durham: Moore Publishing Co., n.d.

———. *Lift Up Your Head, Tom Dooley: The True Story of the Appalachian Murder That Inspired One of America's Most Popular Ballads.* Asheboro, N.C.: Down Home Press, 1993.

West, Robin. *Narrative, Authority, and Law.* Ann Arbor: University of Michigan Press, 1993.

Wheeler, John H. *Reminiscences and Memoirs of North Carolina and Eminent North Carolinians.* Columbus, Ohio: n.p., 1884.

White, B. F. *The Sacred Harp.* Rev. ed. Bremen, Ga.: Sacred Harp Publishing Co., 1991.

White, William E. "A History of Alexander County, N.C." Taylorsville, N.C.: Alexander County Historical Society, n.d.

Wilgus, D. K. "Fiddler's Farewell: The Legend of the Hanged Fiddler." In *Studia Musicologica* (Budapest), 7 (1965): 195–209.

Williams, Jack K. *Vogues in Villainy: Crime and Retribution in Ante-Bellum South Carolina.* Columbia: University of South Carolina Press, 1959.

Winslow, Ola E. *American Broadside Verse from Imprints of the Seventeenth and Eighteenth Centuries.* New Haven, Conn.: Yale University Press, 1930.

Wise, Jim. "About This Here Tom Dooley: Singer Bobby McMillon Sets Record Straight on Dooley's Misdeeds." *Durham Morning Herald,* November 13, 1981, 1D, 8D.

Woody, Albert W. "A Red Ribbon Marker in Woody Family Bible." *Tri-County News* (Spruce Pine, N.C.), December 22, 1960, 9.

Würzbach, Natascha. *The Rise of the English Street Ballad, 1550–1650.* Cambridge: Cambridge University Press, 1990.

Wyatt-Brown, Bertram. *Southern Honor: Ethics and Behavior in the Old South.* New York: Oxford University Press, 1982.

Young, Perry D. "Documents Relating to 'State v. Frances Silver' (Files of the N.C. Supreme Court in the N.C. Archives)," "Documents Relating to the Case of 'State v. Frances Silver'" (Located in the Governor's Letterbooks in the N.C. Archives)," and "Frankie Silver and the Laws of God and Man." In *The Heritage of the Toe River Valley,* edited by Lloyd R. Bailey Sr., 1:66–72. Durham, N.C.: privately printed, 1994.

———. "In the Mountains, There's a Tale of Christmas Death," *Durham Morning Herald,* December 22, 1962.

———. *The Untold Story of Frankie Silver: Was She Unjustly Hanged?* Asheboro, N.C.: Down Home Press, 1998.

———. "Why Frankie Silver Swung." *Ms.,* May 1976, 120–22.

RECORDINGS

Carolina Sampler: Anglo-American Vocal Music from North Carolina, edited by Karen Helms. Audiocassette, Global Village C-312. New York: Global Village Music, 1992.

Cecilia Costello: Recordings from the Sound Archives of the BBC. 33⅓ rpm disc. Leader LEE-4054. London: Leader Records, 1975.

Country and Western Classics: The Women. 33⅓ rpm disc. Chicago: Time-Life Records, 1981.

"Crazy about a Song": Old-Time Ballad Singers and Musicians from Virginia and North Carolina, recorded by Mike Yates, 1979–83. Audiocassette. Vaughn Williams Memorial Library 007. London: English Folk Dance and Song Society, 1992.

Deeper Feeling, A: Bobby McMillon. Audiocassette, Ivy Creek ICR-401. Mars Hill, N.C.: Ivy Creek Recordings, 1994.

Hand-Me-Down Music—Old Songs, Old Friends: 1—Traditional Music of Union County, North Carolina, recorded by Karen G. Helms and Otto Henry. 33⅓ rpm disc. Folkways Records FES-34151. New York: Folkways Records and Service Corp., 1979.

Heather and Glen: A Collection of Folk Songs and Folk Music from Aberdeenshire and the Hebrides, Collected by Alan Lomax, Calum McLean, and Hamish Henderson. 33⅓ rpm disc. Tradition TLP-1047. Los Angeles: Everest Records, n.d.

INDEX

Abrahams, Roger, 163
Abuse: by parent, 89; by spouse, 57–58, 89–90, 134, 138, 156, 187–88 (n. 42)
Adams, Sheila Kay, 11
Adderholt, Louise W., 18
Alexander, William J., 44, 46, 52, 64, 129, 130, 135, 137
Appalachia: patterns of justice in, 50–51; political views in, 10; prejudice against, 5–6; social change in, 9, 11
Asheville, N.C., 128, 141, 148
Ashley, Clarence, 110

Baker, Frankie, 40
Bailey, Lloyd, 63
Bailey, W. W., 84, 169
Baker, David, 72, 151, 187 (nn. 19, 22)
Ball, Jo, 4
Ballads. *See also* Broadside, criminal's farewell; Confessions, dying; "Frankie Silver" ballad; Gallows literature
—flash, 159
—individual, discussed: "The Ballad of Colonel Sharp," 104; "The Ballad of Finley Preston," 108; "Beauchamp's Address" or "Beauchamp's Confession," 103–5; "Birchie Potter," 118; "The Cruel Mother," 95; "Frankie and Albert," 40, 189 (n. 1); "The Gosport Tragedy," 106–7; "The House Carpenter," 95; "Jack Sheppard's Last Epistle," 159; "Little Frankie," 65, 189 (n. 1), "McPherson's Lament," 111, 194 (n. 35); "Mary Hamilton," 93–94; "Patsy Beasly," 96; "Pennington's

Lament," 108; "Pretty Polly," 106–7; "Tom Dooley," 77, 96; "The Triplett Tragedy," 117–18
—murder, 100–101, 104
—topical: local response to, 117–18; on events in North Carolina, 107–8
—traits: effects of oral transmission on, 92–95, 106–7
Barnett, Jessee, 47–48, 150–51, 155
Battered spouse syndrome, 188 (n. 43). *See also* Abuse: by spouse
Battle, Kemp P., 54, 135, 187 (n. 21)
Beauchamp, Jereboam, 103–4, 153
Bevens, W. C., 124
Boone, John, 147, 150
Blackstone, William, 52–53, 58
Broadside, criminal's farewell: function of, 115, 117–20, 195 (n. 62); history and types of, 105–6, 111, 114–15, 193 (n. 22). *See also* Ballads—flash; Ballads—individual, discussed
—examples of: "Levi Ames," 114, 116, 195 (n. 57); "Luke Hutton's Lamentation," 194 (n. 28)
Brookshire, Lou, 20, 22, 71, 79, 107, 109, 157
Bryant, H. E. C., 66, 68, 84, 165–69, 191 (n. 42)
Buchanan, Minnie G., 85
Burke County, N.C., 50–51, 124, 126, 130, 133, 145, 154–55

Carson, John, 61–62, 125, 128
Carson, Joseph M., 50, 128
Carson, Samuel P., 62, 125, 128
Cartwright, Peter, 138
Caruthers, Eli W., 136

*Celebration of American Family Folklore,
A* (Zeitlin et al.), 66
Chapel Hill, N.C., 145–46
Civil War, 138, 142, 146
Cleveland County, N.C., 96, 191–92
   (n. 67)
Collins family (at Somerset Planta-
   tion), 143
Collis, Jake, 36, 86–87, 167, 176, 187
   (n. 19)
Confessions, dying, 158–60, 201 (n.
   36). *See also* Broadside, criminal's
   farewell; Testimonies, dying
Cosby, Tenn., 10, 14, 19–20, 24
Costello, Cecilia, 95
Criminal cases, cited: William W.
   Avery, 154; Sally Barnicastle, 123;
   Boorn-Colvin, 54; Catherine Bos-
   tian, 131–32, 144; Claiborn Car-
   roll, 154; George Craft, 99; Logan
   Henderson, 154; James Lea, 52;
   Aaron Norwood, 59, 134; Osborn,
   100; Robert Potter, 153; George
   Reves, 59; Solomon Roper, 59;
   Benjamin F. Seaborn, 132; "Slave
   named Jerry," 54; Reuben Southard
   (Sudderth), 134; *State v. William
   Hussey*, 57–58; *State v. Rhodes*, 57–
   58; Washington Taburn, 132; Joseph
   Wilson, 99–100

Damon's Hill (Morganton, N.C.), 78
Davenport, Tom, 1–3, 78, 151, 183 (n. 1),
   183–84 (nn. 4, 7)
Dégh, Linda, 77, 81–82, 85–86
DePriest Joe, 192 (n. 67)
Donnell, John R., 44–45, 47, 51, 60, 129
Dooley, Tom. *See* Ballads: individual;
   Dula, Tom
Dowd, Patricia J., 4
Dula, Tom, 26, 96–97

Eller, Richard, 4
Ellison, Rolf, 20, 22–23
Ellison, W. T. ("Bill"), 23, 108

Ervin, Sam J., Jr., 4, 54, 56–57, 184 (n.
   5), 193 (n. 8)
Erwin, Matilda S., 56, 125–26
Erwin, Susan G., 4, 191 (n. 50)
Evidence, rules of, 52–54, 57
Executions: as issue, 197 (n. 26); of
   men, 58; as ritual, 111, 194 (n. 43), 195
   (n. 48); speeches at, 114, 158–59; of
   women, 58, 133, 159, 197 (n. 36)
—of individuals: Levi Ames, 114, 116,
   195 (n. 57); Elijah W. Kimbrough
   and "negro Kelly," 113; Oliver Lewis,
   113, 115; James Morgan, 158; Frankie
   Silver, 38–39, 48, 101, 114–15, 147;
   Joseph Sollis, 114

Farlow, Fran, 4, 128, 190 (n. 19)
Folklore: and popular media, 65–67, 71,
   79, 84, 88–89, 101–11, 114–17, 120,
   159–60; artistry in, 79–84, 86, 93–97,
   160–63; oral transmission in, 106–7
Folk revival, 72
"Frankie Silver" ballad: authorship of,
   103, 193 (n. 8); in criminal's farewell
   tradition, 111, 115, 117, 157; legend
   about, 101, 115, 118; publication of,
   101; response to, 119–20, 163; text
   of, 30–32, 101–3, 109–10, 119–20, 194
   (n. 31); tunes for (scores), 31, 108–9;
   variants, 178–80
—folksong sources: "Barbara Allen,"
   108, 194 (n. 29); "Beauchamp's Address," 103–5; "Devotion," 31, 109,
   194 (n. 30); "Lord Bateman," 108,
   194 (n. 29); unidentified, 109
Frankie Silver legend cycle: artistic
   treatments of, 2–5, 163, 181–82 (*see
   also* McCrumb, Sharyn); creation
   of, 79–86; structure of, 85–87, 90–97,
   159–61
—motifs in (*examples* and discussion
   of): baby's bloody handprint, *34*, 80,
   83, 85, 162, *173, 175–76*; backtracking
   in snow, *35*, 88, *173*; Charlie chops
   wood that will burn him, *33*, 90–

91, *166, 171, 173, 175;* Charlie killed with nail, *42,* 79; Charlie's dog aids search, *36–37,* 87, 94, *170, 174, 176;* Charlie's head hidden in stump, *34, 176;* Charlie's heart, 81; Charlie's lights hidden under rock, *34, 37, 72, 174, 176;* Charlie smiles in sleep, *33,* 82, 94, *175;* Charlie takes nap, *33,* 78, 80, 135, *166, 171, 173, 175;* conjure ball or glass, *35–36,* 84, *167, 176;* "Die with it in you, Frankie," *39,* 88–89, 162, *168, 172, 174, 177;* father's threat as motive for murder, *33–34,* 88, *173, 175;* Frankie catches ball, *38,* 94, *174;* Frankie disguised as man, *38, 168, 174, 176;* Frankie's ghost, *41,* 98, 192 (n. 76); ghostly screams, *42,* 67, 98; "God bless the child," *34,* 80, 83, *166, 175;* hangman's hood, 87–88, *172;* "Her name is Tom," *38,* 83, *168, 177;* jealousy as motive for murder, 88, *168, 177;* money to go west as motive for murder, *41;* multiple graves of Charlie and Frankie, *37, 39,* 71, 95–96; "Now's your time, Frankie," *33,* 88, *173, 175;* red ribbon, 79–80, 88, 190 (n. 31); request for cake, *39,* 84, 162, *172;* self-defense as motive for murder, *41;* sings ballad on scaffold, *39,* 101, 111, 115, 118, 120, *171, 174, 177;* Stewart family cursed, *40,* 96, *168–69;* tree accurst, iii, 43, 71, 148, 163
—variants from: Lattimore Hughes, 172–74; Bobby McMillon, 32–42, 174–77; Lucinda S. Norman, 169–72; Alfred Silver, 165–69

Gaither, Burgess S., 54, 56, 57, 128, 150
Gales, Joseph, 131
Gales, Weston, 131
Gallows literature, 158–60. *See also* Ballads—flash; Ballads—individual, discussed; Broadside, criminal's farewell

Gaston, William, 131
Gender. *See* Abuse; Battered spouse syndrome; Criminal cases, cited; Executions; Honor, male code of; "Madwoman in the attic"; Polite class; Rule of thumb; Silver, Frankie, trial—circumstances affecting: gender bias, legal traditions; Stereotypes: of gender; Swain, David L.: marital dilemma of, views of; Swain, Eleanor W.
Gerould, Gordon H., 92–93
Gilbert, Wade, 20, 97
Glassie, Henry, 163
Grave robbing, 39, 95–96, 191–92 (n. 67)
Gray, Jeffrey, 52, 78, 188 (n. 43), 190 (n. 23)
Green, Clarence, 71
Green Mountain, N.C., 15, 69

Halttunen, Karen, 160
Harbin, Jim, 4–5
Hawthorne, Nathaniel, 162
Heritage Middle School (Valdese, N.C.), 4
Holsclaw, Henry, 107–8
Holt, George, 24
Honor, male code of, 154–56
Hopson family, 15, 23, 67, 71, 185 (n. 1)
Howell, Thomas, 186 (n. 12)
Hughes, Lattimore ("Uncle Latt"), 67, 69–71, 84–89, 172–74
Hunt, James B., 4

Jones, S. C., 192 (n. 76)
Joyner, Charles, 79

Kane, Stuart A., 117, 195 (nn. 61, 62)
Kona, N.C., 3–4, 9, 23, 26–29, 52, 65, 67, 79, 92, 129, 163, 187 (n. 22)

Lane family (Raleigh, N.C.), 143
Legends: artistry in, 81–84, 97; belief,

81–82, 85–86; characteristics of, 76–79, 85–86, 91; distrust of, 77–78, 161; historical, 71, 73, 76, 79, 86, 90–91; relation to ballads, 17, 96–97; value of, 161–63. *See also* Frankie Silver legend cycle

Lenoir, N.C., 20, 25, 111

Lincoln County, N.C., 59, 154–55

Lowry, James, 128–29, 152, 159, 196 (n. 19)

McCall, Maxine, 4

McCrumb, Sharyn, 28, 61, 63, 151–52, 154, 200 (n. 10)

McDowell, Silas, 140

McDowell County, N.C., 105

McMillon, Bobby: acquaintance with ballad writers, 107–8; acquaintance with folklorists, 2, 18; aesthetic of storytelling, 29, 72–73, 79–84, 86–87, 91, 94–98, 161; as factory worker, 25–26; as folksong collector, 18–23, 183 (n. 3); as performer, 23–26, 79, 82–83, 94; family background of, 10–11; homesickness in San Diego, 12–13; honors received by, 2; interest in folklore, 8–9, 11–18, 29, 82; interest in Frankie Silver, 65, 67, 69–72, 163, 189 (n. 13); personal values, 97–98; recordings by, 183 (n. 2); relation to Silver family, 72; view of Frankie Silver, 87–91, 120, 157; writings about, 183 (n. 2); writings by, 1, 189 (n. 13). *See also* "Frankie Silver" ballad; Frankie Silver legend cycle

Macon County, N.C., 129

Madison County, N.C., 104, 112

"Madwoman in the attic," 145–46, 199–200 (n. 98)

"Making of a Ballad Singer, The" (Davenport video), 3

Mandeville, Bernard, 156

Marriage. *See* Abuse: by spouse; Battered spouse syndrome; Criminal cases, cited; Executions; Polite class; Rule of thumb; Swain, David L.: marital dilemma of, views of; Swain, Eleanor W.

Martin, Wayne, 3, 193 (n. 23)

Mechanics, 140–41, 199 (n. 67)

Melton, Ann, 96–97

Methodism, 138, 143, 152–53

Miller, Edmund, 108

Mitchell, Elisha, 123

Monroe, Bill, 5–6

Montell, Lynwood, 50, 192 (n. 77)

Moore, Byrd, 71, 110

Morganton, N.C., 3, 37, 48, 51–52, 61, 63, 78, 112, 114, 125–26, 130, 134, 140

Mull, David S., 4

Newland, David, 60, 188 (n. 58)

Norman, Lucinda Silver, 66–67, 84–85, 87–89, 134, 169–72, 189 (n. 5)

North Carolina Arts Council, 2–3, 25

North Carolina Center for Public Broadcasting, 5

Panaiotis, 4, 28

Patterson, Beverly, 4, 183 (n. 3), 184 (nn. 7, 18), 185 (n. 1), 193 (n. 23)

Phillips, Mae H. ("Maw Maw"), 8, 19–22, 24

Polite class: definition of, 138–39, 148; expectations of males, 153–56; view of marriage, 139–41, 199 (n. 67); view of women, 143–45, 153

Potter, Birchie, 23

Potter, Boone, 23

Primitive Baptists, 17–18, 21, 184 (n. 18)

Punishment: as example to public, 95, 112–15

Riddle, Almeda, 95

Ross, Charlotte T., 157

Rule of thumb, 58, 188 (n. 47)

San Diego, Calif., 10, 12–13

Schilling, Jean, 24

Schilling, Lee, 24
Scotch-Irish, 136–37
Scott, Thomas W., 103–4, 110
Sermons: and executions, 113–15, 158, 160
Sheppard, Muriel E., 66–67, 69, 71, 84–85, 87–88, 91, 165–69
Silver, Alfred, 66, 71, 84–85, 87–88, 134, 157, 165–69, 189 (n. 4)
Silver, Charles ("Charlie"): birth, 186 (n. 9); Bobby McMillon's view of, 90; character of, 92, 133, 136, 165–66; graves of, 37, 71; poverty of, 191 (n. 57)
Silver, Frances ("Frankie"): Bobby McMillon's view of, 37, 41, 87–91; character of, 92, 126, 136, 144–45, 152, 163, 168; confession of, 54–55, 57, 60–61, 124–25, 135, 145, 151, 187 (n. 38); and effect of the murder on the community, 43, 59, 67, 78, 98, 144–45, 158, 192 (n. 76); imprisonment and escape of, 44, 47, 54, 64, 132; motive of, for murder, 41, 88–91, 134–35, 152; petitions on behalf of, 54–56, 60–62, 121, 123–28, 130, 133–34, 144–45, 196; trial of, 44–48, 163. See also "Frankie Silver" ballad; Frankie Silver legend cycle
—execution of, 101, 114–15, 147, 191 (n. 50); ballad sung at, 91, 115, 117–20, 191 (n. 50)
—interest in: Bobby McMillon's, 65–67, 69–72, 163, 189 (n. 13); 20th-century public's, 3–5, 26–29, 66–67
—trial, circumstances affecting: competence of attorney, 59–62, 64, 130; court schedule, 51; gender bias, 132–34, 153, 156; geography, 51–52; legal traditions, 53–54, 57–58, 156; political networks, 128–31; jurors, 51, 123, 132, 134, 186 (nn. 17, 18, 19), 195–96 (n. 1)
Silver, Greenberry, 72, 77, 157
Silver, Jacob, 76, 90, 95–96, 128–29, 196 (n. 19)

Silver, Wayne, 4, 26–29, 78, 151
Silver, Will, 41, 67, 76, 90
Silver family museum, 4, 26–28
Sobol, Joseph, 191–92 (n. 67)
South, Stanley, 73
Spainhour, Henry: character of, 48–49; on the Silver case, 49–50; on the ballad "Frankie Silver," 103–5; on Frankie Silver's confession, 135, 145, 151
Spencer, Cornelia Phillips, 131, 145–46, 148
Spruce Pine, N.C., 25–26, 71, 169
Stereotypes: of class, 138–39, 140; of gender, 132–36, 139–40, 147–48, 153, 199–200 (n. 98); of races, 142–43; of regions, 5–6, 11, 137–38
—of ethnic groups: Germans, 137; Scotch-Irish, 136–37
Stewart family: abuse in, 89; background, 51, 85, 144, 147, 187 (n. 20), 188 (n. 62); character of brother Jackson, 136; effort to bury Frankie, 95–96; involved in Frankie's crime and legal case, 44, 47–48, 59, 85, 88–89, 145, 150–51, 166; involved in Frankie's escape, 47–48, 150–51, 186 (n. 6); reputation of, 89, 96, 144–45; subsequent history of, 40, 151, 192 (n. 68), 200 (n. 3); tragic flaw of, 152
Stokes, Montfort, 52, 54, 60, 113, 122–24, 128, 131, 133, 143, 196 (n. 6)
Storytelling, traditional, 11, 14–17, 19–20, 23, 29, 66–73, 76–79, 81–83, 94–98, 157, 160–63; legal, 78, 135, 149, 190 (n. 25)
Sutton, Maude M., 96–97, 111, 184 (n. 16), 192 (n. 71)
Swain, Anna, 144–46
Swain, Caroline, 152–53, 200–201 (n. 13)
Swain, David L.: awkward appearance of, 142; career of, 141–42; character of, 130–31; family background of, 76, 141, 143–44; friendship with

Thomas W. Wilson, 130; genealogical interests of, 142; marital dilemma of, 146–48; mental illness in family of, 145–47, 152; reason of for missing court session in Burke County, 186 (n. 9)
—as governor: actions, 124, 130–31; pardons granted and denied, 131–32; response to petitions, 124, 125–26, 128
—views of: on books, 131, 197 (n. 28); on class, 138, 141–43, 147–48; on Frankie Silver, 144, 148; on Germans, 137; on race, 142–43; on religion, 144; on women, 143–45, 148
Swain, Eleanor (daughter), 146, 200 (n. 100)
Swain, Eleanor W. (wife), 142, 146–48

Tanz Ensemble Cathy Sharp, 4, 28
Tate, Samuel M., 113
Taylor, John L., 131, 141
Testimonies, dying, 158–60, 201–2 (n. 36). See also Broadside, criminal's goodnight; Confessions, dying
Thomas, Grady, 67
Thomas, Monroe, 72
Thomas, William F., 135
Trivette, Doug, 20, 73, 190 (n. 15)
Trivette, Marina, 3, 20, 89–90, 120, 191 (n. 54)
Turpin, James A., 110

University of North Carolina, 131–32, 141–42, 197 (n. 28)

Vance, Robert B., 128
Vance, Zebulon B., 138, 141–42

Walker, Lenore E., 89
Waller, Altina, 11, 50
Wallin, Doug, 104, 193 (n. 23)
Walters, Minette, 5
West, John F., 77
Williams, Cratis, 18
Williams, Howard, 4
Wilson, Thomas W.: career, 51, 61–64, 130, 187 (n. 21); character of, 61, 63–64; conduct of Frankie's defense, 59–61, 64, 150, 187 (n. 21); emigration to Texas, 61–64; family background, 51; friendship with David L. Swain, 130; knowledge of Frankie Silver's motives, 54; tactical deficiencies, 59–61, 63–64
Wood, Lawrence E., 85, 118
Woodfin, Eliza Grace McDowell, 125, 127
Woodfin, Nicholas W., 53–55, 60, 128, 135, 187 (nn. 21, 31)
Woodmason, Charles, 136
Woody, Dewey, 9–10, 13, 72
Woody, Greenberry, 72, 77, 157
Woody, Rosa, 13, 65–66, 79, 88, 157–58
Wyatt-Brown, Bertram, 155–56, 201 (n. 26)
Wycough, 103–4

Yancey County, N.C., 63, 112
Young, Perry D., 4, 77, 96, 105, 134, 198 (n. 41)